"In the weeks before Hurricane Andrew sweeps down on Cuba in 1992, Dr. Mano Rodriguez is caught up in intrigue in this thoughtful, lushly detailed neo-noir."
—*Publishers Weekly*

"Arellano is masterful in weaving both the physical and the emotional into a story that everyone can relate to in some way, regardless of geography and politics."
—*Multi Cultural Review*

"Cuban-American Arellano sets his noir thriller in Cuba just after the collapse of the Soviet Union, when a divorced and out-of-favor doctor takes on the protection of a teenaged prostitute, quickly discovering that the violence of the underworld is just below the surface."
—*Globe and Mail* (Canada)

"A sad, surreal, beautiful tour of the hell that was Cuba in the immediate aftermath of the collapse of the Soviet Union. The writing is hypnotic, the storytelling superb. *Havana Lunar* is perfect."
—Tim McLoughlin, author of *Heart of the Old Country*

"Written with passion and vision and with a clear, unflinching eye, Robert Arellano's *Havana Lunar* breaks new ground. It is not a Cuban American novel but a Cuban novel written in English. In it the Cuban underworld of chulos and jineteras is revealed and the uber-world of political bosses and apparatchiks unmasked. I am certain that *Havana Lunar* will find a wide and enthusiastic readership."
—Pablo Medina, author of *The Island Kingdom*

Jake Hostetter

Robert Arellano is the award-winning author of six previous novels including *Curse the Names*, *Fast Eddie*, *King of the Bees*, and *Don Dimaio of La Plata*. His nonfiction title *Friki: Rock and Rebellion in the Cuban Revolution*, will be released in 2018. He lives in Oregon. *Havana Libre* is the standalone sequel to his Edgar-nominated *Havana Lunar*.

HAVANA LIBRE

ROBERT ARELLANO

BROOKLYN, NEW YORK, USA
BALLYDEHOB, CO. CORK, IRELAND

This is a work of fiction. All names, characters, places, and incidents are the product of the author's imagination. Any resemblance to real events or persons, living or dead, is entirely coincidental.

Published by Akashic Books
©2017 Robert Arellano

ISBN: 978-1-61775-583-5
Library of Congress Control Number: 2017936109

Akashic Books
Brooklyn, New York, USA
Ballydehob, Co. Cork, Ireland
Twitter: @AkashicBooks
Facebook: AkashicBooks
E-mail: info@akashicbooks.com
Website: www.akashicbooks.com

For Amanda and Robert Casserly

Tú, que llenas todo de alegría y juventud
Y ves fantasmas en la noche de trasluz
Y oyes el canto perfumado del azul,
Vete de mi.

You, that fills everything with happiness and youth
And sees ghosts in the night of backlit moon
And hears the perfumed song of blue,
Get away from me.

—Homero y Virgilio Expósito, "Vete de mí"

LUNES, 1 SEPTIEMBRE 1997
THE TOURIST

On a Monday morning at eight thirty in Havana, a tourist steps off an air-conditioned flight from San Salvador and into eighty-five degrees at José Martí International Airport. He wears ripped jeans, a Kurt Cobain T-shirt, and a plaid flannel shirt tied at the waist. Brand-new Timberlands bolster his stature as an international traveler, because this new style among black rappers and grunge musicians has not yet caught on across Latin America. The huge boots seem a few sizes too large for him, but that is the point: show you're ready any minute for a mosh-pit and plod around with steel toes like you own the dance floor. He is a year or two too old for this look, but maybe that is why he has come to Cuba alone. His act does not work on the girls in El Salvador anymore, so he wants to try it out on the teenagers of Commieland. Perhaps he believes that with a few fulas to throw around, some girl will fall for it.

The traveler approaches customs with only a backpack, and to encourage the possibility that the two unsmiling soldiers might just wave him along, he does not let go of the straps when he places it on the stainless-steel counter before them. "Open the backpack," the tall one says. The zipper is unlocked, and the tourist unzips the top. "All the way." The smaller soldier removes each article of clothing and makes a stack on the counter. He also produces a pair of tennis shoes, toiletries bag, two General Electric travel alarm clocks, and a small calculator. "Why two clocks? Planning on leaving behind a gift?"

"In case the first one fails to wake me. I am a very sound sleeper."

"Lucky you."

From the side pockets the soldier pulls out some felt-tip pens and a fountain pen. The tourist makes a joke: "Don't you want to see if you can find some contraband hidden between my teeth?"

The soldiers do not find this funny. "Put your things in the backpack and come with us."

Together they stomp down a long corridor to a small, windowless room. The tall soldier locks the door behind them and calls the shots; the smaller one pulls on a pair of latex gloves and silently conducts the examination. "Take off your shirt and pull down your pants and underpants." The tourist undoes his belt and lets his pants drop over the tops of his boots, then pulls his underwear down to his knees. "Lift your testicles . . . Separate your buttocks." Finding nothing, the soldier peels off the latex gloves and reexamines the tourist's backpack, switching the calculator on to make sure it functions and trying out the pens on yesterday's copy of *Granma*, while the other one flips through his passport. The tourist does not ask whether it is time to pull up his pants. A few minutes later, the tall soldier says, "Get dressed. You're free to go."

He rides the hotel shuttle from Boyeros to Vedado, and taking in the countryside he feels the power of contempt and invulnerability. He is glad his two-week trip has begun this way. It is typical of Cuba to treat a traveler like this. "Welcome to Havana," the tourist mutters to himself.

The desk agent at check-in is a gorgeous black woman in a tailored skirt suit, and when she asks to see his passport he hands over the one Chávez Abarca obtained for him. He has had black and half-black girlfriends before, but on his last trip to Havana he learned that la negra Cubana is completely different. And the women who work in the tourist industry here are confident, nothing like those in Salvador, with their crude manners and the way they shrink like you're always going to hit them. "Disfrute su estancia, señor—" Boldly she looks him in the eye and calls him by the surname on the passport, and for a second he feels a little off-kilter. Has he let a sleepless night, early travel, the flight, and the trip from the airport get to him? By the banks of lights above the elevators, he takes notice that all six are working and rides the third on the left up to the thirteenth floor.

The window of room 1317 looks onto the block of houses across the way. He closes the curtains, locks the door, and puts the chain on the hook. He also closes the door to the bathroom which is letting in light and noise from the street. He does not want any distractions in his peripheral vision. He carefully removes his boots and unzips his backpack, taking advantage of his insomnia to get organized. First he arranges the clothing in the closet. Then he makes an inventory of materials on the bed.

Inside his toiletries bag he carries toothpaste and toothbrush; razor, shaving cream, and aftershave; a small stack of Band-Aids; a miniature Phillips-head screwdriver, the kind used for repairing eyeglasses; and a little roll of black plastic insulation tape that might have been thrown in there as a last-minute substitute for medical tape.

He takes the screwdriver from his toiletries bag and removes the outer casing of the portable alarm clocks. Each one carries fresh batteries, and the red-and-black connectors have been replaced with extra-long segments of insulated copper wire he soldered himself.

In a side pocket of the backpack, the three felt-tip pens have their ink cartridges removed and they're replaced with detonators. There is one extra, in case one of the others appears to malfunction. They are the length and shape of carpentry nails. The tip of each pen contains enough fresh ink to pass the customs soldier's test. The pocket also holds a fourth pen, a fountain pen full of blue ink.

He unscrews the back of the calculator; this reveals fresh batteries as well as additional wire, and a cavity holds the small firing pins. Finally, from the toes of the Timberlands he pulls the plastic bags containing two banana-shaped masses off gray putty. The morons at customs did not think to make him remove his boots.

When he is done with his inventory, the tourist places the items in the middle of the backpack and locks the zipper on top. He goes to the closet and removes a new shirt from its package. Nobody watching would comprehend the logic behind the strange thing he is about to do. He takes the pristine dress shirt out of its cellophane wrapper, removes the fountain pen from the pocket of the backpack, unpins the shirt, unfolds the sleeves, and lays it out on the bed. He takes the cap off the pen and pushes the tip into the cloth above the breast pocket. He holds it against the fabric for several seconds and watches the blue stain spread unevenly into a map of linked lagoons. The tourist caps the pen and puts it on the bedside table. He holds up the shirt to inspect his work.

Part I

La Habana

LUNES, 1 SEPTIEMBRE 1997
MANOLO

At sunset on the corner of 12 y 23 in Vedado, four men hunker around an upended shipping crate to study their tiles by the meager light of an oil lamp chuffing black smoke. They slam their fiches down to the staccato accompaniment of Radio Reloj, and el viejo Ramírez, victorious, crows, "¡Dominó!" There is no reason to buy a few drops of gas for the Lada because I have nobody to take for a ride. Besides, the driver's-side back tire has a flat I have not fixed for months. But this soon after sunset it will be much too hot in my attic apartment, so I close up the clinic and take myself on a walk along Paseo and Avenida de los Presidentes to try to catch a breeze somewhere along el Malecón.

Another oppressive September has settled over Havana. Heat peels the bark off trees, leaving the streets of Vedado redolent with sweat and regret. It is not yet time for tonight's apagón and all the TVs are tuned to replays of yesterday's big news about the princess, killed in a tunnel.

The entire length of the sea wall is in a dead calm, so I turn up Carlos Tercero. Maybe I'll find a pocket of cool air somewhere along el bosque. I walk past the dark capitolio at the top of the hill and cross broad Paseo del Prado, empty but for a few fareless turistaxis. Taking a seat on one of the wrought-iron benches at the edge of the Parque Central, I smoke a cigarette. The moment anyone who looks like he could be a foreign tourist enters the park, jineteras bustle out of the shadows like pigeons to bread crumbs.

I walk down Zapata all the way to La Madriguera. Cutting between two trails through the woods, I accidentally trample a writhing limb—a human arm or leg. "¡Coño!" a man curses at me for interrupting the couple's lovemaking. "¿Tú estás ciego?"

Not blind, not yet, although la Opción Zero has made everyone in Havana adept at the strategies of the sightless. "Lo siento," I say, and resume my march on Zapata, crossing Paseo back into the heart of Vedado. It is nerve-racking walking alone at night and a nuisance surprising lovers of all combinations tangled in their trysts, but it is better than waiting in my stifling attic for the night's oppressive blanket to never lift.

It has been nearly seven years since Fidel Castro ominously declared the Revolution in an indefinite state of "el Período Especial en Tiempos de Paz" to cope with the end of Soviet subsidies. For a select few, those with family off the island, or access to tourists and their dollars, or connections to crime, the austerity is finally letting up. For the other 95 percent of us, the recovery never arrived. I am still squeaking by on two hundred pesos a month and whatever scraps I can grow at home en el solar or haul back from my infrequent visits to Pinar. I recently turned twenty-eight, and the entire island is rushing headlong into the mouth of the Zero Option. This government slogan for diminishing provisions also fits my sex life. In 1989 I could go out on el Malecón any night of the week and engage one of a thousand young, liberated mujeres revolucionarias to go for a ride in the Lada. Now, even on a Monday night, the best I can get is just a condescending *tsk!* from the jineteras.

"Cómprate unos pantalones que te sirvan," one tells me, throwing a quarter at my feet. I am not too proud to stoop to pick it up. *Why not buy yourself some pants that fit, doctor?* At one time she might have been my patient at the pediátrico or a visitor to my family clinic. Meanwhile, Central American businessmen and Canadian auto mechanics get a graduate degree in beatific mulata ass for the price of entry to a discoteca and a few Tropicolas.

I zigzag back to Avenida 23 along Calle 6 to avoid the cemetery and its sepulchral memories.

Now the apagón has come. It is the new moon and all the streetlights are out along Paseo. There are few cars to get run over by tonight, bitter consolation for gas being impossible to come by. The biggest risk is being hit by a Chinese bicycle with bad brakes; since the beginning of the Período Especial, Cuba has bought two million Flying Pigeons from that factory in Tianjin. The blackout has not stopped the nightly domino match. Listening for the men boasting and bluffing at the corner of 12 y 23, I navigate home through echolocation.

I live in the attic that was once the maid's quarters when this tenement was a Vedado mansion. Could it be that my cramped apartment keeps me here? Not long after my mother died, the Reforma Urbana allocated the main part of the house to Beatrice, the block-watch captain of the neighborhood vigilance committee, but I did not complain. I have access to the private stairs, both front and back, and also the keys to the family clinic, which I open for drop-ins on Mondays and Wednesdays until eight p.m. and for appointments or emergencies when I'm not at the pediátrico. If a case were made to shift me full time to the hospital, the government would close the clinic. My neighbors would grumble at first—in the Período Especial, who doesn't?—but soon they would start going to the clinic on la Calle G instead and not bother the neighborhood doctor anymore—the strange doctor.

Tonight I take the front stairs. When I unlock the door I am prepared for the closed apartment to feel like an oven, but instead a cool breeze informs me that the Florida doors have been left open. In the dim light that reaches Vedado from the skies of central Havana, something out of place on the murky landing catches my eye. Among my collection of empty wine bottles, one is missing. This in itself is not so strange. Many neighbors know of my cache of a couple dozen empties, some sticky with sediment, all drained of the last drop, with the corks back in the top. Some of them will come up and borrow an empty bottle or two upon hearing about a batch of chispe tren selling from a barrel, or in order to split a liter of Tropicola for a child's birthday. Sometimes they even return the empties or their equivalent, but tonight I notice the missing one so quickly because in its place stands a full bottle, never opened. I squint at the ornate label and see it is a good Spanish vintage. Although this attic landing has been the scene of any number of surprises over the years, I do not expect that Beatrice has delivered a belated birthday present.

Suddenly, a thought makes the hairs on the back of my neck prickle to attention, and I peer inside the dark apartment. Silhouetted in front of the balcony in Aurora's old rocking chair sits a man. The line of the hat and overcoat mark him as a familiar Fidelista who might have been handsome, once. When he lights a cigarette, I see he still has his meticulous manicure.

"How long have you been sitting there?" There is a tremor in my voice.

Colonel Emilio Pérez, chief homicide investigator for the Policia Nacional de la Revolución, replies, "Desde que se fue la luz."

My hands are shaking as much from hunger as surprise when I close the door behind me and pat my pockets for my own cigarettes. Pérez is quick to extend his lighter. I inhale and hold it in a long time to make the most of the available nicotine.

He says, "¿Cómo tú andas?"

I exhale. Pérez wants to know how I have been. How have I been since I last saw him five years ago? How have I been lately, the better part of a decade into the Período Especial, now that doctors are malnourished malcontents while dropouts driving tourist taxis are relative millionaires? How have I been this week, when the decision has been whether to take my spare twenty pesos and seek out the neighborhood fermenter who makes "vinos" from guayaba, bananas, pineapple, chícharos, and anything else he can find, or to put it away to spend on something useful someday (a day that might never come), when they open a store for regular Cubans to buy a bar of soap or a razor? The real question should be posed to both Havana and me: how is it that we have held together so long? "I won't pretend; I've been better."

"The clinic is still functioning well enough?"

"The extra supplies made a difference, for a while." A cry comes up from the street in front—the domino match has ended breathtakingly close. "And you? I should think you would be too busy to pay a social call to a humble pediatrician in the national medical service . . . what with the recent bombings."

If I did manage to touch a nerve, Pérez nevertheless holds his game face. "It has been so long; you don't think I could have just called on the teléfono de la vecina, do you?"

He has a point. I feel my way to the kitchen in the dark and find a corkscrew in the top drawer. Two empty fruit-preserve jars serve for glasses. "Shall we open that bottle?"

Pérez does the honors. He pours me a jar and says, "Salud."

Halfheartedly I reply, "Viva Fidel."

Sitting on the sofa across from Detective Pérez, I feel around on the coffee table for an ashtray. The first sip of wine is delicious on my tongue, but before I can swallow he says, "There is an investigation of urgency to State Security with which I wish to request your assistance."

My mouthful turns sour. "Do I have a choice?"

"Your expertise would be valuable only insofar as it is voluntary, although you should take into account that lives are at stake."

I stare into my jar of wine. "In my job, lives are always at stake."

"Yes," Pérez says, pausing to take a long swallow, "and you have requested a weeklong salida to travel to a conference in Tampa later this month."

I look up. How does he know about my conference request? "That may be so, but we both know the exit visa will not be approved in time."

"What makes you so sure?"

"No wife, no dependents. I am what they call an emigration risk."

"Yes, those are the usual reasons. Sad in your case, no? When we both know you would always return to Havana."

Pérez works at Villa Marista, I remind myself. If I even hinted of thinking about deserting the national medical service, he could report me back to the Ministry of Health and the Ministry of the Interior. It would cause many more problems than one denied exit request. Still, the wine, the heat, and a cynical reflex make me risk a response that maybe takes a step too far: "What makes you so sure?"

"Por la misma razón que yo lo haria."

"¿Sí? And what reason is that? What could a

physician in the national medical service possibly have in common with the chief homicide investigator for the PNR?"

By the orange tips of our cigarettes, Pérez and I lock eyes. "No matter your opinion of the Revolution, we are both too devoted to our jobs."

I do not wish to admit it, but once again Pérez has me nailed. I could have left the pediátrico for a comfortable position in medical tourism years ago, except for one thing: put simply, I would never give up the clinic. I cannot abandon Havana.

Pérez says, "I could see to it that your conference request gets favorable consideration."

The last sip of wine is bitter, but it touches my judgment with the sweetest numbness. "I am sorry, colonel, but after our last encounter I made an oath never to cooperate with another one of your investigations."

"Is that your final word?"

"Definitively," I say.

Pérez pulls out his cigarette case. He stubs out the glowing tip against the inside plating and tucks the butt in alongside the unsmoked others. I hear him stand and walk across the dark room before opening the door to the back stairs.

"You came up through the alley?"

"Like I said, I've been here since the apagón started."

In other words, nobody saw him arrive. He points the illuminated face of his digital watch ahead of him to light the way down the stairs.

I call after him, "You've ruined a perfectly good bottle of shiraz." His footsteps, not including the shuffle across the rug on Beatrice's back landing, number twenty-six. I hear the alley door squeak and clap shut. Less than a minute passes before the power comes back on.

Since the lights went out. Who is Pérez kidding? All of Havana is the PNR's interrogation room, and he has been observing me since he first broke into my clinic five years ago, and I followed him—believing that I was the one doing the following!—to the un-marked bar in Chinatown. He has been watching me since the night when one of his unseen minions replaced the broken windowpane while Pérez and I talked about a jinetera and her abusive chulo and how to identify a corpse if you can't seem to find the head.

I put Beny Moré on my father's old tocadiscos. The record is worn and the sound quality is terrible. I have to fashion needles out of bamboo splinters. I lie in bed listening to el Beny and looking at the ceiling.

The letter came in July via courier, on water-marked stationery from the Tampa Medical Extension of the University of Florida, the cuño of the

State of Florida embossed over the bright blue signature of the dean of the medical school: an invitation to a conference on a subject of personal and professional passion. I was not looking for it, and yet it fell into my lap. In '95, the pediátrico received a visit from a group of American doctors, armchair socialists who considered themselves allies against the embargo. They admired my split work model of the big hospital and small family clinic. When the time came for them to invite someone from Cuba to their conference, they also must have considered the notoriety of my own medical case as a kind of bonus, the port-wine stain on my face that became the namesake of its very own thrombosis, *Havana Lunar*. They even offered to pay for the flight and accommodations.

I am not one for conference hopping, but my interest in the topic—pediatric health in third world countries—makes it the opportunity of a lifetime. But where Cuban doctors and scientists are concerned, any invitation to los Estados Unidos carries an exception: my exit permission will never be approved. Or if it is, it will be cruelly too late. Rather than deny the request outright, el Ministerio de Relaciones Exteriores will grant the approval several days after the conference has taken place, and then the US Interests Section will have no choice but to deny the visa. We push and push, and all the while believe we're making progress, but then life gives us a little window into ourselves from above and we see we have not really moved for five, ten, twenty-five years. As the earth circles the sun, so do we circle our destinies. One thing's for certain: death never loses track of the simple circularity she puts us in.

MARTES, 2 SEPTIEMBRE
THE TOURIST

He goes down to dinner early, as soon as the restaurant opens, so as not to run into any friendly fellow tourists. The waiter brings him roast beef that is cut too thin and piled too short, and he chews with contempt, thinking of the sad deprivation of the Revolution that trickles down to every plate. The older couple at the next table eats in silence, an unhappy anniversary or second honeymoon—not newlyweds, in any case. Too jaded. This satisfies him, because even the happy ones, he knows, will become hateful soon enough.

The tourist nurtures hate the way you steep tea or coffee, subverting the awareness that the longer he brews it the more bitter the taste will be, which will allow him to complete his task more effectively. Cold determination, fueled by this paltry beef and insipid au jus, will ensure maximum impact. He believes this much: any foreigner who spends his money in Cuba deserves to go. Tourists, with their euros and their dollars, keep the dying beast on life support. If you support the tourist industry during a time when Communism is destined to die, you are a sympathizer, and to pretend otherwise makes you a cynic and a hypocrite. Send them to hell with the devil.

Does he feel any differently about the common Cubans? They are less contemptible for their poverty. Unlike the tourists, the beast's keepers and feeders, they are the prey, caught in the beast's trap. At the same time, he kisses the cross around his neck and reminds himself that a great majority of them are atheists. If there are any Catholics among them, then they will be martyrs. Communism is on the evil side in a holy war, but their deaths will sanctify them. Let them be cleansed in fire.

A young couple in cheap Chinese business suits approach, and he realizes right away that they are from State Security, even without seeing the telltale earphones. They look too young and too Cuban to be guests at this hotel, and their come-on is deceptively ingenuous. "Are you traveling alone?"

"Sí," he says.

Does it sound like he says it irritably? Why should he jump as if to say, *Is there something wrong with traveling alone?* Is he acting suspiciously? Is he trying to hide something? No, it's just that they did not want to bother him if he was waiting for someone. Seeing as he is not, they might as well sit at his table. Small talk. These employees are early diners by routine, and sitting with a foreigner to get a window into life off the island is their entertainment.

"Mind if we join you? We work here in hotel security." What should he do, the lonely bachelor? Eat his meal in silence? Would it arouse suspicion to be too talkative? Talk. Go ahead, talk.

Their detail is jineteras and black market cigars. No earphones. They are not looking for a bomber. But can't anybody suspicious in this country be subject to search? *Mind if we come up to your room?* Mind or not, they would come up either way. He remembers the materials he laid out on his bedcover, now hidden in the back of the dresser behind the drawer. *What do you need two alarm clocks for?* They're gifts. *Oh, yes? And what's this?*

"Go right ahead. Have a seat."

"Have you been to Havana before? Is this your first time?"

"Sí."

"You mean sí, this is your first time?"

"No . . ." He decides on yes—you better say yes because they may already know. "That is, yes, I have been to Havana on vacation. I like the beaches to the east."

"It is a good time of year to go to the beach."

He thinks he's doing pretty well. "Which do you recommend?"

"If you like las Playas del Este, you should try Guanabo, if you have the time. You'd probably want to share a car. Did you like your dinner?"

"Yes, thank you."

"Well, I hope you meet some friends." That sounded insulting. No, they are just trying to be friendly. "Maybe we'll see you later."

"Maybe."

The tourist returns to his room and checks the lock on the zipper of the backpack. He opens the door to the bathroom and washes his hands. On an island of eleven million people, he is completely alone.

MARTES, 2 SEPTIEMBRE
Manolo

In advance of the weekly staff meeting, Director Gonzalez lets it slip into the gossip mill at the pediátrico that he will introduce a newly appointed physician. The nurses get hold of this information, and it is more effective than if Gonzalez had announced it on the intercom that has not worked since '95. The halls are alive with chatter:

"He's supposed to be some kind of child psychologist."

"Is that even a kind of doctor?"

"What we need is more surgeons."

The nurses do not cut cruel glances at me. Since my tangle with la jinetera a few years back, they rarely cut me any glances at all. In my mind I try referring to her as just *la jinetera,* because it hurts too much to acknowledge her name, her youth, her humanity, knowing how she is wasting away in prison. Julia played the damsel in distress, and she was, but she ended up taking justice into her own hands. She took a scalpel that I used to cut vegetables to the train yard, for protection, she said, but that became circumstantial when she finished the job by laying his neck across the rail beneath a freight car and releasing the brake. There was an unfortunate rumor that briefly circulated on Radio Bemba that it could have been me who had taken the chulo's life, and five years later it still creates a separation between me and the nurses. If beforehand I was unattractive to them, afterward I have become invisible.

"I hope that he's handsome," says the head nurse, "and not such a womanizer as the others."

"Ni tan maricón," chimes in the newest orderly, a mulata from Regla. *Nor such a fag*—this, presumably, in reference to me or any other doctor who has yet to hit on her, she who takes such pains hemming her dingy hospital-issued dress to give us all a good look high up la pierna.

Were there other lovers? Yes, a few. But in five years nobody stands out. It's like that hurricane knocked out my ganas. How can I be so frozen in '92? It is not that I do not hunger, but I know that no invitation to table around here comes without ten forks—in your ass. Especially for those who dare to date across roles: whether nurse to doctor, doctor to administrator, or patient to any of the above. All the currency we have in the Período Especial is these most intimate negotiations, so sex is exchanged like a trinket or a handful of pocket change, but you could be sure of what she would expect in exchange for a taste: *Pero doctor, yo que vengo todo los días de Regla, tan lejos, y tú tan cerca y solito en este apartamento.* We are all better off if, rather than mixing work with pleasure again, I find my lovers far from el pediátrico, preferably as far as Pinar del Rio, better still to stick to the widow with the five orphans.

For the better part of a decade, Director Gonzales has not gone out of his way to improve conditions at the pediátrico. Every July 26 there is a little pep talk for the weary physicians with a modest reception at his apartment: rum, Tropicola, and a salami that gets shorter every year. But when it comes to shaking things up by advocating for better equipment or some new linens for the beds, the director never lifts a finger.

In July I submitted the paperwork for my request to attend the Tampa conference, along with the dean of medicine's invitation letter. There was ample time for my application to get from Gonzalez's desk, where it sat for who knows how long, up the chain of command to the Minister of Health himself, and from there across chasms of bureaucracy to MINREX, el Ministerio de Relaciones Exteriores. But because ministries speak only to ministries, I have no way of knowing when or if he forwarded my application.

"Still waiting to hear back from MINREX,"

he said when I stuck my head in his office. "Here, take some chocolate." It was Belgian and still in the wrapper, so I did not decline.

The summer dragged on, and I knew in my heart that he let it sit on his desk until the last day of the prescribed review period. Every step of the way he has delayed the petition process. I could flatter myself that he does not want to lose me, but since that desire exists only within his architecture of bureaucracy and mediocracy, it is no consolation. He does not think it would be approved in time, and neither do I. He is not cultivating a star clinician and surgeon for the sake of creating one of the best pediatric hospitals on the island. Instead, he is abusing and exhausting one of his only competent doctors because by burning me out, it helps him maintain the status quo at minimal effort and expense, which is exactly what his superior administrators in the national medical service expect of him.

If improved attendance at the meeting was his ulterior motive in leaking the news, then Director Gonzalez got his wish. There's a full house—doctors, nurses, orderlies, and even a few parents of longterm patients—when he enters the staff room followed by the new physician, a pediatric psychiatrist. "Compañeros, I am pleased to introduce to you Doctora Ana Luisa Hernández."

The nurses audibly deflate while the men all

share a barely audible *hmm!* It takes a moment for me to focus because, although she dons a doctor's coat (mercifully no stethoscope), instead of scrubs she's wearing the snug blue jeans popular among the young women of Havana. A psychiatrist's consultations do not often get messy, so she is free to wear what she pleases.

"Thank you, Director Gonzalez." She steps into the hush to examine us. She seems too young to be a physician, but that's what they said about me. She's not pretty—she's gorgeous. The denim flatters the curve of her hip, thrown sideways provocatively even as her crossed arms suggest she takes new business only by referral. Her blouse does not quite reach the top of her pantalones, so if it weren't for the lab coat, every time she bends even the slightest bit—to pick a pencil off the desk, for instance, or to pour herself a little water from the jug on the table—we get a glimpse of midriff. "Colleagues, for the past seven years since the official start of the Período Especial, depression and desperation have been on the rise. Young people experience feelings of hopelessness in home and school environments, and increasing aggression and exploitation. I am very interested in getting to know the makeup of the community, and I hope that before long I can be of some assistance to you and to the people of Havana who use the pediátrico."

The brief meeting concludes with my male co-workers lining up to introduce themselves. I opt out of the reception line and make my way to the broom closet that serves as a break room.

I am stretched out on two chairs in the closet for a brief nap before the start of my shift when the new doctor interrupts me: "Buenos días, Doctor Rodriguez."

"Buenos días, Doctora Hernández, y bienvenida al pediátrico." I endeavor to make my new colleague feel welcome with a dose of the usual teasing reserved for interns and recent arrivals on staff: "So, they make psychiatrists just for children now? How very post-Soviético."

"I would think that you, who could have benefited from one during the medical confusion around your *Havana Lunar,* would be the last to scoff."

Her commentary about the mark on my left cheek is not the anticipated *How did you get that?* or the clueless *This remind me of something I read in a medical journal.* She already knows the case and, being a good psychiatrist, she understands that two decades later any expressions of sympathy would be purely gratuitous and practically insulting. Thank goodness it does not veer into the buffoonish insensitivity I have noticed surfacing more of late, even among otherwise mature medical personnel: *¡Mira!*

¡El famoso Havana Lunar! *Wow, it must be cool to have a syndrome named after you!*

I cannot dislodge myself from my two-chair stretcher in this narrow alcove without an awkard bit of clattering around, so I remain supine while she stands over me. "Let me know if I can be of any assistance, Doctora Hernández, orienting you to our patients and their neuroses."

She pours herself a cup of water from the pitcher on the dusty shelf. "Surely children are much more than just their neurosis."

"Without a doubt."

She is comfortable in conversation, does not mind protracted silences, and has a pleasant smile and pretty eyes. In my mind I am singing, *Que bonitos ojos tienes . . .*

"But yes," she says, "disorders would be a good place to start."

"I agree with your assessment of pervasive desperation," I tell her.

"Yes, except for the occasional pinguero or jinetera, in which case a liaison with a foreigner might lead to delusions of grandeur, thinking they have found a way out."

"Only to be cheated, abused, or otherwise knocked down again."

"In most cases, yes."

"I have to admit, it's a story I hear over and over,

but in so many different versions it will make your head spin: *I have a chance to leave the island . . .*"

"That's right," she says. "It has become a collective hallucination. A form of currency more powerful than the peso or even the dollar: *Tengo un chance de irme . . .*"

"The parents' desperation is frequently worse. Oftentimes the nurses or I will have to calm them down with platitudes and placebos before we are able to conduct an exam on the actual patient."

"The job of the Cuban psychiatrist at the end of the century seems to have become helping 95 percent of the population cope with the Período Especial, and I have a prediction: it will continue to be the case well into the next century."

"¡Que vá!" I say. "Next you're going to say you can tell what I'm thinking."

"No, that's a psychic. There is a slight difference. But I will tell you what I believe some of my new colleagues must be thinking. Something along the lines of: *To what does she owe the privilege of this assignment?*"

"Why do you think that?"

"Because the pediatric hospital needs more real doctors, no? Physicians and surgeons." Although I personally do not believe this, it is difficult to conceal the fleeting reaction on my face: yes, this is probably what many of her new colleagues are thinking.

"Therefore," she contines, "I will also tell you what I believe the director is thinking, and in this he and I see eye to eye. Over the past seven years, one consequence of the Período Especial has been economic hardship in the countryside, and there have been annual increases in the rate of relocados from the provincias. An exponential growth of migration into Havana."

"These are the statistics, yes, as well as my personal experience of my neighborhood in Vedado. Many adolescents who have no savings to get started become jineteros and jineteras, some as young as twelve years old. Even those who do not become prostitutes for tourists are at risk of exploitation by Habaneros."

"These children, some of them barely in their teens, as you say, have become our domestic refugees, and the pediátrico is the place to confront the threat."

She is correct, and pediatric specialists such as myself have been at a loss to address the full spectrum of our patients' afflictions. As crisis responders, we ourselves have been working in crisis mode for too long. The triage at admitting has no protocol for our patients' emotional states; the emergency room is unprepared for such situations. I can set a broken arm or perform an emergency operation to excise a hemorrhaging abscess, but while checking on the

patient's cast or monitoring the postsurgery convalescent I hear stories of persistent trouble in the lives
of young people who are not safe in their homes, or
who have no fixed home, and I am helpless for how
to manage the spectrum of conditions emergent in
an ever-increasing caseload, nor am I trained in the
prognoses or therapies for these conditions.

Relishing her clarity and articulateness, I have
to smile. "I cannot tell you how long I've wished for
a colleague like you—a licensed psychiatrist."

"And yet, why do you already look at me with
faraway eyes?" The way she says this surprises me for
how closely it echoes my internal monologue.

"Are you asking me what I am thinking? If so, I
will tell you."

"Please do."

"I am wondering how long you'll stay. This place
wears on people. Most new physicians pass through
in a year or two."

"It sounds like you are really telling me something about yourself."

"Maybe so, but it is something I dredge up only
when I meet someone like you."

"And what am I like?" she asks.

I hesitate to answer, not because I cannot think
of the word, but because it is so sad: *Someone who
will move on before too long.*

Doctora Hernández places a hand on mine there

on the arm of the chair—she could be taking my pulse—and turns her analytical instrument on me. "You were a prodigy, no? One of the youngest ever to complete Plan G, verdad?" I cannot speak for the lump in my throat, and there is no modest way to say aloud, *In fact the youngest ever.* She continues, "Maybe you wish to feel too good for a place."

"An elegant analysis . . . but not very materialist of you."

"Because you would not know what to do with yourself without your companion."

"What companion?"

"Self-pity. Could you imagine Doctor Rodriguez being just another average doctor among a cohort of the country's most talented physicians? Or maybe you have imagined in great detail. This would be completely alien to practically every defense you have assembled for yourself so far: youngest in medical school, first in Plan G, most precocious physician at the pediátrico. Perhaps you thrive on the self-alienation of the prodigy, and you feed off the envidia of your resentful colleagues, whom you know to be righteous in their resentment . . ." She takes her hand away but not before giving my wrist a little squeeze.

Still semi-prostrate, I say to myself, *I probably could have used you back in the 1970s.* And her eyes seem to be saying, *I wish I had been there to help you.*

She is already walking away when I say aloud, "Is this how you end all of your sessions, Doctora Hernández? With a light touch and an admonition?"

Disregarding my lame comment, she throws a smile over her shoulder and delivers the coup de grâce: "Who could blame you, with all you have been through?"

For the rest of my shift, I think about Doctora Hernández. It always comes down to this with someone new: the fact that I never know quite what to say to the ones who are good. They arrive con muchas ganas, but if they have any talent, they hardly ever stay. The pediátrico has struggled, while SERVIMED hospitals for tourists like Sancti Spíritus soak up the resources. The turnover is exhausting. Just when you have finished training someone and started really getting to know them, you learn that they are moving on. The pediátrico might even be cultivating this way station for the up-and-coming. I should ask Director Gonzalez sometime whether this is by design. I would rather ask Ana Luisa Hernández what she thinks, in private. While finishing my rounds, I also find myself thinking of what Pérez said about my conference request: he told me he could get my exit visa approved on time.

When my shift is over, I exit the pediátrico through the emergency room into the inferno of Havana at four p.m. A sharp hiss from the afternoon shadows stops me on my way across the ambulance parking area. "*Pss!* Rodriguez, don't be a fool." Virgilio Candelario brushes past me on the way to his shift. In medical school, Candelario wanted to be Plan G, but a professor had raised questions about his final exam. A copy had gone missing from department files two days before the test, and while cheating could not be proven incontrovertibly, the quality of Candelario's answers was inconsistent with his previous performance. He got the grade, but not the appointment to Plan G. He turns now to scowl at me. "Why don't you go to la Yuma?"

"Because they would shut down the family clinic in Vedado."

Candelario has an irritating habit of staring at my lunar instead of looking me in the eye. "They would find some young doctor to take it over. He'd move into that attic apartment of yours."

"No, Candelario. There would be no replacement physician. The Ministry of Health would close the family clinic."

"You should consult with that sexy new psychiatrist. You can't be sure that famous clot of yours didn't clog your common sense."

"The clinic is not like the pediátrico. There's not even a nurse to help."

He gets up in my face and does not bother trying

to cover his foul breath. "You mean a nurse to get in the way. In Havana they are such stupid bitches!"

"You're going to work drunk."

Ignoring this remark, Candelario continues, "Turismo Medico sends all the hot nurses to Sancti Spíritus. They are probably just as incompetent as here, but at least they have been handpicked for good looks. They should call it Plan T—for tetas."

"The way you talk, you remind me of my friend Yorki."

"A doctor?"

"No, a dishwasher."

I take the long way home to walk out the anger Candelario has stirred in me. Trudging over the hill between the fallout tunnels and the empty playing fields of the university, here it comes again: the nagging doubt resuming its refrain of what should have been, what could have been, what would be different in another place, another time, another life . . . ? Regret is a noxious weed. Drop it, even on rocky soil, and it will take root and begin to send out shoots.

Have the first thirty-eight years of the Revolution been just a series of dreams? First, the dream of the 1960s, before I was born: the Yanquis on the run while los ricos fled for Miami, and lower-class Cubans experienced the temporary improvements that come with a 180-degree conversion to socialism. Fidel, Camilo, and el Ché all ascendant—until the second and third died under questionable circumstances, and the first became untouchable.

The 1970s, the Days of Food: long, happy afternoons with Aurora and Machado, and then The Accident, which is what Abuela calls my mother's suicide.

Then the early eighties: membership in the Unión de Jóvenes Comunistas and Beisból Juventud, summers in Pinar del Rio and my first infatuation. 1988: Plan G, medical school camaraderie, my compañeros and I dedicated to doctoring the common man, woman, boy, and girl. 1989: my marriage to Elena, the move upstairs, preparing for the exam that would send me and a few select interns to train medics in Angola, and then came the reality shock of watching Germans on television looking through a hole in The Wall.

Suddenly there were shortages of food, clothing, toiletries, cosmetics, and medicine; the abrupt disappearance of professional opportunity; and the gradual, growing suspicion that all which had happened before that scorching autumn day when nobody could believe their TV—that everything Cubans born since '59 remembered was just a dream.

In 1990, Angola is scrapped, along with almost every other intern program except for pediatrics and medical tourism. Cuban coffee—¡café, carajo!— becomes scarce. At first, a few imported instants are available as substitutes. Then, in an international insult, even Sanka gets too expensive for common Cubans, and there aren't too many uncommon Cubans, those higher-ups who orbit within the pull of el Barba's inescapable gravity. Raul, Ricardo, and a few dozen other top ministers get their coffee from Kenya, scotch from Edinburgh, caviar from Leningrad—correction: St. Petersburg. When el Comandante's delicacy jet touches down, the world's seven races all prepare their wares. Meanwhile, for regular Cubans, every reduction in rations hits like a fist in the belly. And in 1990, to top it all off for me, Elena leaves.

By 1991, there is nothing but rice and beans, a pound of each per week for a grown man. Pregnant women, nursing mothers, and children get an additional egg and a small box of Cerelac, some weeks two eggs. What I miss most is bread: thick, wide loaves of bleached wheat. I am lucky if once a month I get one small, stale roll of pan del gobierno—a euphemism for baked sawdust. Years go by without improvement and Cubans tighten their belts, punching extra holes to keep up. Each time I punch a new notch I hear a voice in my head say, *I might have thought . . .*

I might have thought that I would be married by now, with a son or a daughter too. I might have thought that I'd be back in the main part of the house on 12 y 23. I might have thought that I either would have resigned from the pediátrico or passed the clinic along to someone else. (I always believed I would still be practicing medicine, but I hadn't thought that it would be possible to still be juggling both jobs, not this long, not for so little in return.) Instead I visit the penitentiary for young women with whatever I have gathered that month from the black market or Abuelo's garden. I do not ask to see the prisoner, but I always leave a couple of buns of pan integral or a small bunch of carrots with the guards. It has to be something easy to inspect. I believe that some of it makes it through, after the guards take their cut. She might guess who is behind it, but I never send any message. If I keep things strictly business, we will both be better off.

Fidel gives a speech in '96 and declares the Special Period over, but if that's true then it's only for the hotel workers, taxi drivers, and jineteras. The rest of us have to scrape by with our ration books and pesos and whatever we can pick from the kitchen waste behind tourist paladares. It would be comical if it were not so depressing.

I might have thought that I'd be dead now. But my lunar still looks down upon me from the mirror—a mute, indifferent crescent—and refuses to reveal the exact date of its inevitable collapse; or whether it is indeed the grim detonator all the doctors agree that, at least without a very risky surgery, it must be; or how long it will take if it eventually does burst to do its work. I think all these things not in any clear, conscious way of seeing the outcome, but with the grim conviction of a vague double negative: I cannot think of nothing different.

I might have thought it impossible that my misery would continue. I could not conceive of holding it together so long. I could not see myself still in this attic, a crow's nest barely above the constant chaos and cacophony of Vedado. I could not imagine the Período Especial going on this long. I could not imagine Havana. Yes, the aspirin and the hypodermics Pérez sent over made my family clinic popular again, however briefly. For a while, the women would say, "¡Ay, esa cosa con la jinetera!" and wave it away. Even Celia had been so impressed that one of the highest-ranking commanders in the PNR had bothered to come to the building and arrange for the supplies that she settled back from her blockade to a cool embargo: *You keep to your business* . . . Running the family clinic kept me in the apartment, and I remember thinking that if the situation ever changed I might get the whole house back, adiós a Beatrice. Now that we are the better part of a decade into the Período Especial, some of my neighbors are beginning to get their properties appraised for sale to investors from Europe, the US, and Latin America.

To me this seems, to put it lightly, overly optimistic. And through it all, I have known that any moment it could be over thanks to my lunar. A badge, a stain, a watermark as emblematic and recognizable from afar as the silhouette of el Ché.

Contrary to what a drunk and famous poet said, not everything falls apart. Like the crumbling mansions looking hollow-eyed over el Malecón and across the Florida Straits, a thin and yellow film of paint peeling from their stone walls that barely hold up against the buffeting salt water and stinging wind of the Caribbean. If you look at one of those houses funny it could collapse, but other ruins around it prop it up, shoulder to shoulder, the entire stretch along el Malecón a shambling fortress of remorse. The Revolution: the world's longest-running nation-mistake. We are stuck with this mistake because we are already running on fumes and we can't afford the gas to start again. Things barely stick together. The center somehow holds.

Has it all been a series of dreams? Better I should ask myself the question: why is it that I allow oafs like Candelario to get me started? I have to shut off the broken record in my head, but when I get back to the apartment, Cine de las diez is running a Charlie Chaplin film festival, and I relate too closely to the Little Tramp to want to abide all over again his hours of misery, which remind me of other summers I would sooner forget. I don't want to listen to the same Beny Moré record as always, so instead I put on one of Yorki's mixtapes. The first song is AC/DC, "Hell's Bells."

Has living alone made me crazy enough that nobody could bear to live with me ever again? You shall never escape Havana, Rodriguez, nor will you ever escape being Doctor Rodriquez. Like Cuba, I am stuck, embargoed, blockaded. Aloud I admonish myself, "Enough of your self-pity, get some sleep."

MIERCOLES, 3 SEPTIEMBRE
THE TOURIST

Four blocks to the corner of Misión, then left one bock to Agramonte. He could have taken a bus, but the communal taxis leave more frequently, and they're cheaper: forty pesos, about two dollars, if you don't mind riding con los Cubanos.

All the Chevies are there, and the tourist seeks a taxi particular going to Guanabo, Santa Maria del Mar, the last beach on Playas del Este. The driver takes them through the tunnel under Havana Bay and they hurtle eastward on the road to Matanzas. It is the closest thing he has seen to the traffic of San Salvador, with cars following each other perilously close on the highway. Once they make it the thirty kilometers into Guanabo, the traffic starts to thin.

He knows he is taking a risk, but it is worth it. It will give him focus and conviction. Chávez Abarca does not know about it, and he does not need to know. It is essential to the success of his mission, and that is all that matters to the client. Communism is dying a slow death. It has already been eight years. And now they are preparing to deliver the deathblow.

He sits in the beach chair that he rents for five dollars and watches the locals walk by. He does not have to look for the boy—the boy will find him. After less than half an hour, here comes one in a thong bottom, eyeing him while his friend scans the beach ahead. He can't be older than fourteen. Is it the same boy as last time? He's not sure, but it doesn't matter. He can tell by the swagger and the way he holds his arms close to his sides.

The boy's friend walks ahead and positions himself as if admiring the beautiful women sunbathing down the beach, but he's really keeping a lookout for the police. The boy walks up to his chair smiling and says in one breath, "Buenos días. ¿Buscas algo?"

Looking for anything? He knows that he and the boy are probably thinking the same thing, but he will not be drawn in to saying it first. "No sé. ¿Como qué?"

If it isn't the same boy as last time, he has to know this beach well enough to be certain that he is dealing with a real tourist and there's nothing to worry about, because he cheerfully, quietly says, "Coca."

Convenient that if need be he can claim he was talking about a cola. "Es posible."

"Veinte dólares. Ponlo aqui en la arena."

With his slender right foot, the boy traces a circle in the sand beneath the beach chair. Like last time, the tourist is ready and already has the bill in his hand. He drops the crumpled twenty in the sand. The boy pivots, pinching the money with his big toe, and in the same movement lifts his armpit while he spins away: a fat little plastic bindle of white powder, maybe three grams, drops into the sand. Walking away, the boy reaches down to scratch his foot midstride, transferring the money to the cavity of his armpit.

The tourist covers the packet with his shirt. Now he has it in his hand. All he has to do is go somewhere he can safely snort it. And yet he savors the moment—he is already high. This is the feeling, the rush of blood through his aorta like a blast of fuel injection, a hundred shots of café Cubano, an orgasm without the attendant shame or mess. His heart rate goes straight to fifth gear, ninety miles an hour, and it stays there. He is going to do this. He is going to show Castro. He will show the world.

MIERCOLES, 3 SEPTIEMBRE
MANOLO

In the morning my mind is still roiling when I open the clinic. I have barely slept, and here comes that same fat old alcoholic wife-beater complaining of pains again. He collected compensation from a faked fall on a Spanish construction project and used it to start a secret pizzeria out of his back patio. He refuses to serve anyone without a Yanqui dólar—especially not the doctor who wrote a note to the union representative warning that the patient's complaints of chronic pain seemed to be (I couched his exposure in the most merciful terms) at best psychosomatic. He stokes his brick oven with wood he pays the neighborhood kids to drag away from collapsed mansions in Old Havana, lumber impregnated with lead paint and other chemicals that choke the neighborhood with noxious fumes also laced with the delicious odors of tomato sauce (a stolen case of Mexican ketchup he waters down) and melted cheese (soy that his silent, skittish wife curdles in five-gallon buckets in their dirty apartment). When sooner or later he succumbs to heart disease, there will be a brief mourning, and then someone else will come along to pick up the slack in the neighborhood's fast-food offerings. He believes that eventually I will yield and proffer up some of that secret stash of ibuprofen I must be hoarding if he returns once a month with that most unspecified of symptoms, "chronic pain." He is correct about the yielding—my intestines convulse disagreeably every time I see him coming, and I would give every last fula in my wallet and a bottle of my uncle's best country wine just to make him go away, but I assure him that he is wrong about the secret stash—no ibuprofen, not anymore, no end in sight.

Then there is the nice lady from next door who cannot stop talking. She needs some salve for the demented grandmother, whose house they still occupy, who is stuffed in a back room with the grandchildren so that they may rent out the front bedroom to tourists. And the matriarch, her perception wracked by dementia, balbuceando todo el dia, moaning and howling while her daughter—now a grandmother herself—smiles and asks tourists from Sweden and Germany staying in this showpiece of collapsing opulence, *Would you like more café?* She takes the hundred dollars they give her for three nights (breakfast included) and immediately turns it around to buy a twenty-pound bag of flash-frozen Brazilian chicken quarters that somehow found its way to her back door between the InTur distribution center and one of the hotels, and then she offers those quarters at ten dollars a pound through word-of-mouth in the neighborhood. They sell out in less than an hour, and she has doubled her money, buena capitalista en que se ha convertido. What to invest in next?

I close up briefly at noon and use my lunch hour to take my ration book and buy myself some beans and rice from the neighborhood mercado. They come in two half-pound paper bags with the tops torn off. The proprietor uses the excess paper for writing figures.

Sometimes running my family clinic is a little like being the school nurse. In the afternoon I get an eight-year-old girl with a knee scraped up from a bike injury. Her mother cannot stop blabbering about the recent bombings: "No me siento segura caminando por los hoteles."

"Por favor . . ." I cock my head in the direction of her daughter while applying antiseptic to the abrasions.

"¿Y qué?" says the mother. "This is reality, doctor. She has to know to stay on alert around those places." I cannot argue with the mother. I do not wish to say it aloud, because there is a child nearby, but I am also nervous near tourist hotels.

Eighteen months ago, two of our MiG fighters shot down two Cessnas belonging to the exile group Brothers to the Rescue that had repeatedly violated Cuban airspace, killing four men. For the anti-Castro extremists who funded the group, their response has been a terrorism campaign targeting tourist spots. Havana has been on edge since the brutality of this summer's bombings. There have been a half-dozen explosions at hotels already this year, and while miraculously there have been no fatalities, everybody in Havana is uneasy.

The last patient of the day walks in as I am preparing to close up the clinic. Sometimes this is a sign. The egocentric patient will try to get at the neighborhood doctor just when he is about to get off work. An unscrupulous physician might prescribe whatever is requested a bit more freely in order to dispense with the last-minute consult. However, in this case I believe showing up at the last possible moment was just her luck.

"Buenas tardes."

"Buenas."

Her ripped jeans and black T-shirt emblazoned with the dark album art of a German metal band identify her as a rockera, but her coal-black eye makeup is smudged beyond the rockeros' usual display of antisocial disenchantment. She has been crying. Blond hair, pretty face, light skin, and Eastern

European features. I can tell from the way she talks she is a Pinareña.

"¿Ya estaba cerrando?" she asks.

"No importa. Siéntate." I invite her to sit across from me at my desk. I do not go straight to the exam room unless the patient is in pain or is a regular with whom I have established a rapport. I prefer taking new patients on with a casual conversation. In first-world medical communities, physicians do this in order to bill a quick additional consultation to the insurance companies before practicing any actual medicine. In my case, it is a simple matter of making patients feel more comfortable than they would if I went straight to poking them with instruments and examining them.

However, it is vain to speak of a difference between the office and the exam room, because they are in fact sections of the same small basement separated only by a flimsy curtain.

"I haven't seen you around before. Are you from the neighborhood?"

"I'm new here. My aunt died and I have to clean out her apartment. Acabo de llegar de Pinar."

My impulse is to say, *Tengo familia en Pinar*, but I know better than to get personal with a patient too soon. Nevertheless, our encounter is now imbued with a kind of understanding, even if it is only I who recognizes it. Certainly I know this girl. The girls of Pinar City are like this. They want to smile and please, but something more is going on behind the eyes.

"¿Quién era tu tia?"

"Marilyn Delgado."

"Lo siento," I say, leaving it at that. I remember la viuda Delgado—a solitary woman, widowed ever since I was a boy. When she died in the spring, some of the neighbors raided her furniture. It's a good thing the family finally sent someone to protect what was left. The next-door neighbor went so far as to begin renting out one of her rooms to European tourists, the type with the big backpacks who will sleep anywhere in order to save their money for jineteras. There is no way the government will let the apartment go to a single young woman from the provinces. They will come in and apportion it.

"¿En qué te puedo servir?"

She does not stare at my lunar. She has too much on her mind. "Do you do the HIV test in this clinic?"

"Yes."

"I need to know, but I don't want to be sent to a sanatorium."

"I will keep it confidential."

Her name is Mercedes Delgado. She is twenty years old, October birth date, and her ex-boyfriend is HIV-positive. "He is a friki. He wanted to go to el sanatorio." There is something to this brief pause at mentioning him, whether it is discomfort at their unmarried status or something more. She is thinking of someone else, someone not far from her, but someone who has already passed through a door. Just sitting with me is conspiring against him.

"Did you have unprotected sex?"

"Yes, a few times."

"How long has it been since the last time you had intercourse?"

"Two months."

"A full two months?"

"Yes, eight weeks."

Drawing her blood in silence, I inhale the faint fragrance of jasmine from her skin. Internally I annotate: *Anxiety, possible mood disorder, check glucose.* Mercedes Delgado is telling me much more than her request for a blood test. I wonder what Doctora Ana Luisa Hernández would do. Her influence is already rubbing off on me. I tell the patient, "Moving is always difficult, even more so when you go to a new place where you don't know anybody."

"Yes, I feel much better just speaking to someone about it."

The only prescription she needs today is a human to listen to her, a sympathizer, in the absence of a friend, which is lucky, because sympathy is the only thing left in my supplies, though I also feel like there is still something more we have not touched on. "You can come back the day after tomorrow for the results. In the meantime, is there anything else you require?"

She is feeling better, so she remembers something. "Yes, there is just one thing. Can you tell me where there might be a mercado around here?"

"Of course, you just arrived." I go to the shelf where I keep my personal items when the clinic is open. "Here."

"What is this?"

"A pound of rice and beans. A first-night package for newcomers to Havana provided by the Ministry of Health."

"Is this customary?"

I act surprised. "I would have thought you knew, coming in on your first day. Do you need any oil?"

"No, I can manage."

"In the morning, you can make la cola for the market on 12 y 17 to pick up a bit more with your ration book. Is there anything else I can do to be of service?"

She hesitates and says, "Me da pena decirlo."

"There is no shame in telling your doctor what's troubling you."

"I don't want to go back to Pinar. I want to stay here in Havana."

I do not have to ask her why. I can tell: it is

because she wants distance from the ex-boyfriend. "What will you need to get on your feet? I'd like to help you resolve this, if you will permit me."

"I do not wish to be a bother."

She has given me my opening. And I know I need to meet her humility halfway with my own. "No, please, it is absolutely no difficulty whatsoever." I stop short of saying, *In fact, you'll be doing me a favor,* because I trust I have already been obsequious enough.

There is no guile in it when she says, "*¿No me puedes resolver un trabajo por ahí?*" *You couldn't help me find a job somewhere around here?*

This is in the realm of the reasonable for a médico de familia to consider. Even Doctora Hernández would back me up on this one. "I'll see what I can do. Come back day after tomorrow. I get home around five."

"Home?"

"I live in an apartment upstairs. We can meet down here in the clinic."

When I close up, a waxing crescent is setting over Havana Bay. It has cooled off, and Morro Castle is half-cloaked in clouds that, silver and black, portend rain, but not before morning. With the rising barometer, the city will be relatively hushed tonight.

Going up the stairs to my attic apartment, I

become conscious that I feel better than I have in weeks. With the balance and focus that Mercedes has given me, I should be thanking her. I sleep well for the first time since I can remember.

PINAR DEL RIO

MERCEDES

She retraces the twists and turns that led her out of captivity.

She walked down Calle Real in Pinar and everything about the city was charged with significance. The main street had been named José Martí since the Revolution, but all the locals still call it Calle Real. This was her city, noisy today, but she knew it would get sleepy at night. It was the last time Mercedes would see it for a long time.

She turned right on Calle Colón and already smelled it. The entire block around the terminal reeked of urine, from years of ill-mannered men spreading their territorial stench. La Terminal de Ómnibus de Pinar del Río is a two-story building. On the first floor there is a small sala de espera and the parqueadero for the buses. The entire second floor is another open, crumbling waiting room, along with the taquillas where they sell the bus tickets. The line for the taquillas winds up the ramp between the two floors. The walls were blue, once. Now they are defiantly dirty, as if to say, *Look at what the Yanquis are doing to us with their embargo!* The chairs, with their assortment of broken backs and seats, are stained and uninviting, but los Pinareños waiting the three or four days it takes to buy a ticket guard them jealously for the tortuous little snatches of sleep they afford off of the urine-soaked floor.

Mercedes was not able to pay someone to wait for her. The resellers' prices go up to one hundred pesos for a seven-peso ticket, so she allots three days, possibly four, for la cola, a long process of getting in line to take a number, to then be assigned to another line, to finally buying your ticket. *Waiting in line to get a place in line . . .* At night the whole place is a sad, murky, frightening vigil between strangers. She heard some of them go to the bathroom in the dark corners around the salas de espera. It made her wonder how the ticket sellers could stand the smell by day. Didn't it stink as much inside the taquillas, or had they figured out a way to freshen the air behind their plexiglass windows? A small bag with soap, toothbrush, and a few changes of clothes was her only pillow. She brought her own meager supply of stale crackers and cooked cassava because the terminal cafeteria opens rarely and randomly, and when it does it is only to sell some tasteless bread with a "croqueta" inside, some unknown something that Andrés told her was ground toenail clippings held together by a little lard.

On the third day she finally got a ticket. The bus to Havana was a ruin, with seats falling apart and no air-conditioning, but after several hours of warm air blowing over her through the open windows, Mercedes had almost gotten the smell of urine out of her head. She was hungry, but she was happy. She was moving away from Andrés at high speed. She was starting to feel free.

At the halfway point, they stopped to go to the bathroom by the autopista, and briefly she found herself in line again with the same strangers from the past four days. When you begin approaching Havana, things change a bit. You start seeing more concrete structures, people, and buses. On the outskirts of the city, the buildings grow taller. A few passengers asked to be dropped off in Marianao before reaching Vedado. Mercedes looked out the window at the fancy vans printed with names of hotels on the side, shuttling tourists to and from the airport.

Bus journeys from all over the island end on the border of Vedado and El Cerro at the Terminal de Ómnibus de la Habana. Others who were used to this route from Pinar del Rio were already gathering their packs before they reached the terminal to jockey for position in the aisle and be the first to get off the cramped, sweltering bus, but Mercedes remained in her seat and looked out at the majestic Teatro Nacional. She had seen many television programs of concerts by Silvio Rodriguez and ballets with Alicia Alonso that happened inside. She saw el Monumento de la Revolución y la Biblioteca Nacional, but all these familiar place names, famous in her imagination thanks to the stories of cousins and friends who had come back from adventures in the big city, meant nothing to her personal locative scheme. Her spatial computer was empty. In a boundless metropolis teeming with millions of hungry people, her only point of reference was herself, and she felt infinitesimally small among the murderers and rapists, priests and paleros, and, somewhere out there, in the middle of everything and nowhere at all, Fidel.

Now she would have to find her own way walking to the center of Vedado. She did not want anyone to know this was her first time in Havana. When her school took the class trip to el Zoológico Nacional and Parque Lenin, she had been recovering from an appendectomy, and after no other opportunity presented itself she became stubborn, cultivating a grudge throughout her teenage years. She would never go to the city, and that was fine with her. She was busy taking care of her mother in Pinar. Now, with her mother's only sister gone and this problem with the apartment, travel had suddenly become imperative, and she wished she hadn't been such an intransigent country bumpkin.

"We're like a couple of pack horses." She heard an old couple making their strategy for how to carry their bundles; they were going to Vedado via Paseo. She followed them at a short distance to la Plaza de la Revolución, where the Ladas and taxis made their endless circles around the monument to José Martí. The pack horses did a quarter-orbit, and the revolution ejected them up a broad avenue Mercedes knew must be Paseo, and she gained new confidence: she had found her axis, and she believed she could keep her bearings on her own.

She headed down Paseo past the theater and the park. Mercedes was always good at math, and her mother had taught her about Vedado: the odd streets run one way intersecting the even, with Paseo being the even Calle 0, although nobody calls it that, and counting down from 29 to el Malecón, which would be the odd 0 since after that you'd be underwater.

She crossed busy Zapata. Even with the soldiers on the corners, she never saw cars so opposed to slowing down. The next street was Calle 19, and she knew 23 couldn't be far. The camellos went up and down Zapata, blowing their air horns and coughing exhaust. They did not have these in Pinar, and nobody had warned her about them before she left for

ROBERT ARELLANO + 73

Havana. The first one she saw frightened her. Why were these people stuffed inside this three-tier monstrosity pulled along by a tractor? Was something terribly wrong? Were they being evacuated for some reason?

She decided to turn up 25 because she could tell it would be quieter. After the ordeal across Zapata, she wanted to approach her aunt's apartment from behind and see how the regular neighborhood looked. Like they told her, casas particulares were popping up almost every block along Calles 2, 4, 6, 8, and 10. The legal ones hung out their hand-painted signs: *La Casa de Angla, Casa MartaAna, Casa Dora*. Who knew how many more unauthorized hostels hid among these crumbling mansions and dilapidated apartment buildings? Even her poor aunt's had been one for a while after she died.

Mercedes had not planned it, but 25 ended at the towering entrance of the famous cemetery from movies and stories, a separate black-and-white city of cement, stone, and bones. A funeral procession was slowly entering between the majestic pillars and she thought of her aunt who, when she would visit Pinar del Rio once a year while Mercedes was a little girl, would always bring a little gift. Sometimes it had been candy, back in the days when there was candy. Then for a while it was a cone full of peanuts or some other treat you could get just as well in Pinar as in Havana. In the past couple of years before she became too sick to travel, it would be something random from her aunt's personal odds and ends: a hair ribbon, a lapel pin, or a scene of antique Havana. The last present was a color post-card of this very necropolis. *Cemeterio Colón, la Habana*, it read. Mercedes had believed the souvenir photograph was beautiful at the time, the gates of wrought iron and the city of white spires pointing to the blue sky with its angelic wisps of cloud. Now it seemed strange and sad that, the last time she saw her aunt Marilyn Delgado, the woman's final offer-ing had been an advertisement for her own death. Mercedes wept.

The apartment door was closed but unlocked. Thresholds are places that preserve the energy of the living long after they are gone. Her aunt Marilyn had passed through this doorway on tens of thou-sands of occasions over seven decades, and soon it would be someone else's. For the privilege, Tia Mar-ilyn had paid rent to a landlord for roughly half this time, and for the other half she had made her token payments to the Reforma Urbana. This doorway had started as a capitalist doorway, and eventually it turned into a socialist doorway.

Mercedes was not surprised to find her aunt's pantry had been picked clean. She was hungry, and she did not know where to get food. She wanted it to be somewhere they would not treat her like a fool. She had her ration book, but even so, to make la cola for rice and beans could take all day, and they still might run out before she got to the front. However, a cafeteria would be a waste of precious pesos. Beneath the kitchen sink she found a dented aluminum pot keeping a dripping drain from further rotting a hole in the planking that showed clear through to the apartment below. If she could find a mercado that had anything in stock and was open long enough, she would get dried beans and rice and manage with that. Then she would make herself a place to sleep on the floor, because her aunt's bed and chairs had all been stolen, and she refused to use the moldy mattress someone had dragged in and left behind.

Mercedes changed into clean clothes and went back down to the street with her carnét de identidad and the ration book in the pocket of her jeans, clutching to her chest the remaining pesos wrapped in a handkerchief. On the sidewalk she looked right and left. She did not know which direction to go, but she did not wish to ask any of the neighbors. There was no saying which of these people had robbed her dead aunt's food and furniture, or who had rented out the apartment to backpackers from Germany as soon as the body had been removed. Mercedes did not remember seeing a market on her walk into the neighborhood, so she decided to go the opposite way from whence she came, in the direction of a boisterous domino game.

It was almost eight p.m., and she was no less hungry, but when she saw the sign for a clínica de familia, she considered the other preoccupation that had been gnawing at her, and how it would be much harder to remedy than an empty stomach. She put her hand on the knob and felt that it was not locked.

She passes through the door.

JUEVES, 4 SEPTIEMBRE
Manolo

I awaken refreshed to remember the patient from Pinar del Rio, Mercedes, her blood sample in my refrigerator awaiting transport to the lab, and the recognition that there is something I can do for someone who needs and deserves my help.

I take the vial from the refrigerator and make sure it is well stopped, placing it inside the cutout Styrofoam block I keep for transport from the clinic. With Mercedes's blood sample in my backpack, I walk to the pediátrico and drop by the lab to fill out the order before starting my shift. It will be twenty-four hours for the various panels I am requesting.

Midmorning the staff nurse brings me a father who is impatient to check out his daughter, and he and I have to wrangle over hospital policy.

"Why give her more pills if she's already feeling better?"

"Even though her fever has gone down, I wish to finish a series of antibiotics just to be certain. Our pharmaceutical technology is very advanced, but it takes time for the human body to reveal the successive details we need to determine a prognosis."

"But she doesn't like the medicine. It makes her feel nauseous."

"That's how antibiotics work sometimes."

"What kind of doctor are you, making a girl who was already getting better feel sick again?"

"Please, señor, let's speak outside."

"Yes, let's. Let's go straight to your boss to talk about the incompetents who are employed here."

I would like to concede to the father that he is correct: there is something imperfect about Cuban health care, but he storms off in the direction of the director's office. You take her home, and what happens? It seems like her condition is improving, and you get back to the house and something goes wrong. First, you waste time discussing what to do; second, you find a phone to call the hospital; third, you drive back in the car. All that time can affect the treatment. Not only that, but even after returning you waste more time registering, sitting in the waiting room, going for another exam in intensive care—and by then the symptoms have changed again.

The nurse gives me a look that makes me smile. "Don't worry, Juanita, you were only following my orders."

"I'm sorry, doctor."

"Don't be. It's simply that I read people's faces the way other people read the newspaper."

In a quiet moment before lunch I chance upon the child psychiatrist, Hernández, at admitting. She has a full schedule six days a week; nevertheless, between consults she has taken to outreach in the emergency room. On her first day she wore jeans; today she helps the nurses with trauma cases and is wearing scrubs.

"I heard you have an invitation to a conference en los Estados Unidos." It is suggestive, the way she says this, and I suppose that this is understandable. In just a couple of days at the pediátrico, she has picked up the pervasive attitude of gridlock and futility. As jobs in the national medical service go, this is the shortest of dead ends. It is not only unlike the coveted jobs in medical tourism, it is stifling even compared to community clinics and rural hospitals. The director is a gato gordo, a fat cat of the worst breed: lots of purring, but when the time comes to get something done, he does not lift a paw. The jaded staff runs the place, and colleagues like Candelario seem to delight in coping by offering barely adequate care with the most cynical attitude.

"Why do you mention it? Were you hoping to put in an order for whiskey and DVDs, like Candelario?"

"I don't drink and all I have is a broken VHS player."

I find myself thinking that I would like to see where she keeps the TV, would like to sit with her on the couch and not drink and watch a romantic movie. Maybe she smokes, or at least she might try, and we could get high and start giggling until she slumps against me and brushes her fingers gently against my neck, my heart stubbornly pulsing away the years—or maybe it's minutes—left to me. Maybe she would raise those fingers to my cheek and trace the contours of my lunar . . .

She continues, "But it wouldn't do me any good to place an order, would it? The goods would never arrive."

"Oh, no?"

"You're soltero, right? No kids. We'll see you on the Miami news, perhaps, another doctor drawn to the miracles of capitalist medical development and denouncing us to the US. What are you going to do to gain their trust?"

"Why don't you tell me?"

"Perhaps you'll be one of those halfhearted defectors who says, *Well, I support the Revolution, but for the sake of my professional potential I feel it is incumbent upon me to practice and conduct research at facilities more suited to my expertise.*"

"It seems you have already prepared my remarks for me."

"Oh, come on, you've read the stories. There's a

new one every week, sometimes two or three."

She is so sexy with that ass in blue doctor duds that I have to struggle against casting a pathetic piropo like, *Dame el sí, mami, y yo regresaré.* If she did say yes, then cóño, she could bring me back.

For a moment I imagine she is inviting me to believe this, when my better judgment takes over to say, "That's not me, doctora. I have my principles."

"You say that now. But once you see the stores— the supermarkets with their shelves and shelves of wine, meat, coffee . . ."

I offered her the slogan as a placeholder, but what I am really thinking is that if you could get to know me, you would understand that Havana and I are like one organism. "I live in the attic above a family clinic that I operate, in the house where I was born. I can't leave Havana. A hundred types of breakfast cereal could not keep me from coming back to Cuba."

"And the hospitals in the USA are lean sky-scrapers of stainless steel and clean tile. They're like air-conditioned cities."

Her teasing is much more relentless than any of the other doctors'. I have to give her credit for stamina, but I change the subject. "Look, I need to step out at lunch, and I might be a few minutes late coming back. Would you please keep an eye out front for me?"

Her shoulder in the doorway, Hernández leans her hip into one hand. "I'll keep an eye on admitting, but I won't be much help in surgery."

"If something like that arises, the head nurse will contact the surgeon on call, but I'd rather a scared kid who is not feeling well talk to you instead of Candelario."

"If I were a scared kid, I'd rather talk to me too."

"Gracias. Hasta luego."

Yorki has jobs at the Neptuno and at the Havana Libre. He washes dishes at both places, not for the extra pesos but because it doubles his access to black markets for beer, lobsters, and whatever else he and the kitchen staff can smuggle out of there without getting caught. Whenever I go see Yorki, I have to work out which hotel he'll be at that day. Today is Thursday, so it's the Neptuno, three kilometers away. As long as I walk briskly and keep the conversation brief, I have just enough time to get there and back during my lunch hour.

I hike down Paseo all the way to el Malecón, through the túnel de Almendares into Miramar. When it runs at all, the Rio de Almendares is like an open sewer separating the ambassadors' residences from my neighbors and patients in Vedado. On the other side, I cannot stand the traffic of tourists and diplomats on Quinta Avenida, so I make my way five short blocks straight to the stone beaches

that remind me of the rocky coastline of Pinar—
except that for the past seven years there have
been so many abandoned cats and dogs scavenging
the beach for anything to eat: dead fish or trash or
sometimes each other, which does mar the beauty
of the sea.

Out by the Copacabana I see the rafters. Balseros
have been leaving from Varadero, from Mariel, and
now from mero Miramar. The Tritón and Neptuno
are twin sentries overlooking the Florida Straits. I
use the service entrance. The kitchen at the Neptuno is enormous. Navigating it reminds me of that
long take from Yorki's bootlegged copy of *Goodfellas*.

Against one wall are the dishwashers, three of
them at a ludicrous 1950s conveyor system that
the hotel maintenance staff somehow keeps loudly
spouting steam. Yorki, with his skinny fútbol-player
physique like a muscular scarecrow, wearing a Guns
N' Roses bandanna, stands out at the end of the line.
Yorki is my oldest friend, and he almost did not stay
that way. He looks up when I tap him on the shoulder, tips his chin in salute, and raises his fingers to
the corners of his mouth to shriek-whistle over the
noise of the machines by the other two dishwashers.
They nod back and one of them moves down to his
position so he can get out of the din for a minute.

Outside by the trash barrels, Yorki takes the opportunity to smoke a precious Marlboro and crack

a joke: "Did you hear the one about Pepito and the prostíbulo?"

"Either way, I'm sure you're going to tell me."

"Pepito and his father walk past a house of prostitution, and Pepito says, *Papi, what's this place?* His father replies, *It's a factory where they make people.* So Pepito goes the next day and peeks through the curtains to see two queers doing it. When he gets home he says, *Papi, I went to the people factory.* His father answers, *Yes, Pepito, and what did you see?* The boy says, *I saw one that was almost finished. A worker still had his hose attached.*"

"A cousin is moving from Pinar," I tell him when the joke is over. If I do not say *cousin*, Yorki will ask too many questions. I have contemplated what I am planning on doing for Mercedes before I do it. "See if you can get her a situation here or at the Havana Libre, something with a place to stay."

"What's in it for me?"

I do not begrudge Yorki the mordida. He is just trying to get me up to speed on the New World Order, the New Economy, and all the other new things I have missed out on and he has mastered so far this decade. On the walk over to the hotel, I was thinking he might put it this way, so I respond with capitalist confidence, as prepared as a businessman: "I will bring you back those tenis Americanos from Tampa."

ROBERT ARELLANO + 85

"What? Has your salida for the conference been approved?"

"It is looking more likely."

"Your cousin, how old is she?"

"She'll be twenty-one in a few weeks," I say, adding, in a flagrant breach of patient confidentiality because I know of no better way to fend off Yorki, which is essential in circumstances like this, "Naturally this stays between you and me, but she may be HIV-positive."

Yorki pinches the ember off and puts the half-smoked Marlboro back in the pack. "I'll check if there's something in housekeeping at the Havana Libre. The camareras there have a common room with bunk beds."

"Her name is Mercedes. I'll send her around to the Havana Libre to talk to you this weekend."

I take the service exit. On my hike back down Tercera Avenida I have to wonder: *Is this really happening? Would I really do something for Pérez to confirm my seat on that flight to a conference just to bring back running shoes for Yorki so that Mercedes can get a job as a maid at a luxury hotel in Havana?* All symptoms would seem to point to the conclusion that indeed, this is what is happening. And the beauty of it is, I can return with those Nikes and refuse to ever cooperate with the PNR—to hell with Pérez.

I pass the Russian embassy and am so lost in

thought that I walk all the way around the traffic circle twice. By the time I realize my mistake, a thunderclap shakes the earth and rattles all the cars parked on the street. Alarms go off in all the diplomats' and tourists' cars, but the day is clear and bright, so how could there be lightning? Are workers dynamiting rocks nearby for a new hotel going up?

This is when I hear the screams, and turn to see people running out of the Copacabana, smoke pouring from the lobby's shattered windows.

My emergency-room instinct makes me run toward the hotel. I hesitate to enter, not for fear of what I will find, but absurdly because I have come to accept that front doors to expensive hotels are off-limits to anyone with pitiful pesos instead of Yanqui dollars, except for jineteras.

A stout State Security agent in a dark suit approaches menacingly, with both arms held out like an American football player, and in order to hold my hospital ID card out with a shaking hand I have to suppress a decade of reflexes that rendered me a second-class citizen who had given up on ever entering a nice place like this. I notice his earpiece, the outline of a handgun under his jacket, and I see he is confused and in shock himself. He does not recognize the insignia of the national medical service on my card.

"Soy médico."

Without a beat he responds, "Why didn't you say something, damn it, there's a tourist bleeding to death inside here!" He grabs my sleeve and drags me through the entrance into a scene of chaos in the dining room.

The security agent was half right: the tourist is still bleeding, but by the time I get to him and reach for his hand he is already as good as dead.

He is young, looks like he's in his late twenties, and there is a piece of metal embedded near his Adam's apple that appears to have pierced the carotid artery. Whenever I read the phrase *died instantly* in the newspaper, I know that it is usually a euphemism. More often than not, it takes several minutes.

The young man's skin is tan and smooth, and his eyes are open, reflecting mine. Does he see me? It makes no difference, because his desperate gulps for air along with the volume of bleeding from the wound in his neck tell me it will be a short competition between blood loss and asphyxiation until the end. We lock eyes and I let him see my humanity. Watching him gasp for breath is all the more galling for the ridiculous association the mind makes, because one thinks of all the fish one has killed this way, and how it can happen to humans like this man, who has just been dispossessed of a hearty life in precisely the same senseless way. His breathing finally ceases, and I see his corneas cloud over.

The paramedics arrive and a young ambulance driver wants to check me out, but I protest that I am not hurt and he should pay attention to the victims. He tells me that there are enough medical personnel to attend to everyone, and that I may be suffering shock and should go to the emergency room so that they can monitor my condition. I tell him that I am a physician and surgeon and that I work in an emergency room; I will monitor my own condition.

Many more men and women have been hit by the concussion wave, window shards that flew into them just minutes ago. You cannot see blood because the glass pierced the epidermis at such velocity: tiny particles peppering the faces, arms, and legs; glass in their clothing, which would have to be removed delicately, not all at once. I have been trained for this—calming a disaster scene, treating shock victims—but it feels like a hundred years ago. I touch the shoulders of as many as I can. *Be calm. Help is on the way.* Mercifully, there are no injured children in sight.

A PNR investigator asks my name. I tell him, "I was two blocks away at the time of the blast," and he takes a photograph of my ID card. When he asks me to clear the area, I tell him that I am a doctor; when he says the ambulances have all gone and the injured are on their way to the hospital, the fog lifts and I see he is right. "This is a crime scene, and we have to start collecting evidence. We will be in touch if any more information is needed from you." And so the site of an inhumane slaughter turns into a job for forensics experts. I do not know if it has been ten minutes or an hour.

When I leave the hotel, I am crossing the turn-around circle in front when a black Toyota pulls up to the lobby entrance and Pérez gets out; I do not stop to talk to him.

I walk home in a daze. I am too shaken up to return to the pediátrico, so I go home to lie in my bed, but I cannot sleep. There is no turning off the replay of what I saw, or my abiding horror at the inhumanity of the scene. I keep seeing the victim's eyes and his last gasps for breath. It is awful to live in a time when any butcher can leave a bomb in a backpack so it will go off where a family eats their lunch around a table.

This is when I understand something about terrorism. Along with the violence and destruction, there is another brutal level to suffer: arbitrariness. It is dehumanizing, knowing that this young man, bleeding to death, was not selected for revenge, enemy conspiracy, or complicity with evil. This victim was not accounted for whatsoever, he was completely collateral. These and other bitter ruminations keep me awake far into the night.

AGOSTO 1979
MANOLO

While my mother was bedridden and clinically depressed, Aurora was the light of my life. I spent my happiest hours upstairs, gazing out the Florida doors with Machado on my lap and Aurora in her rocking chair. She had lived up there since before I was born, and she remained with us, Revolution or no Revolution, raising me until I was ten. "¿Por qué voy a irme, si tú eres la única familia que yo tengo?" I was Aurora's only family, and she worried about leaving me alone with my mother, who rarely left her room.

There had been talk, from the time I could talk, of my father trying to send for us once he could start his own practice. But he had made one tragic error: he initiated the petition to leave before quietly arranging to get the official transcripts of his medical school records. Without these, he was not eligible to take the Florida medical board exams, and without passing them he could not practice medicine.

The functionaries at the medical school stonewalled him, something not uncommon to this day. It has happened to hundreds of doctor-defectors. The State of Florida obstructs them by requiring proof of schooling in order to qualify for the medical boards, and the medical school in Havana frustrates them by refusing to send the official transcripts needed to prove it: no transcript, no board exam; and no board exam, no permission to practice medicine.

It went on for years with no good news. He started conducting exams on the side, doing consultations for other Cuban exiles who, for whatever reason, did not qualify for Medicare. By the time I was nine, Doctor Juan Rodriguez had taken a job as a pharmacist's assistant that paid about a tenth of what he would have made as a physician, with no family medical coverage. That was the same year my mother was diagnosed with cancer.

I was not allowed to disturb Mamá unless Aurora first determined it was a good day and got her ready, but on the morning of my tenth birthday, Machado followed me down to the basement where Aurora had recently scrubbed the sheets and I found the laundry chute at its terminus above the folding table. The little chamber looked so cozy that I told Machado to stay quiet and decided to crawl up inside. This is how I learned that they build passages into walls that fit only the innocent.

The laundry chute was perfectly constructed

with no ridges in the finish, but it was just the right dimensions for me to brace myself on all fours. It made it possible to lift myself up in space. When I looked up, I saw a dim glow from my mother's bathroom, and I started climbing.

The bathroom opened onto my mamá's room, and even the blackout curtains could not keep Havana's blinding sun from trickling in. Her eyes were closed but her chest slowly rose and fell. The bottle of chemotherapy pills stood on the night table. Undetected, I looked at my mother for a long time. She lay beneath the sheet perfectly still with her arms at her sides. It haunted me, the way she did not move. I did not move either because I feared that if I tried, I might find that I, too, was paralyzed. There is a tongue twister I learned when I was young: *deprimida clinicamente*—clinically depressed.

When I heard Aurora below me hiss, "¡Qué cóño pasó con esto!" I panicked and descended too quickly. I hit the bottom hard, crying more out of surprise than pain, although my butt did smart from the shock. Machado started barking and Aurora was more frightened than I was. When she saw I had no cuts or broken bones, she smothered me with kisses on her folding table while theatrically declaiming that I was in trouble, and that I would not get any of the birthday cake my mother planned to bake unless I promised I would never do that again—all for the benefit of my mother's hearing up the chute.

I emerged no wiser to the causes of my mother's affliction, but older for understanding I had been wrong about something that I was not fully conscious I had been thinking: *She is faking it.* The way I saw her laid out there, it was clear that this depresión clínica must be a condition with great determination to be able to incapacitate her so. It shut her system down like venom and left her entire body in a trance. She was not faking it.

It was Aurora's night off and she put me to bed first, but after she went out I heard Mamá emerge from her room. I called out and asked her what was wrong. "Nothing. I'm going to bake a cake." She found eggs, flour, sugar, and powdered chocolate, and when the batter was almost ready she used a pestle to grind up a special ingredient.

It didn't take long to bake, and she sang "Las Mañanitas" and gave me hugs for the first time in as long as I could remember, and she almost seemed to smile. I wondered, *Is this just a good day, or does this mean Mamá is better?* When it came out of the oven she cut it in two and we ate off the same plate. The kitchen smelled good, but I cringed at the first taste. While she consumed her half, I snuck most of mine beneath the table to Machado.

Two hours later, the doctors identified the poison

by dissecting the dog. The smallest had died first, and Mamá did not make it through the night, but I had ingested very little and the doctors were able to pump my stomach in time. I survived the overdose of my mother's chemotherapy pills with the side effect of a small but noticeable hematoma beneath my right eye, an *infarctus incubatus* that came to be known by Communist doctors from Venezuela to Angola by the name *Havana Lunar*.

VIERNES, 5 SEPTIEMBRE
MANOLO

I am awakened by a shout on the stairs: "¡MaNOlo! ¡TeLÉfono!" My back, my neck, my arms and legs—every centimeter aches with the same penetrating agony; I have been holding my body tense all night. I hate what I have to remember.

It satisfies my cynicism to have to go down to the demon Beatrice to get my calls. I walk past the open door to her bedroom, once my mother's bedroom. Another door opens onto her bathroom, my mother's bathroom, and the laundry chute. Beatrice hands me the receiver and reliably, if rudely, relays messages.

Although I did not ask, when I enter her kitchen Beatrice announces, "El pediátrico," meaning that she has been nosy, because the hospital dispatcher never identifies herself when she calls for me.

The phone is in the old pantry off the kitchen. I take the handset and say, "Rodriguez. ¿Oigo?"

A woman's voice: "Un minuto." And then another voice is on the line. Pérez says, "Repeat after me: *I'm not sure what you're talking about. Can you give me more information on the patient?*"

"I'm not sure what you're talking about. Give me some more information on the patient."

"Listen to me, Doctor Rodriguez: if you knew that you could prevent more random bloodshed like the kind you saw yesterday, would you do something to stop it?"

My heart feels heavy in my chest. The obvious answer is yes, I would do anything to stop it. "Why me? What do you think I can do about it?" I cannot say more with Beatrice eavesdropping.

Pérez says, "Because it involves another doctor. If you wish to know more, it will have to wait until we can meet again in person."

"When?"

"Tonight, in the apagón. Now say, *Thank you for letting me know. I will check in on my rounds.*"

"Thank you for letting me know. I will check in on my rounds."

Pérez concludes, "You know she has a peephole up to your bathroom, don't you?" I look over at Beatrice in the kitchen with her towel, conspicuously rubbing some already-dry dishes. He hangs up.

Immediately the line makes the weak buzzing sound that reminds me, *There is no connection. And there never will be. This is Cuba. Communism has failed, and so has communication.* I tell the dead line, "Adiós."

Beatrice says, "Cierra la puerta," so I close the door on my way out.

Back up in my apartment, I find a knothole in the floorboard beside the toilet. When I push it, it drops through the floor of the bathroom, followed by the sound of frenzied shuffling down in Beatrice's pantry. I plug the hole with a wad of toilet paper and several layers of surgical tape.

I sit on the edge of my bed and think about calling in sick to work—I do not want to walk across Vedado to the pediátrico.

I remember something I read in *Granma* about terrorism, an interview with a psychiatrist that resonated for me. When they terrorize you to the point that you do not wish to go outside, and then you don't go outside, that is when they have won. If you do not wish to show up at work, you have handed them the victory. Is this what I have been doing, ignoring the terrorism as abstract until it was laid bare to me materially? The ostrich burying his head? I do not want to get out of bed, but neither do I want to be absent when something happens that I could help cure or heal. I have to hold onto this plain certainty that I do not want to be gone if something bad happens that I could have prevented.

I swing my feet over the side of the bed and arrive at a decision, although in reality I have no choice.

* * *

At the pediátrico, Hernández greets me with: "Is this what's known as a few minutes late after lunch?"

"I'm sorry I never came back yesterday."

"Packing for Tampa?"

In a daze, I hear myself say, "There was a bombing at the Copacabana."

"I head about it from the director. They treated the injured at Calixto Garcia."

"A man was killed, a tourist. I witnessed it."

"Carajo, Mano." When she calls me *Mano*, I sense a human beneath her usual sarcasm.

"I was outside at the time of the explosion. There was little I could do before the first responders arrived."

"How are you feeling?"

I have to choke back a bitter laugh. "Don't try your psychiatric tricks on me." I change the subject: "Doctora Hernández, may I ask your professional opinion? As long as you give all your patients the best treatment possible in the clinic, is it wrong to give one patient special treatment by helping with problems in the outside world?"

"Well, it would depend on the circumstances. For example, if it contributes to the overall sanitary environment."

"What does that mean?"

"We have a moral obligation to protect at-risk

populations from domestic violence, for instance."

"And if I happen to have personal contact in an area that could be of use to a patient, but it is also because I am especially motivated in this case? I feel more empathy than I have in any other situation for some time."

"It sounds like you are becoming susceptible to one of the oldest distractions ever to blind the physician to his duty."

"What's that?"

"Love."

"¡Que vá!"

"I didn't say romantic love, necessarily."

"What kind, then? Are you suggesting that I am becoming predisposed toward paternalismo?"

"Well," she says, "both Jung and Freud would call it fine, so long as you keep your dirty-old-man hands off her."

"Spoken like a true materialist."

"It takes one to know one."

I leave Hernández to start my rounds. I go by the lab for the results of Mercedes's blood tests, but I do not look at them. Although I would not proceed any differently with my plan, to learn of a serious medical condition could alter this grand, happy feeling of helping her, a country girl with nothing who escaped to a new city where she has nobody, just the ghost of an aunt whose estate is already being reapportioned by the government. Looking at the lab report is not going to change this. But I wish to feel hopeful, even if it is just for a few more hours until the end of the day.

I walk straight home and take a quick, cold shower and put on clean scrubs. This way I will not smell of diesel and the street when my patient and I discuss her tests. I go down to open the clinic and clean the clutter from my desk for some semblance of order and efficiency. I want Mercedes to know that she is in good hands. At 5:25 I look at the lab report so I do not appear surprised when I tell her. Although I am relieved, I compose myself. I need to proceed carefully and monitor her reaction. Because most of my patients in this neighborhood are seniors or young children, I do not often get the chance in this clinic to be the one to tell someone. I am ready the moment she comes through the door.

Mercedes fidgets in her chair. She has been chewing at her fingernails, and they are a ragged mess. They have been blackened by something that may or may not be nail polish. Clearly and evenly I say, "You do not have HIV."

She shudders lightly and exhales a great breath. "Qué alivio."

She starts shaking and I put a hand on her shoulder. "I have more news for you. Please, sit down . . . You are pregnant."

I took her blood. I ran the tests. I ran one more, although she did not ask me to. I wouldn't have told her anything if the results had been negative, and there would have been no harm. *You are pregnant.* Mercifully, it is accompanied by a great, quivering smile that tells me I have confirmed her suspicion.

Tears come to her eyes and she glances around as if expecting to see someone she knows in the room. She looks directly down at her belly, and then up at me. In the absence of anyone else, she throws her arms around my neck and gives me a great squeeze.

She composes herself and I can see through the tears that she is pleased, but then a dark cloud of uncertainty passes over her expression, and she sobs, "No es fácil."

"Mira, sobre lo de resolver un trabajo por ahí. I have a friend at the Havana Libre and you may be able to work and live there for a while."

"You found me a job, and a place to stay too?"

"Drop by the Havana Libre tomorrow and ask for Yorki in the kitchen. I have to prepare for a conference en la Florida next week, but he will be expecting you. If anyone asks, you should tell people that you and I are cousins."

"What if they find out?"

"No te preocupes. It won't come up. Besides," I decide to tell her, "my father's family is from Pinar del Rio, you know."

"¡No me diga!"

"He came to Havana for medical school and met my mother, but he left for la Yuma before I was born. I spent every summer in Pinar growing up, and I've always considered Viñales home."

"I don't know how to thank you, doctor."

"No tienes que agradecerme." I almost forgot that we are speaking as doctor and patient.

"Me da vergüenza."

"No hay pena."

Mercedes smiles, but it is not a self-satisfied smile. She is thinking of her baby. She is in love; she loves blindly, searchingly—and she makes me wonder what it would be like to be loved like that again, just once.

I write down when and where she can find Yorki, and then Mercedes and I say good night.

Closing up the clinic, I grasp that years spent ruminating on the dead ends of my life have been disrupted by the grim reappearance of Pérez and the horror of the Copacabana bombing. I needed Mercedes to appear as much as she needs me. It reminds me of the families in Pinar del Rio, the old timers coming around before harvest, asking, *You don't think you can find me two pounds of frijoles?* Because someone will always be able to help you. In the darkness of these days, for a couple of hours at least, here is a way to clear a new road for someone who really deserves it. Mercedes is becoming more than a patient. I did not wish for this; neither do I resist. It gives me a pleasant but queasy feeling, like a friend I have not seen in five years walking up and punching me in the gut.

The apagón comes before I get back upstairs to my apartment. Pérez is already there in Aurora's old rocking chair. "I thought I would call first this time."

"Qué bueno que llamaste antes," I say. Like last time, he waits until I arrive to light up a smoke, and like last time I join him. It is my last Popular.

"The victim at the Copacabana was thirty-two years old." Pérez pauses either out of respect or to let the victim's age resonate for a moment. And it does: thirty-two, a life cut off less than halfway through. "He was a Canadian citizen of Italian origin on vacation with his father, who was upstairs at the time of the blast. At 11:35 a.m., while he was having lunch with friends at the hotel restaurant, a bomb concealed in a floor-standing ashtray nearby exploded, sending a shard of shrapnel deep into his neck and severing the carotid artery."

I raise the cigarette to my lips and see that my hands are trembling. "Carniceros . . ."

"Bombs also exploded in the lobbies at the Chateau and Tritón at fifteen-minute intervals."

"Long enough for someone to walk from each hotel to the next."

"There were dozens more injuries but no fatalities. Late last night, one more blew at the Bodeguita del Medio after closing time and nobody was hurt. All the bombs were made with the same C-4, and the timer-detonators were assembled from the same primitive components."

"Why are you telling me this? I'm a doctor. How do you expect me to stop a bomber?"

"We already have this bomber."

"¿Qué?"

"Un Salvadoreño. Forty-four years old. DSS took him into custody yesterday evening and he confessed before midnight. He was in possession of detonators and C-4 to make more bombs."

"A Salvadoran? Why?"

"For money. The real butcher is a Cuban exile who pays for it without ever leaving Miami. His contact recruits mercenaries in San Salvador. We have gotten some new intelligence that you are in a position to build on."

"How?"

"Your invitation to the conference in Tampa next week."

"I never expected it to get approved."

"Expect it now."

"This is absolutely crazy. I am not a spy."

"No, but gathering intelligence means quickly getting close to a doctor in Miami, and it will be more credible telling you what to look for than training a spy to impersonate a physician."

"I see the reasoning."

"I cannot tell you any more unless you come with me to a secure location."

"Is my apartment not a secure location?" I am surprised that an insider of Cuban intelligence like Pérez does not feel that everywhere is a secure location.

He stubs out his cigarette and I copy him. We take the back stairs to the alley, where a black Toyota with dark-tinted windows is waiting. It is an inconspicuous sedan, not one of the late-model SUVs that draws attention and makes people in the neighborhood gossip about what ministry someone has gotten mixed up with.

Pérez gets in the front passenger side and I get in back behind the driver, an unsmiling prieto who stares at my lunar in his rearview mirror. I try to catch the driver's eye for some kind of acknowledgment that he knows I have been in the back of a car like this before, that I know I am lucky to be on Pérez's good side—for now—but he consigns for me less regard than the toothpick clenched in his jaw. The moment both doors shut, he hits the gas and accelerates down the alley to Paseo.

I am an atheist, so it is only figuratively that I

say something sent me in a circle through Miramar yesterday. If I had not heard the blast and seen that young man die, I might not be here. Pérez reads my mind. "Look, Doctor Rodriguez, there is no way you could have prevented what happened at the Copacabana, but now the time is short. It is essential you tell me if you feel even the slightest hesitation."

The driver makes a fast, sharp left onto the avenue, pushing me into the empty seat beside me. "No. No hesitation."

"It's a little different, isn't it, when you look a victim in the eye, and you can hear the monster breathing?" It does not escape my notice that Pérez, his expressionless gaze fixed downhill and out to sea, does not need to tell the driver our destination. Things are proceeding as planned—that is, according to Pérez's expectations. A deep, familiar discomfort stirs in the pit of my stomach.

We hurtle down Paseo, the police on the median conspicuously ignoring our government plates. Everyone else leaps back at the intersections. That is usually me standing on the corner, jumping out of the way of a government car's inexorable slipstream. A right on Linea and one block to the tall building I take note of on the corner of Calle A whenever I walk by on my way to el Malecón. There are metal barriers on either end of the sidewalk and, in case there remains any question in your mind whether you must cross Calle A just to walk past, two military guards brandish AK-47s in a bulletproof sentry post by the driveway.

We slow just enough not to bottom out on the tire shredders that the guards lower, waving us into a small underground garage. The only other vehicle is a gleaming Toyota pickup truck. I have never seen something so big, not to mention brand new, except for in pirated American movies. The driver parks beside the pickup but does not shut off the engine. Pérez gets out and when I go to open my door, I discover there is no inside handle. *The simplest traps are the ones you need to keep alert for, Mano.*

Pérez comes around and opens the door for me. We find our way through the dark, damp garage, leaving the driver to torture his toothpick in solitude. There is a set of two elevators: one for floors 1 through 12, and the other for 14 and 15. Pérez pushes *14* and we rise silently inside the fortress.

State security's mission is to protect the Cuban people from rogue and mercenary external threats. The elevator stops but the doors do not open yet. Pérez stays perfectly still, his chin tilted back a little farther than customary. This is when I see he is looking up at a fish-eye lens mounted in the middle of the number 8 above the pocket doors. We are on closed circuit, awaiting authorization to escape this box. *The simplest traps . . .*

The doors open onto a small dining room. It is essentially a converted apartment, but unquestionably it was remodeled with attention to the kind of impenetrable security one would expect of Daniel Caballero, general chief of the DI of the DSS, the Intelligence Directorate of the Department of State Security. He says, "Pérez tells me you have an invitation to a conference."

"That's right."

We sit in the dining room around a glass table with a clean ashtray. The general chief smokes Newports. Pérez pulls out his Camels and also gives me a fresh pack of Populares. "Very thoughtful," I mutter.

We smoke. "Has he told you about the assignment?" Caballero asks, looking at me.

Pérez lets me answer. "Just that I am to contact a doctor who has access to the exile community."

"Yes, but to accomplish this you shall have to miss the conference."

"I don't understand."

"You will have to defect." I look over to Pérez, but he is studying his fingernails.

"¿Cómo?"

"For a little while, at least. If you want to establish credibility quickly among los gusanos, you will have to make your allegiance clear by renouncing Cuban citizenship."

"I have to pretend I'm going to stay?"

"You know the saying. *Every family has one gusano and one gay.*"

Now that we are in a secure location, Pérez becomes talkative and gives me the précis: "The suspect in the Copacabana bombing flew in on September 1 as a tourist, smuggling timers in the linings of his suitcase and C-4 in the bottoms of his boots. He has no clear ideological position. You know the rate for bombing a Cuban hotel?"

"How much?"

Pérez says, "They offered the Salvadoran $1,500."

Caballero interjects, "About the cost of a week at a nice hotel."

"That is a morbid way of looking at it."

"Not enough left to cover a jinetera," says Caballero.

I think about that young Italian's father upstairs in the hotel. When he heard the blast, what had he thought? Could he have imagined at that instant his son dying in the lobby below?

Pérez continues, "He'd intended to hit four targets for $6,000, flying back to El Salvador this weekend. He would have been paid after the backers heard about it on Univisión or Telemundo, but now that he's in prison, Miami and San Salvador have naturally cut him off. He became cooperative after he realized that we have all the forensic evidence we need from his fingernail clippings to put him in front of the firing squad. He has given us much useful information, the most actionable being that there is a second bomber with more C-4 already in Havana."

Caballero remarks, "We cut off a dragon's head, but discovered it is a two-headed dragon."

Pérez unbuttons the inside pocket of his overcoat and removes some papers. He reads from a transcript. *"There is a second bomber who came with a lot of C-4. Before the end of the month he'll try to hit a target that will make a very big impact*—those are his words."

Caballero says, "He knows neither the identity nor the whereabouts of the second bomber, but a link through his recruiter in San Salvador to a Cuban exile in Miami could lead us to the next target and date."

Pérez says, "There is something else you did not need to know until now."

Caballero fixes my gaze. "The exile is a landlord in Little Havana named José Felipe Mendoza. He rents a building to another exile, a former doctor who runs a small pharmacy on Calle 8 in Little Havana." The air in the room turns cold instantly. I know immediately whom he is getting at. "I am talking about Doctor Juan Rodriguez."

I stand in shock and push my chair back from the table. Pérez puts his hand on my arm and says,

"The monster is not a tourist from Central America hiding explosives in his shoes, Rodriguez. It is a relatively small group of men in Miami paying him to do it."

Pérez looks me in the eye. He seems to be asking a question. I understand something, and I have to catch my breath. He is asking me to look the monster in the eye. He is telling me I cannot deny his existence any longer and asking me to take a job nobody could want. Pérez knows that the work he has inherited is detestable, but if he tried to refuse it, either he would have to convince himself like a madman that the monster does not exist, or he would slowly die trying to drown out the sound of his own breathing with strong drink.

"You saw the destruction at the Copacabana," Pérez reminds me. "If we know where the monster plans to strike, we can prevent it. If you can learn the target, we can stop the next one."

"We know this is not easy," Caballero says, "but you must exercise your will as a doctor and separate the person from the problem, which is to get close to Mendoza."

They are both staring at me now. I have been flirting with abandoning the Revolution, but now they are asking me to spy on my own father and risk my life for it. I do not care much about socialist doctrine or preening one's principles, but I do care about saving lives. If I do this, it will not be for Cuba. It will be for decency.

It might not be far from materialist to say that what propels me on this expedition is this new feeling for Mercedes. Pérez is correct: I would do this for life's small triumph over the senseless death of an innocent young person. You cannot pretend any longer, Rodriguez. What are you going to do?

I look at Caballero. "On one condition." He glances at Pérez, not accustomed to being given conditions. "That you will not allow them to close the family clinic I operate in Vedado. I can even tell you how to do it."

Pérez's complete stasis must tell Caballero something, if only, *Go on, this is not unusual; I'll take care of it.* The general chief says flatly, "How?"

"Someone high up in the Ministry of Health will suggest to Director Gonzalez the doctor who will take over in my absence. She's new at the pediátrico and has not become indispensable."

Pérez turns to Caballero and says, "Gonzalez will be helpful." And that seals it.

Caballero says, "All right. We have to move forward quickly. What would your normal routine be leading up to a trip like this?"

"Tomorrow I was planning to go to Pinar to visit my grandparents." Even as I hear myself say it, I am thinking that there is nothing normal about a Cuban doctor getting approved for a salida to go to a conference en los Estados Unidos, with or without the spying.

"Then you will go to Pinar. Anyone there you could ask for your father's telephone number?"

"I would have thought you knew it already."

"We do, but your father will wonder where you got it from."

"I think my primo Emilio has a socio in Miami who once got him the number of the pharmacy."

"Then get the number from Emilio, but if he asks, say that you are only thinking of calling your father from the conference. Can you return from Pinar on Sunday?"

"That was the plan."

"Get back as early as possible. We'll need to meet at a different location. Pérez will arrange for transportation."

On the elevator down, I ask, "What happens on the fifteenth floor?"

Pérez replies, "That's where Caballero lives." In the car I tell him about Doctora Hernández. He says, "I'll take care of it tonight."

The driver stops at the same spot in the alley behind my apartment. It is dark. The apagón is taking extra long tonight. But of course this alley is not the same alley. Everything is different now.

Pérez says, "If you're lucky, sometime in the next

forty-eight hours the Copacabana bomber might give us information that will lead to the second bomber, and instead you get to go to your conference."

Before getting out of the car, I ask him, "How did you people come up with this locura?"

"The analysts created models for thirty-seven discrete scenarios: introducing multiple agents, introducing a female agent, recruiting from disgruntled members of the organization. Yours is the one with the greatest probability of achieving our objective in the shortest amount of time."

"And how long did your analysts say it might take me?"

Pérez can read between the lines, but his expression is inscrutable when he says, "Until you get to Miami, you're the only one who knows you're defecting. Tell your grandparents you're going to Tampa and that you will see them in a week. Tell your cousins about all the things you will bring back for them from la Yuma."

"Just as if I were really planning to return in a week?"

Pérez says, "Just as if you were really planning to defect."

The Toyota pulls away.

In the morning I will have to fix the flat on the Lada. When I get to my apartment at the top of the stairs, the light returns.

SÁBADO, 6 SEPTIEMBRE
MERCEDES

In the basement dormitory for laundry staff and maids at the Havana Libre, her new home, she lies on the top bunk and looks at the ceiling. "Cuídate," her mother told her when she set out for Havana. "Men will look at you and men will look through you. They'll try to do you favors because they believe you will think they deserve something in return." She said it with such gravity that it was clear her mother was talking about the girl's father, whom Mercedes never knew. She refused to believe all men were like this, but it would be useless to argue. In her mother's mind and heart, it was manifest truth.

She is done with Andrés. He told her she would never amount to anything in Havana but a puta jinetera. She should inject with him and go into the sanatorium. Or they could do it without a condom, which were getting harder to find anyway. Fidel would find an antidote in the next year or two. Hell, he probably already has it, he's just waiting to make a big announcement. "Let him wait. Meat every day, milk and eggs—and air-conditioning!"

It disgusted her, how he spoke of it as if he were on vacation in Varadero, when for more than a year already los rockeros in Los Baños have been dying. People told stories of diseases that ate the brain, rendering the dying patient insane.

"You'll never be more than a whore of a jinetera. You'll have to sell your ass just to pay the rent. Fat, ugly Germans will think they deserve a piece for the price of a Coke and entry to a disco. Some of them will want to choke you until you lose consciousness, and the police won't give a shit . . ."

"Stop!" she shouted. "Stop talking!" She left the room. Why wouldn't he stop these barrages?

". . . because you chose to sell a tourist your skin just to pay the rent."

Why wouldn't he stop? It makes her shudder to remember the nights he treated her like this, not much better than the brutal tourists he described, when he knew that she would never turn to prostitution. All the more now that she was carrying his baby, although he had no idea she was pregnant. Something was inside of her that she would never sell, even if she had to die to protect it. She had known she would have to leave Pinar del Rio. She left the apartment and she left Andrés.

It has been so sad, and while she will never

turn her back on her friends, she will not visit them in the sanatorium as long as Andrés is around. Is she hoping he's going to go soon? Is that what she meant by that thought? She doesn't know for sure, but she suspects that Fidel and all his doctors have no fucking idea what to do about AIDS. She hopes that Andrés will be around for one reason: because some day the child will want to know who her father is. Even though he was a scoundrel once, and may still be if he survives until her daughter is four or five, the drive to know your father is something Mercedes understands from experience, and when that time comes she will need to arrange a safe way.

Havana is a new beginning. In Havana she is free to start over, and the doctor is giving her a direction for her to make the first move. He has given her license to make a new start, this doctor who helped her find a job. Why is he treating her so kindly? She wonders at what, in a manner of speaking, she would call his androgyny. Platonism is supposedly his occupational imperative, but that does not mean that she has not noticed the male doctors at the polyclinic in Pinar del Rio, while lifting the stethoscope from her chest, letting their hands linger a little longer, allowing fingers to brush her breasts—not this one. She cannot even imagine him trying.

She is certain he is not a maricón, but he separates his manhood from their consultas for some combination of professionalism and paternalism. Nevertheless, he does not seem like a family man, and that first time they met, he clearly said *I live upstairs*. She opens her eyes and looks at the ceiling, picturing the doctor going to his conference en la Florida, dazzling some blond Americana with his awkward gentleness. She hopes he will be happy. She hopes he will be as happy as he has made her. She hopes that he, too, will find love.

SÁBADO, 6 SEPTIEMBRE
MANOLO

If it gets complicated quickly, it is because I know there isn't much time before I might be gone a long time. Whatever help I might give her will have to be between now and Tuesday, when I leave for the conference. Whatever energy I have left after my shifts at the pediátrico must go to Mercedes. In the morning before leaving for Pinar, I pay a visit to the daughter of a regular patient who now directs the círculo infantil in the neighborhood. "A cousin of mine just moved here from Pinar. Her husband is very ill and the baby is due in March. Can you get her on the wait-list?" I assure the director that the mother has a job at the Havana Libre, and she assures me there will be space for a baby in the spring.

What is happening to me? I have just turned twenty-eight. Is this what it is like to become an old man? If I could break my resolution about collaborating with Pérez, I might forgive myself for falling for a patient again. I need to get away for a time. It could not hurt to put some distance between her and me. What way to feel more chaste than spending the time undertaking a brave and selfless mission? How better to make myself feel noble? I get ready for my drive to Pinar del Rio and go down to the Lada. The flat has been fixed, and when I start the car, I notice that the tank is full.

I never met Juan Rodriguez, who left a few weeks before I was born in '69. Around my tenth birthday he stopped writing, and my mother stopped living. There has been not so much as a postcard in nearly twenty years. So many left in the early sixties that the neighborhood was empty for a while. This was a time of relative peace, but for those remaining from the old families it was terrible anticipating what must be coming. By '61, the expropriations of foreign-owned property were underway, and Reforma Urbana had worked out their draconian redistribution plan. It felt like a free-for-all, a new nightmare every week: people moving into the neighborhood from East Havana and the provinces. The people from the provinces were okay. They were humble, but unaccustomed to others living on top of them.

The ones from East Havana were the worst. Many of them hated Rodriguez unreservedly. Their contempt for the few good families remaining had been pent up all their lives. Moving into Vedado was a kind of revenge: take over the mansions of those snobby Habaneros; throw trash in the alleys and shit in the well water. They called this freedom. These were his new patients, and the idiots from MINSAP told Rodriguez that he had to treat them for free.

These were the people that the criminal and illegitimate government told Rodriguez he had to sacrifice his private practice for, and they abused and exploited the services. After all, everything these dumb doctors did was free! Rodriguez became a puppet of the ignorant and entitled masses, held at gunpoint by the equally uneducated and exploitative soldiers, taking orders from the devil—Fidel—and that shit-eating Argentine who called himself a doctor. By 1963, half of the country's six thousand physicians had left.

It was 1965 when everything blew up in his face. First, Beatrice stopped paying rent. Doctor Rodriguez tried to be dignified about it; the lease would be up soon. He did not renew the lease, and still she did not move out. He paid a server to deliver an eviction notice, and in return he received a notice from the Ministry of the Interior that Beatrice Amarilys Zequeira was petitioning for tenant's rights. The way the wheels of injustice were turning, the Ministry of Interior would be the new landlord, and she would pay *them* rent from now on, and there was nothing he could do about it. By '69, he told Abuelo he had put up with the Revolution for ten years, and that was long enough.

* * *

In Pinar City, everyone is watching the rerun of Diana Spencer's funeral, and if they do not have TVs they're listening on the radio. Once in Viñales, I prefer to follow the road from town to the dark side of the valley on foot, three kilometers up a shadeless, steady slope. It helps me get in the right frame of mind. The poinsettias grow enormous on either side of the trail.

The rains came in May. Now that it is late summer, the river that usually runs between these rocks has gone dry. From June to August, there are times you cannot climb the back way without getting covered in mud. I make my way through groves of palma real, and I can hear Abuelo's voice from when I was a boy: *La palma real is the perfect tree. Con las tablas se puede cubrir la casa completa por afuera y se pueden usar hasta para las paredes. Las pencas se usan pa'l techo, y las yaguas pa' guardar el tabaco y p'arriba del techo. Hasta los palmiches engordan a los puercos.*

When I reach the summit of his mogote, Abuelo is sitting in the chair in front of his house. "I saw you coming an hour ago."

I kiss his cheek. "Tienes ojos de águila, Abuelo."

"Tardaste mucho en subir. ¿Todavía tienes esa gripe?"

"No todavía, Abuelo: otra vez."

"Cúrate, Manolo."

"Me voy, Abuelo. Me voy a curar con el agua."

I sit with Abuelo, watching a pair of hawks spin their valley shadows into mesmeric lace. The up-draft under those broad, efficient wings lets them soar and rise to the sky without flapping a feather. I rustle inside my mochila for the plastic sack and, although Abuelo does not divert his eyes from the hypnotic patterns of the hawks, a discernible tremor in the flesh of his temple makes me smile.

"Te traje un poco de chocolate, Abuelo. Es Bélgico—el mejor del mundo."

"Nunca te olvidas de mi, Manolo. Nunca!"

I help him unwrap the bit of chocolate Direc-tor Gonzalez gave me. We sit quietly and watch the hawks. I listen to the sound of their wings and my grandfather's breath.

Emilio always told me, "When your father was young, people from all around the valley would search him out on the first of January . . . Not just because he's a Juan, but also the son of the most re-spected man on any of the mogotes, and so must be the luckiest to greet for New Year's luck."

Ramón is the strong one. Bernarda came next, but nobody calls her that; everyone calls her Mima. Then Arturo, and Gloria, whom everyone calls Yoya because when Manolito was little, this was all he could say. Sevilla was beautiful, with a face so pretty pink she looked like a delicate rose blossom. She died giving birth to her second child, which nobody has quite gotten over. And then there's Manolito, casado con Lydia, and their two daughters—they live with Abuela and Abuelo. Abuela had children from the time she was sixteen until she finished with Manolito at forty. And if she had known what she was bringing into the world, she would have stopped at Sevilla, a family joke for more than twenty-five years which has become ossified: it is now funny because it is so not funny.

A crazy whoop that would shame Tarzan echoes up the trail from the valley: Manolito is coming home.

Now that Abuelo is so old, it has fallen to the youngest to run the small rancho because he was the last to be born and never left the house. Manolito sees it as his duty to take care of them. Or maybe Abuelo and Abuela knew that the wild streak in Manolito made it important for him to stay close, so they told him they needed him to stay. Who can say? It has become an essential arrangement.

I remember when he landed Lydia. I remember her standing quietly in the threshold the first time he brought her over, with her nicest dress and her pretty legs in her chancletas, and he spread his arms wide like a carnival hawker in an old movie and shouted, as if to drill it into her head and make it her own thought, "¡Mira, una casa con piso y to'!"

as if all she could want in this world would be built on that house with a floor and everything.

I almost wished she would wise up and break it off, but he rushed the wedding and got her pregnant before she realized what she had gotten into. She was awestruck by his cockiness—which she mistook for confidence—and his brazenness—which she attributed to intelligence. In reality Manolito is just an ignorant guajiro so crazy as to shout at the world, even as he drinks himself deeper and deeper into a hole to hide from the ever-multiplying fears of all that he misunderstands. It is an unspoken certainty that she would, could, and probably should leave him—were it not for the old folks. Otherwise, not even their two beautiful daughters would be a force strong enough to stop her. Nobody doubts she would take the girls with her, and she would be completely justified, for the love a mother bears her children and for their own safety, carajo. Nobody would fault her. Manolito is crazy, just plain crazy. Poor Lydia— could she have known what she was getting into? But something about the larger constellation has conspired to keep her there. Manolito manages the farm and takes care of his aging parents, who in turn help with the girls, and all the while Lydia somehow manages to half-tame wild Manolito. A perfect arrangement for everyone, except for miserable Lydia.

"¡Mi sobrino se va pa' la Yuma!" he shouts as

he approaches. "¿Y ahora eres revolucionario? ¡Singa'o! ¡Esto no tiene nada que ver con esos hijos de puta en la Habana y su jodío comunismo!" *This has nothing to do with those sons of bitches in Havana and their screwed-up Communism.* A brief explosion, but one that doesn't even make my heart race anymore. Como los huracanes de Agosto en la Habana, I know that as long as you diminish your own reaction, it will blow by and the streets will be dry before anyone has time to go inside for an umbrella.

First Manolito looks in on his mule to make sure she made it home from town all right. He has no reason to worry, because it was she who carried him, but it seems right and proper to him to check her feet for stones and her ears for any new nicks or bite marks. "Buena, buena Moronga."

He tells me for the hundredth time, "Se llama Moronga, pero el Chino le dice Lapinga." El Chino needing no explanation as another of his drink-drank-drunk buddies from town who finds it funny to call everything a variation on a near-homophone to penis.

In Pinar there is food. We grow yuca, guanábana, y matas grandes de flor de pascuas que vendemos en el pueblo pa' las fiestas. Malanga, tabaco, arroz, frijoles. In Pinar my family shares modest meals, but as Abuelo says, there is always food for a feast. Abuela and Lydia go about preparing one in my honor. There is puerco asado, congris, and fried yucca seasoned with garlic and lime. There is café from the garden for everyone but the youngest cousins, who get a splash of coffee in their milk. Manolito gives my littlest cousin a two-liter bottle to go around to the neighbors and see who is selling wine—"Que sea de platano, o de guayabita, o de caña"—even if it is made out of wood.

Hovering over Abuelo's shoulder, Abuela repeats her litany for my sake, but of course Lydia, washing pots, is within earshot. "Why do wives today have to talk and talk and talk so much at their husbands? He is the father of her children. She should serve him. What does talking and complaining accomplish? In sixty-nine years of marriage, Abuelo has never had to hit me—not once." Lydia might not hear every word, but she is certainly familiar with the timbre of this matriarchal grievance.

Abuela is too old now to do the actual serving, though she refuses to eat until Abuelo is finished. Lydia does most of the work, but Abuela insists on leaning against the counter or a high stool the entire time and remains standing while the men are served. It has always been this way, yet I only notice now since she has slowed down and passed the serving duties along to Manolito's wife. The rest of her children have gone, and her self-exile from the meal is clearly less out of necessity than deference.

Abuela interrupts herself: "¿Todavia no te has casado, Manolo? ¿No quieres tener hijos?"

"Abuela, you got started young."

I will be the first of her immediate family to travel outside of Cuba, but that does not count her firstborn son. Rarely is mention made of my father. This is Abuelo's preference, his seldom-spoken resolution of disownment, and it is also my preference. He first deserted this family when he left for Havana, and then he abandoned his pregnant wife to go to Miami, and now Abuelo knows he will never see him again.

The wine arrives—banana, mercifully. Manolito wants a party. It is a party for the first of his cousins to go to los Estados Unidos. He pours two glasses and I sip slowly, but he goads me, prying my mouth open and tipping my chin back if he has to. He pours it right down my throat from the bottle. Lydia begins preparing a pot of ajiaco.

After we are good and drunk and Manolito passes out, my cousin Emilio arrives. He gives me a hug and goes in to change out of his coast guard uniform. When he comes back he smells the remains of the home-filled bottle of banana wine and winks at me, "That's going to hurt tomorrow, primo." He crumbles up a bud and twists a joint with a tobacco leaf he borrowed from one of the curing houses. We smoke.

"Emilio, quiero preguntarte una cosa sobre mi padre."

"¿En qué tú estás pensando, Mano?"

"¿Por qué él se fué?"

"When your father left, it was not by boat, or raft, or in the dark of night. It was a milk run, a common hopper flight that connected Varadero with Miami."

Emilio takes some more Colombian marijuana and tells me the story while rolling the first roach into another joint.

"The only reason Doctor Juan Rodriguez and his young wife rented out the first floor of the house in Vedado was to get the medical practice started. It was their intent to live up on the second floor and attic for a time, and leave the first floor to a tenant, Beatrice. When his practice got on its feet and was making a modest profit, once he paid off some of the loans he had taken to make it through medical school, and once they had children and needed more space, he would be cordial and professional, and would notify the renter that he was not going to renew the lease, and then he would wish her well. First came the Reforma Urbana, when they were after his country place in La Lisa. Then the nationalizing of medical care. It didn't stop him from marrying your mother in 1967. No elaborate honeymoons in those days, but the government gave them a discount voucher for three days and two nights at the Havana Libre."

Hearing this surprises me. For the first time I think of Juan Rodriguez not as an absent father I never knew, but as the man who was present with my mother at the time of my conception.

"Finally in '68, Fidel gave that endless speech on the Revolutionary Offensive: *Con la revolución, todo; sin la revolución, nada.* It looked like they would expropriate his private practice. The frustration became too much when la segunda Reforma Urbana started sniffing around your mother's place in Vedado. All he could talk about were the thieves and parasites who had taken everything from him, and how much he hated what Cuba had turned into. Your mother couldn't take it. In the last few weeks, it was hard to sit around the table with him. Before he left he came to Pinar and Abuelo blew up at him, told him if he abandoned his wife that Abuelo would no longer consider him a son."

The rooster's crow cleaves my splitting headache. "My father's pharmacy in Miami, do you have the telephone number?"

Emilio squints at me. "Are you planning on coming back, primo?"

"I just want to call him from the conference," I assure him. Thanks to the emergent hangover, I think it sounds just pathetic and credible enough.

Emilio shakes his head. "Forget it, Mano. Some questions have no answers."

In the dawn hours, Manolito seems to be snoozing, blacked out, but I know better. Emilio has managed to miss the self-destructive drunk, and therefore also the hangover. "Don't be fooled. You should never get too close to him when he gets like this."

"Believe me, I know. Get me a stick."

You could argue I should just let him sleep, but it will only make things worse. He will get so deep into his hangover that he'll awaken without wanting a drink, and then it's two or three days of dark, dangerous moods. Better to wake him now and keep him drinking so that he can remain a semifunctioning farmer and we can get some jobs done before I have to head back to Havana.

"Dip the stick in sugar water and hold it to his lips." Sure enough, he sucks the stick, and in a minute is on his feet.

I think about the way Manolito walks, before all the banana wine made him assume a constant, comical jig; a clownish saunter I presume started as a cover for his chronic inebriation, but gradually assumed a life of its own as his way of navigating the world of the sober. Awake, only a little hungover, and just about to get drunk again: this is Manolito at his finest, the sweet, gentle uncle I love, who as a teenager once made it on foot all the way up and back from the Tope de Viñales in one day. I saw it with my own eyes, aided by Abuelo's binoculars.

Deliverance comes served in a plastic cone. Lydia reserves this receptacle exclusively for the morning-after restorative stew. Men sitting around all crudos cannot be trusted with plates, bowls, or even spoons. You cannot set the cone down to rest until you have emptied all the contents, so focusing on holding it upright helps fend off the vertigo. Manolito and I each get an inverted clown's cap to clutch beside the coals of last night's fire, and we sip the only potion known to remedy our hammering headaches. Ajiaco is a wonder that defies medical explanation, a steaming thick broth, chunks of malanga, and every last cut of pig. I find myself chewing on a bit of gristle, and when I pull it out of my mouth I have to choke back a gag when I find it's the snout.

Manolito asks, "¿Tú sabes lo que dicen de los puercos, Mano?"

"¿Qué?"

"You can eat every part of the pig except the—" a pounding assault on my head as Manolito maniacally squeals.

It has been this way since the summer I turned eleven and I started calling Viñales home: ajiaco served in plastic cones. And when I turned fifteen and my uncles first got me drunk, I learned how to clutch the cone against la cruda, and Tio Manolito has always been here to nurse me, sadistically, through the hangover. We come back to the bohío and Lydia has oranges for us, floating in cool water in a metal bowl I once brought her from Havana. Manolito takes his tarnished knife and spins the peel off in one long corkscrew that he throws to the chickens, and then he splits it and gives me half. While I separate the sections the way I was taught en el pre, he squeezes his half straight into his mouth and, using his front teeth as a shovel, scrapes back over the pith and sucks out the fruit. Manolito gives Lydia a slap on the ass and bellows a great "¡CóÑOOOOOO!" and I laugh, and I love my uncle again.

"Ten cuidado por ahí," Abuelo says as I prepare to leave.

I clasp his shoulders in embrace. "I'll be careful, Abuelo."

It is awkward taking Emilio's orders for magazines. "Anything futból, moto, o marino." He forces an American fifty-dollar bill on me.

I try to refuse. "Me pagas cuando regrese."

"Take it with you. These things are expensive, Mano. Five dollars, some of them. Get me ten of the latest, and if there's any money left, buy Abuelo some more chocolate." He lowers his voice and passes me a slip of paper: "Don't tell Abuelo, but I got this from Abuela."

It is an American phone number with the area code 305.

SÁBADO, 6 SEPTIEMBRE
THE TOURIST

He makes a call with his mobile phone. To the man who answers, he says, "It's me."

"Your instincts were correct."

"How so?"

"Rambo is out of work."

"Permanently?"

"Yes. He is beyond hope. It would take an army."

"How do you know?"

"He has called me several times and is trying to get me to admit things over the phone. He is desperate. It was obvious they have him. I hung up . . ."

"The fool."

"It was smart to keep him in the dark. Now just be patient a few more days."

"I will proceed with the client's plan."

"Good man. Do not act before the appointed date in order to assure maximum impact."

"A very big impact. Adiós."

DOMINGO, 7 SEPTIEMBRE
Manolo

At the safe house in Havana, Caballero and Pérez brief me on the latest with the Salvadoran. None of his intelligence has yielded a good lead on the second bomber: the trail has gone cold. "Did you get a number for the pharmacy from your primo?"

I take out the slip of paper with the 305 area code. "Yes, he gave me this and some money for magazines."

"What kind of magazines?" Caballero asks. I understand his implication, although the job of enforcing the pornography ban would be on Pérez's side of the law.

"Just soccer, motorsports, and boating."

"Does this check out with what you got in Pinar?" Caballero recites a telephone number and it matches exactly.

We all smoke and drink strong Cuban coffee, which cuts through my pain from last night and the hungover drive back to Havana. Caballero drills me: "What made you want to defect?"

"I'm in a dead-end job where for the past eight years I have been thwarted by a jealous supervisor."

"Why leave now?"

"It was my plan all along, but the invitation to the conference made it possible. I might never have gotten another chance."

"How will you explain how you got the salida approved?"

"By staking the clinic and my share of the house in Vedado as collateral."

"Now that you have made it to Miami, what is your objective?"

"To get my physician's license."

"Yes, but without your papers and the transcripts from the medical school in the Havana, you will be frustrated."

I think to myself: the same frustration as my father's tragic exile.

Pérez shows me a photo. "José Felipe Mendoza y Paredes."

"Mendoza."

"Yes. He leases commercial real estate and helped your father get his start. He is one of the most powerful men in Miami. The Salvadoran has provided credible intelligence that the recruiter in San Salvador communicates with him by e-mail drafts."

Pérez introduces me to the computer expert, a

young mulatto named Eduardo who does not shake hands. Caballero tells me, "In the morning, after visiting Gonzalez to pick up your passport and the salida, go directly to the US Interests Section in the Swiss Embassy."

"Won't I need an appointment?"

"You have an appointment. You will be allowed through the gate between ten a.m. and noon. Shoot for ten thirty. Now, if you'll excuse me . . ."

"Any last words of advice?"

"When speaking of Cuba among the gusanos, remember to use the past tense." He shakes my hand. "Good luck."

Pérez and I follow Eduardo to an alcove barely larger than a closet where a new laptop computer is set up on a desk. "Last we could ascertain, Mendoza uses an IBM ThinkPad like this one. Do not attempt to boot up a computer that is off. You cannot control the Windows 95 start-up sound, which is loud and lasts for six seconds. But if this little light is green, it's only sleeping. Touch any key to wake it up." Eduardo shows me how to wake it and put it back to sleep. "Here is the Explorer browser running Yahoo, the host Mendoza uses for his e-mail account. Look in this drafts folder first. Have you heard of a *dead drop?*" Eduardo shows me how to look in the drafts folder. "No traces of *send* or *receive*. Keep an eye out for dates and the names of locations." On a slip of paper Eduardo gives me another number with a 305 area code. "Memorize this. It's the number for a pre-paid voice mail account that is secure. Do not have it written in your possession when you fly to Miami. Leave a brief message when you first establish contact with Mendoza, and any subsequent reports by calling from a public telephone."

"A cabina de teléfono? This is the technology currently in use by the DSS?"

"You have to *be* a refugee in Miami, doctor. It could be awhile before you will have access to a mobile phone or computer. Use a pay phone. There will be no greeting, just a tone to signify the start of recording. Calling in a report, you must take every precaution so that nobody should see you. Find a booth in a quiet location. Make your calls at night unless you suspect an immediate threat to Cuban security."

"And if someone discovers I am making pay phone calls despite my precautions?"

Pérez answers: "Tell them that you are trying to contact the conference organizers in Tampa. Explain how you felt guilty about taking the invitation when you knew all along you were going to defect. Perhaps you are hoping they will help establish your medical credentials in Florida." He holds my gaze intently in that way he has always had of completely ignoring my lunar to make a point. "Of course, you should not really try to contact the doctors in Tampa for any reason."

Eduardo gives me the evacuation plan. He unfolds a map emblazoned, *1997 Greater Miami Official Map and Visitor's Guide*. "Just to the north of Calle 8 there is a park named after José Martí. See here, on Southwest 4th Avenue? Do you see how the highway crosses over the Miami River? When it is time to evacuate, you will call the number and this time there will be an announcement. You will not leave a message, but go directly to the park and your handler will make contact."

"This all sounds very Sylvester Stallone."

"Do you know how to fly a plane?"

"No."

"Then when the time comes, a rendezvous at a predetermined location will be the safest, most effective way to get you back to Havana."

I spend some more time familiarizing myself with the laptop computer and we repeat how to check e-mail for a dead drop. It is near dawn when Pérez and his driver give me a ride home.

When we pull up in the alley behind Calle 23, Pérez says, "Just between you and me, take these with you to Miami." He hands me a small pile of papers in the dark car.

"¿Qué es esto?" I flip through the small stack in the murky light from the alley. I can make out two sets of letterhead: the pediátrico and the medical school. These are unauthorized copies of my records. I do not have to say it, because Pérez knows as well as I do that it is illegal for me to have them.

"Take them," he tells me, "to boost your credibility. You are not a fool. Nobody would believe that you planned to leave without at least trying to get unofficial copies."

Pérez's driver stares at me in the rearview. He and I and Pérez make up a tiny archipelago of trust in a vast ocean of suspicion and deceit. The back of this Toyota is a secure location.

"With these papers," I point out, "there is a much greater possibility that I could be allowed to practice medicine if I do decide to stay. Aren't you taking a great risk?"

"I hope not." Pérez looks at me—really looks at me. It reminds me of that first day five years ago, when he fixed his gaze unrepentantly on the mark that has defined me since I was ten and, unbeknownst to me at the time, impassively sized me up for the first job he had in mind for me. "They will want to make you a spokesperson to tell lies about the Revolution. You need to speak the part: be disgruntled, be critical, but don't go believing your own act."

LUNES, 8 SEPTIEMBRE
MERCEDES

Mercedes awakens before hundreds of sleeping tourists in the dormitory of her new job, and it takes her breath away to remember all those floors above her. The air in the laundry room is overpowering with the fresh, clean smells of capitalism. Here in the bowels beneath a city of glass and steel—what Martí might call the belly of the beast—although the atmosphere is suffocating among the driers in the basement, it is also safe and free.

Yorki drops by on the second day. "So what do you think of the dormitory?"

"It's fine. I'm grateful to have a place."

She finds Yorki charmingly awkward. Hyperactive, darting eyes, and rapid-fire patter. "When guests want to complain about housekeeping," he tells her, "they always go first to the front desk, so the manager puts the head of housekeeping where the desk captain can say curtly, *I'm sorry to hear you found the condition of the room unsatisfactory. Al-*

low me to introduce you to the head of housekeeping, and thereby pass the problem along and get back to dealing with other, happier guests, which is, after all, the objective of the front desk." He tells her, "I told Manolo I'd look out for you while he's in la Yuma, so let me know if I can help. I'm here Monday, Wednesday, and Friday, and the rest of the week at the Neptuno."

Manolo, she learns her second day of work, is her guardian-doctor's first name. A small protocol that gives her great comfort is that he has never told her, *Please, just call me Manolo.* Neither did he invite her up to his apartment. That would have been a big red flag. She felt safe around him, in her element. She hesitated to say *at home.* There's something more about him, something to do with that mark on his face. Mercedes would like to know about it, but she is naturally ashamed to ask. Instead, she accepted him as not unhandsome because of it. She closes her eyes and tries to picture him without it, and in fact he is not as handsome.

LUNES, 8 SEPTIEMBRE
MANOLO

I go to the pediátrico for my consulta with Director Gonzalez. We sit in his air-conditioned office. It is a window unit, the only one in the entire hospital. I once heard him justify it in an offhand comment that it helped to refrigerate irate parents into complacency when they came to make specious complaints about nurses acting surly, or overworked doctors' malpractice.

Director Gonzalez says, "Your salida got approved, and your passport too." I see them sitting on his desk.

"Yes, something of a surprise." I am taking to my new role of pretending to be someone who is pretending not to defect.

I know he has not even read my petition when he says, "Remind me again how long you're gone?"

"The conference lasts five days. I'll travel back on Monday the fifteenth."

"Very well. Give yourself a rest day and we'll put you on the schedule for Wednesday the seventeenth." Gonzalez, not one to be only a half-cynic, cajoles me with a casual reference to finally reviewing a long-requested schedule revision, adding, "You're one of my best doctors, Manolo. You are sure you're coming back?" He is searching my expression. If it is to tell whether my complexion betrays any hint of duplicity, the only discoloration on my face is my *Havana Lunar*.

I am amused at how calm I feel. Deceiving him is such a delight, I realize I'm being introduced to one of the distinct pleasures of espionage: the experience of betraying the small-minded people who, for superficial reasons, have pestered, pigeonholed, and procrastinated you to death if for no more motive than—than what? Envy? No, something more than that: a backward-headed misinterpretation of un dicho made into a lyric by Silvio Rodriguez: *Qué no van lejos los de alante si los de atras corren bien.* That is, if your mediocrity means you are falling behind, then by all means put snares out to trip up the front-runners.

I say, "I am sure."

"Then enjoy the conference. Bring back new developments to share with your colleagues." It remains unspoken, but by his expression Director Gonzalez appends his constant caution: *As long as it involves no expensive equipment.* He hands me my passport with the salida. In terms of what a lowly doctor is capable of exacting from his obstructive boss in the doldrums of the Período Especial, my defection will be the ultimate vengeance. Here is one person I will be glad to let swallow the deception. Go fuck yourself, Gonzalez.

At ten forty-five I take my passport to the US Interests Section in the Swiss Embassy, and by eleven forty-five I am holding my visa.

On my last afternoon before leaving for Miami, I visit the Havana Libre. Sol Melina has undertaken extensive renovations of the onetime Havana Hilton. They have even restored the enormous Amelia Peláez mural over the main entrance, which has been hidden behind construction scaffolding ever since I can remember. Calle 23 slopes so steeply on the Calle L side, where guests arrive, that the entrance is three floors higher than the street behind, and the service entrance leads to a level that is mostly underground beneath a plinth that supports the rest of the hotel's twenty-seven stories.

I stop off in the subterranean kitchen and find Yorki. He looks around to make sure nobody is listening, a pantomime that is just for my sake, to let me know he has something on me, because there is no way anyone not standing right next to us could hear over the dishwashers' clatter. Yorki says, "It was crazy what happened at the Copacabana on Thursday. I heard you were there."

"How the hell did you hear that?"

"From one of the busboys. He was lucky—he'd just walked past the ashtray with the bomb and only got the left half of his face peppered with glass shards. He told me that after the explosion, he saw my friend with the splotch on his face." Yorki pauses and a satisfied smile forms in anticipation of what he has to say next. "That cousin of yours started work yesterday."

"That was quick."

He shrugs. "Ever since the renovation they've been hiring maids, but it speeds things up when you supply the head housekeeper a lobster tail."

"I owe you one."

"Damn right you do. Mano, that girl is not your cousin."

I do not conceal my surprise at Yorki's forthrightness. "Does it make a difference?"

"Yes. For the job, no, not now that she's in. But it seems to me it does make a difference to you. Is that old frozen Mano finally thawing out—has it been five years?—from hibernation and falling for a patient again?"

"Look out for her, Yorki."

He puts a sweaty hand on the back of my neck and says close to my ear, "Is it yours?"

"¿Qué?"

"That seed she's growing—you the farmer?"

"Nice figure of speech. No, I'm not the farmer."

"Cuidado que no te claven otra vez."

Play with a hammer and you might get nailed," I quote Yorki's patented comeback to the common warning. He appreciates this. "I want to say good-bye to Mercedes. Can you point me to the maids' quarters?"

"Careful what you see. Some of those viejas are in their sixties. Make sure to knock so you don't get a look at anything madness-inducing. One of them has a paunch and breasts that hang so low, you can't tell where one begins and the others end—it looks like three tits."

"Thanks. I'll cover my eyes."

Yorki reaches into his pocket and pulls out a green bill. "Bring me a pair of tenis Americano, marca Nike—make sure they're not fakes, either. They have to have that wave along the side and on the little tag inside. The fakes are as common as the real thing en la Florida." He hands me a twenty-dollar note.

Although there is no telling whether I will ever get to buy him those Nikes, I have to take it to maintain the profile. "Are you sure that twenty will cover it?"

"Sure it will, if you don't let yourself get ripped off like some asshole guajiro. Feliz viaje. Don't come back without my Nikes."

It is surreal playing the part and pretending I will be gone just one week. No long goodbyes of uncertain future; just get it over with. *You will soon hear something shocking about me, but I assure you that someday I am coming back, Yorki.*

Down in the basement, past the deafening clatter of the washers and the suffocating heat of the driers, are the maids' dormitories. It is almost time for their shift change, so the doors are open to several rooms, dozens of bunk beds in each. I find Mercedes. She has a top bunk, spare and neat. The uniform looks good on her. She gives me a hug and exclaims, "I came in on Saturday and your friend Yorki got me the job the same day!"

"He works fast." My own hands are shaking from excitement or from hunger—it's hard to tell the difference—when I tell her about the círculo infantil. "Havana Libre will give you a maternity leave, and there is a good place nearby for the baby beginning at six weeks." I distract her with a simple printed pamphlet from the infant day care in the neighborhood of the Havana Libre because I do not wish to overwhelm her with the portentous accumulation of happy details around her destiny that fate and I have conspired to expedite. She holds the pamphlet and delicately traces the services with a finger: feedings, nap times, and just seven infants for every licensed caregiver.

"Thank you, doctor."

"They will take the baby for up to eight hours a day. And you can spend a lunch break together. I want to help you find a long-term place where you can stay with the baby, when I return."

I say *cuando regrese* deliberately and emphatically. She will remember this moment in a little over a week when she hears the news of my defection, and hopefully she will guard a spark of hope inside. It could be many months, but I have to believe she will hold on.

She says, "Pa' cuando tú vuelvas todavía no hay niño hasta dentro de seis meses." *When you return there won't be any baby, not for six more months.*

I draw a breath. "Of course not, but we will start looking at your options when I get back."

She walks me to the service entrance in silence. In the back shadows of the Havana Libre, Mercedes says, "Nos vemos pronto."

Walking away, I turn and see she is looking after me. *Guajira, you are family to me. Te conozco, pinareña Mercedes. I will come back from this conference.*

Part II

MANOLO EN MIAMI

MARTES, 9 SEPTIEMBRE

The once-daily flight from Havana to Miami departs at 7:30 a.m. The immigration agent inspects my passport and permiso de salida and gives them a bored stamp, and then the security agent checks my bag. All I take is a carry-on with four pairs of socks, two pairs of black pants, three pairs of underwear, three black T-shirts, and a toothbrush. Tucked beneath the shirts are my medical papers, along with the invitation letter from the American doctor and the conference program that accompanied it. I'll get razors in Miami. "¿Cómo te vas a llevar maquinillas plásticas a la Yuma," Yorki taunted, "si hasta las máquinas chinas sin filo cuentan el doble en la Habana?" He was right. Even dull Chinese razors cost twice as much in Havana.

When I finally get through security, the salida does not matter anymore. I could take the token paper Gonzalez gave me and toss it in the trash, but I do not. However worthless it has just become, it will be my souvenir.

I get a window seat. Cóño, pero la Habana is

beautiful from above! The bay a sparkling jewel, I see where the name of my medical case comes from: the inverted contour of Havana Bay *is* shaped like my lunar. I see the city below, identify the Havana Libre, and think about Mercedes and the possibility of something better for this city.

The guajiro sitting next to me, an old Cubano on a first-time visit to an exile sister and a half-dozen nephews and nieces he's never met, wonders aloud how long the flight will take. "About forty minutes," I tell him.

I look out the window at the Florida Straits and try to distract myself from the overwhelming unknown by thinking in English. Every Cuban's exile is solitary and unique. Even on a raft full of family, each person makes the crossing individually, and in the act of abandoning la patria and sailing ahead to face the unknown, everyone is alone. It is a supremely egoistic act. The father is thinking one thing: *I will make a better life for my wife and children; I will get a job that pays in dollars; I will have a car, and a TV, and money to go out drinking.* All the altruistic excuses about doing it for family cannot conceal that, at heart, all our motives are ultimately selfish. To my knowledge, nobody ever tried to construct a homemade raft to go back to Cuba.

In the airplane I take out the twenty-dollar bill Yorki gave me and the fifty from Emilio. It is not that I think customs won't let me carry them in. It is myself I do not trust with the money. If it is in my pocket, I will lose it, or in my ignorance of American exorbitance throw it away on the wrong basura. Como dijo Yorki, I'll probably get ripped off like some asshole. I take both bills, fold them together, and slip them beneath my right heel into the lining of my shoe. This seems like the right place not to lose it, with what I am about to go through. It makes me feel better to have an emergency fund stashed away somewhere sweaty and secure. And it makes me feel superstitious that the twenty is from Yorki, the perennial Habanero, as if carrying it on my person has talismanic powers to ensure my safe return.

The Cubano sitting next to me watches. "Will they take away our money?"

"No, I just don't trust myself not to lose it."

He does the same with his own small collection of crumpled fives and ones.

I fall asleep and miss the descent into Miami, but the guajiro shakes me awake just in time to see the runway coming up under the wing. Off the jetway at Miami International Airport, there are televisions everywhere: beautiful, thousand-dollar, Japanese televisions; screens so slender you want to look behind them. How can they be so slim and still show all those brilliant colors?

I will have to go through customs before getting

156 + HAVANA LIBRE

on the connecting flight to Tampa. Of course, I will not be getting on the connecting flight to Tampa, but the drill would be the same either way in order to get out of international arrivals. I will have to keep playing a part, or rather I'll be playing a new part. It occurs to me that I will have to play multiple parts, and now I am approaching a moment of transformation between parts which all exilados who come by air must play: from emigrant to immigrant, from tourist to exile.

Whether you are a trained professional attending a conference in a high-tech field, or an overqualified but uncertified specialist seeking a green card; whether you are someone hitting the beaches and spending a few hundred dollars at a hotel, or a refugee about to become a problem for immigration and naturalization: you go from playing one part to be allowed to leave Cuba, to playing another role that will allow you to enter los Estados Unidos.

My passport and visa are all in order, but approaching US customs my heart pounds all the same. The lines are short and move steadily, and as I approach the booth I notice that there are mirrors in all the corners. Even when it comes to examination, these Americanos are expensive.

The unauthorized copies of my medical records are in my bag, and for the first time since Pérez handed them to me in the back of the Toyota, I realize that it is no longer incriminating for me to be carrying them. Just like the permiso de salida does not matter anymore. Havana has no more authority over me. I am free—almost.

The counter is at eye level, and the man in the customs booth stands on a platform that makes him several feet taller. The little steel slot in the plexiglass is large enough to slip a passport through, but not to poke a gun barrel. "Plan on making any connections?" he says in English.

"Tampa." I am curious about his accent, which is Spanish but not Cuban, and nervousness makes me garrulous. I ask him, "¿De dónde es usted?" To my surprise, he tells me he is Central American, a naturalized Nicaraguan, and the United States customs agent from Nicaragua will make use of this detention by imparting a brief English lesson.

"What is the purpose of your travel?"

I say in *berry good Ingles*: "I am here for a conference at the invitation of Professor B.A. Shapiro of the Tampa Medical Extension of the University of Florida."

"How long are you planning on staying?"

"I intend to return to Havana on the fifteenth of September."

"No, you don't." I am speechless. This is a welcome that Caballero and his men never prepared me for. "Mira, yo lo he visto todo. I have seen it all.

What's going to happen is you're gonna ask the medical school in Havana for your records, and you ain't gonna get 'em, so you won't be able to take the Florida state exam, mucho menos pass the puto examen. Mira, it's your funeral, compadre. But if I were you, I would take your time to declare your intent to stay. I'll give you an extra day, until the sixteenth." He stamps me seven days. He has seen it all.

At the baggage inspection, American dogs sniff my pockets and million-dollar X-ray machines expose the contents of my bag. Sweating in the air-conditioned international terminal, I know I conceal something more dangerous than the contents of my carry-on: I harbor hidden intent. But I get through easily. It is Tuesday at nine a.m., and I am in los Estados Unidos.

Instead of turning left toward domestic departures, I head right to parking and ground transportation. In my mind I'm saying, like a prayer, *Dear Doctor Shapiro, please accept my deepest regrets, but I will not be able to fulfill my acceptance of your invitation to attend the conference in Tampa . . .* Knowing that I will neither write nor call him. No such courtesy is permitted of me.

I wait to make the phone call. Eduardo suggested that I first make a survey of José Martí Park. At ground transportation I find the right bus route for Little Havana and take the twenty from the wad in my shoe to buy a two-dollar ticket for the 42 bus to Calle 8. I ask the cashier for change for the pay phone, and I decide that I am comfortable enough to carry eighteen dollars in bills and coins in my pants pocket, the back left one with the button.

Miami is an endless ocean of mammoth buildings and their shadows, surrounded by great migrations of cars. The buses here are much better than the camellos in Havana. It is clean, has air-conditioning, and I have two seats all to myself. Then I look out the window and know I have descended into the belly of the beast. The sigil of the devil is everywhere: dollar signs wink at me from every window, doorway, and sidewalk clothing rack. The electronic stores' prices all have five digits that always end in .99: *JUST $199.99! JUST $279.99! JUST $999.99!* What about Yorki's order for twenty-dollar Nikes? Olvídalo, forget it. In bright glass storefronts shouting *SAVE!* and *DEALS!* even the knockoffs start at $59.99. I see a Ferrari racing its engine at a red light and rattling the windows of the sushi restaurants. I see more Porsches than I can count. I see a real Maserati. It peels around the corner with a shriek. There goes one hundred Cuban doctors' lifetime fortunes on four wheels. I see men walking in under a great, lighted marquee for a strip club that announces, *NUDE! NUDE! NUDE!* and I cannot believe the pictures they show on the street.

It takes under an hour to go the five miles to Little Havana. At José Martí Park, the people are tan and well fed and their clothes are clean. There is one man in a torn T-shirt fishing in the river, and a rico wearing a Polo shirt and Gucci sunglasses walks up to interact with him. I look out over the river at the sun climbing between the skyscrapers downtown and eavesdrop on their exchange.

"How are they biting?" el rico says in Spanish, and it occurs to me that although this is America, the expectation of one stranger approaching another here is that Spanish will most likely be the common tongue.

"Más o menos," says the ragged fisherman without looking up from his idle line.

The rich man of the people takes this as an opportunity to recount aloud to anyone in the park who can hear about the marlin he caught on a fishing excursion the other day, one assumes with the dual objective of at once boasting of his own prowess as a sportfisherman, and of edifying the poor peasant trying to catch a simple bonefish—and nobody begrudges him the entitlement.

Their mouths emanate the familiar accents and cadences of Cuban Spanish, but everything else about them is so different that it seems I am on another planet from Havana. Instead of talking about apartment swaps, prostitution, and how to find

some scrap to eat, they shout about skimpy swim-
suits, how the fishing is, and what they have had
or are about to have to eat and drink. The rich are
so rich they do not comprehend their own solipsism
when they brag about their privilege to a worker of
the lower classes. Solipsism. It reminds me of the
second bomber. He is out there somewhere, eating,
breathing, planning the destruction of innocent life,
and somehow reconciling his conscience to his decision. The ultimate egomaniac.

I take in the surroundings at José Martí Park. In
several weeks or several months I will have to come
back here. I am thinking—I have to suppress laughing cynically to avoid calling attention to myself—
here I am, planning like a spy. At the edge of the
park I find a pay phone. I look at the phone number
Emilio gave me and prepare to make the most awkward telephone call of my life. I put in the coins and
push the buttons. The connection comes through
instantly, and for a moment I am impressed by this
country, but it rings a long time and I am about to
give up.

"Farmacia Rodriguez. ¿Aló?"

"¿Por favor, puedo hablar con Juan Rodriguez?"

A crisp "¿Quién habla?"

I can tell it is not my father. Rather than com-
manding the authority of a former physician in Cuba
who now owns his own pharmacy in Miami, the ac-

cented voice betrays the customary paranoia of the Miami Cuban combined with some of the petty suspicion of an underling whose duty is to answer the phone and triage calls by order of importance.

"Me llamo Manolo Rodriguez."

A pause on the other end of the line. If there is any recognition, it is only a dim connection that the same surname could mean a cousin or other relative, if it isn't just a joke or a coincidence.

The sycophant says, "Un minuto, por favor."

Not nearly a minute, maybe six endless seconds later, a voice says, "¿Quién es?" These two words sound so much like Emilio and, in younger days, Abuelo, that I know it has to be him. He asks who is speaking.

"It's Manolo Rodriguez calling."

"¿Cómo?"

"Tu hijo Manolo."

Silence on the line. I am so used to CubaTel that after a full fifteen seconds I believe we must have been cut off, but I finally hear his response and know that America's phone lines have not let us down: "Cóño."

"Estoy en Miami." There is another long silence. "¿Me oyes todavia?"

"Sí."

I say, "Soy médico."

"Yes, I heard you became a doctor. When did you get here?"

"This morning. I was invited to a conference."

"Where did you find the number for my pharmacy?"

I say what I know I must—"Primo Emilio got it from Abuela"—adding, like someone who might never see his beloved grandfather again, "I was in Pinar last weekend to say goodbye to her and Abuelo."

My father, like someone who could care less that he'll never see his own father again, says, "How is he? Still taking the water?"

"He's well, and yes, un Acuático hasta la muerte." *An Acuático until death.*

He lets that hang on the line. Maybe he is not completely immune to the discomfort of hearing about family he hasn't spoken with in two decades, although I cannot verify this without seeing his mannerisms in person. "Well," he says, "would you like to meet for lunch?"

To meet my father for the first time? But for the assignment, I am not sure there is any part of me that actually wants to. "Yes. When?"

"Today, if you'd like. Say eleven thirty. That way we'll beat the second wave."

The second wave: the exiles who left Cuba in the 1960s. "Okay," I say. "Name the place."

"How about Habana Vieja? That's on Calle 8. You think you can find it?"

"No problem."

It's hard to tell over the phone whether I hear a chuckle or a sigh, and he hangs up with something I never thought I'd hear from this man: "Hasta luego."

I am not sure that I will get used to this.

I stand in front of the restaurant at the appointed time, *eleven thirty . . . to beat the second wave*, but he is not there. I look inside. Other diners who shared my father's idea of getting in and out before the second wave crowd the tables in nice suits, with Ray-Bans on their heads, Rolex watches on their wrists, and beepers and cell phones in their hands. It is louder than any restaurant I have ever been in, louder than any party I have been to with one exception: the end of my fiesta in Viñales when Manolito started singing.

The hostess is kind. She does not stare at my lunar or down at my cheap shoes. Looking me in the eye, she tells me I may sit in the waiting area before leading a couple back to the dining rooms. Her pants are of a cut and cloth that have yet to make it to Havana, or maybe that Cubanas saw coming but nevertheless have foresworn for their favored Lycra. And I, no novice at detecting the exemplary culo de Cubana, am nevertheless mindful of my impoverishment trying to visualize the possibilities through the rushed cut of slacks and scrubs around the pediátrico: it has nothing on this stretchy black fabric, probably synthetic, but not shiny like Lycra, and the fine specimen tolling like a cathedral bell.

Enter a man in white guayabera and tan chinos whose features resemble not his nephew Emilio but instead his father, mi abuelo. He is my father, Juan Rodriguez, and he is fat. He looks at my lunar and takes it in along with the rest of me. If he thinks I am handsome, he doesn't let it show. I am a version of him thirty years younger and a hundred pounds lighter, with a large blemish under the left eye. I take note of the broken capillaries in his cheeks. It could just be rosacea, but I doubt my father would leave that undiagnosed and untreated. I estimate twenty or twenty-five years of heavy drinking.

I expected the similarities to Manolito and Abuelo, but now, no matter how much I thought I prepared myself for this moment, the strangest thing is actually believing it is him, this father I never met. I had to bury him. Until this moment, I have not believed it impossible that I would show up and learn he is dead. It was someone's farce, someone in the family: those letters from the early years, never sending pictures. Now there is no question.

The actual fact of finding him alive makes me feel so uncomfortable that I focus on the hostess. She takes two menus the size of washboards and leads us through the crowded restaurant. Her swagger and pace transfix my father and myself alike. Charmed snakes, we follow.

I watch how my father walks, touching tables and doorframes as he passes—and I can see Abuelo twenty years younger. It is unmistakable: that's the Rodriguez walk. The hostess does not look back, and that makes us tail her swiftly through the crowded dining rooms. Brushing by so many well-dressed elbows and shoulders feels self-aggrandizing, exhilarating, and a little dangerous. We have money. This is America. We are going to eat a good lunch.

On every wall in each room there are murals and dioramas depicting cartoonish, prerevolutionary street scenes of Old Havana. In South Florida, exiles have created a cardboard Cuba. Little Havana is a Disney attraction complete with streets, restaurants, and even a country club named after their nostalgic version of the lost island. It is a labyrinth of longing that envelops every cavity of the restaurant. The hostess stops at an empty table for two along the wall and lays the huge menus at the place settings, not even stopping her delightful pendulum, just pivoting while chirping, "Buen provecho," and then she's already on her way back to her station to seat the next early birds. In a breath a busboy is there with a pitcher of ice water.

Most of the diners around us are young, my age.

They are powerless to put away their beepers even for a meal, checking them between bites. "Yuccas," my father says, settling into his chair while the mozo decorously pours chilled water into our glasses from on high. "You heard of them? Like yuppies, but Cuban Americans."

The waiter shows up immediately and asks, "¿Algo de tomar?" My father orders a cerveza Hatuey. *Habana Vieja, second wave, Hatuey*—my head is spinning. Is it a coincidence, or does my father use filial instincts when he says, "Don't worry, you'll get used to it"? He asks, "You want a suggestion? You like steak?"

"Sí."

"¿Estilo criollo?"

"Cómo no."

"Let me get you the ropa vieja."

My father orders picadillo, and the waiter, a mulatto who does not look Cuban, but is possibly Venezuelan or Puerto Rican, takes our orders to the kitchen.

The clock on the wall reads 11:35—the same time of day less than a week ago that the young Italian staying at the Copacabana with his father was murdered while eating lunch.

Despite more than two decades between them, my father's resemblance to Tio Manolito is certainly there in his jaw and thick black hair, in his gestures and pauses. Instead of muscles from years of farm work and climbing the tope de Viñales, there is a luxurious layer of cellulite from decades inside an air-conditioned pharmacy and sauntering along Calle 8. I wonder if he shares Manolito's bloodshot eyes when he removes his dark sunglasses. My father surely feels as nervous as I do, but he brushes off intimacy and awkwardness with efficiency. "Did my old records get saved?"

He has switched the subject so abruptly that I have to say, "¿Cómo?"

"Los discos. The LPs."

"Yes, and the record player."

"¿Todavia funciona el tocadiscos?" He leans forward, incredulous.

"Sí. Still working." Remember to speak of Cuba in the past tense. "Some days I would open the French doors to the balcony and put on Pérez Prado."

"Y el Bola de Nieve?"

"Still there, but most mornings I chose Beny Moré."

My father sits back in his chair and smiles. He looks around as if he might see 1960s Havana here in the dining room of restaurante Habana Vieja. He says, "I saw Aurora one time, you know."

"When?"

"More than ten years after she came over. She never looked me up. I think it was '90."

"That's when the letters stopped."

"Yes, she was near the end of her life. I bumped into her at Costco, where she was buying groceries for the family she worked for. She spoke of you as if you were still a child, but she told me you were already done with medical school. I was proud of you."

I think, *But not proud enough to write.*

The drinks come. The waiter pours half the beer in a short glass, and my father quenches his thirst with it in three swift gulps, his greedy Adam's apple bobbing through the folds of flesh at his neck. My Coke comes in a tall plastic cup filled to the brim with ice. It is the sweetest soft drink I have ever tasted. The carbonation is delirious when I raise the tumbler to my lips, stinging my eyes and tickling my nose, making me wince. Looking past my shoulder, hoping the food will come and interrupt the uncomfortable pause, my father says, "This is strange, isn't it, meeting for the first time over ropa vieja and a Coke?"

"Yes."

"We have much in common."

I was thinking the same thing. I look at his hands—elegant hands, not rough like a man's. The fingers taper subtly like dinner candles, and he trims his nails carefully. They are surgeon's hands. They are my hands.

When the food arrives, it is not on two plates,

but on eight: the ropa vieja and picadillo arrive in their own boats with ample sauce, and each of us gets separate life rafts of platanos, arroz, and frijoles. And the bread: beautiful, white pan Cubano bathed in garlicky butter comes in a big basket. My eyes tear up at the sight of it, and I look at my father as a child might, for permission. "Go on," he says with a mouth already half full, "take all you want. They'll bring more."

The dishes are piled high and every taste is delicious. In Vedado this much food would feed a dozen neighborhood kids for a week. My father and I eat in silence, and I understand that despite the similar mannerisms, common speech cadences, and familiar fingers, there are many innate differences between us. He eats fast, attacking his plate with relish and treating the waiter, who dizzies me by returning three, then four times to ask if everything is all right, with cool contempt.

I chew slowly, savoring each bite. My father makes his disappear in ten minutes, washing it down with a second beer, and orders two flans. I can't eat this much or this fast, and my stomach rebels noisily, making somersaults at the awkwardness of this encounter.

My father does most of the eating and all of the talking. He mostly talks about the pharmacy. He is the sole owner of the business, although he does not own the building the pharmacy is in. He pays rent to the landlord, whom he calls a friend. My father characterizes himself as an irreplaceable tenant who makes his own decisions about property management, maintenance, and improvements. I do not ask any questions, noting privately that by *landlord* he means *Mendoza*.

I take what I can't finish of the ropa vieja in what my father unsarcastically calls a "doggy bag." Dogs in Miami eat better than people do in Cuba. The waiter even lets me take the remaining bread from the basket. In Havana the camarero would have removed it to the kitchen and served it to the next customer.

The flan comes accompanied by café Cubano: dark, strong, sugary, and delicious. I finish the flan. Without a block of ice to keep it from melting in the Miami heat, it would never do to try to take it to go.

My heart is pounding and my voice quavers, but the meal is over, so I must say it now or never. "Listen, I don't expect anything from you, but I would be grateful for a little advice on how to get the process started."

"Which process?"

"Permanent residency."

Abruptly he says, "¿Que es lo que tú quieres, Manolo?"

To buy a little time, I repeat his question back to him: "What is it that I want?"

"Yes, coming here now."

I am a little dumbfounded by the brusqueness of his question. "To get residency. To work as a doctor. To practice medicine under suitable conditions for a change."

"No, I mean, why now?"

"What exactly do you mean?"

"Mira," he says, "you know that it is something of an anxious time in Miami."

They briefed me for this at DSS, and I have been practicing under my breath from the time I boarded the plane. My answer is an automatic "How so?"

"Some people believe last year's killing of the four Brothers to the Rescue pilots was an open declaration of war. They might wonder about you." If there is a trace of suspicion in his word choice, it does not permeate his tone. "After all that time in Havana, why did you choose to come now?"

"The conference invitation made it possible. It took me years of planning to get cleared for a visit."

"Yet, in the end, your salida got approved. How come?"

"They decided I was no longer a flight risk."

"But why now? No wife, no kids. Why did they think you would come back if you didn't have to?"

"The house in Vedado. They figured I would never let it go."

My father is silent in a way that says, *This is plausible to me, even if I do not decide I believe it.* A house is worth something, and so is a clinic. He knows this. He says, "You didn't waste any time declaring your intention to stay."

I was prepared for this. It is the first thing that comes up among los recién llegados: ¿Qué pasa con la Inmigración? ¿Cómo andan los trámites? ¿Cuando llegará el permiso de trabajo? "I did not want to delay the process for even one day."

My father nods approvingly. "You could get your green card in a year."

"In the meantime, I'll request un permiso de trabajo. I should be able to get a job in ninety days."

"Yes, three or four months, unless you mean doctoring. The work authorization won't do you any good without a chance to take the medical exam. Did you bring your official transcripts?"

"No, but I will request them from the medical school."

Bitterly, my father mutters, "Good luck."

I take the photocopies out of my bag. "I do have these."

My father pulls a pair of reading glasses from the pocket of his guayabera to examine the papers. In an instant I appreciate the importance of Pérez giving me these, how they bolster the part I have to play. And I also understand how cynical Caballero is—to have known I would need them, but letting Pérez do it unauthorized anyway. A just-in-case for Caballero. As los Americanos say: a CYA.

"They don't have the cuño?"

"No. They're copies."

"Nevertheless, you may have something." He hands back the papers, adding, with his seasoned knowledge of under-the-table work, "De alguna manera consiguerás un trabajo." *You'll find yourself a job somehow.*

"Do you think I will be able to practice medicine?"

My father lowers his sunglasses and I see into his bloodshot eyes. "If you're really decided, I can talk with someone I know on the state medical board."

"I am decided," I tell my father.

"Oye, Manolo, you might have a preconceived notion about me from the influence of your mother and years living in Communism, but I make a living, which stands for something here, and I have earned the trust and support of powerful people who can just as easily make it very difficult for a person to get by in Miami." Before I have time to respond, he leans back to relieve the tension of an abrupt close-ness long postponed, and with a grandiose gesture that is our common doctors' manner, he hands me a slip of paper with a phone number. It is different from the number that was in the phone book. It must be his mobile phone. "Let me make a few calls. Meanwhile, I need you to think about if this is what you really want."

"Okay."

We walk out into the Miami heat, fiercer for all the new steel and glass and concrete rising up from the streets. On the sidewalk, there is one comforting reminder of the real Havana: la cola. The line of perfumed, bejeweled gusanos with their beepers, cellular phones, and overlapping chatter winds out the door and into the parking lot. It occurs to me: our waiter's busy, bustling fussing was all a capitalist-consumerist tactic to push us, the unctuous customers, along from the trough faster so they could strap the feed bags on some other porcine-in-a-Porsche and double the boss's profits during the lunch-hour rush. The profit margin is an engine that runs on the hurried dyspep-sia of obese malcontents.

I walk my father to his car in the parking lot. It is a boxy Buick, dark brown, which strikes me as odd for my father, because the only pictures I have of him from Havana in the sixties show him sport-ing always-white suits and guayaberas. The seats are real leather. The one time I have seen upholstery like this was in medical school when we visited a prerevolutionary mortuary.

Through the driver's-side window my father says, "Call me around four o'clock."

"Okay."

He drives away. *It's Tuesday,* I say to myself, *Martes, the day named after the god of war. I am twenty-eight years old and I have just met my father for the first time.*

Midafternoon I consume the remainder of my ropa vieja from the doggy bag. Now I can finally enjoy it, because my stomach is no longer doing somersaults from meeting the man who is technically my father and whom I will have to betray if I am to complete my assignment. Yorki and my cousin placed their orders for magazines, Nikes, and whiskey, and now they will tell themselves I will never be bringing it back. They will hear I renounced Cuban citizenship, and they will say to each other, *We knew it. Just like his father, he gave up on us.*

At four p.m. I find a pay telephone to call the number my father gave me. I put in the coins and when I am done pushing the buttons, my father answers after the first ring.

He says, "Have you thought about what I asked you?"

"Yes."

"Do you have any hesitation about your decision to defect?"

"No. I am resolved."

"Are your principles compromised in any way? Because if they are, please leave me out of it."

"Listen," I tell my father, "I am not going back."

"I always knew this day would come," he says. "Gusano como yo."

No, I reflect privately, *never a worm like you*. I could go into the rumors that no doubt he has heard in Miami about how, now that we are the better part of a decade into the Período Especial, Habaneros are getting their properties appraised for the waves of speculators expected from Europe, the US, and Latin America. Or I could repeat the part about being an excellent physician in a corrupt system, frustration with the poor state of the hospitals, blaming this on Communist Party graft. But I do not have to, because he does something that strikes me as very typically Rodriguez. Doctor Juan Rodriguez, likewise resolved, gives me the address of his pharmacy in Little Havana—this is how my father offers me a job.

It is a short walk to the pharmacy in Little Havana. On Calle 8 there is a faux-deco storefront that has been preserved since 1970. Neon tubing that hasn't been ignited for some time still spells the familiar code, a salivary stimulant to OTC junkies and other aficionados of chronic pain, so to speak: *Rx*.

Signs for *Farmacia* and *Mercado* in Spanish, advertisements for local brands of milk and eggs, specials painted with soap in the windows. I crane my neck to look up the side of the building at the second floor's apartment windows.

This is what my father gave it all up for. Well, at least he has something. I do not pity him. He needed a place to put his energy, and it makes sense that it was another business. All that effort to get the clinic open in Havana, just to have it nationalized. Start from zero at age thirty, with a few favors from some other exilados who got their head start in '59 and '60, and twenty-seven years later he's able to make a decent living. If the storefront seems stuck in the fifties, then it should console the viejitos who come for their consultas. This vestige of prerevolutionary medicine could be as much at home on Calle 23 in Vedado as it is on Calle 8 in Miami . . . if this were 1959.

My father is waiting for me in front of the store. We shake hands. "There's an empty one-bedroom above the pharmacy," he says. "I'll ask the landlord if you can get in there this weekend."

"Thank you. What kind of work will I do?"

"Inventory, shine up the windows and mirrors, take the trash out for a while. If I don't start you out as his assistant, Coroalles will have a fit."

"Who's Coroalles?"

The corner of my father's mouth curls into a lopsided smile. "You'll see."

a counter from the processing lab retrieves them and returns prints twice every day. This is what I would write home about, if I had somebody besides Emilio to write home to: the farmacia with the film-developing business inside, and fat little exile children running in to drop off a roll and picking up a one-dollar ice cream bar from the freezer on the way out.

There are freezer chests full of ice cream in every grocery store, gas station, and pharmacy in Miami. My father's store also sells vacuum-packed bricks of café Cubano, candles in glass containers with prayers and pictures of saints on the side, bottles of cheap cologne, and something called *Florida Water*—the whole spectrum of Caribbean specialty items. It is impossible to compare this to the same universe as my paltry dispensary. At the clinic in Vedado, I have a dusty cabinet with empty shelves above the faded surgical tape marked *Aspirina*. Here, the drugs are kept behind a blasted-bright counter high above where the patients wait with mirrors and cameras all around.

My father introduces me to Coroalles, his shop-keeper. "Coroalles takes care of everything this side of the pharmacist's desk," he says, and I see through the bald man's solemn nod that he accepts this dignity with great diffidence. "Well, I'll leave you two."

"Adelante, doctor."

It catches me off guard to hear Coroalles address my father as a doctor. Those credentials have been no good for decades. But should I be so dismissive? I find myself questioning my own judgment. What makes this man, who went to medical school and practiced in my same clinic for ten years, any less a doctor? A piece of paper from the state?

My father returns behind the pharmacist's counter and Coroalles right away begins my training: "Coffee, milk, bread, and soft drinks—that's how the store makes money. We could sell beer, but with prescription drugs in the same store it draws too much crime." The meds are a slim margin, and this is the man who makes sure we make the money. It hits me that this man is the reason my father told me to call him at four when we were done with lunch. After he checked me out, the next step was to check with Coroalles.

"You will keep the aisles tidy and rotate the stock," Coroalles says. Just the concept takes some getting used to, when in Cuban peso stores the stock consists of one or two items. Here, someone picks a

dates behind. We have to sell the older stuff first. It's very irritating when products expire on the shelves, especially in the refrigerators."

"Don't customers check to get the freshest?" It is incredible to me that someone spending three dollars on a half-gallon of juice would not make sure he's getting the freshest.

Coroalles's smile shows the weary bemusement of almost thirty years of this. "Only the viejitos and newcomers. Americanos and Yuccas are in too much of a hurry, too much corre-corre, to stop and check and get the freshest stuff. You'll see, amigo." In a few days, he says, he will teach me how to manage the electronic cash register. Meanwhile, I am to keep the coolers bursting with milk, juice, and soft drinks. Mostly the soft drinks, from Coca-Cola to coco agua.

I am beginning to feel good, although it makes me uncomfortable, about this little victory on my first day in the United States. Last week I found a young Pinareña a job at a hotel in Havana, and now my long-lost father in Miami takes me in. After closing the pharmacy at eight p.m., he invites me to get in his Buick. "You can sleep on my sofa until we get you in that apartment." This is how my father welcomes me to move in with him, temporarily.

I tell him, "I appreciate this."

"You don't have to thank me. Some people helped me get on my feet when I first arrived. It's what gusanos do."

Although it is less than a mile away, we drive to his apartment in Little Havana. People's lives center around intersections, and on my father's corner there is an Eckerd, one of the big chain "drugstores," with the actual pharmacy in the back, selling nearly everything except prescription drugs. Every aisle is as big as an entire store in Cuba, and there are twenty aisles. In Havana it would be like visiting twenty separate businesses. The diamond-bright lights shine above, making it a perpetual daytime where you may spend some time in Pueblo del Cereal, some more en Ciudad Pizza. If behind every mirror in the ceiling crouches a spotter with binoculars looking for shoplifters, so be it. I am a documented applicant for immigration with special classification, and I am here stealing nothing but secrets. Your store detectives don't have anything on me.

"What kinds of things do you like?"

"You don't have to buy me things, I have a little

the cereal aisle, he gestures toward a brand called Raisin Bran.

"I'm not sure about the raisins," I tell him.

"Wait until you try these." There is a small box, a large box, and then the biggest of all is emblazoned with the words *Family Size*. He picks that one. Does this make us a family?

There is an entire beer aisle: a section the size of a whole store in Havana lined with refrigerators full of beer. Other men walk out of there with cartons full of cans, but my father drinks from six-packs of bottles with the foil on top. He chooses two. "One for each of us."

Near the intersection outside the Eckerd, I note the location of a pay phone booth. It is not exactly what I would call a quiet location, but it is recessed against the side of the building, and although the sidewalks in Little Havana all glow with the lights off Calle 8, the alcove with the phone is in a gap between two bright streetlights. If I am nimble inserting the coins and pressing the buttons, I could complete a call in less than a minute on the walk back to my father's house.

We return to his apartment, both exhausted. For dinner we make sandwiches. The plastic packages he bought contain ham, turkey, and roast beef. I take two slices of the fluffiest white bread I have ever touched and delicately insert one cut of ham. My father pushes my hand out of the way and takes over. He layers on generous wads of all three meats and shows me how to squeeze mustard and mayonnaise straight from the plastic bottles without dirtying so much as one fork. We eat on paper towels for plates.

For the second course he opens the box of cereal. He fills one bowl and I get another. It is more food than I would see in a week in Havana. He pours in milk and gives me a spoon.

I try the Raisin Bran. "¡Dios mio! These aren't raisins at all. This is candy."

"I told you." He goads me and I eat one bowl, and then another. We make it to the bottom of the family-sized box.

For dessert we start on one of the six-packs. Bohemia, a Mexican beer, delicious like the dark Hatuey they serve at the hotels in Havana. So far my father has had beers with lunch and dinner, and it's only Tuesday. But he is too old to be lectured on his drinking, and besides, who am I—neither his per-

MIERCOLES, 10 SEPTIEMBRE

On my second day in America, I see that Coroalles is right: 90 percent of customers are in too much of a hurry to check the expiration dates. It is impressive to me, the conversion rate: five, ten, twenty dollars per transaction. Laborers younger than me with money. Children with money. Kids with "allowances" from their parents—so that they'll "take care of themselves"—for the most part buying chips and sodas at our store instead of eating nutritional meals cooked at home. Kids with fives and tens and twenties crumpled in their pockets, smoothing them out at the cash register to see what they have, never thinking about paying four dollars for an eight-ounce bag of chips—and with every price, the ubiquitous .99 on the end, one cent shy of next dollar amount, deceiving them that they are only paying four instead of five.

The one population that does not seem to have money to throw away is the senior citizens, again: they-who-check-the-dates. Only the viejitos look at the prices and count their change, Cubano or Amer-

icano, their children and grandchildren too busy to
check in on them except for birthdays and holidays

g .... what merited
a warning. Instead, it is their domesticity. I should
say infantilism. Breeds of every variety get walked,
carried, and pushed in strollers into the store wearing little tailored clothes. Rich ladies share licked
kisses with poodles and pugs whose tongues just seconds ago were probing their own butts. It makes me
dizzy to see it. I overhear some customers joke about
it: "My little Chula's food is more expensive than a
meal at a fine restaurant!" I do not find this funny
at all. I watch them walk their pampered pets back
home past old women pushing all that they own in
stolen shopping carts down Calle 8. If anything, this
is the most aberrant perversion of capitalism's ex-
tremes: dogs living better than people. Martí, I am
glad you did not live to pass through this particular intestine of the beast's belly, but I do wonder
whether you could have turned it into poetry, and
if so, how.

Coroalles extends his address of my father as

doctor into the public. *Doctor Rodriguez*, although appearing nowhere on the signs inside the store or on any of the pharmacy's printed materials, is frequently heard in the aisles and around the counter, and emanating nowhere more than from the mouth of Martín Coroalles. He calls me *amigo*. Is it sarcastic? He does not pronounce it with the least overtone of irony, but the word selection alone makes me wonder. It sounds to me like the choice of someone who would rather not remember my name, rather not decide whether he wants to assign me a name at all, hedging that I might not be around long enough to matter, not just betting but baiting: wish fulfillment. *Amigo.* Could Coroalles really see me, in any sense, as a friend?

Las consultas make up the bulk of my father's work. Viejitos come to see him for a variety of conditions and with a spectrum of explanations for choosing him over a licensed physician. Either their Medicare is not active or up-to-date, or they don't like that new doctor who pronounces their name wrong down at the clínica, or they don't have six weeks to wait for the next appointment at the public clinic, or—and this seems to be la clave, the key, to brisk business at this Calle 8 pharmacy—for certain ailments my father will dispense a prescription without the need for anything written; no scrip, with perpetual refills. How convenient, qué cómodo, in this America of limitations and regulations to just get what you need by asking for it!

Sometimes my father goes away for an hour or more. It is Coroalles's job to say, "Drop off your prescription. Doctor Rodriguez will fill it when he gets back and you can pick it up later this afternoon." It's like he knows my father's patterns. Even when my father says nothing and slips out the back, Coroalles's estimates for when patients can pick up their prescriptions is never off by more than a few minutes. Coroalles does what he's told. He does not make waves. He clearly sees an opportunity to advance by keeping his mouth shut.

We are stocking the bottom shelf with coffee when Coroalles undertakes it to educate me in the ways of gusano communication. The store is quiet for a moment between customers, and he tells me he is going to show me how to grind the coffee. He sets me stocking coffees that come in vacuum-sealed bricks: Bustelo, Goya, Caribe, Pilon, and La Llave. Beside these shelves is an industrial grinder, because the store also sells cheap pounds from sackfuls of roasted beans they buy in bulk. Most of the customers will pay an extra fifty cents for the convenience of not having to grind it themselves, so we have a daily ritual of measuring scoopfuls from the sack to make preground pounds.

Coroalles flips on the grinder, and while the machine whines he leans in close to me, shelving bricks. He speaks beneath his breath in a soothing undertone as if he is talking to a convalescent or a child. "You know, you have to be careful what you say around here."

I modulate my tone to match his. "You mean in the store?"

"The store, the street, the neighborhood. Anywhere in Little Havana. This place draws a certain amount of attention, and they are paying attention."

"*They?*"

"El FBI y la CIA." Coroalles pours in another scoop.

I wonder if I should risk asking, and I remind myself that any reasonable person would ask, especially a new arrival meeting his father for the first time in twenty-eight years. "Why would they be interested in listening to what goes on in my father's store?"

"They don't know who to watch, so they watch everybody."

"You mean people are listening who are infor-
mants? Or are you saying this place may be bugged?"

don't really want to catch anybody. They just want
to say they were watching, so that when something
happens, the director can claim that they tried but
that the Cubans were too tricky. Not devious—
tricky. Everyone wins."

Did I say the right thing? Did I say the wrong
thing? Here in Miami you have to cool them down
before they get too hot. They'll lure you in with their
doublespeak of talking not-politics, and before you
know it you're paralyzed in a snare of you-started-it.

Coroalles pours in another pound and says, "Miami is a little crazy, know what I mean?"

"What do you mean?"

"I'm only saying that other cities are much more
tranquilas for a Cubano. In New York and Chicago,
nobody gives a shit about Fidel."

Equivocation is an art I learned well in the national medical service, and I decide that I can tell
Coroalles the cover concocted by DSS: "When I get
the approval from the state medical board, I might

try to get in touch with the doctors in Tampa." I think this might be the time to insert a small word of deferral to let Coroalles know I am on his side, that I do not mean to replace him, in case he is concerned. "I just feel lucky my father is here to help me get a start."

"No you don't," Coroalles says.

"¿Cómo?" I reply, taken aback.

Coroalles pours in one more pound. "I just mean that you shouldn't feel lucky. Or if you do, you'd better wake up. This place is a hornet's nest. You'd be better off if you'd gone straight to Catholic Relief Services."

A big, exquisitely waxed, late-model SUV pulls up outside the pharmacy. It is hot as hell outside, but a fat man emerges in a dress shirt buttoned at the collar, the sleeves gold-cuffed at the wrists. How does he survive in there?

When he enters the store, my father greets him at the door and introduces us. Mendoza holds both of my shoulders in hands bedecked with gold rings and exclaims, "¡Hijo de Rodriguez es hijo mio!" I am anxious for a chance to practice communicating the criteria for my immigration request, and Mendoza does not let me down. "What were the hospitals like, hijo de Rodriguez?"

This is a good start. Just that he asks me in the perfect tense would intimate that we share an epistemology of pastness to that life. They buy it, that I want to defect. I cultivate a contained bitterness: "Getting worse every day. They expected me to conduct outpatient treatment with no painkillers. Even the anesthesia was rationed."

If this last statement was too far a stretch, my interlocutor's expression does not betray any skepticism when he goads me further: "So the Communists at the top take all the money?"

I capitulate: "The director lives in a posh apartment, and the physicians can't even get new scrubs."

A slight flaring of Mendoza's nostrils accompanies an unconcealed sarcasm of the perpetually suspicious. "You should write a booklet about this, hijo de Rodriguez." It is apparently too much for him to learn my first name. "Maybe la Fundación will publish it, ¿no?"

I catch my breath at this reference to the CANF. They published the autobiography of Juan Pablo Roque, now known to be an elaborate front for a Cuban agent sent to spy on them. I do not know how to think like a Florida Republican, but I do know Cuban irony, so I reply, "Don't you think I could find a better publisher than that?"

"Hahaha!" He smacks me on the back, his big Rolex worn loose and dangling conspicuously outside his shirt cuff. "Sure you can! Simón y SHOOster, ¿cómo no? Call it *Doctor Defector.*"

I should not be surprised that Mendoza displays the canny Cuban charisma. I remind myself: this man kills. This is the monster from my nightmares.

Less than a week ago, a young man was alive and enjoying his vacation in Havana when a bomb ex-

man's SUV and entered the store. They both have short, scruffy beards that do little to improve their acne-scarred faces. The older one is Eusebio, "pero call me Yuyo," he says. Yuyo, sociably aggressive, goads me, "You happy, huh? You the lucky one, mang!" He pulls a rice cooker off the shelf in the small kitchen section of my father's store and puts his other arm around my neck halfway between brotherly hug and choke hold. "You should be happy: couple of days you could own your own rice cooker! Your own wallet with diez fulas inside! You could have it all!"

Yuyo introduces the younger one. No cute name, no smile. Just: "Y éste es mi hermanito Carlos." Carlos keeps his distance and holds his tongue, but even as he mutters, "Mucho gusto," he cannot conceal a pent-up rage that has misshapen his face around a jaw clenched like a disqualified Olympian's. It is apparent that he looks forward to the possibility that Mendoza might someday find an excuse to unleash him on me.

We talk a little longer about the bad conditions in Cuba, and I find that I am beginning to feel comfortable with the rhetoric of exile resentment: the monotony and exhaustion of treating such a heavy caseload of patients for a cafeteria-worker's salary, all the while knowing that anyplace else in the world I'd be living like a king with half as much work. I am learning the persona that needs to be played, because in fact it is not far from the truth. There is an opportunism, a materialism, that these Rolex-wearing, cologne-smelling gusanos would be only too happy to accommodate.

Mendoza and the Riveras go upstairs. Their offices are accessed from the back of the store, by the double-padlocked doors at the bottom of the stairs I assume are off-limits to my father, and certainly to me.

Back home that night, my father heats the spaghetti from a can. The sauce is so good. As it says on the can, *Boy-o-boy*. He opens two beers. I tell him, "You've done very well for yourself here. The pharmacy is so opulent compared to Cuba."

"The main problem is derelicts coming in to steal painkillers."

"What kind?"

"Codeine and other opiates."

"Do they have guns?"

rush, breaking off conversations, behaving like he has somewhere to be when in reality he is running from something he'll never escape—at least not this way. Pain. He is in constant, chronic back pain. This makes him cranky, but it also makes him piti-able. His state of permanent hurry, coupled with a gusano's reflex mistrust, cause him to be jumpy. He will self-medicate whatever it takes. When he drags on his cigarettes, he is sucking on heated nicotine rather than savoring the smoke.

I tell my father, "I think I'll go to Eckerd for some razors. Do you want anything?"

"Nothing. You need money?"

"I've got a little, thanks . . ." We both sense the awkward pause. No, I am not going to just go and start saying *Papá*.

If I stand out on the intersection, the axis of my father's life in Miami, there is nothing to compare it to 12 y 23 in Vedado. Here there was a swamp, but all that capital and ingenuity that came with the Cuban immigration in the 1960s spread across southeast Florida like—perdóname, Edmundo Desnoes—a monstrous plant with great, glistening leaves but no fruit. A gas station at every crossroads, and irritable exiles in gas-guzzling SUVs speeding in to fill up, and then speeding out to make more money, but nobody shoots the breeze with a neighbor on the sidewalk or sets up their chair on the porch to watch the telenovela. There are no porches. Havana, they say, is stuck in 1958—but at least it is a *living* '58.

At the Eckerd near my father's apartment, a pack of the cheapest disposable razors is six dollars. After this and the calls to my father and the bus ride, Yorki's twenty is already down to $11.50. I will never be able to buy his new Nikes, not even for twice that much, so I choose to use it on smokes. The nearest to the black tobacco of Populares is an expensive French brand called Gauloise. I could get filterless Camels, but that's still blond tobacco. I finally settle on Marlboro Reds. I pay for my razors and smokes and make sure that the change contains a quarter.

Outside the Eckerd, I break the filter off a Marlboro to make it taste like something and light up. I smoke for a minute on the quiet corner. I think before I make the call. It will have to be very brief. I want to make it in and out of the phone booth in less than a minute. I would be terrified to step

out and see one of my father's friends. Lives center around intersections. There is sure to be gossip

the number I memorized. After one ring, there
is a brief tone and I say, "I met the landlord." I
hang up and exit the booth with my heart in my
throat, but there is still nobody on the street.

Back at the apartment, my father is drunker still.
"Ay, Manolo, it is very difficult to talk about." *Which
part?* I want to say. Instead I wait while he stands
up, grabbing his lumbar—"¡Carajo!"—and stag-
gers from his chair to the refrigerator to get us both
another beer. He puts one in front of me, sits back
down with his bottle, and raises the shredded gold
foil to his lips to take a long pull. "That place in
Vedado belongs to us," he says. "We'll get it back
cuando se muera Fidel."

Now I understand. It is difficult for him to talk
about losing the house. Can I blame my father for
betraying a more sentimental connection to the
property than to the wife he left behind and the

child he never knew? I use this instant to let Caballero's advice sink in: separate the person from the problem. This man, although my biological father, has drifted many lifetimes away from my values.

He says, "I remember them coming, functionaries from Reforma Urbana, barely literate. Taking my coffee and looking around at the sala, estimating the square footage, like it already belonged to them. Like it already belonged to that campesina-turned-spy—what was her name?"

"Beatrice. She's still there."

"You wait. Cuando se muera Fidel, we'll kick her out on her ass." When Fidel is dead. I wonder: *What does he mean by "we"?* Beatrice. His medical school. Fidel Castro. Cuba. Who is going to try screwing him next? The bitterness. He is always running like he has to go to the bathroom. He, the perpetual refugee: running from, running to, on a treadmill, never getting away. Take whatever he can. He is rich, and yet he must grab at the tendrils of desperation. Because deep in his heart he knows that, someday again, someone will take it all away. I am thinking this when he gets up from his chair with another carajo, and I see he has finished the six-pack as well as who knows how much rum. I feel sorry for him. The only thing that makes it tolerable is concentrating on the role I must play. I must press my own ambition.

I break the silence: "I am eager to get the application started."

My father goes on, blaming Beatrice for his exile, when in reality it was his own vanity and stubbornness that sent him packing. I am convinced this is true, and I feel a bittersweet surge of pride at this tidy analysis. *Doctora Hernández, you would be proud of me.*

Then I see how cruel my analysis is, however accurate. Yes, it was his own arrogance that pushed him to leave Cuba. He had spent half his lifetime harboring an open wound. And refusing to treat it or even let it heal. Picking the scab off every morning, pouring beer and rum over it every night. Horrible. Sad. And when he blamed it on Beatrice, he not only nurtured a bottomless bitterness, he forestalled ever getting over it. He would take it to his death. His defeat at the hands of a woman—uneducated, a proletarian of the nonworking peasant class— this is what ate away at him and gave him ulcers. Consumed him with anger. Crushed him beneath bitterness. Sad, tragic memories: twenty-eight years trapped in a labyrinth of what could have been.

"Beatrice, la descarada, la enredadora, la engañadora—she will live forever." He nods in his chair over the glass of rum. I have to lead him stumbling to his bed to get the living room to myself.

bring me along. I am not certain whether my father is happy that Mendoza has extended this invitation to me, but he must grudgingly accept that I am a curiosity. I have escaped Castro's Cuba. I am the latest harbinger on the exiles' horizon, and so far I would seem to portend fair weather: a competent doctor, a second-generation gusano, a worm begotten of a worm.

My father asks if I want to borrow a shirt. My favorite black T-shirt is clean from his small washing machine, so I decline.

Driving the Buick to Mendoza's house, he is unusually quiet. "¿Qué te pasa?" I ask.

Looking at the traffic ahead, he says, "There were those explosions in Havana last week."

Caballero instructed me not to indicate that I had been anywhere near the Copacabana on Thursday, September 4, so I am cautious when my father brings it up. "Yes, I heard about it on the news. An Italian tourist was killed."

"Around here, the thinking goes that someone who chooses to visit Havana in wartime collaborates with the enemy."

"That's a bit of a stretch, isn't it?"

"Yes, but in other words, they say that the money for those MiGs that shot down the Brothers came from tourists who stay in those hotels."

"Do you believe that?"

"As a doctor," he says, "I find such justifications for violence deplorable."

"And as a human being?"

"¡Qué vá! Do not badger me, Manolo. As a human being, I live in Miami."

When we arrive at Mendoza's, I realize immediately that I should have accepted my father's offer to let me borrow a shirt. Every other man is wearing a pressed white guayabera. I assumed that, like in Cuba, I could just show up in a clean T-shirt. This proves how thoroughly my mind-set is stuck in the proletariat.

In Havana, we would call Mendoza's house a mansion. Here, hundreds of Miami Cubans of his profile—landowners, land developers, landlords—have palaces like this. Mendoza welcomes us and says, "¿Pasamos al bar?" At first I believe he is moving the party and we are all going to relocate to a bar somewhere in the neighborhood. Following him into the back of his castle, however, I see that he has his own bar. There is a long counter, and behind it dozens of gleaming bottles against a lighted mirror.

out on the ocean, half of them smoking cigars and half of the rest smoking cigarettes. The older men politely introduce themselves. There is interest in my defection. "Was it hard to get out?"

"Did they hold you up at the airport?"

The Riveras invite me to go work out with them sometime. Yuyo: "You want to see a Gold's Gym?"

I cannot imagine myself in one of those gleaming Miami gyms, even in borrowed workout clothes, anywhere alongside these two. "Some other time."

Mendoza introduces me first to a doctor, Centurión, a retired geriatrician who visibly sniffs when my father says that I, too, am a physician and that I have just escaped Cuba. Acabado de llegar. I think of the annual pediátrico mixer that Gonzalez calls a cocktail party: a bottle of ron paticrusados and a scrawny salami that disappears too quickly. Here in the US, this is how doctors do it every Friday: with heaping platters of food and a full bar.

I am able to add some authenticity to my litany by referring to the abusive system of ever-expanding work overloads. Let them exploit it for their propaganda. I tell them about the corruption, the frustration with the poor state of the hospitals, the Communist Party graft, all in the past tense. "The director would get funds for staffing and instead spend it on personal travel and perks for his office—everything from air-conditioning to chocolate. In order to function, any doctor with a conscience had to work twice as hard." For once, Director Gonzalez is proving useful. It is not hard for me to summon real resentment for him before this audience. I am beginning to believe my own rap.

My father interjects, "There's a saying aquí: *If you want something done, give it to someone who is busy.*" The cruel logic of el capitalismo, encapsulated in an aphorism like this, occasionally rings truer than all the socialist slogans of my youth.

"¿Cuánto tiempo practicaste en la Habana?" asks Centurión.

I tell him that I finished medical school early, so it had been almost eight years practicing at the pediatric hospital.

"Yo no me jactaría de haber trabajado tanto tiempo en ese infierno para el diablo." *I would not brag about working so long in hell for the devil.*

He is not being ironic. This subdues the party

a bit. It is an affront for one Cuban to thus challenge another, although it all seems a bit absurd to

ence in personality and removes me to the kitchen,
where Coroalles pulls us two beers from a refrigerator the size of a small apartment. I ask to use the
bathroom, but the one off the kitchen is locked.
"Must be the Rivera boys," says Mendoza, the joc-
ular godfather, parent to none but uncle to all. He
bangs on the door. "We know what you're doing in
there, hombres! Coroalles, take him to the one in
my office."

"Follow me, amigo," Coroalles says, leading me
through vaulted hallways to the other end of the
house, adding, "I needed to go anyway," as if to em-
phasize that he does not usually take orders from
Mendoza. It strikes me how strict the caste system
is in Cuban America: for twenty-five years Coroalles
has been el mozo, the gopher, busboy, stockboy, and
shopboy, but who would ever expect him to ask for
more? These men are his only family, and my father
is both his brother and his bread-and-butter.

Mendoza's office is a typically bombastic arrangement: walls lined with lots of books whose spines have never been cracked, and on the great oak desk, one elegant late-model laptop.

"You mind if I go first?" Coroalles says, and I know that he has considered for a moment what, in the worst-case scenario, someone like me might be thinking. But he has probably decided that the odds are better someone like me will seize up and merely *deliberate* the possibility of snooping should I be left alone so suddenly, whereas standing at the throne to go I could build up my courage. Therefore, he will go first, and I will wait outside and listen for the flush.

Coroalles, if only your modesty had not allowed you to shut the door all the way while peeing, you could have kept an eye on the situation through the crack. Thus I find myself alone in Mendoza's office, where the little yellow light on the top edge of the laptop means the computer is asleep, but breathing. I press the space bar to wake it up. The screen comes to life. I touch the trackball and click the task bar, and there is the Explorer icon. I tap it twice and it opens to Yahoo. Mendoza is already logged in. In the drafts folder there is an unsent message. It is not made up of full sentences, so I stare at the numbers and words and repeat them to myself several times until they are memorized as groupings.

26-9
José Martí

the name of our great liberator. And then the number 4,500, which I immediately recognize as a multiple of the same amount paid to the Salvadoran for bombing the Copacabana.

I hear Coroalles press the handle and my heart leaps into my throat. I flip the laptop shut and fortunately the little smack sound coincides with the crescendo of Coroalles's flush, and I am glad I have enough of my wits about me to take a sidestep, one long sidestep that matches the apogee of what is visible in the room from the inward-opening door of Mendoza's bathroom. With a glance over my shoulder I verify this, and I raise a finger that says to anyone who cares to ask themselves, *This finger has been running along the spines from the top shelf for the last minute and a half or so, for as long as you have been hastily peeing and quickly zipping up.* Coroalles, his conscience needling him, has not bothered to wash his hands. There are a few dark spots where the last drops of pee sprinkled on his fly while he zipped up too hastily.

He takes in the room—the new gusano apparently absorbed in the fascinating titles from Mendoza's august collection, the laptop shut—and he seems satisfied. "You go ahead," he says.

"Ah, sí." I act as if I have lost myself for a moment in literary contemplation and have almost forgotten that I needed to go, and like a good spy I add what I consider a small masterstroke of authenticity: "I can find my way back." Do not try to seem innocent in his eyes. He wants to be useful, and yet the men in the caste above his, who have been above him since long before the Revolution in Havana, wish to ridicule him. *Ah, Coroalles thinks el hijo de Rodriquez is too curious. A touch of jealousy? Did you really think el doctor was going to leave you the store when he retired?* It can only be in my favor if I go ahead and validate his legitimate suspicions.

"Mm," Coroalles says, taking my full measure when I brush past him to the bathroom. I close the door with a click and don't bother to lock it, but my hands are shaking so bad I have trouble unzipping, and when I am unzipped, it takes a full minute for my taut bladder to let loose, as I repeat to myself, *José Martí, 26-9, 4,500.* I flush and turn the faucet on full bore, washing my hands like I plan to go into surgery. *José Martí, 26-9, 4,500.*

When I emerge from the bathroom, Coroalles is pretending to study the first page of a book from the

arm and shows me a little white powder. "Come on, have a blast."

It takes me a moment to understand that he is offering me cocaine. There is nothing quite so distasteful as two men crammed into a bathroom together to bend over a little mound of addictive powder that has been cut with talc and contaminated by various poisons to gorge their noses on aggression, and I wish nothing more than to leave the party with my father as soon as possible. I must get to a pay phone.

"Try it, mang. It will let you drink more."

"Please excuse me. I already have to drive my father home, and I don't even have an American license." Yuyo leaves me to go get high. My hands are wet with perspiration.

Down the hall I hear Mendoza telling Centurión: "It's the only way on or off the island. Think of what it will do to tourism when tourists decide it isn't safe." When I enter the living room, Mendoza lowers his voice.

It gets late and I tell my father it's time to go home, thinking, *I will have to get him drunker*.

Compared to the Lada with its clunky gears, driving the Buick is a piece of cake. Although my left foot keeps pushing the floorboard for a ghost clutch, the transmission is automatic, and it shifts gears as smoothly as silk. It's not even audible— that's Yanqui know-how.

Back at my father's apartment, he is so drunk I have to help him up the stairs. He soliloquizes: "For a while I thought we might be able to work through it. The ocean sounds coming up on a clear, quiet night at your mother's house made Havana tolerable for a few hours; it felt all the more precious, knowing that all the evil down below could not harass us around the clock. They took everything, Manolo, the house, the business, my dream: a private practice. We worked for that. Ten years of hard work. We put a lot of money into that. Then Fidel makes one speech and it all evaporates. A voucher for two nights at the Havana Libre. Then they took away half of our house in Vedado, your mother's childhood home, and we are supposed to thank them? They let your mother die."

It is everything I can do not to choke him when

he says that. Drunken fool. It was he who let my
mother die. *Do not try to twist your conscience to feed*

What to make of *26-9*? At first I did not see it, only
memorized it. Outside of Eckerd there's some graffiti on the wall and it hits me: it may be a date. I
might not have thought of it were it not for the *26*,
the first part of the graffiti that before 1959 could
cost a Fidelista his life. If you were caught writing
it on the side of a building, you would be accused of
supporting the 26th of July Movement: M-26-7. If
the numbers do mean September 26, that is just two
weeks away. But José Martí? The name on my lips is
reverent as only José Martí can be to both exile and
barbudo alike. Could it be a cynical code name for
the mercenary?

I think before I make the call. *When will it be safe
to evacuate? Should I walk straight to the rendezvous?*
No, in the morning I will make the follow-up call,
and, according to the instructions, only if there is a
message will I walk to José Martí Park. This is when I
realize what is meant by *José Martí*. It is not the man.

I almost forgot what all has been named, on both sides of the Florida Straits, after our patriot, both before and after the Revolution. Not José Martí the name. José Martí the place. *It is the airport named José Martí.* José Martí Airport is the most crowded place in all Havana every day from five a.m. until midnight. Surely Mendoza has this in mind; he knows a deadly airport bombing will destroy tourism in one blow.

I enter the phone booth in the alcove, insert a quarter, and push the buttons. The line clicks, the tone bursts, and I whisper into the mouthpiece. I could be a doctor reciting notes on a patient's chart into a dictation machine, including an estimate of expenses (except that Cuban doctors take their own chart notes, and patients do not pay): "E-mail draft, 26-9, José Martí, 4,500."

If the person answering the phone doesn't know, Pérez and Caballero will. *José Martí*: the airport. *September 26*: two weeks away. *4,500*: three bombs.

When I get back to my father's apartment, he is still passed out on my sofa. I want to say, *We could have taken it the other way, Papá. It could have become us against Beatrice. Maybe Mamá would have made it. The cancer could have gone into remission. The witch to make us stronger.* In the morning I will meet my father's friend on the medical board and begin the immigration process. I will have to renounce my Cuban citizenship. I will go through the motions until

deserted during the day. She is out, and while the door to the apartment is not locked, I have to put my shoulder into it to get it open for the mountain of mail and unread papers that has piled up beneath the slot. Although my mother comes home every night, she must just push over them as I have just done, spreading the mess even further as stack after stack of unread correspondence gets shuffled and crumpled. I have more to add, because I borrowed two newspapers just the other day, knowing she wouldn't read them anyway. Someday, maybe, if she starts feeling better. And so I drop them back onto the pile, including today's paper, which I bought with my own dollar. I'll leave her my paper. Maybe she'll see it when she comes home. I have to go now. Soon she'll be back.

SÁBADO, 13 SEPTIEMBRE

It is early morning, before dawn, when I awake to the ringing of the phone in my father's apartment. The sofa is empty. I am cramped from sleeping in the chair, and I pick up the receiver and mutter, "¿Oigo?"

"Getting your beauty sleep?" It is my father. "Can you come down to the pharmacy and help with some boxes? The store got an early delivery and it's Coroalles's day off."

I walk down a quiet Calle 8 and get to the pharmacy in less than fifteen minutes. It is still dark outside, but the service door is unlocked. Emerging from the storeroom, I discover the store lights are out except for over the pharmacist's counter, where my father has poured himself a good rum, Bacardi Añejo. He pours me one in a nice glass. We sit side by side in chairs where customers usually wait for prescriptions to be filled.

I take a small sip. It is very good, as smooth as Havana Club, but without a certain musty antiquity I associate with the taste of real Cuban rum. "What are we celebrating this morning?"

"La vida," my father answers, "just like every morning."

are shaking, it is hard to picture that this man was once capable with a scalpel. Slouching back in the chair, he refills his glass and takes another swallow. "There are times a surgeon walks into an emergent situation with a severe trauma of some kind—a knife wound, auto accident, or a bad fall—and he knows the patient is not going to make it. Certainly, you know what I am talking about?" I can think of at least a half-dozen occasions, and I am just waiting for the day when there are more than I can count on both hands. "And there is a human inside here," he says, tapping his head, "who knows, despite all the protocols and oaths, who just knows the right thing is *not* to attempt heroic measures, and so he takes his time applying the tourniquets. He hesitates."

My father is right. I now have no doubt that he once worked in an OR, but I am nevertheless uncomfortable with the direction this conversation is taking, so I try changing the subject: "What about those boxes?"

My father lowers the sunglasses. His eyes are very red. "What I am trying to say is this: you and I are both men who have looked horror in the face, and once you have locked eyes with horror, without turning away, you never look at the world the same again."

Coroalles enters from the front of the store and my heart races. It was supposed to be his day off. He carries a handheld recorder. It still bears the sticker from the store advertising that it is *Voice-activated!* I feel the burning rum I just swallowed rising in my throat, and I have to choke it back to say, "Where did you get that?"

Coroalles says, "$39.99 at Eckerd." The simplest traps.

My father says, "Cóño, Manolo. How could you have been so foolish? Everyone knows everyone in Little Havana. When you ask the cashier for quarters and he sees you using the pay phone outside, he's got to mention it to Mendoza."

Coroalles adds, "I wondered, who could you be calling that you would not ask one of us to use the store telephone? Last night I noticed you flipped Mendoza's laptop shut, so I hid this inside the phone booth." Coroalles presses play and I hear the sound of my own voice come out. It is soft and tinny, but unmistakably mine: "*E-mail draft, 26-9, José Martí, 4,500.*"

Precisely how I could have been so foolish becomes a secondary consideration when I hear the

and scoops his fingers against the back of my glottis. I stifle another hot ball of nausea welling up in my esophagus. They have watched too many James Bond movies, assuming I carry cyanide clenched in the back of my mouth.

Yuyo takes his hand out of my throat and a Rivera on either side pins a wrist to the arm of my chair. The world tilts and a shudder passes through me. My body becomes no longer my property. All these years of hardship, and the past few weeks of fear weighing on me like an old man, radiate from my sore bones. Mendoza says, "¿Tú no pensaste que estábamos esperando algo así?"

Of course I thought they would be looking out for something like this.

He takes the cordless phone from its cradle on the pharmacist's counter and pushes it in my face. "A ti te gusta hacer llamadas por teléfono. Vamos, llama a tus jefes."

Call my masters. I glance at my father and he looks down at his glass. He is already drunk, and he pours himself another. And why not? How could anyone do this sober? I understand he is as much a prisoner as I am.

I hold the phone in shaking hands and it strikes me with alacrity that Mendoza is correct about one thing: all I have is a number, but he does not know it is an untraceable voice mail, and Eduardo told me never to leave a message from anywhere but a pay phone. Making this call from my father's pharmacy could be my only chance to indicate that I am in trouble. I push the buttons slowly, my hands shaking. Carlos watches and copies the number onto a pad of yellow paper.

When I am done dialing, Mendoza takes the phone. The line clicks, the tone bursts, and Mendoza listens. After a few seconds of silence, his face contorts in disgust. He presses the button to end the call. "Who did you signal? Is it Giro?"

"No sé."

"Mentiroso sinvergüenza." Mendoza grabs my throat. "Fidel is breeding these wasps like so many worthless pesos. You are disposable, hijo de Rodriguez." To Yuyo he says, "¿Ya está listo el cuarto?"

"Listo."

The room is ready.

Part III

HAVANA LIBRE

carceration, freedom from torture and cruelty, even freedom of thought. The lies about free enterprise vs. free health care, free choice vs. free education— to the educated citizen, these are afterthoughts. Bodily freedom is first, last, and indispensable.

They take me up the stairs to the hallway of the vacant apartment, where a radio is turned up very loud on a gusano talk station. Yuyo tells me to take off my shoes. I have heard of prisoners getting shoe-laces taken away to forestall attempts at suicide by asphyxiation, but in my case they leave me barefoot altogether. When Yuyo takes away the right shoe, I remember that my cousin Emilio's fifty-dollar bill is in there. They also take my belt and tell me to remove my black T-shirt.

Carlos pushes me into the small room and they lock the door behind me, leaving me in darkness. I am trapped in the bathroom of an empty apartment. My surroundings consist of a sink, a shower-tub, and a toilet. I try flipping on the light but nothing happens. When I reach for the faucet and turn it, the vacuum backfills with a whoosh of air from the room. I try the valves under the sink, but it's no use: the line has been shut off downstairs and the pipes have been purged. With the shower it is the same. The toilet is drained of water and both seat and lid have been removed. And when I lift the top off the back to feel in the dark tank, I find the float on the dry bottom.

At dawn, enough light comes through the high window for me to see two brass screws holding the thick trim of the single pane flush to the frame. I touch the edges of the frosted glass, a chicken-wire pane about fifty by forty centimeters. The futility of my situation makes me swoon. I am numb with the rum of the night before, but without any of the pleasant effects of intoxication.

Situation analysis. Reconstruct to my best ability the past forty-eight hours from the captor's perspective: My father suspected me, and he did not hesitate to betray me before I could him. Mendoza aided him to lay a trap on his computer, and Coroalles set the recorder in the phone booth. Maybe my father feigned being drunker than he really was. Coroalles went out and retrieved the recorder while I slept. Perhaps he had been trying to warn me when he said

I would have been better off had I gone to Catholic Relief Services, but they are not bombing hotels in

the store. This is Mendoza's building, in the heart of Little Havana. He is the king of Little Havana. The bathroom easily made into a jail cell. The objective seems to have been to get me into captivity as quickly as possible and to make the conditions as uncomfortable as possible. No food, no water. Although I do not yet feel parched, I am thirsty. I have experienced severe dehydration before, and I do not wish to again.

Triage. In my early days as a medical intern in Cuba's national health-care system, pulling double and triple shifts, days which never really ended as the conscientious physician still works twice and three times as hard, I had to constantly inventory my resources and assess my options. Despite the narrow probability that it would serve me for much more than a psychological diversion, we must do this as physicians and as Cubans. Now, in my current predicament, I fall back on it as an only alternative to surrender, a stratagem for self-preservation against complete collapse. I must focus my faculties and attenuate: deliberating conscientiously either on the biggest problem, the most soluble problem, or some combination, before the onset of soreness, hunger, and complete exhaustion. Right now, while I am still reasonably conscious. Who is Giro? What does Mendoza mean by wasps?

Just outside the door, the radio's ceaseless onslaught. The hosts' hollered diatribes and occasional conversations with callers; advertisements for grocery stores, car dealerships, and impossibilities such as fat-reducing pills and get-rich-quick schemes with a maddening machine gun of disclaimers crammed into five seconds at the end of each—such is the orthodoxy of Little Havana that no neighbor would call in a noise complaint against Radio Mambí, WAQI Miami 710 AM. There hardly ever passes a beat of silence. Not only does the dissonance keep me from trying with much enthusiasm to cry for help, it will also deprive me of sleep.

The room lightens and all I have is porcelain tile, talk radio, and sleep deprivation. I perceive that there is no shower curtain or rod for one above the bathtub, and the bar for the towel rack is gone too. No easy way of hanging myself, should I elect the only option for exit. Anything metal that was not fixed in position has been removed. Even the drain covers in the sink and tub are gone. I cannot imagine what mischief they thought I might stir up with these.

I recognize it is an oven thermometer, my stomach tightens like a fist. The needle rests at the bottom, where the temperature starts at 120 degrees Fahrenheit.

Hopeless schemes spin through my half-awareness. *My screwed-shut window: break it, squeeze through, drop to the alley below* . . . Even though I know that, at about 0.2 square meter, there would be no way for more than a small child to fit through. There is no hardware to hang a curtain, nor is there an edge to hang some scrap of fabric and keep out the direct sun. I have to block these thoughts and stop the spiral. It is useless. It is burning up what cognitive energy I have left.

I really need to shit, but I hold it. Without water in the toilet, there will be no pressure to flush. I pee down the bathtub drain because the P trap is behind the wall and not in the middle of the room and it could keep bad odors down, depending on how long I am in here. I experience severe abdominal pangs.

My intestinal contortions are redoubled by the absurdity of the configuration: locked in a room with a toilet, but no way to go. The sun shines directly onto the tile floor through my window. The morning drags on and by midday the temperature reaches 130 degrees.

It is no longer possible to hold it and I have no recourse. I sit on the toilet and let myself go. Naturally there is no paper. I take off my black T-shirt and tear it into strips to wipe with, throwing the rags in the dry toilet on top of the shit. In my prison-oven, the stench remains close in my throat. By early afternoon, the radio says it's 95 degrees outside. Inside the bathroom, the oven thermometer says it is 140.

Nothing happening, nobody else is in the apartment except for the person guarding my room right outside the door. In the split-second breaks from the radio's cacophony I hear him flip the pages of a newspaper or magazine. I think it is currently Carlos because when he shifts in the chair it creaks louder than it did this morning. He is taking alternating shifts with Yuyo. While the temperature inside rises, their job is to mind the oven. Whoever it is, he does not want to look at me. He does not want to smell me. By midafternoon it is 150 degrees.

They finally come and get me. Yuyo hollers, "Woo! It stinks in here!" He guides me shirtless across the hallway to the bedroom. Carlos is there, and there is a single metal folding chair in the middle of the

had a rest. The Rivera boys remain, but my father is conspicuously missing.

Mendoza's tone is cold, calm, imperative—not pleading, not threatening. He says, "Four men, unarmed, were shot out of the sky last year by Russian-made fighter jets in Castro's air force because of sinvergüenzas like you. I stood alongside the wives of those pilots at the funerals, weeping."

The radio in the hallway blares Radio Mambí. I have told him the number, but he is doubly angry because it was a prepaid voice mail. Now all I have left is José Martí Park. These are the only words I have that might be of value to him, but they are also my only hope, however slim. José Martí Park. I will not say it.

"They abandoned you," Mendoza says. He wants something from me—Giro—and all he has gotten is a prepaid voice mail. To know whom Roque was feeding information, the one who in turn conveyed it to Havana, coordinating with others who made the decision to shoot down the planes and kill those four men. This would be a real catch.

Mendoza repeats, "¿Quién es Giro?"

He waits for a reply, but I look at the floor. Mendoza is not a professional interrogator. Like a dull knife, this can be more dangerous. He is a new and lazy jailer, one who believes that deprivation and dehydration will prevail. He tells the Riveras, "Bring him back to his air-conditioned studio."

When they return me to the bathroom and the stench of hot feces, the sun is just passing out of my window zone and the temperature is 160. I breathe through the fabric of what's left of my shirt, but the stench is unbearable. I gag in the fetid air, dry-heaving through painful convulsions of my throat and abdomen. A recorder in a phone booth. I was not careful. The bathroom a prison cell. The bedroom an interrogation chamber.

Who is Giro? What does Mendoza mean by wasp? Five years and what, roughly five weeks? That is how long it has been since the first time I lost my freedom. I said I would not let them lock me up again. I meant anybody, ever. Now, half a decade later, I find myself in this ridiculous situation. Blame Pérez and Caballero? No. Blame some Salvadoran asshole willing to blow people up for $1,500? Yes, but not as much as my father and these other

moneyed motherfuckers. Blame myself. Privación
de libertad. Deprivation of liberty—this is what the

the first eighteen hours, I will lose nearly two liters of
water and two kilograms of body mass. The heat and
thirst are already disrupting my metabolic processes.
And the discomfort caused by hypernatremia, loss of
free water, and the attendant excess concentration
of salt is considerable. Gout. Weighing sixty-three
kilos, I could lose almost eight relatively safely. It
would be uncomfortable. It would be very uncomfortable. But it would not be lethal. I would begin
to break down at 15 percent. But the greater risk, I
know, is hypovolemia: loss of blood volume, particularly plasma, could be critical.

The effects of the physical discomfort combined
with dehydration create an agony like that of the
acute arthritis sufferer: every inch of joint and muscle
saturated with uric acid, the onset of gout. I languish
on my left side, bent double, arms wrenched behind
my back. Despite the agony of the position, the soreness throughout my body prevents me from moving.

Mercedes is probably asleep in the basement at the Havana Libre. Or with the baby in her belly in the water on the beach in Miramar. She has taken herself on a walk after her shift to cool down. Regardless, she could have heard the news by now: I did not show up at the conference. Maybe I have requested residency. Maybe I have defected.

Either she is brushing it off and saying, *El egoismo: just another refugee doctor who thought he deserved better than other Cubans.* Or she is thinking what I must have been thinking when I told her goodbye and saying to herself, *Ese hijo de puta. Me dijo que me iba a ayudar. Él se hizo el que quería ayudarme a mi con el niño. Con esos ojos con que me dijo adiós. Me hirió a propósito. Me engañó.* He told me he would help me. He pretended he wanted to take care of me and my baby. He said it with his eyes when he said goodbye. He hurt me on purpose.

A virtuous voice inside me says, *I hope she believes it was just egoism, but if she does, and if I die here, then what is left of me? I am nothing.* An iron hand seems to have nailed me to the spot where I stood last night. I am motionless with my eyes fixed on the window. I stand and stare at it. The moon moves slowly, blurily behind the frosted glass. I hum verses of "Guantanamera" to mark the time. *I am an honest man . . . And before I die . . . Verses from my soul . . .*

week on the job, and so Mercedes decides she can take a little bit of her savings—the pesos, not the dollars—and treat herself to ice cream. She crosses the street from the hotel to El Coppelia and sees the famous Cine Yara on the other corner. Tourists have their own entrance. Mercedes gets in line with the Cubans.

Across Calle 23 people line up for the guaguas going all across Havana. The camellos go up and down la Rampa. Blowing their air horns and coughing exhaust, they maneuver around the taxis and bici-taxis. The couple in front assure her that today it is a short line: an hour at most. She tells them it is her first time and the woman explains, "The glasses of water, plates, and spoons are dirty and smell like rotten milk, but don't complain! They'll serve you even more slowly."

There's a Coppelia in Pinar del Rio too, but it's much smaller compared to the one in Havana, which is shaped like un gran OVNI and at least it still sells ice cream. She wishes she had a friend to stand in line with, but that will happen in time. When the doctor returns from his trip she will ask him to join her for her October ice cream. In the meantime, she knows she is not alone.

The attendant in charge of distributing people to tables as they become available calls, "Una persona sola," and she is seated on the upstairs level at a table of hyperactive teenagers who pay no attention to her.

Clutching the pesos in her handkerchief, she looks around at her surroundings and despite herself thinks, *I expected it to be prettier.* She closes her eyes and tries to picture how pretty it was before everything began to fall apart.

She is trying to save for her baby, so she calculates what she might order for as little as possible to treat herself. How many flavors are available? What's the name for a bowl with just one scoop, as opposed to una ensalada?

The server's shirt is dingy white and his black pants are stained. He is tired and overworked. All the good servers are on the tourist side where tips are in dollars. He tells her it is seven pesos for una ensalada of five scoops, otherwise 1.50 per bola. The only flavor is vanilla. She orders one scoop of vanilla.

While she waits, she looks across the street at

the Havana Libre, her place of employment, and it makes her feel good for herself and for her child.

She was not able to conceive it otherwise. It was a sacrifice for the well-being of the child. If she had not been in love with him once, she would not be here now. If he had not become abusive and as such unrecognizable from the man she once loved, she could not have made the decision. But that did not mean that she couldn't tell her daughter someday about her father. She could tell her about the one that her mother had loved.

It takes thirty minutes for her scoop to arrive and she gives the server the money. There is no paper or ink for him to write the check. It is bad ice cream, very watery, and the bola has a hole on the inside, but to Mercedes it is refreshing and delicious. *This is vanilla*, she tells her baby, *ice cream the flavor of vanilla.*

MIAMI: THE ROOM

I do not hear Yuyo enter. He taps me on the shoulder and I shudder alert.

"Have you not slept?"

I shake my head. "I don't know."

"Are you not hungry?"

"I do not know." I know it would be futile to plead for water, and my head hurts too much to speak.

Yuyo grabs my underarms and helps me up. "Woo! It *really* stinks in here, man!" He drags me into the bedroom and props me up in the metal folding chair. The relative dimness is a balm to my eyes, but my sight is troubled with bursts of red fireworks. The men, three of them, are blurry blotches, and I realize my father is still not here. I close my eyes to preserve whatever moisture remains in them, but my parched lips are stuck painfully open, exposing my swollen tongue to the bone-dry room, and when I try to close my mouth the blistered skin at the corners splits open.

I am laughing to myself. Mendoza looks at me

strangely, which gives me a slight twinge of hope
that these are not such bad men, because I have

your captive. Just turn up the volume on the TV in
the adjoining room as loud as it will go.

"Who is Giro?" Sore, swollen eyes cannot see
against the harsh light, but I know from the voice
that it is Mendoza. "How many more wasps?"

"Leave me alone!" I shout this to offer something besides *José Martí Park*. The one thing I cannot say, my only thread of hope. If I do ever get out
of here, it's my only way back to Cuba. I could tell
them about Pérez. I could tell them about Caballero.
I probably would if they only asked me, just to be
able to say something, to give them something to cut
off the misery of repetition. *Who is Giro? How many
wasps?* I don't know.

Mendoza has me now, but I have obtained the
objective. I take solace in that, and I believe I might
make it through whatever deprivation Mendoza has
in mind. Even as I absorb the grim situation, I remember: I did it. I completed my mission. Havana is

safe. And it gives me strength. Focus on this through the heat and dehydration. Corazón, hombre. Have heart.

Yuyo comes up from the store with a fresh roll of duct tape. He removes the plastic and hands the roll to Carlos, and then Yuyo takes my right arm, pressing it into the arm of the chair with all his weight. Carlos unwraps the end of the tape with his teeth. Crushing my hand, he unrolls the tape four turns, binding my wrists to the arm of the chair. He is quick and clumsy, though I do not resist because it is Carlos. I am disgusted with myself but glad that he has not hit me. He repeats the process on my right arm. Mendoza tells the Rivera boys to turn up the radio in the hall and close the door behind them, and after they do he removes something from a plastic bag in his pants pocket.

He holds it in the palm of his hand for me to see: a little rubber ball of the size used by physical therapists. "I want you to feel this." He takes the ball and he rolls it over my bare arms above the restraints. It is soft like clay, smooth and warm from being in his pocket, and smells like motor oil. "Hit it with a hammer? Nothing happens. It can be shot with bullets, microwaved, or even set on fire—nothing. But zap it with a little electrical charge from a small battery . . . *Boom!*" He rolls the ball across my bare shoulders and continues low and soothing, "Do you feel it? That is all it took Posada to blow the Copacabana lobby to hell."

me what I want to know is that you still think there is something you can do. I have some bad news for you: the information you relayed to Havana was false."

"¿Cómo?" I rasp.

"We identified a target with more potential for the other Salvadoran. What you saw, what you reported to your masters, was actually a snippet of a rejected plan. Now the wasps are swarming to José Martí, but it is not happening on the 26th, and it will not be at the airport. A hotel in Havana, thirty floors, three of them below a plinth that is at grade on the north side. And it will happen mañana."

I am too dazed to make sense of his meaning and I seize on the word *mañana,* the most beautiful word in the Spanish language, which resonates in the misery of my captivity. "Tomorrow?"

"The 15th, shortly after dawn." He rolls the ball up my naked back. "I want you to understand which hotel I speak of. It underwent a renovation recently, and one of our friends in Havana who worked construction on the project sent us some photographs of the architect's report. He pointed out that the steep incline of the substructure below the plinth makes the building vulnerable to collapse if the two main structural supports are compromised. My masterstroke."

I let out a groan. "Havana Libre."

"It will fall like a domino." He presses the C-4 firmly into the base of my neck, at the top of the spinal column where the cervical vertebrae meet the skull. "Two charges about this size, set to go off simultaneously, at two junctures of steel beams in the basement. It was a marvel of its time, and its Achilles' heel is just two supports beneath the plinth. Take those out, and every floor, every room, will collapse to the north with approximately five hundred sleeping tourists. Fidel's infamous private floor will be in the basement, and thirty stories of steel and concrete will decimate the surrounding neighborhood: among Cubans, another 750 to 1,000 casualties are anticipated." Now Mendoza smiles. "Look on the bright side: most of the victims will die in their sleep, or at least half-asleep. There is nothing else you can do but tell us everything you know about Giro, and the other avispas, and maybe save your own skin." He pockets the putty and opens the door. "Take him back to his cooler."

SÁBADO, 13 SEPTIEMBRE
THE TOURIST

He walks down the hall to the door marked *Servicio*, the stained shirt draped over his backpack. The service stairwell is lit not with decorative fixtures like up on the main floors, but with a single bulb behind an institutional cage. He notes that it is the kind of light casing that makes the bulb tamper-proof in the type of habitat where you cannot trust the residents not to steal. The hotel's proprietors do not even trust their own employees not to steal a lightbulb: no wonder the service is so meager and skittish. He has noticed it not just here, but in the restaurants and nightclubs as well. Lots of *señor* and *en qué le puedo servir* and *a su orden*, but when he catches them thinking he's not looking, he sees the avarice and fear of abused dogs who are desperate for the merest rations. And this is supposed to be one of the country's finer hotels!

As he descends the stairs he knows that it would normally be unadvisable to think about staying in the facility that is the target, but in this case it makes more sense to assume the risk for the better development of the plan. As a guest, he can bum-

aquí? ¿Quién es el manager?

He opens the door to the service basement and peeks down the hall. He waits until a pair of house-keepers disappear into their dormitory, and before anyone else emerges he makes his way down the hall to the door that says, *Sólo Empleados.* He rolls the shirt up lengthwise, draping it over his shoulders like a scarf, and takes out a key that he got from the recruiter in San Salvador. He unlocks the door and steps inside to the semidarkness, reaching into his backpack and slowly pulling on a pair of gloves.

When he is finished scouting, he returns to the service door and opens it a crack to listen. There are no noises, not even a footfall. He takes the shirt from around his shoulders, holding it in his hands along with the empty backpack, and steps out into the hush.

The moment the service door clicks behind him, a housekeeper emerges from the dormitory. She starts, surprised to see him, and catches her breath to say clearly, firmly, and with much deference, "¿Lo puedo ayudar en algo?"

"Ahí estás," he spouts. "I need this shirt laundered right away. A terrible stain . . ."

"I'll do my best to get it out. What room are you staying in?"

"Actually, never mind, it's ruined now. Too late." He pushes through the stairwell doors and rushes up the steps.

met him last week at the Habana Vieja restaurant that he does not appear hungover or drunk. Carlos turns down Radio Mambí to medium-loud and listens in the doorway. Anything I say, he will tell Mendoza. They want to know if I will tell my father anything. I know it is Sunday because I can hear the church bells.

My father stares at me coldly. It was he who betrayed me, and yet he thinks it is the other way around. I am a nuisance who showed up in his life uninvited. The only compensation may be if they get an answer out of me. *Who is Giro?* My father says calmly, "I am going to Tampa for a few days. I am going to speak with the American doctor and explain how you defected and chose not to go to the conference. Y quiero que sepas algo antes de irme." *I want to tell you something before I leave.*

Half-lucid, I hear the implied meaning: he wants to say something now because I might not be here when he gets back.

"You came here as an enemy. Nevertheless, there is something that I wish you to understand. Not speaking as your father—because who can claim fatherhood with three decades of absence?—but as a man, a serious, moral, free man, I say of these people you work for: they took our lives away. You have become a human sacrifice for Communism: you rendered your life worthless for this. And what have they done for you? Twenty years of brainwashing, plus eight more of a worthless career in medicine where you get paid less than a cab driver. And now that you are no longer useful to them, they leave you here to rot."

It may sound delirious to him, but I must exert my focus to speak. My voice is hoarse: "I was there at the Copacabana. I was powerless to help him. He was thirty-two years old, just four years more than me."

My father shakes his head. He pays no attention to my raving.

"A chunk of ashtray pierced his carotid. I saw him bleed to death on the floor of the restaurant. Y ahora . . ." I think of the ones to come. Hundreds of innocent victims. Tourists as well as employees—Cubans without a penny to their names sleeping in the basement. I am trying to say that one of them is my patient and she's pregnant, but I cannot form the words. There are other things I'd like to say as well. *You and Mamá on your honeymoon. Three days and two nights at the Havana Libre. Carlos is stand-*

with me, and I have a flash of dread similar to when I watched as the young Italian's life was extinguished. "You know, Manolo, in the beginning stages of dehydration a person loses a lot of body mass, 10 to 15 percent, just before the greatest risk." He swivels to look into the mirrorless medicine cabinet. Carlos returns to his post to pretend he's not listening. Clearly but dispassionately, like an automaton, my father says, "Este baño me recuerda el baño en la casa de tu madre." *This reminds me of the bathroom in your mother's house.*

My father turns and leaves the bathroom without giving me a last look. Carlos shuts the door and turns up Radio Mambí.

SÁBADO, 13 SEPTIEMBRE
MERCEDES

The encounter with the tourist leaves Mercedes with a terrible feeling. She wonders if she should tell the management. Would they offer to replace the shirt for him if she brought it to their attention? Or would they take the cost of a new dress shirt out of her own salary? Surely it would cost as much as her first month's wages. She looks at the shirt. With a scrub brush, some bleach, and a minor miracle, she could get the spot out.

Merecedes considers how strange it is that the tourist managed to get the kind of stain a man makes when he absently inserts an uncapped pen into his breast pocket, but that the shirt still has the creases of folds straight from the store. It is a ruined shirt that has never been worn.

■■ jumble of impressions. The flies. The smell of day-old shit. The cacophony of Radio Mambí. This bathroom. Why would my father say, *This reminds me of the bathroom in your mother's house?* It is actually nothing like that bathroom, which is now Beatrice's bathroom, with its claw-foot tub, its double sinks, its ornate fixtures, and the large closet with the laundry chute. And he never called it *your mother's house*, even that day when we first spoke over lunch at the Habana Vieja restaurant, a day we still trusted each other.

I am outside the door trying to get in. There are two voices in there, two versions of my father.

We're coming, they say.

Come now, I tell them.

It will be soon, hold on.

Not sure I can hold on.

The sun shines so hot on my back, which part of me knows is impossible in the shady hallway, but I reason to myself that the roof has been torn off. The sun beats hot on my back and I am in so much pain, every wiggle of a finger sends agony ricocheting all through my central nervous system. I would do anything to get out of the sun. Take off my own skin and use it as a blanket to cover my head. But I am too, too weak. If I can wake up, fully wake up, I might be able to stand, reach the knob, turn it, go in. Well, I can wake up. I can feel it. I can fully make myself awake. Fully awake. And with a great exertion of focus and what faculties remain, I do.

When the ceiling spins into focus, I see I am inside already. *Oh, that's good.* But where is my father? I hear the blaring of the radio, and I remember. There is someone out there who will gladly give me a thump on the head if I even touch the doorknob. I can hear him breathing in the break between songs.

Reminds me of the bathroom in your mother's house. He was calling my attention to it. *I want to tell you something before I leave.* Enough! I am only confusing myself, when all that is left is to give them the words *José Martí Park*, or to quietly let myself disappear— probably both. I will die, and she will die. And all of a sudden, I am struck by a crazy idea. An absolutely crazy idea.

■ ■ conferences the week of the fourteenth, and by Monday morning the hotel will be at maximum occupancy. The coke courses through his aorta, and his conscience has never been cleaner. There is a utility corridor in the subbasement that runs along the entire north side, the downhill wall of the hotel. Two charges is all it will take to sweep the hotel's legs out from under it. Like felling a tree, the entire building will collapse downhill.

It will make a spectacular sight for anyone fortunate enough to be in a position to see it at this early hour. A couple of workers at Coppelia, perhaps, churning ice cream or cleaning in preparation for opening, or the projectionist at Cine Yara, who has arrived early to prepare the week's reels, might hear the explosion and look up. Immediately after the explosion, it will be silent for a few seconds, and then the entire structure—he estimates from reading construction manuals more than a million tons of concrete, glass, and steel—will groan and list gruesomely in the direction of el Malecón and fall like a thirty-story domino. The lobby and everything down to the subbasement will be decimated, and the upper twenty-seven floors as well as ten surrounding blocks of Vedado will also be destroyed by the fall.

He looks out the window. Most guests at the Havana Libre look straight to the ocean and say, *What a beautiful view!* He pulls his chin to his chest and looks straight down at Calle M. The soundproof glass makes the children playing and the old people leaning from their second-floor windows look like the first shot of a silent film. He counts up the streets and makes an educated guess. The room he is sitting in right now should fall just about on Calle P, on the roof of that house with the peeling red paint. He turns to look at the bed, wonders who will be sleeping in it Monday morning. A Spaniard? A Canadian? Another Salvadoran? A sympathizer, he reminds himself, whatever the nationality. The guest who will be here that morning will wake with a start. Did he hear thunder? And then he will feel his bed lurching slowly to the right. He will be rolled out of bed, but it will not be his bed's fault.

He closes the curtains and bathroom door, lays all the materials on the bed again, and makes the final preparations with the TV turned down low. He unfolds the diagram and spreads it on the bed.

The bedcover is an awful pattern of green and gold squares that remind him of the chambers of a hon-

He is meditative, almost in a trance, placing them at the top corners of the diagram. He wants to visualize this spatially, in microcosm. He takes the detonator pins and bell and attaches two wires to the ends, and the other ends he twines around the terminals on a nine-volt battery and caps with black tape.

Finally, he takes the two banana-shaped sections of gray putty and rolls them into neat balls of equal size, placing them alongside the two travel clocks. Here on this rough fabric, on a space no more than three meters square, rests the fate of hundreds upon hundreds of human lives. It could be more than a thousand. The body count will be a measure of his success.

The feeling he gets is tremendous when he contemplates what he knows in his heart: how a man, a Salvadoran man, can kill Communism. *Comunista*— he hates the word. *Kill them.* He has already killed Communists, and now he will kill Communism.

He laughs out loud, convulsing with a brief sob he catches in his throat: not sorrow, but another emotion, something more akin to scorn or contempt for how easy it is, with a little bit of plastic and a ten-dollar travel clock, to alter history. To show the world. To beat the devil. To bring in a new world. To deliver the fatal blow.

The power to kill not just Communists, but Communism itself. And, of course, he is aware of the power that money brings—the money that will come to him out of this will be enough to start a business in San Salvador. No longer just the son of a lowly pupusa vendor, he will have more power than Cruz Abarca, the car dealer/bomb-broker who hired him. He will be as powerful, among Salvadorans, as the unknown men in Miami who fund it.

He emerges from his reverie when he realizes that the TV has been carrying a report on his failed compatriot. He catches only the last part: . . . *ha confesado de haber puesto la bomba en la Copacabana* . . . The Cubans have finally acknowledged it was a bomb, and Rambo has confessed. Before he can learn more, the newscaster is on to the next story. He is so excited that he decides to go down to the lobby right then and see whether it is also in the newspapers. He puts the sign on the door: *No Molestar*. He is wearing the tennis shoes, not the boots.

All of Havana is alert to the danger of public

spaces, and he has learned over the past week that his hotel is no exception: A suitcase is left unat-

with his assignment, but he knows he can use this to his advantage: How many complaints does each employee get pardoned? Who is keeping track? It would be easier to track who is *not* keeping track. Nobody. Nobody wants to be at the bottom with their neck sticking out when the time comes for a sacrifice to management. No severance. No pension. Do not be the one they make an example. They are thinking about how quiet it is, and how suddenly this quiet can be ripped like silk by lightning on a sunny day. Their hearts are already pounding with thunder.

He notices these things. He counts the occupants and the employees. He takes note of these numbers dispassionately. He exercises his capacity for indifference. This tourist might not be staying here tomorrow. This housekeeper likely will still be here. It makes no difference to him. The client wants it to be on Monday the fifteenth, when 630 rooms will be at capacity, in the early-morning hours.

In the lobby, potted palm trees create an indoor jungle. There are newspapers from London and Madrid as well as the ubiquitous *Granma*. He finds a short report in the Cuban newspaper that covers up at least half the story—how the captured Salvadoran would have killed many more, for instance, had he not been so inept. The article rushes to point the blame at Cubans in Miami, which of course is legitimate, anybody could have told you that, but now they have a Salvadoran's mouth to put it in, and it's not just Castro and Robaina frothing at the teeth as usual.

The photograph of Rambo is precious. ¡Qué guaje! That, the tourist says to himself, is how a coward makes the news. Today is Sunday, September 14. Tomorrow, they are planning a television confession. Poor Rambo will be shitting his pants under the stern gaze of the director of State Security, the man the tourist knows must right now be looking for him. He delights in the certainty that before they can show their pathetic television confession for the clumsy job that Rambo made—lucky that he killed one Italian—there will be news of a much bigger impact.

glass. The box is approximately ten centimeters deep. An adult at his most dehydrated, his most emaciated, is thicker than this. With just ten centimeters, my skeleton alone would get stuck. But I have to consider that the shelf depth is probably only half the space of the cavity in the wall. There would have to be room for the pipe chase or for the back of another cabinet to butt up against this one. Twenty centimeters, then. I might never have considered breaking glass to hurt myself, but by taking the mirror off the front of the cabinet they gave me the idea of using the pipe chase to escape. This makes sense: an American two-by-four plus room for the pipes—eight inches, maybe. Twenty centimeters of space to work with.

There are only six nails keeping the cabinet from getting pulled off its ledge, and I am easily able to back these out of the drywall. Now I should be able to slide the cabinet out of its box in the wall—

Stop! Put the nails back! They could come any time, and if they look closely they might see that I have tampered with the cabinet.

No, I tell myself, careful in my near-delirium not to speak aloud, there is no turning back. Cheap construction; cheap American construction—or was it that they have already been loosened? It seems possible: they might have been removed with a hammer claw, then replaced with slightly smaller nails reinserted in the holes loosely enough to pull free with the fingertips.

My heart in my throat; I pry at the sides and the cabinet shimmies out of the wall. When it is free of the framing I concentrate on lowering it gently to the floor. I cannot let this cabinet drop, and I am afraid to look because I know that any remaining hope depends on what I find lies behind.

I look inside the box and let out a sigh of despair. The rectangular hole left by the cabinet is approximately forty-by-fifty centimeters, about the dimensions of one of those family-sized boxes of cereal my father likes to buy, and the space behind the two-by-four construction is about as deep as the box of Raisin Bran I ate. It cannot be more than twenty centimeters deep.

Fifteen percent of body weight in just three days. That would put me from sixty-three kilograms to fifty-five. Hard to believe, but possible. Now that

I have begun, there is no turning back. There is no way of putting the cabinet back without them notic-

propped up on the floor inside the wall. It has been left there to shine the way. My father is two hundred miles away in Tampa on purpose. I silently say, *Thank you,* and like a boy spying on his depressed and bedridden mother from the laundry chute in her bathroom, I step inside the wall.

The human head is close to twenty-five centimeters long, but just eighteen wide, so I have to choose a direction to face sideways if I am going to be able to slide down. I go in face-right. *Goodbye, room. Goodbye, shit smell.* If there is one thing that propels me feet-first into the hole, it is this image I hold of Mercedes.

DOMINGO, 14 SEPTIEMBRE
MERCEDES

It's a good thing that the ink was blue and the shirt was bright white so she could use bleach. Although it is as good as new, she never got the room number of the guest. He may have even checked out already. While she is trying to decide what to do with the shirt, she gets the idea to ask the head of housekeeping. Maybe the man, who was so irritated by losing his shirt, did make a complaint, and the head of housekeeping will remember and know how to find him, return the clean shirt. She takes the shirt with her and rides the service elevator up to the main level to a little windowless room where the head of housekeeping, armed with a telephone, a two-way radio, and a computer connecting her to the front desk, manages to get all the rooms cleaned before check-in time, four p.m., on any given day for arriving guests.

When Mercedes peeks around the corner, however, the head of housekeeping has stepped away from her desk, and so as not to call attention to herself she turns quickly to return to the subbasement, but when she looks across the lobby—qué casualidad—she sees him, the guest, in the lobby,

haughty and contemptuous to everyone in service except for the head of housekeeping. Clutching the shirt on a hanger, Mercedes comes to a decision.

To get the desk captain's attention, she says. "Perdóname—"

"Haven't you learned to use the subfloor entrance?" the desk captain interrupts.

"Excuse me. I just wanted to return this shirt, but the guest forgot to give me his room number."

"And this is my problem how?"

She points through the palms. "That's him over there."

The pretty desk captain looks slyly at Mercedes, one woman to another. "How long have you been in Havana?"

Intuiting her implication, Mercedes looks down at the floor. "One week. Soy de Pinar."

"Mm. It shows. Well, he's been here almost two weeks, traveling alone. Unusual last name: Salvadoran, starting with a J." She types something into the computer to jog her memory. "Yes, here he is. Room 1317. Go hang it in his closet."

"Thank you, but I'm down in laundry. To gain access to the room I would have to find the head of housekeeping."

The woman slips a plastic card through a slot along the side of her computer screen. "Here, bring this right back. What's your name?"

"Mercedes."

"Okay, Mercedes. It's a good thing you did not approach him yourself here in the lobby. That would have been grounds for reporting you to the head of housekeeping."

She takes the service elevator to the thirteenth floor. There is a sign, *No Molestar*, on the door of room 1317. But she saw him in the lobby, absorbed in the newspaper, and she has the card. The pretty desk captain did not mention anything about signs on the doorknobs, but what harm could there be in opening the door just long enough to reach into the closet?

The door clicks shut behind her. She knows she shouldn't delay, but she can't help it. This is her first time in a tourist's room. She lets her gaze linger for a moment on the objects on the vanity in the entry-way: a modern electric razor, neat cotton socks, and a calculator. Where is he from? Where did he get these things? He does not look especially sophisticated, but she has heard stories about how in other

bed is made, she guesses by the guest, because it would not pass the head of housekeeping's expectations, and she can tell the carpet has not been vacuumed. There is a map on the bedcover, some electronic items, and two balls of something that looks like clay. Could it be drugs? The door opens and she jumps.

"¡Qué coño—!"

"Perdone, señor," she says, reaching into the closet to show him the shirt wrapped in plastic. "Tengo su camisa aquí."

He is looking over her shoulder at the bed that he made, and she feels a sudden shame when he finds his voice. "Can't you read? I don't want to be disturbed."

"I'm very sorry, señor." She puts the hanger on the rod in the closet.

"Eres una berreca. ¿Cómo te llamas?"

She tells him her name. He stands there holding

the heavy fireproof door, and for a moment she does not know how to get past him. Is he trying to block her way?

In a move she practiced dozens of times with Andrés, Mercedes straightens her shoulders, bows her head, and steps forward into uncertainty. Fortunately, the guest's manners return and he yields. Brushing his shoulder, Mercedes passes through the space between the guest and the doorway.

She makes her way down the hall to the service elevator and does not look back. She hears her own footsteps on the padded carpeting and does not hear his door close. When the elevator doors open, she turns around and sees his door click shut.

Riding down, she feels her face and neck burn with disgrace. What had she been thinking, bringing the shirt up here? She should have given it to an experienced housekeeper, one who would know what to say. Should she report that she thought she might have seen drugs? No, she would just make more of a fool of herself. She would not know illegal narcotics from cow dung. Now she is certain she will get a complaint. She should never have taken herself out for ice cream.

Mercedes gives the plastic card back to the woman at the front desk and returns to her basement room. The second encounter with this irritable guest leaves her with an even worse feeling than the first.

age twenty-eight, get so old so suddenly? I am a spent skin, an empty bag of bones. Nerve endings, deprived of water for days and riddled by gout, sing with pain. Muscles burn. Every shred of tissue is pickled in lactic acid. The descent is accomplished not so much by shimmying as by surrendering to gravity and fatigue. Drop, drop in painful lurches down inside the walls, and hear Radio Mambí blaring from the upstairs hall. Meant to deprive me of sleep and preclude my own attempts to cry for help, the booming beats and screaming deejays now cover up the noise of my escape.

The rough plywood scrapes my stomach, arms, and legs. A stray screw scratches my face, and I feel something wet against my left cheek and taste a trickle of blood in the corner of my mouth. If I had gone down facing left, and if what the doctors speculated about my *Havana Lunar* is correct, such a cut would mean my death in a matter of minutes.

I finally make it to the bottom and the wall panel is already loose. I slide it aside and step into the basement. I take the flashlight and next to it find a Miami Dolphins T-shirt and a can of Goya coconut water. I take a small sip of water and pull on the shirt. There is also a fresh pair of running shoes. I step into them. They are loose, a size or two too big, but they are clean, new, and feel good on my feet after forty-eight hours barefoot and dehumanized. When I feel something inside the right shoe, I take it off and reach inside: a crumpled twenty-dollar bill. Turn off the flashlight, but take it. To leave the flashlight would be to implicate my father. I flip it off.

Now, put one foot in front of the other. The thought paralyzes me with terror. *Turn around. Do not try to leave. Go up, put everything back in place.* Could I possibly climb back up the pipes? Not in my state. *Go up the stairs.* Carlos or Yuyo is right outside the room. What could I do? *Ask to be let in.* Insanity. I am raving. I am raving. If I tell myself this, will I listen? *Put one foot in front of the other.* The fatigue is crushing. But I must plow on through the pain. I go to the back of the basement and open the bulkhead doors. I have to try to get to José Martí Park, but first I have to make one more call.

Every step is more agony, but I'm no longer caged and I must keep going. One step and then another. One step in front of the other. Five steps.

Stop. Lean against the wall. No: I cannot do this. Not for long. I have to think of a way to trick myself

LUNES, 15 SEPTIEMBRE
THE TOURIST

That housekeeper with the shirt: why is she hounding him? How many times has she entered his room? He has to get this over with and check out before dawn. He has everything he needs, so he returns to the basement for the final time.

When his eyes have adjusted, he finds his way to the first corner and pushes a ball of gray putty into the joint at the juncture of two girders. He secures the travel clock and the detonator to the section of putty with duct tape, and he activates the alarm.

In the next corner, he does the same thing, though he does not rip the duct tape, leaving the roll attached to the bomb. He won't be needing it any longer.

The tourist returns to his room and packs in a hurry. He knows that nothing will happen for close to an hour, but it makes him uneasy just being inside the building, knowing what he has set in motion.

The beautiful black front desk captain is kind to him. Will she still be on duty at sunrise? He knows

he must dissimulate this thought just to go from moment to moment, knowing what he was holding in

to expedite the inevitable.

Just before dawn, the tourist checks out.

MIAMI: THE STREET

A desolate strip of red lights stretches straight for five miles to downtown. I must stay off Calle 8, so I stick to the callejones between the backs of storefronts and go up to 6th. Make my way east, toward the ocean and the sunrise, and keep an eye out for pay phones on the corners. Pain. Daze. Fatigue. Coco agua. Small sips. Should be resting. Should have an IV with saline. But have to keep moving. Get away from Little Havana. First a pay phone . . . but I have no quarters. I have no change whatsoever. I check the coin return on the telephone and it is empty. How do I do this?

I almost do not remember the number. In a daze, I let my fingers find the pattern in the buttons. *"Please deposit twenty-five cents."* I do not have twenty-five cents. There is no more important telephone call that needs to take place at this hour, on this day, anywhere in the world. In any world. Of this I am certain. Important for peace. Important for humanity. And yet I have no money. *"Please deposit twenty-five cents."* How the hell do I do this! I have no quarter. Look for a gas station or convenience store that is open. Stay away from 8th. Hear a car

She does emerge, and I raise myself up as straight as possible and hold up my father's twenty-dollar bill. I summon all possible composure despite my dirty and decrepit state, not so much because I feel shame but because I know the short transaction required to make change must proceed without delay, and it will proceed more quickly if she and I tacitly observe the rituals of the complicit customer and cashier.

"¿Por favor, me puede dar cambio para hacer una llamada?"

"Lo siento, mi amor, pero no puedo darte cambio sin que compres algo."

She calls me *my love*, but she still can't make change without a purchase. There is much I would want to buy: Comida por libra. Croquetas de pollo. Croquetas de jamón. I am starving; I have not eaten in days. But I know better than to make any of these my first meal—they would ruin me. I hold this authentic president, Andrew Jackson. We will part ways without incident. And no closed-circuit camera will record our exchange for storage longer than the proscribed erasure time. A banana—that is what I find. A one-dollar banana.

"May I please have four quarters?"

"Cómo no, mi amor." She must notice how bad I smell, but she pretends not to.

Good. I need to make a call. A very important call. Do not stand between me and the change from my banana.

I push the buttons and insert a quarter. The machine takes the coin and I fall to my knees in the phone booth. It is five a.m. Light is dawning on Miami ten minutes earlier than it does in Havana. But there is no ring. A robotic female voice intones, *"This number is no longer in service."* I must have dialed wrong. I push the buttons again, very slowly, and there is still no ring. *"This number is no longer in service."* The machine spits back the quarter.

How could the number be out of service? How could the line be dead? "Hello! Hello!" I yell. This is a trick. This has to be a trick. I feed the machine all four quarters and dial again. It has to be a decoy recording. Could this be what DSS meant when they said that there would be an announcement to signal the evacuation? *"This number is no longer in service."* Are they listening? Although I want to yell, I whisper, "Havana Libre Hotel, that is the real target—" but am interrupted by loud buzzing, a harsh staccato connoting *hang up now* so much

to get to José Martí Park. The cashier looks at me from the bright windows of the 7-Eleven as I run away down Calle 6. All that separates me from the safety of Mercedes's and hundreds of lives at the Havana Libre is a vast, hostile country of concrete.

Miami at dawn.

LUNES, 15 SEPTIEMBRE
MERCEDES

The sun, coming up over the hill behind the Capitol, shines its everyday drama on the Havana Libre from the top floor on down all the eastern windows. Mercedes awakens before the light has reached the bottom. Today she has to decide whether to spend her seven dollars in tips for the week on a liter of milk or a dozen eggs.

Mercedes chooses to save it, tucking the money into the hem she has made in her apron. She has a few pesos she'll spend to get herself a treat. But the dollars she sews up in her hem so she won't lose them or spend them. They are for her baby. She will need them.

At the other end of the hall, Mercedes starts her day in the hotel laundry room. Up above, hundreds of tourists sleep and watch TV and make love. Mercedes launders their sheets. She is free.

stopped by a hiss from the edge of the Miami River where on my first day I saw the ragged fisherman. I look over the railing and see a figure at the bottom of the steps. "Follow me."

When they told me the park, I did not know I would be getting into the river. I descend the concrete steps to the moorings below. Alongside a nice fishing boat stands a man: it is Eduardo, the computer expert from DSS. "Suba, doctor." Someone calling me doctor is comforting, and I climb aboard. Again he does not offer a hand.

"Wait!" I stop him before I get in the boat. "There is an urgent message to get to Havana. The Havana Libre—"

"Ya lo sabemos, doctor. Cogieron al segundo terrorista. El hotel y la gente están a salvo." *We know, doctor. The second bomber has been caught. The hotel and the people are safe.*

I have to back up to catch what I have heard.

"The people at the Havana Libre are safe?"

"I know you have a lot of questions, but right now the essential thing is to very quickly get you far from Florida."

I have no words. Eduardo works efficiently and quickly to untie us from a piling. Only when we are slowly motoring through downtown Miami does he break the spell by saying, "It was good of you to come alone."

"How did you get here so fast?" I ask.

"I live in Miami."

"Are you Giro?"

"No, I'm not Giro."

"Avispa?"

"Wasp, yes, if you wish. I come and go because I was born in the US. It will be very noisy for the next couple of hours. There are some blankets down in the cabin. Why don't you get some rest? You will have ample opportunity to get debriefed in Havana." He gives me a bottle of oral rehydration solution, the kind I would administer to a child with severe diarrhea. "You're a doctor, so I don't have to tell you to drink slowly."

I climb the ladder down into the dimly lit cabin. There is a wraparound sofa, a V-shaped berth with a stainless-steel sink and a cooler, and a tiny dinette area. I sit on the edge of the berth and take small sips to slowly bring myself back to life. The lights are

suddenly turned off and I sense a change in course.
When we make it into open water, Eduardo throws

HAVANA LIBRE

When the engine powers down I awaken with a start and briefly panic. It takes a few seconds to realize that the motor is not a sound effect on Radio Mambí, the footsteps above not one of the Rivera brothers about to come and get me. I reassure myself that there will be no more *Who is Giro?* and I never told anyone anything about José Martí Park.

I drag my sore body out of the berth and climb the ladder to the deck. Havana flickers in the distance. This is not the bright skyline of a great capital of Latin America, but it relieves me all the same to see el Castillo del Moro. No cities of cereal. No dogs in little ballerina costumes. No six-packs of beer for dessert. Mi Habana.

I know from my cousin Emilio that the coast guard has a station not five miles from here, but the way Eduardo pilots us in, we look entirely at home among the multimillion-dollar fishing boats of Marina Hemingway. Eduardo says to me, "Look, I know how badly you must want to get out of here, but Pérez would like to debrief here and wait until nightfall to move you off the boat. Would you mind

and pair of sweatpants, and several new bars of soap still in packages. Peeling off the filthy clothes of my captivity, I find eighteen dollars in my pocket. I spend a long time under the stream of hot water. After rinsing once, I discard the first bar of soap and open a second. When I emerge from the bathroom in the clean clothes, a doctor is there waiting for me. He checks me out and gives me more drinks in more flavors of rehydration salts. He also brings some vegetable broth and flavored gelatin.

His care is thorough, and he is not in a hurry. I have been in America for fewer than seven days, but I find myself wondering who will get the bill. "What's your name?" I ask him.

"Martinez."

"Where did you intern?"

"Calixto Garcia."

"What year?"

"'95."

Nineteen ninety-five. Two years ago. Five years behind me. It makes me proud to know there are young physicians this good.

When Pérez comes aboard, he brings a fine bottle of wine. "You are probably not ready to drink this yet, so I won't open it."

"Never again shall I accept an invitation to share a bottle of wine with you, colonel, no matter how good the vintage."

"Take it home with you tonight." I drink rehydration salts while he sips water and debriefs me. "The bomber's work was somewhat clumsy insofar as concealment goes, but if they had been detonated, the charges would in all likelihood have caused the intended and horrible effect. The hotel was never evacuated. During interviews, a Spanish subcontractor confessed to copying the plans but claimed he had no knowledge of how they would be used. This led us to the bomber, a Salvadoran who was foolish enough to meet with the Spaniard in the same neighborhood where he often stayed in the home of a jinetera."

Although I still feel tired, these details finally convince me that she is fine. All the people in and around the Havana Libre are fine, and I finally believe it. Everyone is safe.

"We were getting chatter about José Martí from several sources. More than half of our agents were at the airport. It was incapacitating: daily searches of the facility, from top to bottom, not to mention

the locations of the devices, which were crude but could have been lethal—massively lethal."

"How did you get the intelligence in time?"

"A voice mail."

"When I called, there was a recording that said the number was disconnected."

"The message came in the night. We had the number disconnected after we knew we had the right information about the target."

"¿Pero cómo? ¿Quién?"

Pérez fixes my gaze. "It would appear it was your father who left the message."

"Cóño . . ." I let that sink in. Dazed, I tell Pérez, "He helped me escape."

"I suspected that might be the case."

"How did he know the number of the voice mail?"

"That's what I was going to ask you. Was there a time he would have seen you dial it or seen it written? Maybe when Mendoza made you call that time . . . ?"

"He watched me push the buttons; he watched Carlos write it."

"His message, partially, was, *Hotel Havana Libre, very soon, early this morning, I think.* This was immediately relayed to Havana, and we had a bomb squad at the hotel within minutes."

"Will he be okay?"

"Your father left the message from a pay phone. He made it to Tampa, two hundred miles away, at the time of your escape. Did you leave behind any evidence that could implicate him?"

I took the flashlight, the T-shirt, and the coconut water. I am still wearing the Nikes. And Carlos heard our entire conversation. *This reminds me of the bathroom in your mother's house.* "I don't think so."

"Good." Pérez does not hesitate with his calculations. No doubt his analysts have provided him with thirty-seven possible scenarios for what might happen next. "A certain asset you have, doctor, is that you know nothing of Giro or la Red Avispa."

"You're saying there's an entire network?"

Pérez ignores this. "Mendoza learned nothing new, and we crushed what should have been the Revolution's death blow. He will keep what has happened to you a secret for as long as it is convenient, and until we can get the recruiter, so will we."

I swoon with vertigo from a flash of what Pérez might be getting at. "How long do I have to stay on

hardly left your room." *True enough*, I reflect with bitter satisfaction. "Here, for your cousin—you got these at the Miami airport before your return flight." Pérez gives me a small stack of American magazines: soccer, motorsports, and boating.

"If this is as close as I am ever likely to get to an apology from you, colonel, I would like to tell you that in no way do I accept it."

"Listen, Manolo, I know that our trust has been compromised, but I would like to offer you something to assure you of my personal confidence in you. It's classified. To be quite honest, Caballero instructed me that under no circumstances was I to discuss this detail with you. Your father also left a brief personal message that seems to be intended for you." He has my attention. "In its entirety, the exact transcript of the recording was: *Hotel Havana Libre, very soon, early this morning, I think. Tell him to listen to the Bola.*"

Pérez is such a considerate gentleman with me, his staked goat, that he knows the resultant curiosity must lead to a strong impulse—the yearning to get the record and try to figure out what the message means. Then he says, "I apologize for keeping you here all day." The way he says this makes me appreciate that all along he has been calling the shots: whether to send me to Miami, how to allow me to get captured, whether to attempt a rescue or let death take me. And I do not take it in the least personally, because I apprehend that the only way to make decisions in his position is with the calculus of massive fatalities. But just because I don't take it personally does not mean that I hate him any less.

I hear footsteps on deck and look up the wooden ladder. Pérez rises to leave. I see her coming feet first. If I had stood up I would have fallen over.

"How was your conference?" she says.

My head feels heavy when I wheel to face Pérez. "She knows?"

Doctora Hernández answers the question: "In fact, Doctor Rodriguez, it was my objective to evaluate you and your fitness for this mission."

I feel dizzy and try to cast my memory back. Has it been ten days or a thousand years since Hernández's first shift at the hospital? She wore this same cool demeanor and these same snug jeans, but all I see in my mind's eye is Director Gonzalez's simpering grin. Why hadn't I seen it at the time? He had been on a sycophantic high. Some minister

double-blind counterespionage job that had a high probability of failure. In baseball, I would be called a sacrifice fly. And Gonzalez, without knowing it, had set me up. *Hijo de puta este Gonzales.*

They give me a moment to recover.

"Are you okay?" Hernández finally asks.

"Cabrón," I say.

Doctora Hernández gives me a little smile. They know I am referring to myself, and we leave it at that.

A slight readjustment of her shoulders to indicate her resumed role, and Hernández repeats, "How was your conference?"

I take a deep breath. "Boring. I had to stay shut up in my room the whole time."

"The whole time? That's a very American exaggeration!"

"Diarrhea, dehydration. First chance to visit la Yuma, and I get food poisoning."

"Food poisoning? I thought the Americanos had eradicated such ailments."

"If that were the case, there would be no more need for doctors."

"No, verdad?" Breaking character, she says, "When you're back at work, you can ask me on a date."

"Is this part of your objective?"

Pérez interrupts: "Along these lines will do fine. Do it again Wednesday at the pediátrico."

to Vedado, the blackout has not stopped the nightly domino game in front of my apartment. I take a long, cold shower in the dark.

After the electricity returns, I find the record: Bola de Nieve, *Este sí es Bola*. In the upper left, the logo and motto: *Sonotone, el sello de los grandes éxitos*. The record slips into my hand, but there is nothing unusual about it. Printed in the center are the songs and composers, fourteen tracks between the two sides, and the year the disk was recorded: *1960*. I have flipped past the dust jacket hundreds of times. On the cover there's a clever photograph, a portrait of el Bola, famous for his blackness, and so Rita Montaner nicknamed him *Snowball*: his face is almost indistinguishable from the black background, except for the unforgettable smile.

The jacket art is so black that nobody, not even with a long passage of time, would notice the discoloring effect of the adhesive showing through the cardboard. I part the edges of the dust jacket: inside, the cellophane tape, yellowed with age, is affixed to all four edges of the folded sheet so that slipping the record in and out will not dislodge it. *Tell him to listen to the Bola.*

I delicately peel back the tape, thinking, *If he'd left the message in the Beny Moré instead, I would have found it long ago.*

The letter is dated one month before I was born.

12 July 1969

Mi querido hijo o hija,

 What does one write to a son or daughter whom one might not meet until they are seven, or twenty, or never? You have to know that I will be far away, and I will be apart from you for a long time. I am leaving at a difficult period in our country, when each man and his neighbor are enemies. You will have the privilege of living in another era, and you have to be worthy of it. You must strive to be the best in school, better in every way. You know what I am trying to say. Forget me. There is something Bola de Nieve sings:

  In your life I'll be the best
  Of the fog of yesterday.

When you learn to forget,
Better: like that verse

Take care of your mother.
Juan Rodriguez

I put the record on my father's old tocadisco and listen. The lyrics Juan Rodriguez copied in his letter before I was born are from the end of the fourth song on side A, titled "Vete de mi." Earlier, Bola de Nieve sings:

You, who fill everything with happiness and youth,
And sees ghosts in the night of twilight,
And today are the perfumed song of blue—get away from me.
Do not stop to look at the dead branches of the rosebush
That go away without flower;
Look at love's landscape,

That is the reason to dream and to love.
I, who have already fought against all evil,
Have ruined my hands so from holding on
I cannot hold you—get away from me.

eans, and I follow. Mercedes stands between the ocean and me, smiling at some faraway secret.

"Buenas tardes, doctor. ¿Cómo fue la conferencia?" I try to make out the delicate curve of her abdomen beneath the maid's uniform. She looks good, like she is starting to put on weight from the employee meals here.

"Terrible. I was shut up in my room the whole time."

"You're lying."

"No, no es mentira."

"¿Qué te pasó?"

"Un virus del estómago."

"I'm so sorry, doctor. Your first trip . . ." Like me, she is probably thinking, *Your only trip*.

"It wasn't so bad. I watched TV in a comfortable bed and took hot showers every day . . . So this is where you work?"

"Yes, they have me in the hottest room. But I drink plenty of water, and the food for employees is very good."

"¿Y tu apetito?"

"Healthy. I saw the obstetrician. It's too early for kicks, but sometimes I feel flutters."

"¡Qué maravilla!"

"Mira, se está moviendo." *I feel her growing.* She takes my hand and puts it on her belly. The maid's uniform is made of rough, durable polyester, but beneath is soft, warm, and alive. Mercedes says, "I start break now. Want to go for a walk to el Malecón with me?"

"Absolutamente."

While she changes out of the maid's uniform, I wait in the hall clutching the eighteen dollars in my pocket.

Our walk takes us past Cafetería La Rampa, Cine Yara, and the lines outside Coppelia ice cream parlor. Mercedes wears cutoff jeans and a T-shirt, and I notice that she has the wide, careful gait of someone from the provinces. It is pleasant walking beside her and letting approaching men pass us appraisingly.

Mercedes says, "I have already saved seven dollars in tips. To celebrate my first week, I went out to Coppelia."

"Your first time?"

"Sí."

"¡No me digas! I hope you didn't pay in dollars."

"Of course not. I used pesos and waited en la

cola Cubana. I went early so the wait w[...] of minutes. I was seated up in the big fl[...] o[...] the side facing away from the Havan[...] a beautiful day in the park. You shoul[...] next time."

"What flavor did you order?"

"Vanilla."

"That's my favorite."

"Really?" She lets me have a pri[...] smile. "Hers too."

"And you're so sure she is a girl?"

"Of course I'm sure."

For the remainder of our walk to[...] is no need for conversation becaus[...] Pinareños.

When we get to el Malecón, [...] "You didn't think about staying?"

"¿Dónde, en la Yuma? ¡Qué va!"

"I wondered. Whenever anyone [...] brief visit, we always have to wonder[...]

"No need to wonder with me. M[...] solid."

"I want to go for a swim."

I take the eighteen dollars out of[...] tuck the money up inside a rolled-u[...] keep dry. Mercedes slips off her shirt t[...] est black bra. She climbs over to the[...] rocks on the other side in her Chines[...]

his Skylark and Lensman series novels. This is his newest novel — all about a future world in which all the creative energies of the West have been turned to space. All the ingredients are here — the Nameless One of the East, psionics, Communists, conflict on Earth and in outer space, prophecy — well, you name it. Those who dote on space opera will like this one . . . its entertainment value is well up there with the best.

" 'Doc' Smith's nomination to the Science Fiction Hall of Fame was certainly no accident. By any reckoning, he belongs with the pioneers of the form. His novels are fast-paced, hard-hitting, filled with action and dialogue . . ."

— August Derleth
Madison Capital Times

SUBSPACE
EXPLORERS

BERKLEY BOOKS, NEW YORK

SUBSPACE EXPLORERS

A Berkley Book / published by arrangement with
the author's estate

PRINTING HISTORY
Ace edition published 1965
Berkley edition / July 1983

ISBN: 0-425-06245-7

AT TIME zero minus nine minutes First Officer Carlyle Deston, Chief Electronicist of the starliner *Procyon,* sat attentively at his board. He was five feet eight inches tall and weighed one hundred sixty two pounds. Just a little guy, as spacemen go. Although narrow-waisted and, for his heft, broad-shouldered, he was built for speed and maneuverability, not to handle freight.

Watching a hundred lights and half that many instruments; listening to four telephone circuits, two with each ear; hands flashing to toggles and buttons and knobs; he was completely informed as to the instant-by-instant condition of everything in his department during countdown. Everything had been and still was in condition GO.

Nevertheless, he was bothered; bothered as he had never been bothered before in all his three years of subspacing. He had always had hunches and they had always been right, but this one was utterly ridiculous. It wasn't the ship or the trip—nothing was yelling "DANGER!" into his mind—it was something down in the Middle that was pulling at him like a cat tractor and it didn't make sense. He *never* went down into passenger territory. He had no business there and flirting with vacskulled girls was not his dish.

So he fought his hunch down and concentrated on his job. Lift-off was uneventful; so was the climb out to a safe distance from Earth. At time zero minus two seconds Deston poised a fingertip over the red button, but everything stayed in condition GO and immergence into

7

subspace was perfectly normal. All the green lights except one went out; all the needles dropped to zero; all four phones went dead; all signals stopped. He plugged a jack into the socket under the remaining green light and said:

"*Procyon* One to Control Six. Flight eight four nine. Subspace radio test number one. How do you read me, Control Six?"

"Control Six to *Procyon* One. I read you ten and zero. How do you read me, *Procyon* One?"

"Ten and zero. Out." The solitary green light went out and Deston unplugged.

Perfect signal and zero noise. That was that. From now until Emergence—unless some robot or computer called for help—he might as well be a passenger. He leaned back in his seat, lit a cigarette, and began really to study this wild hunch, that was getting worse all the time. It was all he could do to keep from calling his relief and going down there right then; but he couldn't and wouldn't do that. He was on until plus three hours. He couldn't possibly explain any such break as that would be, so he stuck it out.

At time zero plus one hundred seventy nine minutes his relief appeared. "All black, Babe?" the newcomer asked.

"As the pit, Eddie. Take over. You've picked out your girl-friend for the trip, I suppose?"

While taking the bucket seat, Eddie said, "Not yet. I got sidetracked watching Bobby Warner . . ."

A wave of psychic force hit Deston's mind hard enough almost to turn it inside out; but he clenched his teeth and held his pose.

". . . and after seeing her just walk across the lounge once, all the other women looked like a dime's worth of catmeat. Talk about poetry in motion!" Eddie rolled his eyes, made motions with his hands, and whistled expressively. "Oh, *brother!*"

"Okay, okay, don't blow a fuse," Deston said, in what

known to man and never puts down a dry hole. All gushers that blow their rigs clear up into the stratosphere. Everybody wonders how come. The poop is, his wife's an oil-witch, is why he lugs her around with him all the time. Why else would he?"

"Maybe he loves her. It happens, you know."

"Huh? After twenty-some years of her? Comet-gas! Anyway, would *you* have the sublime gall to make a pass at WarnOil's heiress, with more millions in her own sock than you've got dimes? If you ever made passes, I mean."

"Uh-uh. Negative. For sure."

"You nor me neither. But *what* a dish! *Brother*, what a lovely, luscious, toothsome *dish!*"

"Cheer up; you'll be raving about another one tomorrow," Deston said callously, turning away.

"I don't know . . . maybe; but even if I do, *she* won't be anything like *her*," Eddie mourned, to the closing door.

Deston didn't go to his cabin; didn't take off his sidearm. He didn't even think of it; the .41 automatic at his hip was as much a part of his uniform as his pants.

Entering the lounge, he did not have to look around. She was playing contract, and as eyes met eyes and she rose to her feet a shock-wave went through him that made him feel as though every hair he had was standing straight on end.

She was about five feet four. Her hair was a startlingly brilliant artificial yellow; her eyes a deep, cool blue. She could have made the Miss Western Hemisphere finals.

Deston, however, did not notice any of these details—then.

"Excuse me, please," she said to the other three at her table. "I must go now." She tossed her cards down onto the table and walked straight toward him; eyes still holding eyes.

He backed hastily out into the corridor, and as the door closed behind her they went naturally and wordlessly into each other's arms. Lips met lips in a kiss that lasted for a long time. It was not a passionate embrace—passion would come later—it was as though each of them, after endless years of bootless, fruitless longing, had come at long last home.

"Come with me, dear, where we can talk," she said finally, eyeing with disfavor the half-dozen spectators; and, in her suite a few minutes later, Deston said:

"So *this* is why I had to come down into passenger territory. You came aboard at exactly zero seven forty three."

"Uh-uh." She shook her head. "A few minutes before that; that was when I read your name on the board. First Officer, Carlyle Deston. It simply unraveled me; I came completely unzipped. It's wonderful that you're so strongly psychic, too."

"I don't know about that," he said, thoughtfully. "Psionics says that that the map is the territory, but all my training has been based on the axiom that it isn't. I've had hunches all my life, but the signal doesn't carry much information. Like hearing a siren while you're driving a ground-car. You know you have to pull over and stop, but that's all you know. It could be police, fire, ambulance—*anything*. Anybody with any psionic ability at all ought to do a lot better than that, I should think."

"Not necessarily. You don't *want* to believe it, so you've been fighting it; beating it down. So it has to force its way through whillions and skillions of ohms of resistance to get through to you at all. But I *know* you're very strongly psychic, or you wouldn't've come down here . . ."

... and you'd've jumped clear

any job in the universe there's no choice.

"I knew you'd say that, Carl." She hugged his elbow against her side. "I'd *love* to get married right now. . . ." She paused.

"Except for what?" he asked.

"I thought at first I'd tell my parents first—they're aboard, you know—but I won't. She'd scream and he'd roar and neither of them could make me change my mind, so we *will* do it right now."

He looked at her questioningly; she shrugged and went on, "We aren't what you could call a happy family. She's been trying to make me marry an old goat of a prince and I finally told her to go roll her hoop—to get a divorce and marry the foul old beast herself. And he's been pushing me to marry an oil-man—to consolidate two empires—that it makes me sick at the stomach just to look at! Last week he *insisted* on it and I blew an atomic bomb. I'd keep on finding oil and stuff for him, I said, but . . ." She broke off as Deston stiffened involuntarily.

"Oil?" he asked, too quietly. "You're the oil-witch, then; not your mother. Besides having more megabucks in your own right than any. . . ."

"Don't say it, dearest!" She seized both his hands in hers. "I know how you feel. I don't like to let you ruin your career, either, but *nothing* can come between us now that we've found each other. So I'll tell you this." Her eyes looked steadily into his. "If it bothers you that much

I'll give every dollar I own to some foundation or other. I swear it."

He laughed shamefacedly as he took her into his arms. "*That's* knocking me for the well-known loop, sweetheart. I'll live with it and like it."

Then, to get away from that subject, he explored with knowing fingers the muscles of her arms and back. "You're trained down as fine as I am and it's my business to be—how come?"

"I majored in Phys. Ed. and I love it. And I'm a Newmartian, you know, so I teach a few courses. . . ."

"Newmartian? But I thought—aren't the headquarters of all the big outfits, including WarnOil, on Tellus?"

"In a way. Management, yes, but very little property. Everything possible is owned on Newmars and we Warners have always lived there. The tax situation, you know."

"I didn't know; taxes don't bother me much. But go ahead. You teach a few courses. In?"

"Oh, bars, trapeze, ground-and-lofty tumbling, acrobatics, aerialistics, highwire work, muscle-control, unarmed combat—all that sort of thing."

"Ouch! So if you ever happen accidentally to get mad at me you'll tie me up into a pretzel?"

She laughed. "A pleasant thought; but you know as well as I do that a good big man can take a good little one every time."

"But I'm not big. I'm just a little squirt."

"You outweigh me by forty pounds and I know just how good space officers have to be. You're *exactly* the right size."

"For the first time in my life I'm beginning to think so." Laughing, he put his arm around her and led her up to a full-length mirror. "We're a mighty well-matched pair . . . I like us immensely . . . well, shall we go see the chaplain? Or should we look for a priest—or maybe a rabbi?"

"We *don't* know each other very well, do we? But we'll

"Dowsing? Oh, witching stuff. Of course not."

"Listen, darling. All the time I've been touching you I've been learning about you—and you've been learning about me."

"Yes but . . ."

"No buts, buster. You actually have tremendous powers; ever so much greater than mine. All I can do is feel oil, water, coal, and gas. I'm no good at all on metals—I couldn't feel gold if I were perched right on the ridgepole of Fort Knox. But if you'll stop fighting that terrific power of yours and really *use* it I'm positive that you can dowse anything you want to. Even uranium."

He didn't believe it, and the argument went on until they reached the chaplain's office. Then, of course, it was dropped automatically; and the next five days were deliciously, deliriously, ecstatically happy days for them both.

At the time of this chronicle starships were the safest means of transportation ever used by man; but there was, of course, an occasional accident. Worse than the accidents however—but fortunately much rarer—were the complete disappearances: starships from which no distress signal was ever received and of which no trace was ever found.

And on the Great Wheel of Fate the *Procyon*'s number came up.

In the middle of the night Carlyle Deston came instan-

13

taneously awake—deep down in his mind a huge, terribly silent voice was roaring "DANGER! DANGER! DANGER!" He did not take time to think or to reason: he grabbed Barbara around the waist and leaped out of bed with her.

"Trouble, Bobby! Get into your suit—quick!"

"But . . . but I've *got* to dress!"

"No time! Snap it up!" He stuffed her into her suit; leaped into his own. "Control!" he snapped into its microphone. "Disaster! Abandon Ship!"

The alarm bells clanged once; the big red lights flashed once; the sirens barely started to growl, then quit. The whole vast fabric of the ship shuddered as though it were being mauled by a thousand and impossibly gigantic hammers.

And out in the corridor: "Come on, girl, sprint!" He put his hand under her arm and urged her along.

She tried, but her best wasn't good. "I've never been checked out on sprinting in space-suits, so you'd better . . ."

Everything went out. Lights, artificial gravity, air-circulation—everything.

"You've never been checked out on null-gee, either, so hang on and we'll travel."

"Where to?" she asked, hurtling through the air faster than she would have believed possible.

"Baby Two—Lifecraft Number Two, that is—my crash assignment. Good thing I was down here with you—I don't think anybody'll make it from the Top. Next turn left, then right. I'll swing you."

At the lifecraft he kicked a lever and a port swung open—to reveal a blaze of light and a startled gray-haired man who, half-floating in air, was hanging on to a fixture with both hands.

"What happened?" the man asked. "I didn't know whether . . ."

"Wrecked. Null-gee and high radiation. I'll have to put you in the safe for a while." Deston shoved the oldster

14

he came to a room in which a man in a space-suit was floundering helplessly in the air. He glanced at his tell-tale. Thirty two. High red. Time to go.

In the lifecraft he closed the port, cut in the launcher, and slammed on a one-gravity drive away from the ship. Then he shucked Barbara out of her suit and shed his own. He unclamped a fire-extinguisher-like affair; opened the door of a tiny room. "In here!" He shut the door behind them. "Strip, quick!" He cradled the device and opened four valves.

Fast as he was, she was naked and ready for the gush of thick, creamy foam from the multiplex nozzle. "Oh, Dekon?" she asked. "I've read about it. I rub it in good, all over me?"

"That's right. Short for 'Decontaminant, Complete; Compound, Absorbant, and Chelating; Type DCQ.' It takes care of radiation, but speed is of the essence. All over you is right." He placed the foam-gun on the floor and went vigorously to work. "Eyes, too, yes. *Everywhere.* Just that. And swallow six gulps of it . . . that's it. I slap a gob of it over your nose and mouth and you in-hale once—hard and deep. One good one's enough, but if it isn't a good one you die of lung cancer, so I'll have to knock you out and give it to you while you're unconscious, and that isn't good—complications. So make it good and deep?"

"Will do. Good and deep." She emptied her lungs.

He put a headlock on her and slapped the Dekon on.

15

She inhaled, hard and deep, and went into paroxysms of coughing. He held her in his arms until the worst of it was over; but she was still coughing hard when she pulled herself away from him.

"But—you? Lemme—help—you—quick!"

"No need, sweetheart. The old man won't need it—I got him into the safe in time—the other guy and I will work on each other. Lie down on the bunk there and take it easy for half an hour."

Forty minutes later, while all four were still cleaning up the messes of foam, the chattering sender stopped sending and the communicator came on. Since everything about a starship is designed to fail safe, they were of course in normal space. On the screens many hundreds of stars blazed, in half the colors of the spectrum.

"Baby Three acknowledging," the speaker said. "Jones and four—deconned—who's calling and how's your subspace communicator?"

"Baby Two, Deston and three. Mine's dead, too. Thank God, Herc! With *you* to astrogate us maybe we'll make it. But how'd you get away? Not down from the Top, that's for sure."

Vision came on; a big, square-jawed, lean, tanned face appeared upon the screen. "We were in Baby Three already."

"Oh." Deston was quick on the uptake. "You, too?"

"That's right. But the way the old man chewed you out, I knew he'd slap me in irons, so we hid out. We found three men before high red. I deconned Bun, then . . ."

"Bun?" Barbara exclaimed. "Bernice Burns? How *wonderful!*"

"Bobby!" The face of a silver-haired beauty appeared beside Jones'. "*Am* I glad you got away too!"

"Just a sec," Deston said. "Data for rendezvous, Herc. . . . Hey! My watch stopped—so did the chron!"

"Here too," Jones said. "So I'll handle it on visual."

"But it's non-magnetic—and *nothing* can stop an atomi-chron!" Deston protested.

16

Vincent Lopresto, financer, and his two bodyguards. They were sleeping in their suits. Grounders."

"Just so," the old man said. "Insulated, we acquired the charge very gradually. What did the bodies look like?"

Deston thought for a moment. "Almost as if they had exploded."

"Precisely." Gray-Hair beamed. "That eliminates all the others except three—Morton's, Rothstein's, and my own."

"You're a specialist in subspace, sir?"

"Oh, no, I'm not a specialist at all. I'm a dabbler; a . . ."

"In the College?" Deston asked, and the other nodded.

"With doctorates in everything from astronomy to zoology? I'm mighty glad you were using this lifecraft for an observatory when we got it, Doctor . . . ?"

"Adams. Andrew Adams. But I have only eight at the moment. Earned degrees, that is."

"And you have a lot of apparatus in the hold?"

"Less than six tons. Just what I must have in order to . . ."

"Babe." Jones' voice broke in. "Got you figured. Power two, alpha eighteen, beta forty three. . . ."

Rendezvous with the *Procyon*'s hulk was made; both lifecrafts hung motionless relative to it. No other lifecraft had escaped. A conference was held. Weeks of work would be necessary to determine the ship's condition. Hundreds of other tasks would have to be performed, and there were only nine survivors. Everyone would have to work, and work hard.

The two girls wanted to be together. So did the two officers; since, as long as they lived or until the *Procyon* made port, all responsibility rested: first, upon First Officer Carlyle Deston; and second, upon Second Officer Theodore Jones. Therefore Jones and Bernice came a-board Lifecraft Two and Deston asked Newman to go over to Lifecraft Three.

"Uh-uh, I like the scenery here a lot better." Newman's eyes raked Bernice's five feet nine of scantily-clad sheer beauty from ankles to coiffure.

"As you were, Mister Jones!" Deston rasped, and Jones subsided. Deston went on, very quietly, "As crew chief, Newman, you know the law. I am in command."

"You ain't in command of *me*, pretty boy. Not out here where nobody has ever come back from. I make my own law—with *this*." Newman patted his side pocket.

"Draw it, then, or crawl." Deston's face was coldly calm; his right hand still hung motionless at his side.

Newman glanced at the girls, both of whom were frozen; then at Jones, who smiled at him pityingly. "I . . . my . . . but yours is right where you can get at it," he faltered.

"You should have thought of that sooner. I'm waiting, Newman."

"Just wing him, Babe," Jones said then. "He's strong enough, except in the head. We may need his back."

"Uh-uh. I'll have to kill him sometime, so it might as well be now. Square between the eyes. A hundred bucks I'm two millimeters off dead center?"

Both girls gasped and stared at each other in horror; but Jones said calmly, without losing any part of his smile, "Not a dime; I've lost too much that way already,"—at which outrageous statement both girls realized what was going on and smiled in relief.

And Newman misinterpreted those smiles completely;

have to. So she said, instead,

"Why'd you let him keep his pistol? The . . . the *slime!* And after you saved his life, too!"

"Typical of the type. One gun won't make any difference."

"But you can lock up *all* their guns, can't you?"

"I'm afraid not. Lopresto's a mobster, isn't he, Herc?"

"If he's a financier I'm an angel—complete with wings and halo. They'll have guns hidden out all over the place."

"Check. You and I'll go over and . . ."

"And I," Adams said. "I must tridi everything, and do some autopsies, and . . ."

"Of course," Deston agreed. "With a Big Brain along —oh, excuse that crack, please, Doctor Adams. It slipped out on me."

Adams laughed. "In context, I regard that as the highest compliment I have ever received. In these circumstances you need not 'Doctor' me. 'Adams' will do very nicely."

"I'm going to call you 'Uncle Andy'," Barbara said with a grin. "Now, Uncle Andy, in view of what you said, one of your eight doctorates is in medicine."

"Naturally."

"Are you any good at obstetrics?"

"In the present instance I feel perfectly safe in saying . . ."

"Wait a minute!" Deston snapped. "Bobby, you are *not* . . ."

"I am too! That is, I don't suppose I *am* yet, but with

him aboard I'm certainly *going* to. I *want* to, and if *we* don't get back both Bun and I will *have* to. Castaways' Code. So there!"

Deston started to say something, but Barbara forestalled him. "But for right now, it's high time we all got some sleep."

It was and they did; and next morning the three men wafted themselves across a few hundred yards of space to the crippled liner. Floodlights were rigged.

"What . . . a . . . mess." Deston's voice was low and wondering. "The Top especially . . . but the Middle and the Tail don't look too bad."

Inside, however, devastation had gone deep into the Middle. Walls, floors, and structural members were sheared and torn and twisted into shapes impossible to understand or explain. And, even worse, there were *absences*. In dozens of volumes, of as many sizes and of shapes incompatible with any three-dimensional geometry, every solid thing had simply vanished—vanished without leaving any clue whatever as to how or where it could possibly have gone.

It took four days to clean the ship of Dekon foam and to treat the hot spots that the automatics had missed. Four long days of heartbreaking labor in weightlessness and four too-short nights of sleep in the heavenly—to seven of them, at least—artificial gravity of the lifecraft. With the hulk deconned to zero (all ruptured radiators had of course been blown automatically at the time of catastrophe) Jones and Deston went over the engine rooms item by item.

The subspace drives were fused ruins. Enough normal-space gear was in working order, however, so that they could put on one gravity of drive, which was a vast relief to all. Then Jones began to jury-rig an astrogation set-up and Deston went to help Adams.

A few evenings later Adams said, "Well, that covers all the preliminary observations I am equipped to make.

Thanks a lot for your help, Babe. I won't bother you any

Blasting at normal, it'll be a mighty long time before we have to worry about that."

"Not as long as you think, Babe," Jones said. "We're in toward the center of the galaxy somewhere; stars are a lot thicker here. It's only about a third of a light-year to the nearest one. Point three five, I make it."

"But what's the chance of its having a Tellus-Type planet?"

"Oh, that isn't necessary," Adams said. "Any planet will, it is virtually certain, enable us to restore subspace communication."

"It'll still be a mighty long haul," Deston said. "The shape the engines are in, I doubt if they'll stand up under more than about one gee on a long pull. We can't do much better than that anyway, because we've got no grav-control—the Q-converters are all shot and we can't fix 'em."

"We'll travel at *one* gravity," Barbara said. "Babies; remember?"

"I'll figure it that way," Deston said, and went to work with his slide-rule. A few minutes later he reported, "Neglecting the Einstein Effect, which is altogether too hairy for a slipstick, I make it about fourteen months. But since velocity at turnover will be crowding six tenths of a light, that neglect makes it just a guess."

"We'll compute it tomorrow morning," Jones said. "For your information, all, we're heading for that star now."

21

II

THE ZETA FIELD

THE tremendous Chaytor engines of the *Procyon* were again putting out their wonted torrents of power. The starship, now a mere spaceship, was on course at one gravity. The lifecraft were in their berths, but the five and the four still lived in them rather than in the vast and oppressive emptiness that the liner then was. And outside of working hours the two groups did not mix.

In Lifecraft Three, four men sat at two tables. Ferdy Blaine and Moose Mordan were playing cards for small stakes. Ferdy was of medium size, lithe and poised, built of rawhide and spring steel. Moose the Muscle was six feet five and weighed a good two sixty. The two at the other table had been planning for days. They had had many vitriolic arguments, but neither had made any motion toward his weapon.

"Play it my way and we've got it made, I tell you!" Newman pounded the table with his fist. "Seventy five *megabucks* if it's a dime! Heavier loot than your second-string syndicate ever even *thought* of in one haul! I'm almost as good an astrogator as Jones is and a better engineer, and at *practical* electronics I'm just as good as Pretty Boy Deston is."

"Oh, yeah?" Lopresto sneered. "How come you're only a crew-chief, then?"

"*Only* a crew-chief!" Newman yelled. "D'ya think I'm dumb or something? Or don't know where the big moola is at? Or ain't in exactly the right spot to collect right and left? Or I ain't got exactly the right connections? With Mister Big himself? You ain't *that* dumb!"

"Dumb or not, before I make a move I've got to be *sure* that we can get back without 'em."

"You can be *damn* sure. I got to get back myself, don't I? But paste this in your hat—*I* get the big platinum blonde."

22

tance, turnover—all that stuff. They can do it a lot faster and some better than I can. I'll tell you when."

"Okay, and I'll give the signal. When I yell NOW we give 'em the business."

Newman went to his cabin and the muscle called Moose said, "I don't like that ape, boss. Before you gun him, let me work him over a little, huh?"

"We'll let him think he's top dog for a while yet; then you can have him."

A few evenings later, in Lifecraft Two, Barbara said, "You're worried, Babe, and everything's going so smoothly. Why?"

"Too smoothly altogether. That's why. Newman ought to be doing a slow burn and goldbricking all he dares, and he isn't. And I wouldn't trust Lopresto as far as I can throw a brick chimney by its smoke. I smell trouble. Shooting trouble."

"But they couldn't do *anything* without you two!" Bernice protested. "*Could* they, Ted, possibly?"

"They could, and I think they intend to. Being a crew chief, Newman is a jackleg engineer, a good practical 'troncist, and a rule-of-thumb astrogator, and we're computing every element of the flight. And if he's what I *think* he is . . ." Jones paused.

"Could be," Deston said. "One of an organized ring of pirate-smugglers. But there isn't enough plunder that they could get away with to make it pay."

"No? Think again. Not plunder; salvage. With either of us alive, none. With both of us dead, can you guess within ten megabucks of how much they'll collect?"

"*Blockhead!*" Deston slapped himself on the forehead. "And they aren't planning on killing the girls until the last act."

Both girls shrank visibly and Barbara said, "I see."

Deston went on, "They know they'll have to get both of us at once—the survivor would lock the ship in null-G and they'd be sitting ducks . . . and it won't be until we've finished the computations. We very seldom work together. If we make it a point *never* to be together on duty . . ."

"And be sure to always have our talkies turned on," Jones put in, grimly.

"Check. They'll have to think up some reason for getting everybody together, which will be the tip-off. Blaine will probably draw on me . . ."

"And he'll kill you," Jones said, flatly. "You're fast, I know, but he's a professional—probably one of the fastest guns in all space."

"Yes, but . . . I've got a . . . I mean I think I can . . ."

Bernice, smiling now, stopped Deston's floundering. "Why don't you fellows tell each other that you're both very strongly psionic? Bobby and I let our back hair down long ago."

"Oh—so you'll have warning, too, Babe?" Jones asked.

"That's right; but the girls can't start packing pistols now."

Bernice laughed. "I wouldn't know how to shoot one if I did. I'll throw things—I'm very good at that."

Jones didn't know his new wife very well yet, either. "What can you throw hard enough and straight enough to do any good?"

"Anything that weighs less than fifty pounds," she replied, confidently. "In this case . . . chairs, I think. Flying chairs are really hard to cope with. I'll start wearing a couple of knives in leg-sheaths, but I won't throw 'em

Really?

"Especially against a man-mountain like him. I'm that good. Really. And we should have a signal—an unusual word—so the first one of us to sense their intent yells 'BRAHMS!' Okay?"

That was okay, and the four went to bed.

Three days later, the intended victims allowed themselves to be inveigled into the lounge. All was peace and friendship—until suddenly a four-fold "BRAHMS!" rang out an instant ahead of Lopresto's stentorian "NOW!"

It was all a very good thing that Deston had had warning for he was indeed competing out of his class. As it was, his bullet crashed through Blaine's head, while the gunman's went into the carpet. The other pistol duel wasn't even close and Newman didn't get to aim his gun at Adams at all.

Bernice, even while shrieking the battle-cry, leaped to her feet, hurled her chair, and reached for another; but one chair was enough. It knocked the half-drawn pistol from Newman's hand and sent his body crashing to the floor, where Deston's second bullet made it certain that he would stay there.

If Moose Mordan had had time to get set, he might have had a chance. His thought processes, however, were lamentably slow; and Barbara Deston was very, very fast. She reached him before he even realized that this pint-sized girl actually intended to hit him; thus his belly-

25

muscles were still completely relaxed when her left fist sank half-forearm-deep into his solar plexus.

With an agonized "WHOOSH!" he began to double up, but she scarcely allowed him to bend. The fingers of her right hand, tightly bunched, were already boring savagely into a spot at the base of his neck. Then, left hand at his throat and right hand pulling hard at his belt, she put the totalized and concentrated power of her whole body behind the knee she drove into his groin.

That ended it. To make sure, however—or to keep Barbara from knowing that she had killed a man?—Deston and Jones each put a bullet through the falling head before it struck the floor.

Both girls flung themselves into their husbands' arms.

"Oh, I *killed* him, Carl!" Barbara sobbed. "And the worst of it is, I really *meant* to! I *never* did anything like that before in . . ."

"You didn't kill him, Barbara," Adams said.

"Huh?" She raised her head from Deston's shoulder; the contrast between streaming eyes and dawning relief was almost funny. "Why, I did too! I *know* I did!"

"By no means, my dear. Nor did Bernice kill Newman. Fists and knees and chairs do not kill instantly; bullets through the brain do. The autopsies will show, I'm quite certain, that these four men died instantly of gunshot wounds."

With the gangsters out of the way, life aboardship settled down, but not into a routine. When two spacemen and two grounder girls are trying to do the work of a full crew, no routine is possible. Adams, much older than the others and working even longer hours, became haggard and thin.

"But this work is *necessary*, my dear children," he informed the two girls when they remonstrated with him. "This material is all new. There are many extremely difficult problems involved and I have less than a year left to work on them. *Less than one year,* and it is a task for many men and all the resources of a research

more or less analogous to the electromagnetic field. This residuum either is or is not dischargeable to an object of planetary mass. I am now virtually certain that it is; and I am of the opinion that its discharge is ordinarily of such violence as to destroy the starship carrying it."

"Good God!" Deston exclaimed. "Oh—*that* was what you meant by 'fantastic precautions'?"

"Precisely."

"Any idea of what those precautions will have to be?"

"No. This is all *so* new . . . and I know *so* little . . . and am working with pitifully inadequate instrumentation . . . however, we have months of time yet, and if I an unable to derive a solution before arrival—I don't mean a rigorous analysis, of course; merely a method of discharge having a probability of success of at least point nine—we will remain in orbit around that sun until I do."

The *Procyon* bored on through space at one gravity of acceleration; and one gravity, maintained for months, builds up to an extremely high velocity. And, despite the Einstein Effect, that acceleration was maintained, for there was no lack of power. The *Procyon*'s uranium-driven Wesleys did not drive the ship, but only energized the Chaytor Effect engines that tapped the total energy of the universe.

Thus, in seven months of flight, the spaceship had probably attained a velocity of about six-tenths that of light.

The men did not know the day or date or what their actual velocity was, since the brute-force machine that was their only clock could not be depended upon for either accuracy or uniformity. Also, and worse, there was of course no possibility of determining what, if anything, the Einstein Effect was doing to their time rate.

At the estimated midpoint of the flight the *Procyon* was turned end for end; and, a few days later, Barbara and Deston cornered Adams in his laboratory.

"Listen, you egregious clam!" she began. "I *know* that Bun and I both have been pregnant for at *least* eight months and we ought to be *twice* as big as we are. You've been studying us constantly with a hundred machines that nobody ever heard of before and all you've said is blah. Now, Uncle Andy, I want the *truth*. *Are* we in a lot of trouble?"

"Trouble?" Adams was amazed. "Of course not. None at all. Perfectly normal fetuses, both of them. Perfectly."

"But for what *age?*" she demanded. "Four months, maybe?"

"But that's the crux!" Adams enthused. "Fascinating; and indubitably supremely important. A key datum. If this zeta field is causing it, that gives me a tremendously powerful new tool, for certain time vectors in the generalized matrix become parameters. Thus certain determinants, notably the all-important delta-prime-sub-mu, become manipulable by . . . but you aren't *listening!*"

"I'm listening, pops, but nothing is coming through. But I'm *awfully* glad I'm not going to give birth to a monster," and she led Deston away. "Carl, have you got the *foggiest* idea of what he was talking about?"

"Not the foggiest—that was over my head like a cirrus cloud—but if you gals' slowness in producing will help the old boy lick this thing I'm all for it, believe me."

Months passed. Two perfect babies—Theodore Warner Deston and Barbara Bernice Jones—were born, four days apart, in perfectly normal fashion. Adams made out birth certificates which were unusual in only one respect;

28

the order of magnitude of ten thousand average dis-
charges of lightning. I do not know what it is, but it is
virtually certain that we will be able to discharge it, not
in the one tremendous blast of contact with the planet,
but in successive decrements by the use of long, thin leads
extending downward toward a high point of the planet."

"Wire, you mean? What kind?"

"The material is unimportant except in that it should
have sufficient tensile strength to support as many miles
as possible of its own length."

"We've got dozens of coils of hook-up wire," Deston
said, "but not too many *miles* and it's soft stuff."

Jones snapped his finger. "*Graham* wire!"

"Of course," Deston agreed. "Hundreds of miles of it
aboard. We'll float the senser down on a Hotchkiss. . . ."

"Tear-out," Jones objected.

"Bailey it—and spider the Bailey out to eighteen or
twenty pads. We can cannibal the whole Middle for
metal."

"Sure. But surges—backlash. We'll have to remote it."

"No, problem there; servos all over the place. To Baby
Two."

"Would you mind delousing *your* signal?" Adams asked
caustically.

" 'Scuse, please, Doc. A guy *does* talk better in his
own lingo, doesn't he? Graham wire is used for re-wrap-
ping the Grahams, you know."

"No, I don't know. What are Grahams?"

"Why, they're the intermediates between the Wesleys and the Chaytors . . . okay, okay; Graham wire is one-point-three-millimeter-diameter ultra-high-tensile alloy wire. Used for re-enforcing hollow containers that have to stand terrific pressure."

"Such wire is exactly what will be required. Note now that our bodies will have to be grounded very thoroughly to the metal of the ship."

"You're so right. We'll wrap up to the eyballs in silver mesh and run leads as big as my arm to the frame."

They approached their target planet. It was twice as massive as Earth; its surface was rugged and jagged; its mountain ranges had sharp peaks over forty thousand feet high.

"There's one more thing we must do," Adams said. "This zeta field may very well be irreplaceable. We must therefore launch all the lifecraft except Number Two into separate orbits, so that a properly-staffed and properly-equipped force may study that field."

It was done; and in a few hours the *Procyon* hung motionless, a thousand miles high, directly above an isolated and sharp mountain peak.

The Bailey boom, with its spider-web-like network of grounding cables and with a large pulley at its end, extended two hundred feet straight out from the *Procyon*'s side. A twenty-five-mile coil of Graham wire had been mounted on the remote-controlled Hotchkiss reel. The end of the wire had been run out over the pulley; a fifteen-pound weight, to act both as a "senser" and to keep the wire from fouling, had been attached; and the controls had been tested.

Now, in Lifecraft Two—as far away from the "business district" as they could be—the human bodies were grounded and Deston started the reel. The whole coil ran out, as expected, with no action. Then, slowly and carefully, Deston let the big ship float straight downward. Until, suddenly, it happened.

There was a blast beside which the most terrific flash

of lightning ever seen on Earth would have seemed like

plate and gulped. Without saying a word he waved a hand and the others looked. The sharp tip of the mountain was gone: it had become a seething, flaming lake of incandescent lava.

"And what," Deston managed, "do you suppose happened to the other side of the ship?"

The boom was gone. So were all twenty of the grounding cables that had fanned out in all directions to anchorages welded to the vessel's skin and frame. The anchorages, too, were gone; and tons upon tons of steel plating and of structural members for many feet around where each anchorage had been. Many tons of steel had been completely volatilized; other tons had run like water.

"Shall I try the subspace radio now, Doc?" Deston asked.

"By no means. This first blast would of course be the worst, but there will be several more, of decreasing violence."

There were. The second, while it volatilized the boom and its grounding network, merely fused small portions of the anchorages. The third took only the boom itself; the fourth, only the dangling miles of wire. At the fifth trial nothing—apparently—happened; whereupon the wire was drawn in and a two-hundred-pound mass of steel was lowered into firm contact with solid rock.

"Now you may try your radio," Adams said.

Deston flipped a switch and spoke into his microphone. "*Procyon* One to Control Six. Flight eight four nine.

Subspace radio test number nine five—I think. How do you read me, Control Six?"

The reply was highly unorthodox. It was a wild yell, followed by words not addressed to Deston at all. "Captain Reamer! Captain French! Captain Holloway! ANYBODY! It's the *Procyon,* that was lost over a year ago! IT'S THE *PROCYON!*"

"Line it up! If it's some damn fool's idea of a joke . . ." a crisp authoritative voice grew louder as its source approached the distant pickup ". . . he'll rot in jail for a hundred years!"

"*Procyon* One to Control Six," Deston said again. His voice was not quite steady this time; both girls were crying openly and joyfully. "How do you read me, Frenchy old horse?"

"It *is* the *Procyon*—that's the Runt himself—hi, Babe! I read you nine and one. Survivors?"

"Five. Second Officer Jones, our wives, and Doctor Andrew Adams, a fellow of the College of Study."

"It can't be a lifecraft after this long—what shape is the hulk in?"

"Bad. Can't immerge. The whole Top is an ungodly mess and some of the rest of her won't hold air—air, hell! Section Fourteen won't hold shipping crates! The Chaytors are okay, but five of the Wesleys are shot, and all of the Q-converters. Most of the Grahams are leaking like sieves, and . . ."

"Hold it, Babe. They want this on a recorder downstairs, too. The newshawks are knocking the doors down. This marriage bit. The brides—who are they?"

Deston told him. Just that; no more.

"Okay. They want a lot more than that; especially the sobbers, but that can wait. What happened?"

"I don't know. You'd better fly a Fellow of the College over there to talk to Doc Adams. Maybe he can explain it to another Big Brain, but I wouldn't bet, even on that."

"Okay. Downstairs is hooked in and so is Brass. Give us everything you know or can guess at."

Deston spoke steadily for thirty minutes. He did not

the galaxy, but also of the standard reference points, such as S-Doradus, lying outside it. "When you get that stuff all plotted you'll find a hell of a big confusion, but I hope there aren't enough stars in it but what you'll be able to find us sometime."

"Mark off. Don't make me laugh, Herc; your probable center will spear it. If there's ever more than one star in any confusion *you* set up I'll eat all the extras. But there's a dozen Big Brains, gnawing their nails off to the elbows to talk to Adams. So put him on and let's get back to sleep, huh? They're cutting this mike now."

"Hold it!" Deston snapped. "I want some information too, dammit! What's your Greenwich?"

"Zero seven one four plus thirty seven seconds. So go to bed, you night-prowling owl."

"Of what day, month, and year?" Deston insisted.

"Friday, Sep . . ." French's voice was replaced by that of a much older man; very evidently that of a Fellow of the College.

After listening for less than a minute, Barbara took Deston's arm and led him away. "Any at all of *that* gibberish is exactly that much too much, husband mine. So I think we'd better take Captain French's advice, don't you?"

Since there was only one star in Jones' "confusion" (by the book, "Volume of Uncertainty") finding the *Procyon* was no problem at all. High Brass came in quantity and the whole story, except for one bit of biology, was told. Two huge subspacegoing machine-shops also came, and a battalion of mechanics, who worked on the crippled liner for over three weeks.

Then the *Procyon* started back for Earth under her own subspace drive, under the command of Captain Theodore Jones. His first and only command for the Interstellar Corporation, of course, since he was a married man. Deston had tendered his resignation while still a First Officer, but his superiors would not accept it until after his promotion "for outstanding services" had come through. Thus Captain Carlyle Deston and his wife and son were dead-heading, not quite back to Earth, but to the transfer point for Newmars.

Just before that transfer point was reached, Deston went "up Top" to take leave of his friend, and Jones greeted him with:

"I've been trying to talk to Doc again; but wherever he starts or whatever the angle of approach he *always* boils it down to this: 'Subjective time is measured by the number of learning events experienced.' I ask you, Babe, what in *hell* does that mean? If anything?"

"I know. Me, too. It sounds like it ought to mean *something*, but I'll be damned if I know what. However, if it makes the old boy happy and gives the College a toehold on subspace, what do *we* care?"

And at this same time Barbara had been visiting Bernice. They had of course been talking about the babies, and an awkward silence had fallen.

"Oh," Barbara licked her lips. "So you get those feelings too."

"Too?" Bernice's face paled. "But they're absolutely normal, Bobby. Perfect. Absolutely perfect in every respect."

"I know . . . but once in a while . . . an aura or something . . . it scares me simply witless."

34

"I have them too. Not often, but . . . well, they began

the mystery. They have the same thing we have, except more of it. But they *can't* have real powers without experience or knowledge, so when they grow up they'll be stronger than we are and we'll learn from them."

"That's the way it is. I'm sure of it."

"So am I, now. I feel a lot better, Bun. I've got to gallop. This isn't goodbye, dear—I'll see you soon and often—it's just so long."

III

DESTON THE DOWSER

For a week the Destons were busy settling down in their low, sprawling home on Newmars. Deston had not had time to think about a job, and Barbara did not intend to let him think about one. Wherefore, the first free evening they had, while they were sitting close together on a davenport near the fireplace in their living-room, she said:

"I know how much you really want to explore deep space. I do, too. I'm sure we could accomplish something worth while, and I'd like very much to leave a size five-bee footprint on the sands of time, too. There's a way we can do it."

Deston stiffened. "I'd like to believe that, pet. I'd give my right leg to the hip and one eye—but what's the use of kidding ourselves? Your last buck, even if I'd lay it on that kind of a line, wouldn't cover the nut."

"The way things are now, no. But listen. What is the one single thing that all civilization needs most desperately?"

"Uranium. You know that as well as I do."

"I know; but I want you to think very seriously about the reality, the intensity, and the importance of that need. So elucidate."

"Okay." Deston shrugged his shoulders. "It's the *sine qua non* of interstellar flight; of running the Chaytor engine. While all the uranium does is trigger the power intake, the bigger the Chaytor the bigger its Wesley has to be and the faster the uranium gets used up. Uranium's so scarce that except for controls its price would be fantastic. Hence the black market, where its price *is* fantastic. Hence bribery, corruption, and so forth. Half of the deviltry and skulduggery on all ninety six planets

36

is due to the hard fact that the supply of uranium can-

Tightening his arm, he swung her around and stared into her eyes. "I know all about things that way. Hunches. So how do I go about learning to dowse metal?"

"Like I did. I started on coal, holding a lump in my hand. I concentrated on it until I could sense everything about it, clear down to its atomic structure. Then, looking at a map and spreading it out, I could see every coal deposit on the planet. So here's a piece of copper tube and a blueprint of this house. Concentrate as hard as you possibly can; then you'll know what I mean."

"Oh—so you've been laying for me."

"Of course I have. This is the first time we've had any time."

"Okay. I'll give it the good old college try."

He tried it. He tried over and over again. For half an hour he put everything he had into the effort. Then, coming out of his near-trance, he wiped his sweating face and said, "I can't swing it alone, pet. There must be some way for you to show me how the damn thing goes—if I've got what it takes."

"Of course you have!" she snapped. "Don't think for a single second you haven't—I know you have, I tell you!"

"If you know it, it's so and I believe it. But the question still is—how? But say, you can read my mind, can't you?"

Her eyes widened. "Why, I don't know. I never tried to, of course . . . but what good would that do?"

"Just a hunch. With that close a contact, maybe some of your knowledge will rub off onto me. Especially if you push."

"I'll push, all right; but remember, no resistance. With such a chilled-steel mind as yours, *nothing* could get through."

"No resistance. Just the opposite. I'll pull you in with every tractor I can bring to bear. Across a table?"

"Uh-uh, this is better. Closer."

They gripped hands and stared into each other's eyes. For a long two minutes nothing happened; then Barbara broke contact. "I got a little," she said. "You were fighting with a boy twice your size. A red-haired boy with a lot of freckles."

"Huh? Spike McGonigle—that was twelve or fifteen years ago and I haven't thought of the guy since! But I got something, too. You were at a party, wearing a red dress cut down to here and emerald ear-rings. You put a slightly pie-eyed chicken colonel flat on his face because he wouldn't take 'no' for an answer."

"Not on his *face*, surely . . . oh, yes, I remember. But *this* isn't what we wanted, at all. However, it's something; so let's keep on with it, shall we?"

They kept it up until bed-time, and went at it again immediately after breakfast next morning. Progress was maddeningly slow, but it was progress. Progress marked by a succession of stabbing, fleeting pains, each of which was followed by the opening of an entire vista of one-ness. They did not complete the operation that day, or in three more, or in a week; but finally, the last vista opened, they sat for minutes in what was neither ecstasy nor consternation, but something having the prime elements of both. For full mental rapport is the ultimate intimacy; more intimate by far than any other union possible.

Barbara licked her bloodless lips and said, not in words but purely in thought, "Oh, Carl! So *this* is what telepathy really is!"

"Must be." He was not speaking aloud, either. "*What*

the people who talk about telepathy don't know about it!"

self? How did you ever learn it?"

"Looked at that way . . . I guess maybe I didn't. I must have been born with it."

"That makes sense. Now let's link up and take that copper atom apart clear down to whatever makes up its theta, mu, and pi mesons."

But they didn't. Much to the dismayed surprise of both, their combined attack was no more effective than Deston's alone had been. He frowned at the sample in thought, then said, "Okay. The thing's beginning to make sense."

"What sense?" she demanded. "Not to me, it isn't. Is this another of your hunches?"

"No. Logic. I'm not sure yet, but one more test and I will be. Water. You won't need a sample?"

"No more than with oil. It's just about the same technique. Like this . . . there. But it doesn't get me anywhere. Does it you?"

"Definitely. Look, Bobby. Water, gas, oil, and coal. Oxygen, hydrogen, and carbon. Oxygen, the highest, is atomic number eight. Maybe you can—what'll we call it? 'Handle'?—handle the lower elements, but not the higher ones. So maybe both of us together can handle 'em all. If this hypothesis is valid, you already know helium, lithium, beryllium. . . ."

"Wait up!" she broke in. "I wouldn't recognize any one of them if it should stop me on the street and say hello."

"You just think you wouldn't. How about boron, as in boric acid? Eye-wash, to you?"

Her mind flashed to the medicine cabinet in the bathroom. "I *do* know it, at that. I've never handled it, but I can."

"Nice. How about sodium, as in common salt?"

"Can do."

"Chlorine, the other half of salt?"

"That hurt a little—took a little time—but I made it."

"Fine! The hypothesis begins to look good. Now we'll tackle calcium together. In bones—my thick skull, for instance."

"*Ouch!* That really hurt, Carl. And you did it. I couldn't have, possibly, but I followed you in and I know it now. But golly, it felt like . . . like it was stretching my brain all out of shape. Like giving birth to a child, something. I *told* you you're stronger than I am, Carl, but I want to learn it all. So go right ahead, but take it a little slower, please."

"Slow it is, sweetheart," and they went ahead.

And in a couple of days they could handle all the elements of the periodic table.

Then and only then did they go back to what they had started out to do. Seated side by side, each grasping the short length of metal, they stared at the blueprint and allowed—or, rather, impelled—their perception to pervade the entire volume of the house.

"We've *got* it!" Deston yelled, aloud. "It *is* a new sense—a sixth sense—and *what* a sense!"

They could see—sense—perceive—every bit of copper in, under, and around the building; the network of tubes and pipes stood out like the blood-vessels in a plastic model of the human body. While the metal was not transparent in the optical sense, they could perceive in detail the outside, the inside, and the ultimately fine structure of the material of each component part of the whole gas-and-water-supply installation.

"Oh, you *did* it, Carl!"

"*We* did it—whatever it is. But I can do it alone now;

"Not by chance, no. I done it on purpose. Here they are."

There is no need to go into detail as to the exact fashion in which they explored the enormous volume of the planet, or as to exactly what they found. It is enough to say that they learned; and that, having learned, the techniques became almost automatic and the work itself became comparatively easy.

The next morning Deston made another suggestion. "Bobby, what do you say about seeing what we can do with that forty-eight-inch globe of Tellus?"

"*Tellus!* Light-years and light-years from ` here? Are you completely out of your mind?"

"Maybe I'm a little mad with power, but listen. If the map actually is the territory it's scale that counts, not distance. It's inconceivable, of course, that there isn't a limit somewhere—but where is it? I've got an urge to spread our wings a little."

"A highly laudable objective, I'd say, but I'll bet you a cookie that Tellus is 'way beyond that limit. Drag out the globe . . . ah, there you are, sweet mother world of the race! Now watch out, Mom; ready or not, here we come!"

They went; and when they found out that they could scan and analyze the entire volume of Earth, mile by plotted cubic mile, as easily and as completely as they could that of Newmars on whose surface they were, they stared at each other, appalled.

"Well . . . I . . . that is . . ." Barbara licked her lips and gulped. "I owe you a cookie, I guess, Carl."

"Yeah." But Deston was not thinking of cookies. "That tears it. It really does. Wide open. Rips it up and down and sideways."

"It does for a fact. But it makes the objective even more laudable than ever, I'd say. How do you think we should go about it?"

"There's only one way I can see. I said I'd never spend a dime of your money, remember? I take it back. I think we'd better charter one of WarnOil's fast subspacers and buy all the off-Earth maps, star-charts, and such-like gear we can get hold of."

"Charter? Pfooie! We own WarnOil, silly, subspacers and everything else. In fee simple. So we'll just take one. I'll arrange that; so you can take off right now after your maps and charts and whatever. Scoot!"

"Wait up a bit, sweet. We'll have to have Doc Adams."

"Of course. He'll be tickled silly to go."

"And Herc Jones for captain."

"I'm not so sure about that." Barbara nibbled at her lower lip. "A little premature, don't you think, to unsettle him and Bun—raise hopes that may very well turn out to be false—before we find out what we can actually do?"

"Could be. Okay, fellow explorer—the count-down is on and all stations are in condition GO."

Of all the preparations for the first expedition into the unknown, only one is really noteworthy; the interview with Doctor Adams in his home. For months he had been concentrating on the subether and his zeta field; and when he learned what the purpose of the trip was, and that he would have a free hand and an ample budget, he became enthusiastic indeed.

To a mind of such tremendous power and range as his, it was evident from the first that his young friends had

changed markedly since he had last seen them. This fact
~~~~~ ~~ ~~~~~~ ~ ~~~~~~~~~ Adams was tall and lean and

ly, and completely informatively—a thing that, to my
knowledge, has never before been demonstrated."

"Oh?" Barbara's eyes widened. "When we thought we
were talking did we sometimes forget to?"

"Only in part. Mainly because of a depth of understanding—deduced, to be sure, but actual nonetheless—
impossible to language." Then, Adams-like, he went
straight to the point. "Will you try to teach it to me?"

"Why, of course!" Barbara exclaimed. "That, Uncle
Andy, was very much on the agenda."

"Thank you. And Stella, too, please? Her mind is of
precisionist grade and is of greater sensitivity than my
own."

"Certainly," Deston assured him. "The more we can
spread this ability around the better it will be for everybody."

Adams left the room then, and in a minute or so came
back with his wife; a slender, graceful, gray-haired woman of fifty-odd.

Both Andrew and Stella Adams had been students all
their lives. They knew how to study. They had the brain
capacity—the blocked or latent cells—to learn telepathy
and many other things. They learned rapidly and thoroughly. Neither of them, however, could or ever did
learn how to "handle" any substance. In fact, very few
persons of their time, male or female, ever did learn

more than an insignificant fraction of the Destons' unique ability to dowse.

In compensation, however, the Adamses had nascent powers peculiarly their own. Thus, before they went to bed that night, Andrew and Stella Adams were exploring vistas of reality that neither of the Destons would ever be able to perceive.

Out in deep space, the Destons worked slowly at first. They actually landed on Cerealia, the most fully surveyed of all the colonized planets; and on Galmetia, only a little less so, as it was owned *in toto* by Galactic Metals; and on Lactia, the dairy planet.

Deston worked first on copper; worked on it so long and so intensively that he could find and handle and tridi any deposit of the free metal or of any of its ores with speed and precision, wherever any such might be in a planet's crust. Then he went on up the line of atomic numbers, taking big jumps—molybdenum and barium and tungsten and bismuth—up to uranium, which was what he was after.

Barbara did not work with him on metals very long; just long enough to be sure that she could be of no more help. She didn't really like metals, and she had her own work to do. It was just as important to have on file all possible data concerning water, oil, gas, and coal.

They worked together, however, at perfecting their techniques. Any thought of determining the working limits of psionic abilities had been abandoned long since; they were trying with everything they had to minimize the necessity of using maps and charts. They succeeded. Just as Barbara, while still a child, had become able to work without samples; so both of them learned how to work without maps. All they had to know, finally, was where a solar system was; they could fix their sense of perception upon any star they could see, and hence could study all its planets. They tried to work independently of star-charts—to direct their attention to any point in space at will—but it was to be years before they were

ble only to full mental rapport. She did not like it; and
she, who had never had a money problem in her whole
life, could not fully understand it. He should be big
enough, she thought deep down and a little disappointed-
ly, not to boggle so at such an unimportant thing as
money.

But that attitude was innate and so much a part of
Deston's very make-up that he could not have changed
it had he tried, and he would not try. Almost everyone
who knew them had him labelled as a fortune-hunter,
and that label irked him to the core. It would continue
to irk him as long as it stuck, and the only way he could
unstick it was to do something—or make money enough
—to make him as important as she was. A mountain of
uranium—even a small mountain—would do it two ways.
It would make him a public benefactor and a multi-
millionaire. So—by the living God!—he would find uranium before he went back to civilization.

Adams and his scientists and engineers had developed
an ultra-long-range detector for zeta fields, and they had
not been able to find any other hazards to subspace flight.
Hence they had been constantly stepping up their vessel's
speed. Originally a very fast ship, she was now covering
in hours distances that had formerly required days.

On and on, then, faster and faster, deeper and deeper
into the unexplored immensities of deep space the mighty
flyer bored; and Deston finally found his uranium. They

landed upon a mountainous, barren continent of a lifeless world. They put on radiation armor and labored busily for nineteen hours.

Then Deston told the captain, "Line out for Newmars, please, and don't drag your feet."

And that night, in the Destons' cabin: "Why so glum, chum?" Barbara asked. "That's the best thing for civilization that ever was and the biggest bonanza there ever was. I'd think you'd be shrieking with joy—I've almost been—but you look as though you'd just lost your pet hound."

Deston shrugged off his black mood and smiled. "The trouble is, petsy, it's *too* big. Too damned big altogether. And *look* at our planet Barbizon. Considering the size of the deposits and what and where the planet is, nobody except Galactic Metals could handle the project the way it should be handled."

"Well, would that be bad? To sell it or lease it to them?"

"Not bad, honey; impossible. All those big outfits are murder in the first degree. Before I could get anywhere with them—if they find out I found it, even—GalMet would own not only Barbizon, but my shirt and pants, too."

Barbara laughed gleefully. "How well I know *that* routine! Do you think they don't do it in oil, too? But WarnOil's legal eagles know all about skulduggery and monkey business and fine print—none better. So here's what let's do. File by proxy . . . and maybe you and I had better incorporate ourselves. Just us two; Deston and Deston, say. Develop it by another proxy, making darn sure that they don't find any uranium at all and nothing else that's worth more than three or four dollars a ton. . . ."

"Huh? Why not?"

"Because GalMet's spy system, darling, is very good indeed."

"All right, but we've *still* got to make the approach . . .

dammit, I'd give it to GalMet for *nothing* if it'd give us

hard."

"Fine, gal—fine! So I'll write to Herc; tell him he can
start getting organized. He'll be tickled to death—he
doesn't like flying a desk any better than I do."

"Write? Call him up, right now."

"I'll do that, at that. I'm not used yet to not caring
whether a call is across the street or across half of space."

"And I want to talk to Bun, anyway."

The call was put through and Barbara talked to Bernice for some fifteen minutes. Then Deston took over,
finding that Jones was anything but in love with his desk
job. When Deston concluded, ". . . family quarters aboard.
Full authority and full responsibility of station. Full captain's pay and rank plus a nice bonus in stock," Captain
Theodore Jones was fairly drooling.

IV

ORGANIZATION OF THE LITTLE GEM

In comparison with silicon or aluminum, which together make up almost thirty six percent of the Earth's crust, copper is a very scarce metal indeed, amounting to only a very small fraction of one percent. Yet it is one of the oldest-worked and most widely useful of all metals, having been in continuous demand for well over six thousand Tellurian years.

Yet of all the skills of man, that of mining cuprous ores had perhaps advanced the least. There had been some progress, of course. Miners of old could not go down very deep or go in very far; there was too much water and not enough air. The steam engine helped; it removed water and supplied air. Electricity helped still more. Tools also had improved; instead of wooden sticks and animal-fat candles there was a complex gadgetry of air drills and electric saws and explosives, and there was plenty of light.

Basically, however, since automation could not be economically applied to tiny, twisting, erratic veins of ore, the situation remained unchanged. Men still crawled and wriggled to where the copper was. Brawny men, by sheer power of muscle, still jackassed the heavy stuff out to where the automatics could get hold of it.

And men still died, in various horrible fashions and in callously recorded numbers, in the mines that were trying to satisfy the insatiable demand for the red metal that is one of the prime bases upon which the technology of all civilization rests.

And the United Copper Miners, under the leadership of its president, Burley Hoadman, refused to tolerate any advancement whatever in automation. Also, UCM was approaching, and rapidly, its goal—the complete unionization of every copper mine of the Western Hemisphere

was hard meat, gristle, and bone. His leather-padded
right knee was jammed against the wall of his tiny work-
space; the hobnail-studded sole of his left boot was
jammed even more solidly into a foot-hole cut into the
hard rock of the floor. With his right shoulder and both
huge hands he was holding the Sullivan to its work—the
work of driving an inch-and-a-quarter steel into the face.
And the monstrous, bellowing, thundering, shrieking Slug-
ger, even though mounted upon a short and very heavy
bar, sent visible tremors through the big man's whole
body, clear down to his solidly-anchored feet.

In his shockingly cramped quarters Purvis changed
steel; shifted the position of his Sullivan's mounting bar;
cut new foot-holes; kept on at his man-killing task until
the set of powder-holes was in. Then he dismounted the
heavy drill and, wriggling backwards, lugged it and its
appurtenances out into the main stope to make room for
the powderman.

As he straightened up, half paralyzed by the position
and the strain of his recent labors, another big man lunged
roughly against him.

"Wot tha hell—sock *me*, willya?" the man roared, and
swung his steel-backed timberman's glove against Purvis'
mouth and jaw.

Purvis went down.

"Watcha tryin' ta pull off, Frank?" the shift-boss yelled,
rushing up and jerking his thumb toward the rise. "You

know better'n that—fightin' underground. You're fired—
go on top an' get yer time."

"Wha'd'ya mean, fired?" Frank growled. "He started it,
the crumb. He slugged me first."

"You're a goddam liar," the powderman spoke up,
setting his soft-leather bag of low explosive carefully
down against the foot of the hanging wall. "I seen it.
Purve didn't do nothin'. Not a goddam thing. Besides, he
wasn't in no shape to. He didn't lift a finger. You socked
him fer nothin'."

"Oh, yeah?" Frank sneered. "Stone blind all of a
sudden, I guess? I leave it to tha rest of 'em—" waving
a massive arm at the two muckers and the electrician,
now standing idly by, "—if he didn't sock me first. They
all seen it."

All three nodded, and the electrician said, positively,
"Sure Purve socked him first. We all seen 'im do it."

Purvis struggled to his feet. He shook off a glove,
wiped his bleeding mouth, and stared for a moment at
the blood-smeared back of his hand. Then, and still without a word, he bent over and picked up a three-foot
length of inch-and-a-quarter steel.

"Hold it, Purve—hold it!" The shift-boss put both hands
against the big man's chest and pushed, and the atrocious
weapon dropped with a clang to the hard-rock floor.
"Thass better. They's somethin' damn screwy here. It
just don't jibe."

He crossed over to his telephone and dialed. "Say boss,
what do I do when I fire a nape fer startin' a fight underground an' he won't go out on top? An' three other bastards say somethin' I saw good an' plain with my own
eyes didn't hap . . . okay, I'll hold . . . okay . . . yeah . . .
but listen. Mr. *Speers'* office! Thass takin' it awful high
up, ain't it, just to fire a nogoodnik that . . . okay, okay,
now you hold it." Turning his head, the shift-boss said,
"They want us all up on top an' they wanta know if
you wanta go up under yer own air or will they send

down some guards an' drag y'all tha way up there by

"You said it, Mac, about it's bein' a hell of a long ways up to have to take firin' a louse like him. What'd they say?"

"Nothin'," McGuire said. "Nothin' at all."

"The higher the better," the electrician—who had done most of the talking up in the stope—growled. "The bigger the man we can get up to with this thing, the harder you three finkin' bastards are goin' ta get the boots put to ya. You ain't got a prayer. It's four ta three, see?"

"Hold it, Purve—I said *hold it!*" McGuire shouted, grabbing the miner's right arm with both hands and hanging on—and Purvis did stop his savage motion. "Like I said, Purve, this whole deal stinks. It don't add up—noways. An' what surprised me most was that nobody up on top was surprised at all."

"Huh?" the electrician demanded, with a sudden change in manner and expression. "Why not? Why wasn't they?"

"I wouldn't know," the shift-boss replied, quietly, "but we'll maybe find out when we get up there. But I'm tellin' you four apes somethin' right now. Shut up and stay shut up. If any one of you opens his trap just one more time I'll let Purve here push a mouthful of teeth down his goddam throat."

Wherefore the rest of the trip to the office of Superintendent Speers, the Big Noise of the Little Gem, was made in silence.

Charles Speers was a well-built, well-preserved man nearing sixty. His hair, although more white than brown, was still thick and bushy. His eyes, behind stainless-steel-rimmed trifocals, were a clear, sharp gray. His narrow, close-clipped mustache was brown. When his visitors were all seated he pushed a button on his desk, looked at the shift-boss and said:

"Mr. McGuire, please tell me what happened; exactly as you saw it happen." McGuire told him and he looked at the powderman. "Mr. Bailey, I realize that no two eyewitnesses ever see any event in precisely the same way, but have you anything of significance to add to or subtract from Mr. McGuire's statement of fact?"

"No, sir. That's the way it went."

"Mr. Purvis, did you or did you not strike the first blow?"

"I did not, sir. I'll swear to that. I didn't lift a finger—not 'til after, I mean. Then I lifted a piece of steel, but Mac here stopped me before I could hit him with it."

"Thank you. This is interesting. Very." Speers' voice was as clipped as his mustache. "Now, Mr. Grover C. Shields —or whatever your real name may be—as a non-participating witness and as spokesman apparent for the majority of those present at the scene of violence, please give me your version of the affair."

"They're lyin' in their teeth, all three of 'em," the electrician growled, sullenly. "But what's that 'real name' crack supposed to mean? An' say, are ya puttin' all this crap on a record?"

"Certainly. Why not? However, this is not a court of law and you are not under oath, so go ahead."

"Not me. Not by a damsight, you fine-feathered slicker. Not without a mouthpiece, an' nobody else does, neither."

"That's smart of you. And you're still sticking to the argot, eh, Mr.—ah—Shields?" The mine superintendent's smile was exactly as humorous as the edge of a cut-throat razor. "Such camouflage is of course to be ex-

him, exclaiming as he did so, "An' *that's* on record, too, wise guy!"

"I'm afraid it may not be," Speers said, gently, shaking his head. "This machine is not a new model; it misses an item occasionally. But you see what I mean?" Speers paused, and from the ceiling above there came the almost inaudible click of a camera shutter. "When did those hands ever do any real work? Resume your seat, please." The alleged electrician did so. "I have here seven personnel cards, from which I will read certain data into the record. George J. McGuire, Shift Boss, length of service twenty four years, black spots—demerits, that is—nineteen. Clinton F. Bailey, Powderman, fifteen years, ten demerits. Grant H. Purvis, Top Miner, twelve years, eight demerits. Each of these three has four or five times as many stars as black spots.

"On the other hand, John J. Smith, Mucker, forty three days and thirty three demerits. Thomas J. Jones, Mucker, twenty nine days and thirty one demerits. Frank D. Ormsby, Timberman, twelve days and twenty demerits. Grover C. Shields, Electrician, five days and eleven demerits. There are no stars in this group. These data speak for themselves. The discharge of Ormsby is sustained. I hereby discharge the other three—Sheilds, Smith, and Jones—myself. You four go back, change your clothes, pick up your own property, turn in company property, and leave.

Your termination papers and checks will be in the mail tonight. Get out."

They got.

Speers pressed a button and his secretary, a gray-haired, chilled-steel virgin of fifty, came in. "Yes, sir?"

"Please take Mr. Purvis there," he pointed, "over across and let the doctors look at him."

"Oh, this ain't nothin' . . ." the miner began.

"It would be if I had it." Speers smiled; a genuine smile. "You do exactly what the doctors tell you to do. Okay?"

"Okay, sir. Thanks."

"And Miss Mills, he's on full time until they let him go back to work full time."

"Yes, sir. Come with me, young man," and she led the big miner out of the room.

Still smiling, Speers turned to the two remaining men. "Are you wondering what this is all about, or do you know?"

"I could maybe guess, if there'd been any UCM organizers around," McGuire said, "but I ain't heard of any. Have you, Clint?"

"Uh-uh." The powderman shook his head. "I been kinda expectin' some, but there ain't been even a rumble yet."

"Those four men were undoubtedly UCM goons. They will claim that Ormsby was assaulted and that all four of them were fired because of talking about unionization —for merely sounding out our people's attitude toward unionization. Tomorrow, or the next day at latest, the UCM will bottle us up tight with a picket line."

"But it'd be a goddam lie!" Bailey protested.

"Sure it would," McGuire agreed. "But they've pulled some awful raw stuff before now an' got away with it. D'you think they can get away with it here, Mr. Speers?"

"That's the jackpot question. With the Labor Relations Board, yes. Higher up, it depends . . . but I want to do a little sounding out myself. When we close down, we'll try to place everyone somewhere, of course; but in the event of a very long shut-down, McGuire, how would

"Precisely."

McGuire pondered this shockingly revolutionary thought for a long minute, his callused right palm rasping against the stiff stubble on his chin. "I still couldn't," he decided, finally. "Not just 'cause the union'd win, neither. I like it a hell of a lot better here on Earth. If I was young an' single, maybe. But I ain't so young yet—" he was all of forty two years old, "—an' three of tha kids're still home yet an' my old woman'd raise hell an' put a chunk under it. Besides, me an' her both like ta know where we're at. So when they get us organized I'll join tha union an' work 'til I'm sixty an' then retire an' live easy on my pension an' old-age benefits. Thataway I'll know all tha time just where I'm at."

"I see." Speers' voice was almost a sigh. "And you, Bailey?"

"Not fer me," the powdermen said, with no hesitation at all. "George chirped it—" he jerked his left thumb at the shift-boss, "—about wantin' ta know where yer at. I got nothin' much against tha union. It costs, but between it an' tha outplanets I'll take the UCM any day in tha week. Hoady Hoadman takes care of his men, an' out on tha outplanets ya never know what's gonna happen. Yer takin' awful big chances all tha time. Too goddam big."

"I see, and thanks, both of you. Call Personnel about replacements and go ahead as usual—until you run into a picket line. That is all for now."

As the two men left Speers' office he flipped the switch of his squawk box. "Get me GalMet, please. Maynard's FirSec, Miss Champ . . ."

"Miss *Champion!*" The switchboard girl committed the almost incredible offense of interrupting the Super. "*Herself?*"

"Herself," Speers said, dryly. "As I was about to say, the password in this case is as follows: 'Gem—Little—Operation'. In that order, please."

"Oh—excuse me, sir, please. I'll get right at it."

It took seven minutes, but finally Miss Champion's face appeared upon Speers' screen; a face startlingly young and startlingly comely to be that of one of the top Fir Secs of all Earth.

"Good afternoon, Mr. Speers." Her contralto voice was as smooth and as rich as whipping cream. "It has broken, then?"

"Yes. Four men made themselves so obnoxious that we had to discharge them just now. There has been no talk whatever of unionization as yet, but I expect a picket line tomorrow."

"Thanks for letting us know so promptly, Mr. Speers. I can't get at him myself for fifteen minutes or so yet, but I'll tell him at the earliest possible moment."

"That'll be fine, Miss Champion. Good-bye."

envelopes—herself. She pushed a button. A girl came into her office. Miss Champion said, "Here are two letters, Bessie. One is to Hatfield of InStell, the other to Lansing of WarnOil. Each is to be delivered by special messenger. Delivery is to be strictly-personal-signature-required. Thanks."

So, within a very few days after UCM's picket line had sealed the Little Gem mine as tight as a bottle, fourteen men and one woman met in GalMet's palatial conference room in the Metals Building, in New York City on Earth. Men representing such a tremendous aggregate of power had never before met in any one room. Maynard called the meeting to order, then said:

"Many of you know most of the others here, but most of you do not know us all. Please stand as I introduce you. The lady first, of course. Miss Champion, my First Secretary."

The lady, seated at a small desk off to one side of the great table, rose to her feet, bowed gracefully—not directly toward the camera—and resumed her position.

"Bryce of Metals." A slender man of fifty, with an unruly shock of graying black hair, rose, nodded, and sat down.

"Wellington of Construction." A tall, loose-jointed, sandy-haired man did the same.

"Zeckendorff of the Stockmen ... Stelling of Grain ... Killingsworth of the Producers ... Raymer of Transportation . . . Holbrook of Communications . . . these seven men are the presidents of the seven largest organizations of the Planetsmen—the organized production and service men and women of ninety five planets.

"Will you stand up, please, Mr. Speers? . . . Superintendent Speers, of the Little Gem, now being struck, one of the very few non-union copper mines in existence. Speers is sitting on a situation that very well may develop into the gravest crisis our civilization has ever known.

"Next, Admiral Guerdon Dann of Interstellar . . . who may or may not, depending pretty largely upon the outcome of this meeting, become our Galaxians' Secretary of War."

There was a concerted gasp at this, and Maynard smiled grimly. "I speak advisedly. Each of us knows something, but not one of us knows it all. The whole, I think, will shock us all.

"DuPuy of Warner Oil . . . represents the law; Interplanetary Law in particular.

"Phelps of Galactic Metals . . . is our money man.

"Hatfield of Interstellar . . . Lansing of Warner Oil . . . and I, Maynard of Galactic Metals . . . represent top management.

"Now to business. For almost two hundred years most managements have adhered to the Principle of Enlightened Self-Interest; so that, while both automation and pay-per-man-hour increased, production per man-hour increased at such a rate—especially on the planets —that there was no inflation. In fact, just slightly the opposite; for over a hundred and fifty years the purchasing power of the dollar showed a slight rising trend.

"Then, for reasons upon which there is no agreement —each faction arguing its case according to its own bias —the economic situation began to deteriorate and inflation set in. It has been spiralling. For instance, of the present price of copper, about two dollars and a half a pound, only twenty five cents is . . . Phelps?"

"Rate One, Anaconda, electrolytic, FOB smelter," the

moneyman said, "is two point four five seven dollars per

produced exclusively on Tellus. There are two reasons for this. First, automation cannot be economically applied to copper mining on Tellus or anywhere else we know of; there are no known lodes or deposits big enough. Second, the UCM is the only union that has been able to enforce the dictum that its craft shall be confined absolutely to Tellus.

"So far, I have stated facts, with no attempt to allocate responsibility or blame. I will now begin to prophesy. Information has been obtained, from sources which need not be named . . ." Most of the men chuckled; only a few of them only smiled, ". . . which leads us to believe as follows:

"Burley Hoadman is in trouble in his UCM—internal trouble. There are several local leaders, one in particular being very strong, who do not like him hogging so much of the gravy for himself. They want to get their own snouts into the gravy trough, and are gathering a lot of votes. The best way he can consolidate his position is by making a spectacular play. The Little Gem affair is his opening wedge. If he can make us fight this issue very hard, he will pull a WestHem-wide copper strike. He will refuse to settle that strike for less than a seventy five or one hundred percent increase in scale. Since the UCM's scale is already the highest in existence, that will make him a tin god on wheels.

"There hasn't been a really important strike for over

fifty years; and this one will not be important unless we ourselves make it so by putting up a real fight. Gentlemen, we have two, and only two, alternatives; we can surrender or we can fight.

"If we surrender, every other union in existence will demand a similar increase and the Labor Relations Board will grant it—and I don't need to tell you that West-Hem's corrupt judiciary and government will support the LRB. Neither do I need to dwell upon what these events will do to the already vicious spiral of inflation.

"It's easy to say 'fight', but how far must we be prepared to go? The LRB will rule against us. We will appeal. While that appeal is pending, Hoadman will call all his copper miners out. That strike will be completely effective, and as all industry slows down the public will scream for GalMet's blood. All the mass media of West-Hem will crucify me personally. As I said, we will lose the appeal—or perhaps, even before that, the government will seize the mines and give Hoadman everything he wants. In either case, if we stop at that point, we will be in even worse shape than if we had surrendered without fighting at all."

"But how much farther than that can we possibly go?" Zeckendorff demanded.

"I'm coming to that. If we fight at all, we must be prepared to go the full route. We'll drag the legal proceedings out as long as we can. Meanwhile we'll be developing copper mines on the planets. We have maps and your Metalsmen and Builders will be very good at that. We'll ram planetary copper down WestHem's collective throat. However, that ramming will not be easy. The government is very strong and it will do its utmost to block every move we make. So the most logical conclusion is that we will have to form a government of the planets and declare our complete independence of Tellus.

"We are already calling ourselves the Galaxians; that would be as good a name as any for the new government. That would probably involve a massive and effective blockade of Tellus, which in turn might cause the

a government which is to adhere strictly to the Principle of Enlightened Self-Interest.

"What we can accomplish remains to be seen. We will have to exert extreme caution; we must keep ahead of the opposition; above all, we must be able at all times to pull up short of ultimate catastrophe to Tellus.

"Whether or not we fight at all depends absolutely upon the attitude of the Planetsmen. We must have solidarity. Hoadman expects the full support of Labor, even to the extremity of a general strike of all the unions of WestHem. This would necessitate the cooperation of the Planetsmen, and he expects even that. It is psychologically impossible for any man of Hoadman's stripe to understand that on the planets there is neither Capital nor Labor; that we Galaxians are all labor and are all capitalists. Hence it is clear that unless we are sure of virtual unanimity of all Galaxians we cannot fight Hoadman at all.

"I now ask the supremely vital question— Do the Planetsmen, the most important segment by far of the Galaxians, want to go the route for a stable dollar and all that it means? You seven may retire to a private room for discussion, if you like. . . .

"But I see you don't need to," Maynard went on, as all seven men spoke practically at once; Holbrook of Communications being first by an instant. "Peter Holbrook, president of the Associated Wavesmen, has the floor."

Holbrook of Communications was the youngest man there. He was scarcely out of his twenties and was so deeply tanned that his crew-cut, sun-bleached hair seemed almost white. He looked like a professional football player; or like the expert "pole-climber" he had been until a year before. He stood up, cleared his throat, and said, "You're right, Mr. Maynard, we don't need to discuss that point. We've thought about it and talked about it a lot. We have been and are highly concerned. But I'm not the one to talk about it here. I yield the floor to Mr. Egbert Bryce, President of the Society of Metalsmen, who has been coordinating us all along on this very thing."

"*You*, Eggie?" Maynard asked, with a grin, and the tone of the meeting became less formal all of a sudden. "And you never let me in on it?"

"Me," the wiry, intense Bryce agreed. "Naturally not. You're always beating somebody's ears down about presenting a half-developed program and ours isn't developed yet at all. But you've apparently made plans for a long time ahead."

"Plenty of them, but they're all fluid. Nothing to go into at this point. Go ahead."

"All right. On this basic factor there's no disagreement whatever. No doubt or question. Tellurian labor is a bunch of plain damned fools. Idiots. Cretins. However, that's only to be expected because everybody with any brains or any guts left Tellus years ago. There's scarcely any good breeding stock left, even. So about the only ones with brains left—except for the connivers, chiselers, boodlers, gangsters, and bastardly crooked politicians—and that goes for most Tellurian capitalists, too. Right?"

"Dead right, and we don't like it one bit better than you do. That's why so much Tellurian capital is all set to join us Galaxians when we leave Tellus."

"Oh? You've gone that far? That's some of the stuff you'll go into later?"

"Yes. Go ahead."

"All right. Every time I think of Tellurian labor it makes

thought would fracture their brainless damned skulls. And as long as they get a dollar an hour more than they're worth they don't give a cockeyed tinker's damn that their bosses are stealing everything in sight that isn't welded down—and sometimes even some of that. So you can paste it in your tall silk hat, Mayn, that the Planetsmen are free men, not brainless stupid serfs. Burley Hoadman won't get any help at all from us in stealing any more megabucks than he already has stolen. Not by seven thousand spans of Steinman truss."

"Serf labor versus free men," Maynard said, thoughtfully. "Very well put, Eggie. In that connection, Speers of the Little Gem made a tape that shows the attitude of two of his best men. Will you play it, please, Miss Champion?"

She played it and Maynard went on, "We have thousands of similar recordings. The serf attitude is characteristic of non-union, as well as of union labor, and also of white-collar people as a class. In fact, it is characteristic of Tellus as a planet. In contrast to that attitude, Zeckendorff of the Stockmen brought along a tape, of which we will hear the last few sentences. Scene, a meeting of Local 3856 of the Stockmen. Occasion, the voting upon a resolution presented by a Tellurian union organizer after weeks of work. Miss Champion?"

She flipped a switch and the speaker said, "The vote is nine hundred seventy eight against; none for. That kind of crap doesn't go on the planets, Gaylord, and if you had the brain God gave a goose you'd know it. That kind of security is what life-termers on the Rock have and we don't want any part of it. Nobody but ourselves is *ever* going to tell us what we can or can't do; so you'd better get the hell out of here and back to Tellus before somebody parts your hair with a routing iron."

"I like that," Maynard said. "I like it very much. We knew in general what the sentiment is. However, pure Galaxianism—everybody pulling together harmoniously for the common good—is an ideal and as such can never be realized. The question is, can we approach it nearly enough to make it work?"

"We can try—and I think we can do it," Bryce said. "Anyway, Mayn, this first hurdle was the biggest one, and it's solid. We can guarantee that."

"Wonderful!" Maynard said. "Then we're in business —so let's get on with it."

And the meeting went on; not only for all the rest of that day, but all day and every day for two solid weeks.

Shortly after the Deston Uranium Expedition got back to Newmars, the Deston family went to Earth and to the Warner-owned, luxury-type Hotel Warner; arriving there early of an evening.

Barbara was thoroughly accustomed to red-carpet treatment. She nodded and smiled; she used first names abundantly in greeting; to a few VIP's she introduced her "husband and business partner, Carlyle Deston." A retinue escorted them up to their penthouse suite; the manager himself made sure that everything was on the beam. Lock, stock, and barrel, the place was theirs.

Deston was not used to high life, but he made a good stab at it. Even when, at the imposing portals of the Deep Space Room, the velvet rope was whisked aside and the crowd of waiting standees was ignored. But when, at the end of the long and perfect meal and of the

ly business-like office worthy in every respect of being the *sanctum sanctorum* of the second-largest firm in existence.

As has been said, Warner Oil was not a corporation. It was not even a partnership. It had been owned *in toto* by Barbara's parents as community property; it was now owned in the same way by Carlyle and Barbara Deston. Thus, it had no stock and no bonds and published no reports of any kind. It had no officers, no board of directors. It had one general manager and a few department heads; men who, despite the unimportance of their titles, were high on the list of the most powerful operators of Earth.

The Destons' first appointment was with General Manager Lansing; a big, bear-like man who picked Barbara up on sight and kissed her vigorously. "*Mighty* glad to see you again, Barbry. Glad to meet you, Carl." He engulfed Deston's hand in a huge, hard paw. "I apologize for thinking you were something that crawled out from under a rock. What you've been putting out is the damndest hairiest line of stuff I've seen since the old gut-cutting days when the old man and I were pups. But go ahead, Barbry."

"First, I want to assure you, Uncle Paul, that neither Carl nor I will bother you any more than father did. Not as much, in fact, because neither of us has any delusions as to who is running WarnOil and we both want you to keep on running it."

"Thanks, both of you. I was hoping, of course, but I got a little dubious when Carl here started showing so many long, sharp, curly teeth."

"I understand. Second, I'm very glad that all of you— all that count, I mean—approve of Carl's program."

"Should have incorporated long ago. As for the hell-raising—wow!" He slapped himself resoundingly on the leg. "If we can push *half* of that stuff through it'll rock the whole damned galaxy on its foundations."

"Third, how is the probate coming along?"

"I'd better call DuPuy in here for that, I. . . ."

"Uh-uh, listen! We don't want two solid hours of whereases and hereinbefores. You talk our language."

"We're steam-rollering 'em and it tickles me a foot up . . ." Lansing broke off and into a bellow of laughter. "Every damn shyster the government has got is screaming bloody murder and threatening everything he can think of, including complete confiscation, but they haven't got a leg to stand on. They *can't* tax anything except what little stuff we have here on Tellus, and the inheritance tax on that will be only a few megabucks. Everything else belongs to Newmars, where there's no inheritance tax, no income tax, and hardly any property tax; and the fact that DuPuy writes Newmars' laws has nothing to do with the case. So after DuPuy and his crew get tired of quibbling and horsing around we'll pay it out of petty cash and never miss it."

The Destons, during the next few days, held conference after conference, during which hundreds of details were ironed out; and as a by-product of which the news spread abroad that the heiress was very active indeed in the management of civilization-wide Warner Oil.

One morning, then, at nine o'clock, Barbara herself punched the series of letters and numerals that was the unlisted and close-held number of Doris Champion, the First Secretary of Upton Maynard, the president of

Galactic Metals, the largest firm that civilization had ever

thought." I'm Barbara Warner Deston of WarnOil. Please arrange a half-hour face-to-face for Mr. Deston and me with Mr. Maynard. There's no *great* hurry about it; any time today will do."

"A half *hour! Today?* I'm terribly sorry, Mrs. Deston, but it's simply impossible. Why, he's booked solid for . . ."

"I know he's busy, Miss Champion, but so are we. Just tell him, please, that he is the first metals man we have called, and that tomorrow morning we will call Ajax."

"Very well. If you'll give me a ten-second brief I'll see what we can possibly do and call you back."

"No briefing. You have my private number. We'll be here until twelve o'clock." Barbara's hand moved toward the cut-off switch; but Miss Champion, being a really smart girl, smelled a deal so big that even a top-bracket FirSec should duck—and *fast.* Wherefore:

"Hold the beam for fifty seconds, please, Mrs. Deston," she said, and snapped down the button that made her office as tight as the vault of a bank. Then, "I'm sorry to interrupt, Mr. Maynard, but Mrs. Deston of WarnOil is on." She cut the audio then, but kept on speaking rapidly.

In thirty seconds the keen, taut face of Upton Maynard appeared upon Barbara's plate. "Good morning,

Mrs. Deston. Something about metal, I gather? A little out of your line, isn't it?"

"That's right, Mr. Maynard," Barbara agreed. She added nothing and for a moment he, too, was silent. Then:

"It'll have to be after closing," Maynard said.

"That's quite all right. We'll fit our time to yours and you may name the place."

"Seventeen ten. Your office. Satisfactory?"

"Perfectly. Thank you, Mr. Maynard," and as Barbara's hand moved to cut com Maynard's voice went on:

"Get my wife, Miss Champion. Tell her I'll be late again getting home this evening."

"How do you do, Mister Maynard." Barbara shook his hard cordially. "You haven't met my husband. Carlyle Deston of Deston and Deston, Incorporated."

As the two men shook hands, Maynard said, "Incorporated, eh? This room is spy-proof, of course."

"Solid," Deston assured him.

"Okay, Mrs. Deston; what have you got?"

"Oh, it's Carl's party, really. My part of this project was just to bring you two men together," and Deston took over.

"This is such a weirdie, Mr. Maynard, that I'll have to give it to you in stages." He opened a bulging accordion-pleated case and began to spread its contents out over the table. "Barbara and I discovered a planet that's thousands of parsecs beyond where any human being had ever been before. We named it 'Barbizon'. We did, by proxy, all the development work necessary to establish full ownership of the entire planet.

"Here's an envelope-full of astronautic and planetological data. Here's the file on registration, work, proveup, transfer, and so on. Here's the certification, by Earth's most eminent firm of consulting engineers—Littleton, Bayless, Clifton, and Snelling itself, no less—that said planet Barbizon is a new discovery; that it is exactly where we said it was; that all required work has been done; that the bodies of manganese ore actually exist; that the *in situ* values run as high as three dollars and seventy one cents per ton; that. . . ."

"*Suckered*, by God!" Maynard smacked his right hand flat down against the table's top. "You *mouse-trapped* us —and that hasn't been done before for twenty five years." His sharp gray eyes bored into Deston's with rapidly-mounting respect. "To skip the rest of the preliminaries for the moment, what have you two actually got?"

"I told you he's quick on the uptake, Carl," Barbara laughed, and Deston said, "Uranium, Mr. Maynard. Solid enough for full automation and enough of it to supply every possible demand of all civilization from now on."

"My . . . good . . . God." Maynard almost collapsed back into his chair. "I knew it would have to be something big . . . but *automated uranium*—okay. Go ahead. Somebody told you I like fully-developed presentations?"

"That's right. So here are the applications complete, and here are the final patents—not only from Tellus, but also from Galmetia and Newmars as well. All this is proof of ownership; with—according to DuPuy of Warn-Oil—no possibility whatever of successful challenge."

The tycoon, who had begun to examine the documents, replaced them in the envelope and nodded approvingly. "If Pete DuPuy says it's ironclad it really is. So I'm ready for Stage Two."

"Here's a large-scale tri-di, in dilometers, of the largest ore-body. There are a lot of others, but this whole plateau is one solid mass of jewelry ore. It isn't pure pitchblende or pure anything else; it's been altered down by heat and pressure to an average specific gravity of about ten point one. So it will run well over ten metric gigatons to the cubic kilometer, and you can read the cubage for yourself. Do you wonder that we wouldn't talk to anyone except you in person about it?"

"That's evident—quite." For ten silent minutes Maynard scanned data with practised ease. Then, "There are a few points that need clarification. I know that there are a lot of crackpot planetary claims allowed every year; on planets so worthless that they lapse into the public domain as soon as the crackpots lose interest, go

"That did take a little doing," Deston admitted, and Barbara laughed again. "Our development work was done by the stupidest people we could find, and the man we made foreman was the stupidest one of the whole lot. We didn't appear at any Bureau of Planets ourselves, of course. Our proxies were a couple of very good actors who had studied being crackpots until they were letter-perfect. Then we waited until all *LitBay*'s field men were out on jobs. Our proxies were in such a tearing rush to get Barbizon nailed down that they opened negotiations by offering double fees—and you know what *LitBay*'s usual fees are—for fast action. So since it was so obviously just another crackpot location, who was ever to know or care that it was a couple of office-boys who went out? And, some way or other, their scintillometers happened to get swapped temporarily for a pair of slightly finagled ones we had on board."

"I see." Maynard shook his head admiringly. "So the thing never got upstairs in their office . . . and I can't twit Littleton about it because it never got anywhere near me, either. Okay. Barbizon is of course lifeless—and the whole planet reeks—this ninety-hour limit on the manganese location is the coolest spot on the planet, I suppose."

"That's right. We couldn't put anybody in armor, so we didn't let anybody work over ten six-hour days."

"Refresh my memory." Maynard flipped pages; came

up with a single sheet of paper. "Ah. All your men were over sixty five—and the *LitBay* kids were on the ground only nine hours. So when this is over you'll notify them that they've had ten percent of a year's permissible radiation, I suppose."

Barbara smiled meaningly. "No, Mr. Maynard. It has just occurred to me that you might like to tell Mr. Littleton about that yourself."

"So he'll think I mousetrapped him?" Maynard blushed to the top of his bald head. "And I'm small-souled enough to take advantage of that face-saving offer. Thanks. But to get on with it, there's a glaring vacancy in these data—about that incredible tri-di. . . ."

"It's there, Mr. Maynard," Barbara put in. "It really is."

"I know it is. With a planet whose radiation would trip a scanner at four or five astronomical units out, and what it has cost you to nail it down, faking would be completely pointless. No, the missing information is, how did you make that tri-di? We know of *one* honest-to-God oil-witch . . ." He paused and looked pointedly at Barbara, "but I've never heard of anyone who ever witched enough virgin ore of any kind to load a shotgun shell. Do you, Deston, claim to be the first metal-witch? Excuse me—'warlock', I suppose I should have said."

"I most emphatically do not. Such crackpot stuff as that? No: 'Improved instrumentation and techniques' is the full explanation. Secret, of course—obviously. And whatever made you think Barbara is an oil-witch? They're sinking as many dry holes as anybody."

"Yeah." As Maynard said it, the word was the essence of disbelief. "Lately. I've noticed. You don't want to get her shot. Smart boy—if I were you I wouldn't either."

"But sir, I assure . . ."

"Yeah," Maynard said again. "I'm assured, and I don't leak. So go ahead with Stage Three."

"Thank you. Stage Three is to sell you the planet

72

Barbizon, lock, stock, and barrel, for the sum of one

a Santa Claus, making us a free-gratis-for-nothing Christmas present of God-knows-how-many mega—hell, no; not megabucks, it'll be billions. With production equalling full demand and the price set by the PESI formula it'll be God-knows-how-many gigabucks over the long pull. So you'll have to do some more explaining, Deston."

"I was going to; but first, who else could possibly handle a project that big the way it should be handled?"

"Granted. We're geared for it; no one else is. But you know and I know that with Barbizon nailed down tight you can set and get any royalty you please."

"I know." Deston smiled suddenly. "We just did. We toyed with the idea of socking you, but everything was against it and nothing for it. First; we, too, adhere to the Principle of Enlightened Self-Interest."

"I see." Maynard relaxed and his mien lightened tremendously. "That shaft, son, dead-centered the gold. Go ahead."

"Second; since metal isn't our dish, our take will be pure gravy, and the easier the bite we put on you and the deeper you get into the planet Barbizon, the more convinced you will become that we knew what we're doing."

"It's beginning to make sense. All this will soften me up for the real whingo. So what will Santa Claus, as represented by Deston and Deston Ink, do then?"

"Having established the fact beyond question that we

have, by means of our highly advanced instrumentation and techniques, found an immense amount of one highly desirable natural resource, we will ask you what you want next. We will look for it and we will probably find it."

"And, having found it?"

"Are you sold, up to this point?"

"Definitely." Maynard's fingers drummed lightly upon the soft plastic covering of the arm of his chair. "If the stuff were not there you wouldn't be here: none of this would make any sense at all."

"We will then prove to you that we have found whatever it was that you wanted. The next step will be to merge GalMet and WarnOil—Barbara thinks that 'Metals And Energy' would be a good name for the new corporation. Now, considering . . ."

"You're leaving out one element, Carl," Barbara put in.

"Not exactly. That's speculation, and at the moment I'm . . ."

"He'll be interested in that particular speculation," Barbara broke in, "so I'll tell him. Mr. Maynard, DuPuy says that while it is not yet politically feasible to even suggest including InStell in this proposed merger, he thinks that the present gentlemen's agreement would not only continue, but would become even more so."

Maynard nodded. "I was beginning to think along that same line myself. Go ahead, Deston."

"Considering the size and scope of the proposed firm, and the fact that it would not have to explore, but would have at its command any amount of any natural resource—how fast could it grow?"

"*What* a program . . . what a *program!*" Rock-still, Maynard thought for minutes. "I've always insisted on a fully-developed presentation, but *this* . . . the three biggest firms in existence, all pulling together and with everything they need. . . ." He paused.

"Lansing and DuPuy both said the trouble would be to

keep it from growing too fast—getting all porous and

both of you playing footsie with Hatfield of InStell—with the figurehead president not necessarily knowing quite everything that goes on."

"That sounds good. Lansing's an operator, and so is Hatfield."

"Last, the stock classes will be such, and Deston and Deston's payments will be such, that voting control will be . . . oh, yes, 'conserved' was the word DuPuy used. That's all, sir."

"Not by several stages that isn't all. You've done altogether too much work on this to have it stop at this point. Next stage, please."

Deston looked baffledly at Barbara; who gave him an I-told-you-so smile and said, "You knew darn well you'd have to tell him the whole wild thing, so go right ahead and do it."

"You certainly will, son," Maynard agreed. He had thought that Deston, like so many other space officers, had used the glamor of his status to marry money. That idea was out. He wasn't the type. Neither was Barbara; glamor-boys by the score had been trying to marry her ever since she was fifteen . . . and they *could* find metal . . . and this whole deal showed honest-to-God *brains.* After a very brief pause he went on, "Neither of you cares any more about money *as money* than I do. So it's something else. I'm beginning to think, Barbara, that you were right in ascribing most of this to Carl, here."

"Of course I was." Barbara grinned wickedly; she had known exactly what Maynard had been thinking. "*My* mind doesn't work that way at all. It really doesn't."

"Okay, okay; don't rub it in." Maynard answered her grin, not her words. "I'm sure we'll go along, but after all this you'll *have* to tell me what you're really after."

"The trouble is, I can't, at all exactly." Deston spread out both hands. "Too much extrapolation—altogether too many unknowns—at this point the picture becomes ver-*ee* unclear."

"Okay. Your thinking so far has been eminently precise; I'd like to hear your extrapolations and speculations."

"Okay. MetEnge, or whatever the new firm turns out to be, will employ DesDes as consulting geologists; that is, we would work independently of, and eventually replace, your geological staff and your prospectors and wildcatters and so on. If you should wish to employ us on an exclusive basis . . . ?"

"That goes without saying."

"We would require a very substantial annual fee, payable in MetEnge voting stock at the market. All of our new discoveries, including the find not theretofore revealed, will be leased, not sold, to MetEnge."

"Ah. 'Conserve' is right. Pete has a very fine Italian hand indeed. I'm going to like this. Not money at all, but power."

"Not exactly—or rather, we want power back of us. We want to explore subspace and deep space in ways and to depths that have never even been thought of before. There must be thousands of things not only undiscovered, but not even imagined yet. Barbara and I want to go out after some of them; and, since nobody can have any idea whatever of what we may run into, it is clear that the highly special ship may turn out to be the smallest part of what we'll need. So we'll want the full backing of the biggest private organization it is possible to build. A firm big enough and strong enough to operate on a scale now possible only to governments—one able

fifty, DesDes will be on a non-retainer basis all the time you are out and will have to split fifty-fifty."

"But there isn't going to be anything the least bit commercial about it!" Barbara protested.

"You're wrong there, young lady. Research always has paid off big, in hard dollars. So I'll buy the package." Maynard got up and shook hands with them both. "I'll take this stuff along. WarnOil's legal department is acting for you, I suppose?"

"Yes."

"In the morning we'll send them a check for one dollar, with a firm binder, by special messenger and start things rolling."

"Oh, you don't think it's silly, then?" Barbara asked. "I was awfully afraid you'd think this last part of it was."

"Far from it. I'm sure it will be immensely profitable."

"In that case we have some more news for you." Both Destons were smiling happily. "We also found a deposit of native copper and copper ores big enough and solid enough for full automation."

"*Copper!*" Maynard yelled, jumping out of his chair. "Why the hell didn't you bring that up first?"

"When would this other thing have been settled if we had?"

"You've got a point there. Where is it?"

"Belmark. Strulsa Three, you know."

"*Belmark!* We *prospected* Belmark—it's colonized—

fairly well along. We didn't find any more copper there than anywhere else."

"It'd be impossible to find by any usual method, and it's over five hundred miles from the nearest town. Our finding it was a . . . not an accident, but a byproduct—while we were training for uranium. If we'd known then what we know now I'd've found you a big one, but we weren't interested in copper."

"How big is this one?"

"It'll smelt something over a hundred million tons of metal. It'll tide you over, but I don't know about amortizing the plant."

"We can cut the price in half and still amortize in months . . . but amortization cuts no ice here . . . let's see, production of primary copper runs about six million tons . . . but if we cut the price to the bone, God knows what the sales potential is. . . ."

Maynard immersed himself in thought, then went on, "Definitely. That's the way to do it. Hit 'em hard. Really slug 'em . . . that is, if . . . how sure are you, Carl, that you can find us another big deposit? Within, say, a year?"

Deston's mind flashed back over the comparatively few copper surveys he had made. "Copper isn't too scarce and it tends to aggregate. I'll guarantee to find you one at least three times that big within thirty days."

"Good! Let's cut the chatter, then. I can use your com?"

"Of course," Barbara said; but Maynard's question had been purely a matter of form. He was already punching his call.

"Miss Champion," Maynard said, when his FirSec's face showed on the screen. "I hope you don't have any engagements for tonight."

"I have a date, but it's with Don, so he'll understand perfectly when I break it." She did not ask any questions; she merely raised her perfectly-sculptured black eyebrows.

"I want him, too, so bring him downtown as soon as you can. And please get hold of Quisenberry and Felton and tell them to get to the office jet-propelled. That's

"You've got the dope on it here in your office?"

"Yes." Deston went to his desk and brought back a briefcase. "Here's everything necessary."

"Thanks immensely. We'll own it shortly. As for your royalties, we've been accused of claim-stealing, but we usually pay discoverers' royalties and we'll be glad to on this one. *Brother*, will we be glad to! So Phelps will— no, he'd take it for nothing, the skinflint, and lick his chops. I'll have Don Smith take care of it tonight. And now that that's settled," Maynard smiled as he had not smiled in weeks, "about that trip of yours. I envy you. If we were twenty five years younger I'd talk my wife into going along with you. I'd better call her; and I'd like to have her meet both of you."

"Why, we'd be *delighted* to meet her!" Barbara exclaimed.

Mrs. Maynard proved to be a willowy, strong-featured, gracious woman with whom the years had dealt very lightly. She was as glad to meet the Destons, about whom she had heard so much, as they were to meet her. And so on.

"I'm very sorry, Mrs. Maynard," Barbara said, finally, "that we had to keep your husband so . . ."

"Think nothing of it," Maynard interrupted, briskly. "Just one of those things. If you'd like to come downtown to the office, Floss, I'll take you out to dinner sometime during the evening."

"I would like to, Upton, thanks. I'll be down in an hour or so."

The Destons escorted Maynard up to the roof and to his waiting aircar; and after it had taken off:

"What do you suppose he meant by that 'just one of those things' crack?" Deston asked.

"Why, he was on a *com*, silly, so he was *afraid* to say anything! Even that he was going to work all night!" Barbara explained, excitedly. "*That's* how big he knows it is!" and the two went enthusiastically into each other's arms.

Quisenberry and Felton got to Calmet's main office almost as soon as Maynard himself did. When the two engineers came in Maynard looked at them with the well-known expression of the canary-containing cat.

"Good evening, gentlemen," he said, with a wide and cryptic grin. "I trust that your hearts are in good shape? And your nerves? That you are both sufficiently well integrated to withstand the shock of your trouble-making young lives?"

"Try us," Quisenberry said. He was a black-haired, black-eyed, deeply-tanned man, a little past thirty, who had worked himself up the hard way; clear up from the lowest low of a copper mine. He looked—if not exactly sullen, at least as though he was very sure that what he had been doing on his own was vastly more important than any piffling, niggling conference with THE BIG BOSS. "I'll live through it, I'm sure."

"Okay. Each of you take a table; you'll need lots of room. Quisenberry, here's everything you'll need on a deposit of copper. Felton, ditto, uranium. I want preliminary roughouts of those projects as fast as you can get them. Very rough: plus-or-minus twenty five percent will be close enough. Now, Don and Miss Champion, what we'll have to do tonight is rough out a full operational on copper in the light of information that has just come to hand."

After what may have been an hour Mrs. Maynard came in and Quisenberry came up for air. His table was littered with hand-books, machine-tapes of various kinds, graphs, charts, and wadded-up scratch-paper; much of which had overflowed onto the floor.

"But this is *incredible*, sir." It was the first time either engineer had called Maynard "sir" in over a year. "Of course I can't say that it's absolutely impossible for any such deposit as this to occur, but . . ." Quisenberry paused.

Maynard grinned again, but pleasantly, this time. "Do you think I'd have all that stuff faked up and then come down here and work all night myself just to put you two through the wringer?"

"Put that way, of course not . . . but . . ." Quisenberry paused again and Felton, who had stopped work and was listening with both ears, came in with:

"Quizz said it, Mr. Maynard, and mine's ten to the fourth as hard to swallow as his. I can't make myself believe that there's that much uranium in one place anywhere in the universe."

"I know exactly how you feel," Maynard assured them. "I was flabbergasted myself. You may take it as a fact, however, that all that data is accurate to within the appropriate limits of error. I myself am so convinced of its reliability that I am going to give you two men all the authorization you'll need and full authority to build and to operate fully-automated plants. Satisfactory? That's what you've been getting ready for all this time, isn't it?"

"Yes, *sir!*" Quisenberry said, and:

"You *said* it, sir!" Felton agreed.

At seven fifty five Maynard asked the group at large, "Everybody ready to eat? I'll call Beardsley's."

Neither engineer would leave his job; so, after Miss Champion had ordered up two one-gallon hot-pots of coffee and a good spread of smorgasbord, the two couples went to Beardsley's for dinner—a dinner that lasted for an hour and a half and cost Maynard exactly forty dollars (including tip). Then a GalMet aircar took Mrs.

Maynard home and another one took the other three

ding, so we'll have to pay top prices and bonuses. Check to here?"

"Check and okay."

"Plant capacity. Assuming that you want to cut the price down to somewhere between eleven and twelve cents. . . ."

"You're right on the beam, Quizz. Nearer eleven, I think."

"Extrapolating on that basis, my guessometer says that we'll have to be producing at the rate of fifteen million tons by the end of the first year. That's a mighty big plant, boss. That's one supreme *hell* of a big plant."

"I know. I like those figures very much."

"You won't like these next ones, I'm afraid. On this rush-and-bonus basis it'll take pretty close to twenty five megabucks in the first couple of months, and the total—well, it's a very rough guess at this point. All I'm sure of is the order of magnitude, but the total to first pour will probably run somewhere in the neighborhood of seventy five megabucks."

"Thanks. That's close enough for now. Just so we don't get caught short of cash in the till."

"But listen—sir—Phelps will have a litter of lizards!"

"He'll be amenable to reason when he finds out that we are entering a completely new era in metals. Felton, how about you?"

Felton—a brawny youth with butch-cut straw-colored

hair and blue eyes—could not answer immediately because his mouth was full of *shrimp a la Creole*. He swallowed hastily, then said:

"Since this will have to be a crash-pri job, too, everything Quizz said will apply. Add high radiation to all that, and a hostile dead planet clear out to hellangone beyond anywhere, and the tab gets no smaller fast. My best guesstimate as of now is that the total will crowd a hundred megabucks."

"Fair enough. Thanks a . . ."

"One thing first," Felton interrupted. "Are you sure enough of this—this super-bonanza—for me to roust Bassler out right now? Tell him to cut out all this ten-cent petty-larceny rock-scratching we're doing now, break out all the armor we've got and order more, and start—but quick—jassacking some of that high-grade out of there and hauling it to Galmetia?"

"An excellent idea. Splendid! If I'd thought of it I would have suggested it hours ago. Go ahead."

Felton did so and Maynard went on, "Since you fellows made these estimates in hours instead of weeks I'll give you plenty of leeway. Miss Champion, please issue two preliminary authorizations: Quisenberry, seventy five megabucks; Felton, a hundred."

Preliminaries! Not maxes! Staring at each other as though they could not believe their ears, the two engineers shook hands solemnly with each other, and then with all three of the others. Then they poured themselves two more cups of strong black coffee and went back to work.

Work went on until half past five. Then, since each would have to be on the job by nine o'clock, Maynard broke it up so that each could get three hours' sleep. All top-echelon private offices were equipped for that. Night work was an essential part of such man-killing jobs as theirs; a part that envious underlings knew nothing about. It had happened before and it would happen again. And again and again.

This entire episode was just another one of those

"Nice going. Are you sure we can stay out a few months? I'll locate enough copper while we're gone, of course, to last you for a thousand years."

"Positive. We'll drop the price of copper to where Hoadman will think he's been hit by a pile-driver."

"So solly . . . and the effect on all industry of cheap and plentiful copper—added to your widely-advertised fact that in a few months everybody can buy all the uranium they want for less than thirty cents per pound —will take the curse off of the public image GalMet will get when you smash UCM flat?"

"Not quite all of it, perhaps, but it will certainly help."

"That's for sure. Okay; what do you want firstest and mostest of, now that copper and uranium are out of the way?"

"I wish I could tell you." Maynard's fingers drummed quietly on his desk. "You thought it would be simple? It isn't. It's all fouled up in the personnel situation I told you I'd tell you about. We have six good people— damned good people—each of whom wants a planetary project so passionately that if I stack the deck in favor of any one of them, all the others will blast me to a cinder and run, not walk, to the nearest exit."

Deston did not say anything and after a moment the older man went on, "Platinum and iridium, of course. Osmium, tungsten . . ."

"Tungsten isn't too scarce, is it?"

"For the possible demand, very much so. I'd like to sell it for fifteen cents a pound. Beryllium, tantalum, titanium, thorium, cerium—and, for the grand climax to end all climaxes—*rhenium*."

"Huh? I don't think I've ever heard rhenium even mentioned since my freshman chemistry."

"Not too many people have, but right now I'm as full of information as the dog that sniffed at the third rail. It's so rare that no mineral of it is known; it exists only as a trace of impurity in a very few minerals. Strangely enough, practically only in molybdenite."

"Just a minute." Deston went to a book-case, took out a hand-book, and flipped pages. "Um . . . um . . . mm. Dwimanganese. *Not* usually associated with manganese. *Maybe* it occurs in molybdenite as the sulphide—ReS_2 and/or Re_2S_7—commercial source, flue dust from the roasting of Arizona molybdenite. . . ."

"Right. We own the outfit. That's *why* we own it. It produces a few tons a *year* of Cottrell dust, which yields just about enough rhenium to irritate one eyeball. Production cost, five dollars and seventeen cents per gram."

"But what's it *good* for? Contact points . . . cat mass . . . heavy duty igniters, it says here." Deston tapped the page with his forefinger. "No tonnage outlet there."

"What would you think of an alloy that had a yield point—not ultimate tensile, mind you, but *yield*—of well over a million pounds, and yet an elongation of better than five percent?"

Deston whistled. "I *would* have said it was a pure pipe dream. What else is in it?"

"Mostly tungsten. A lot of tantalum. Rhenium around ten percent. The research isn't done yet, but they're far enough along to know that they'll have something utterly fantastic. The problem, Byrd tells me, is to determine the optimum formula and environment for the growth and matting of single crystals of metal—tungsten 'whiskers', you know—you know about them."

"A little, of course, but not too much. I'm a 'troncist."

"I know. Well, they're playing around now with soak-

rhenium runs less than one part in billions. So if there is any big mass of it anywhere the others are apt to be there too, and a hell of a lot more of 'em."

"All the better, even from a project standpoint. Two prime sources of anything are a lot better than one."

"I didn't mean that. All that stuff is terrifically heavy, and it's got to be close enough to the surface to get at. I simply can't visualize what kind of a planet could possibly have what we want. It *won't* be Tellus-Type, that's for damn certain sure."

"I couldn't care less about that. We can set up automation on anything that isn't hotter than dull red."

"Okay. That brings us back, then, to personnel. This Byrd—has he got what it takes to run such a weirdie as this rhenium thing will almost have to be?"

"Definitely, but Doctor Cecily Byrd isn't a man. Very much the opposite, which is exactly what is thickening the soup. If we could get hold of as little as one megaton of rhenium, so as to add this new alloy leybyrdite to cheap uranium and copper, it would make MetEnge such a public benefactor that it'd be a case of 'the King can do no wrong'. But if I deal one card from the bottom of the deck to 'Curly' Byrd all hell will be out for noon."

"That sounds like something more than ordinary sex antagonism."

"It is. Much more. She not only uses weapons men don't have—and she's got 'em, believe me—but she brags about it. She's a carrot-topped, freckle-faced, shanty-Irish mick, with the shape men drool about and itching to use it—with a megavac for a brain and an ice-cube for a heart. She's half cobra, half black widow, half bitch, and one hundred percent hell-cat on wheels."

"She must be quite a gal, to add up to two hundred and fifty percent."

"She adds up to all that. So do the others. I would have fired her a year ago—she hadn't been on the job three weeks before she started making passes at me—but I haven't been able to find anyone else nearly as good as she is."

"That's a mighty tough signal to read."

"It's a unique situation. I've been gathering those people for over two years, getting ready to expand, and we haven't found anything big enough to expand into. I had eight of them. They were hard enough to handle before I gave Felton and Quisenberry their projects, but ever since then the other six have been damn near impossible. Each has tremendous ability and drive; each is as good as either Felton or Quisenberry and knows it. All working at about ten percent load; with nowhere in the galaxy to go to do any better. Frustrated—tense—sore as boils and touchy as fulminate—knives out, not only for each other, but also for Smith and me. Four men and two women. Purdom hasn't got any sex-appeal at all; Byrd oozes it at every pore. So I tell you rhenium first and the sex-pot is first out. So the other five *know* she got it by sleeping with me, and she—the God damned bitch!—grins like the Chesire cat and rubs it in that *she* has got what it takes to land the big ones."

"That's a hell of a picture, chief. I simply can't visualize top-bracket executives acting that way."

"You haven't handled enough people for years enough. They can't act any other way. What I've been wanting to do, every time she sticks her damned sexy neck out, is wring it . . . wait a minute; that gives me an idea . . . yes, that'll work. The minute they find out for sure—

they must all suspect it already—that you're an honest-

"Could be, at that . . . so maybe we'd better make it a straight tri-di survey for everything you're interested in. That would save time, in fact, over all. What kind of a list would that be?"

"Here." Maynard reached into a drawer and sailed a sheet of paper across his desk. "The full want list, which we boiled down to the must-haves."

Deston caught the paper and read it. "Is that all?"

"Isn't that enough? You're a brute for punishment."

"I'm surprised, is all, that gold isn't on it."

"*Gold!*" Maynard snorted. "Besides currency base, jewelry, and show, what's it good for? We've never touched it and never intend to—produce a few tons too much and you upset the economy instead of benefitting it."

"I never thought of it that way, but that's right. Okay, chief, we'll flit. I'll keep you posted. 'Bye."

Deston strode out and Maynard flipped a switch. "Please get Wharton, Bender, Camp, Byrd, Train, and Purdom and bring 'em into the conference room. No note-pads and no recorder."

"Very well, sir," Miss Champion said; and in a few minutes four men and three women were walking toward the long table at the head of which Maynard sat.

"I for one was *busy*, Mister Maynard!" Cecily Byrd snapped. She was something under thirty, five feet ten in her nylons, and beautifully built. She moved with the lithe grace of a trained dancer. Her thick, brick-red, medium-bobbed hair was naturally and stubbornly curly; with a curliness no hair-dresser had ever been able to subdue. Her untannable skin was heavily freckled and, except for a touch of lipstick, she wore no make-up. Her features, while regular enough, were too bold and too strong by far for prettiness. Her mien was sullen and defiant; her eyes—smoldering green fires—swept the bare expanse of table. "What? No pads and pencils? No mikes? Isn't this conference going to be of such gravid and world-shaking import that its every word and nuance should be preserved for the edification of all ages to come?"

"Shut up, Byrd, and all of you sit down."

The red-head gasped and all the others stared; for this was something new. President Maynard had never before spoken to any one of them except in formal terms. Wondering and silent, they all sat down and Maynard smiled at them wolfishly one by one. After a long half minute of this he spoke.

"I've been looking forward to this moment for a long long time" he gloated. "But first, I wonder if any one of you has any idea of why I put up with all eight of you so long? Such intractable, intransigent hellions; such knuckle-dusting, back stabbing, rampaging jerks as you all have been?"

"That's easy!" the red-head snapped, before any one of the eager others could say a word. "Hog-the-talent. Dog-in-the-manager. Standard Operating Procedure."

"Wrong. You're also wrong in claiming to be busy. Not one of you has even the remotest inkling of what the word means. But you are all going to find out. *How* you'll find out! As soon as this meeting is over each of you will be handed a planetary-project authorization and will . . ."

"*What?*" "Huh?" "Where?" "How come?" Six voices shouted or shrieked almost as one.

"Whereupon each of you will proceed to design and

staff a full-scale, optimum-tonnage plant, exactly as you

"From me?" Maynard asked quietly.

"Well . . . no."

"Nor will you. You'll be on your own; subject to Top Management only in matters of policy—such as no pirating of personnel from each other, for instance. That's so none of you can come around later, bitching and belly-aching that your flop was due to the way we cramped your style. If each of you does a job, and I hope you will; fine. Anybody who doesn't will get fired. I would enjoy firing you, Train, and Byrd. Any questions?"

The six looked at each other, almost in consternation. Even "Curly" Byrd was mute. Finally Train spoke.

"Maybe . . . to be tossing out *that* kind of money . . . this, on top of Barbizon and Belmark, really blows the plug. But I still don't think that Mrs. Deston is a metal-witch. It doesn't make sense."

"Of course she isn't," Rose Purdom, a plumpish, forty-ish blonde put in. "Or she'd have done it before. It's a new talent. *Mister* Deston. Those huge finds were just to prove to a certain hard-nosed tycoon that he could do it. That's what's really back of this gigantic super-merg-er."

"If any or all of you want to believe in that super-natural twaddle it's all right with me," Maynard said, dryly. "What I am authorized to say is that the firm of Deston and Deston Incorporated has, by marked im-provements in instrumentation and techniques, been able to take noteworthy strides in the science or art of locating large deposits of certain metals."

"Comet-gas!" Train rasped. "You're right, Rose, it's Deston. *Es macht mir garnichts aus* who finds the stuff, or how; but just one question, Mr. Maynard. Are you going to play this straight, on a first-found-first-out basis?"

"Absolutely. Thus, either Wharton or Camp will probably be first, the lady Byrd here last. Probably all of you, however, except Byrd, will have your locations before you're ready for them."

"But if probability governs, I *might* come in first," Cecily Byrd said, looking pointedly at Maynard.

"The possibility, although vanishingly small, does exist," Maynard admitted. "Therefore, *if* that event occurs, I want you all to know now as a fact that it will be because rhenium is discovered first in a non-selective survey, and *not* because. . . ." He paused and his icy gray eyes scanned as much of a highly-sculptured green garment as was visible above the table's top, "I repeat, *not* because of our Doctor Byrd's generosity with her charms; which, by the exercise of super-human self-control, I have managed so far to resist. Now go back to your offices, all of you, and start earning part of your pay."

The red-head flushed hotly—it was the first time anyone there had seen her blush—but not even that blast could dampen the enthusiasm of the melee that followed. They shook hands all around; they whacked each other—including Maynard and Miss Champion—on the back; the men kissed the women—including Miss Champion—vigorously; and they all babbled excitedly. In fact, it took fifteen minutes for Maynard to get them out of the conference room.

And the six engineer-scientist-executives who finally left that room were very different from the six who had entered it such a short time before.

The Destons and MetEnge, on a fifty-fifty basis, had

bought from InStell the *Procyon's* hulk, as is, at its an-

of the couples had children. Every man and every wo-man had passed a series of physical, mental, and psy-chological examinations.

With this special ship, then, and with this super-spe-cial crew, the Destons set out.

In the con-room there was now a forty-foot tri-di of the galaxy, with an eight-inch, roughly globular cluster of red dots in a spiral arm, much nearer to one edge than to the center of the huge lens. The Destons sat at two bewildering-instrumented desks. Behind them stood big, hard, tough Captain Theodore Jones, with his plat-inum-blonde wife Bernice. Her left hand rested upon his right shoulder; her spectacular head rested thought-fully upon her hand.

At Jones' left, toward the massed control-boards of the ship, his fifteen top officers stood at ease; at his right was a group of twenty-odd scientists.

"So *that's* what all explored space amounts to." Jones pointed at the tiny globe in the enormous, discus-shaped, light-point-filled volume which represented the galaxy. "I simply would not have believed it. Damn it, Babe, are you *sure* that thing is to scale?"

"To within one percent, yes. That's why Bobby and I are going to work fourteen hours a day instead of six. I'm not going to try to tell any of you what to do"—Des-ton's eyes swept both groups—"because each of you knows more about his own job than I do. So let's get at it."

The *Procyon* flashed to the nearest one of the ninety five colonized planets and Carlyle and Barbara Deston taped their three-dimensional surveys; the man on metals, the woman on oil, coal, water and natural gas. Nor was her part any less important than his. The use of fuels as such, while large, was insignificant in comparison with their use in petrochemistry. Led by Plastics, that industry had grown so fast that not even WarnOil's fantastic expansion had been able to keep up with it.

Day after day, planet after planet, they surveyed the ninety five colonized and all the virgin planets they had scanned so sketchily on their first trip. Deston found immense deposits of several of the "wanted" metals, including copper, and Barbara found plenty of water and fuels. Tungsten and tantalum, however, were no more abundant on any of those planets than they were on Earth; and rhenium existed only in almost imperceptible traces. Therefore the *Procyon* set out, on an immensely helical course, toward the center of the galaxy.

On their first expedition the Destons had learned so much that they could work any planet whose sun they could see. Now, as their psionic powers kept on increasing, their astronomers had to push the *Procyon's* telescopes farther and farther out into the immensity of space to keep them busy.

Days lengthened into weeks, and life aboard the immense sky-rover settled down into a routine. Adults worked, read, studied, loafed, and tuned in programs of entertainment and of instruction. Children went to school and/or played just as though they were at home. In fact, they *were* at home. Except that physical travel outside the hull was forbidden, life aboard the starship was very similar to, and in many ways more rewarding than, life in any village of civilization.

Deston and Barbara, however, worked and slept and

ate, and that was all. Fourteen hours per day every day

VIII

THE BATTLE OF NEW YORK SPACEPORT

GALACTIC METALS moved its main office from Earth to Galmetia. WarnOil's was already on Newmars. InStell moved to Newmars. Many other very large firms moved from Earth to various "outplanets." Thus, while there was a great deal of objection to the formation of such a gigantic "trust" as METALS AND ENERGY, INCORPORATED, there was nothing that WestHem's government could do about it. While GalMet was now a wholly-owned subsidiary of MetEnge, neither its name nor its operation had been changed in any way.

In GalMet's vast new building on Galmetia, President Upton Maynard sat at the head of a conference table. At his left sat Executive Vice-President Eldon Smith and Comptroller Desmond Phelps. At his right were Darrell Stearns, head of GalMet's legal staff, and Ward Q. Wilson, Chief Mediator of WestHem. Miss Champion sat at her desk, off to one side. Wilson was speaking.

". . . no over-riding authority, of course, since MetEnge is a Newmars corporation and GalMet's legal domicile and principal place of business is here on Galmetia. While such tax evasion is not . . ."

"Let's keep the record straight, Mr. Wilson," Maynard said sharply. "Not evasion; avoidance. Avoidance of Earth's ruthlessly confiscatory taxation was necessary to our continued existence. Under such taxation our basic principle of operation, which the founders of GalMet inaugurated over two hundred years ago, could not possibly have remained implemented.

"Do you think it's accidental that we are the largest firm in existence? It isn't; it is due absolutely to the fact that, very unlike capital in general, we have adhered strictly to the Principle of Enlightened Self-Interest.

Simply stated, that Principle is: Don't be a hog. You

ing—cradle-to-grave security—reckless, foolhardy install-
ment buying—the whole inflated credit situation. We, on
the other hand, do not use credit. We buy sight-draft-
attached-to-bill-of-lading and sell the same way. Hard
money and cash on the barrelhead. We have it before we
spend it."

"I'm not saying that your principle hasn't worked very
well for you, up to now. You haven't had a real strike
for half a century, until now. Not because of the stable
dollar or of your principle of operation, however, but
simply because no union was strong enough to fight you
to a finish. Now, there is one. The UCM controls all
copper mining and Burley Hoadman controls the UCM.
The situation, gentlemen, is now desperate; it is a civilization-wide emergency. It is intolerable that all industry
should come to a halt because of your refusal to settle
this strike. You know that all industry must have at least
some new copper to operate at all."

."We do," Maynard said. "You are saying that since
Hoadman will not settle for anything less than double
the present scale—already tops—we must cave in and
pay it? And surrender to all the other unions that will
jump onto the gravy train? That the subsequent inevitable surge of inflation won't hurt? You know exactly
what the spiral will be."

Wilson glanced at his microphone and said nothing.

Miss Champion entered a couple of pot-hooks in her notebook. Maynard went on:

"Your opinion is not for the record. I understand. This is an election year, and because the dear pe-pul are getting out of hand the administration sent you here to tell us to give Hoadman everything he wants—or else. They're junking financial stability completely to get themselves re-elected."

"No, I was not going to . . ."

"Not so crudely, of course; but nobody has put any pressure at all on Hoadman."

"We can't." Wilson spread his hands out helplessly and Miss Champion made a few more marks in her book. "All popular sentiment is for the union and against you. You are altogether too big."

"Or not big enough—yet," Maynard said, savagely.

"Also, in the public mind, the salaries of all you tycoons are altogether too high."

"High, hell!" Smith snarled. "How about Hoadman's take? He drags down more than all four of us put together!"

"Whether or not it is true, that point is irrelevant. The pertinent fact is that Senator Wrigley of California is preparing a bill to annex both Newmars and Galmetia to the Western Hemisphere."

Smith whistled. "*Brother!* They went a hell of a long ways out after *that* one!"

Wilson said nothing.

Stearns stared thoughtfully at the mediator, then said, "It's unconstitutional. Obviously. It violates every principle of Interplanetary law."

"Better yet, it's unenforceable," Smith said. "Admiral Porter knows as well as we do that his handful of tomato-juice cans wouldn't stand the chance of the proverbial nitrocellulose cat in hell."

"One more thing," Maynard said. "Ninety five other planets wouldn't like it, either. Have you thought about what a good, solid boycott would do to Earth?"

"The possibility has been considered, and the concep...

Wilson pursed his lips in hesitation and Smith said, "I'll answer that for you, then, Mr. Wilson. They want security, period, but they don't want to have to earn it. They want everything handed to them on a platter. Advancement by seniority only—all they have to do is stay alive. No changes allowed except more pay and more benefits for fewer hours of exactly the same work. Strictly serf labor and that's the way they like it. Security, hell! It's exactly the same kind of security, if they had brains enough to realize it, as they'd have in jail."

"It has been computed," Wilson said, ignoring Smith's barbed opinion, "that in an emergency outplanet Labor will support that of Earth. Furthermore, public opinion is very strongly opposed to such gigantic trusts, combines, and monopolies as you are. And finally, at the worst, the inevitable litigation would take a long time, which would . . . ?" Wilson paused, delicately.

"It would," Maynard agreed, grimly. "It would cramp us plenty and cost us plenty; and the administration could and would pull a lot of other stuff just as slimy."

Wilson neither confirmed nor denied the statement and Maynard went on. "Okay. We'll sign up for everything Hoadman demands; even the voice in management and the feather-bedding. Also, we'll make the wage scales and fringe benefits retroactive to cover all hours worked on and after July first."

"May I ask why? They might yield that one point."

"Why should they?" Smith sneered. "It's just out of

the goodness of our hearts. You may quote me on that."

"And that isn't all," Maynard went on. "We wanted a three-year contract, but Hoadman wouldn't add a day to his one-year position. So we'll do even better than that. Type a memo, please, Miss Champion. What we've said, and add, 'Cancellable by either party on ten days' notice in writing'!"

"*What?*" The mediator was shaken out of his calm. When Maynard handed him the signed memorandum he handled it as though it might bite. "Just what have you robber barons got up your sleeves?"

"Nothing but our arms," Smith assured him. "What *could* we have? Haven't your spies kept you informed of our every move?"

(No outsider as yet knew anything about Project Belmark, which was ready to go into full production.)

"I don't like this at all—not any part of it," Wilson said, thoughtfully. "I don't think I will recommend signing any contract containing a cancellation clause. Even though I can't see it, I know there's a hook in it somewhere . . . and I think I know what it is . . . but Hoadman is perfectly sure that . . . ?"

"Go ahead, ask me," Smith said. "I'll answer—I'm not under oath. You smell something because you can think. Hoadman can't. Even if he could, and even if there were a hook in the thing, he'll grab it. He'll have to. If he doesn't, the miners will throw him out on his ear. Besides, he'll love it. Imagine the headlines—'BURLEY HOADMAN, GIANT BRAIN OF LABOR, BRINGS MIGHTY GALMET TO ITS KNEES'."

"Mr. Maynard," Wilson said, "please erase Mr. Smith's remarks and this sentence from the record."

"By no means. Hoadman will of course listen to this supposedly top secret recording, and to hear this bit may—just conceivably—be good for what ails him."

Wilson wriggled uncomfortably and Miss Champion wrote another line of shorthand.

Discussion continued for another hour or so, after

rumblings in other unions, none of which had time to develop into serious strikes—for a couple of weeks. Then GalMet cancelled its contract with the UCM. Simultaneously it announced a reduction in the price of copper to eleven point three six one cents per pound FOB spaceport and began to supply all its competitors with all the copper they wanted. (It did not develop until later that Ajax, Revere, and all other large producers were merging with MetEnge). All mines worked by United Copper Miners shut down. Salaried people were transferred. All machinery was scrapped. All properties and buildings were either sold or simply abandoned. Then Maynard talked to the reporters who had for many days been demanding a statement.

"In an economy subscribing fully to the Principle of Enlightened Self-Interest neither stupidly avaricious capital nor serf labor would exist. Nor would such a corrupt government as we now have. While it may be true that any people deserves the government it gets, this three-pronged blight now threatening all civilization is intolerable and something must be done about it. We have begun doing something about it by making an example of Burley Hoadman and his unconscionably greedy United Copper Miners, who . . ."

"One question, Mr. Maynard!" a reporter broke in. "In using the word 'we' do you claim to be represent. . . ."

"I claim nothing!" Maynard snapped. "I state as a fact

SUBSPACE EXPLORERS

that I am speaking for the Galaxians—the free men and
women and the intelligent capital of the planets. These
two component halves of production, eternally irreconcilable on Earth, work together on the planets for the
best good of all. To resume: the closed copper mines
will not be re-opened. There will never, in the foreseeable future, be any employment anywhere for the skilled
craftsmen known as copper miners. We have deliberately automated the entire craft out of existence.

"We do not know whether Hoadman will believe this
statement or not. Nor do we care. If he wishes to use
up his union's funds in supporting the men in idleness
rather than in expediting their absorption into other
industries, that is his privilege.

"It has been threatened that other unions will, in spite
of contractual obligations, walk out in sympathy with
the UCM, to enforce Hoadman's demand that we pay
four men double-scale wages to sit on cushioned chairs
and play stud poker while one machine does the work.
In reply to these threats I say now that we are prepared
to cope with such retaliation at any level of action required.

"We are ready even for a complete general strike by
all the unions of WestHem. In that case all imports to
and all exports from Earth will stop. Earth will stew in
its own juice until the vast majority of WestHem's people, the unorganized people, decide to get themselves
out of the mess into which, by their own stupidity, lazi-
ness, and lack of interest, they got themselves."

This blast was broadcast immediately; and in less than
an hour Antonio Grimes, president of the Brotherhood
of Professional Drivers, was on Miss Champion's com,
demanding access to Maynard.

Since she was expecting the call, he was put on at
once.

"Good morning, Mr. Maynard," he began. He was a
short man, inclined to fat, with heavy jowls and small,
piercing eyes. At the table with him were his three

102

major lieutenants and—not much to Maynard's surprise

shedding in the instant his veneer of gentility. "I'll *show* you who's got a brain, you . . ."

"Shut up and listen!" Maynard snapped. "If you had had any fraction of a brain you would have known that we knew exactly what you would do."

"Like hell you knew! If you did you wouldn't've . . ." Grimes paused; it became evident that his train of thought had all of a sudden been derailed.

"The only question is, how big a battle do you want for an opener? All over WestHem at once, or just one spaceport at first, to see what we have? If you can think at all you'd better start doing it, because the bigger a flop you make the deader you'll be when it's over."

"Comet-gas! You can't scare *me!*"

"I can't? That's nice."

"Who'd want to shoot the whole wad at once? One at a time; one day apart. Tomorrow morning I seal New York Spaceport so tight a cockroach can't get in or out."

"And we'll open it. Here's your one and only warning. Before we send our freight-copters in . . ."

"Just how do you think you'll get any copters off the ground?"

"Wait and see. Before a copter lofts we'll come in on the ground. East on Carter Avenue. Through Gate Twelve. Along Way Twelve to the *Cygnus.* I'm telling you this because I don't want our machines to kill anybody. They'll be fully automatic, so programmed that we won't be able to stop them ourselves. Hence any goons along that designated route who can't get out of the way in time will be committing suicide. If you shoot down any of our copters your gun-crews will be killed. That is all."

"Hot-dog!" Grimes gloated. "Drawing us a map—handing it to us on a platter! What you'll run into a-long . . ."

Miss Champion flipped a switch and the screen went blank.

Carter Avenue became a very busy street. The biggest and heaviest trucks available, loaded to capacity with broken concrete and rock, were jammed into that avenue, blocking it solidly—pavement, parkway, and sidewalk—from building wall to building wall for one full mile. Riflemen with magnums sat at windows; fifty-caliber machine-guns and forty-millimeter quick-firing rifles peered down from roofs; anti-tank weapons of all kinds commanded every yard of that soon-to-be-disputed mile.

Grimes and his strategists had expected a fleet of heavy tanks. What appeared, however, exceeded their expectations by ten raised to a power. They were—in a way—tanks; but tanks of a size, type, and heft never before seen on Earth. There were only two of them; but each one was twenty feet high, sixty feet wide, and a hundred and eighty feet long. They were not going fast, but when they reached the barricade, side by side and a couple of feet apart, they did not even pause. Both front ends reared up as one, but they did not climb very high. Under that terrific tonnage the blocking trucks were crushed flat; the steel of their structures and the concrete and stone of their loads subsided noisily to form a compacted mass only a few feet thick.

Guns of all calibers yammered and thundered, but there was nothing to shoot at except blankly invulnerable expanses of immensely thick high-alloy armor-plate. Flames-throwers, flammable gels, and incendiaries were of no avail. Inside those monstrosities there was nothing of life, nor anything to be harmed by any ordinary

horizontal sheets of fiercely-driven pulverized pavement and soil. Then another, and fifteen more. But not even the heaviest mines could stop those land-going super-dreadnoughts. They wallowed a little in the craters, but that was all. They were simply too big and too heavy and too stable to lift or to tip over; their belly-armor was twelve inches thick and was buttressed and braced internally to withstand anything short of atomic energy. Nor could their treads be blown; since all that was exposed to blast were their stubby, sharply pyramidal, immensely strong driving teeth.

Along Way Twelve the strike-breakers rumbled, and up to GalMet's subspacer *Cygnus*. They stopped. A Gal-Met copter began to descend, to pick up its load of copper. There was a blast of anti-aircraft fire. The copter disintegrated in air.

This time, however, GalMet struck back. Gun-ports snapped open along the nearer behemoth's grim side and a dozen one-hundred-five-millimeter shells lobbed in high arcs across the few hundreds of yards of intervening distance. They exploded, and a few parts recognizable as arms, legs, and heads, together with uncountable grisly scraps of flesh and bone, were mingled with the shattered remains of the anti-aircraft battery.

That ended it.

In Maynard's conference room this time there were, in addition to the GalMet men, Lansing and DuPuy of Warner Oil, Hatfield and Spehn of Interstellar, and seven other men. With Grimes and his minions, were, as before, Deissner and Wilson of WestHem.

Secretary of Labor Deissner looked once at the fourteen men seated at Maynard's table and his ruddy complexion paled.

"Have you had enough, Grimes, or do you want to go the route?" Maynard asked. "You *may* be able to hold your Drivers after this one beating, but one more will plow you under."

"You're *murderers* now and you'll hang!" Grimes snarled.

"What will you use for law, fat-head?"

"To hell with law. I've got WestHem's law in my pants pocket and you'll hang higher than . . ."

"Close your fat mouth, Tony," Deissner said, bruskly. "With WarnOil, InStell, and all the labor of the out-planets in on this, it may be a little . . ." He paused.

"You're wrong, Deissner, it'll be much worse," Smith sneered. "Your computations will all have to be recomputed."

After a short silence Maynard said, "Mr. Secretary; besides WarnOil and InStell, I see that you recognize the presidents of the seven largest organizations of the Planetsmen. Mr. Bryce, President of the Metalsmen, has something to say."

And fiery little Bryce said it. "This Committee of Seven, of which I am the chairman, represents the Planetsmen, the organized production and service personnel of the ninety five planets of the Galactic Federation. Our present trip has two purposes. First, here on Galmetia, to tell you Tellurians that the organized personnel of the planets—not the *out*-planets, you will note, but the *planets*—will not support the purely Tellurian institution of serf labor. We do no featherbedding and we will not support the practice anywhere. We welcome any innovation that will produce more goods or services at lower cost by using our brains more and our muscles less.

"Our second objective is to let the people of Tellus

planets—know exactly what Westfrem's law is: a hood-bossed, hood-riddled mob of abysmally corrupt snolly-gosters. We also know that static, greedy capital is as bad as—yes, even worse than—serf labor. Therefore we Galax-ians have formed a new government, the Galactic Federa-tion; that, among other things, will not—I repeat, NOT —permit any spiral of inflation."

"But *some* inflation is now necessary!" Deissner pro-tested.

"It is not. We're not asking you; we're telling you. If you do not stabilize the dollar we will stabilize it for you."

"Delusions of grandeur, eh? How do you think you can?"

"By isolating Earth until the resulting panic puts the dollar back where it belongs. Earth can't stand a block-ade. The planets can, and would much rather have a complete severance from Earth than have a dollar that will not mail a letter from one town to the next. Hence we of the Galactic Federation hereby serve notice upon the governments and upon the peoples of Earth: it will be either a stable dollar or a strict blockade of every item of commerce except food. Take your choice."

"Serve notice!" Deissner gasped. "Surely you don't mean . . . you can't *possibly* mean . . ."

"We do mean. Just that." Maynard smiled; a thin, cold smile. "This has not been a secret meeting. You tell 'em, Steve."

And Stevens Spehn, Executive Vice-President of vast

Interstellar, told them. "This whole conference has been on every channel, line, wavelength and station that In-Stell operates—ether and subether, radio and teevee, tri-di and flat, in black-and-white and in color."

. And Miss Champion flipped her switch.

New York Spaceport and the conference that followed it took place in the middle of the starship's "night", both were played in full on the regular morning news program. So was one solid hour of bi-partisan and extremely heated discussion by the big-name commentators of Earth.

To say that this news created a sensation is the understatement of the month. Nor was sentiment entirely in favor of GalMet, even though all the men aboard except Deston, and many of the women, were salaried employees and the whole expedition was on MetEnge-DesDes business.

"Shocking!" "Outrageous!" "Cold-blooded murder!"

"Who murdered first?" "Land-mines, Seventy fives, and Bofors!" "Shot down the copter and killed everybody aboard!"

"But they should have settled the strike!" "GalMet was utterly lawless!"

"I suppose it's lawful to use land-mines and anti-aircraft guns and make a full-war-scale battlefield inside New York City?"

And so on.

The top echelon was, of course, solidly in favor of Maynard, and Captain Jones summed up their attitude very neatly when he said, "What the hoodlums are belly-aching about is that they were out-guessed, out-thunk, and outgunned in the ratio of a hundred and five millimeters to seventy five."

"But listen," Bernice said. "Do you think, Babe, that there were any men aboard that copter?"

"One gets you a thousand there weren't. Maynard didn't say there were any."

"He didn't say there weren't any, either," Barbara argued, "like he did for the tanks. What makes you so sure?"

"He knew what was going to happen—he let them think it was manned, probably as a deterrent—so you can paste it in your Easter bonnet, pet, that the only brains aboard that copter were tapes."

Time wore on; the strife on Earth, which did not flare into the news again, was just about forgotten. Deston found several enormous deposits of copper. He found all the other most-wanted metals except rhenium in quantity sufficient to supply even the most extravagant demand. But of rhenium he still found only insignificant traces.

Each tremendous deposit of metal had been reported as soon as it was found. Crew after crew had been sent out. Plant after plant had been built; each one of which would be not only immensely profitable, but also of inestimable benefit to humanity as a whole, since all those highly important metals would soon be on the market at a mere fraction of their former high prices.

Still rhenium did not appear. "I don't believe there *is* any such damn thing, anywhere in the whole galaxy," Deston said, over and over, but he did not give up.

The starship bored along on its hugely helical course, deeper and deeper into unexplored space toward the Center. Until, after weeks of futile seeking, Deston did find rhenium. After a quick once-over, without waiting to get close enough to the planet for the physical scientists to make any kind of survey, he called Galmetia and Miss Champion.

"Hi, Doris!" he greeted her happily. "I've got some good news for you at last. We found it."

"Oh? Rhenium? In quantity? How wonderful!"

"Yes. Oodles and gobs of it. All anybody and everybody can ever use. So how about busting in on the

or . . ."

"That's what *you* think. Usually, Babe—practically *always*—he gives me my head, but this time he swore he'd shoot me right through the brain and hang my carcass out of the window on a hook if I cut in on him with anything whatever or anybody whoever until this brawl is over . . . but I know *damn* well he'll boil me in oil if I hold *this* up for even a minute. . . . Well, I think I'd rather be shot. Wouldn't you?"

"It'd be quicker, anyway."

"Well, a girl can die only once." She shrugged her shapely shoulders and cut Deston in.

"What the *hell*, Champion!" Maynard blazed; then, as he saw what was on the screen, his expression and attitude changed completely. "Okay. Tell you-know-who to roll. Cut."

Deston's image flipped back onto Miss Champion's screen and breathed a deep sigh of relief. "Believe me, Babe, that was one brass-bound toughie to guess."

"Check. But you're a smartie, doll, or you wouldn't be holding *that* fort. So let's get you-know-who and tell her to cut her gravs, huh?"

"Cutting her shoulder-straps would be enough. *B-z-z-z-z-zzt!* She'd take off without an anti-grav, let alone a ship."

"She's been taking it big?"

" 'Immense' would be a much better word . . . Doctor

Byrd, they have found your rhenium. Here's Mister Deston."

It was evident that "The Byrd" had been fighting with someone and was still in a vicious mood. When she saw Deston, however, her stormy face cleared and she became instantly the keen, competent executive. "Have you *really* found some?" she demanded. "Enough of it to make a fully-automated plant pay out?"

"Well, since the stuff runs well over twenty billion metric tons to the cubic kilometer and it's here by the hundreds of cubic kilometers in solid masses, what do *you* think?"

"Oh my God! What's the planet like? A stinker, as expected?"

"All of that. No survey yet, but it's vicious. Several gees. Super-dense atmosphere, probably bad. No listing for it or anything like it—mountains and mesas of solid metal. You'll need personal armor, anti-gravs, skyhooks —the works. Pretty much like theory, from this distance. Closer up, it may get worse."

"Everything anybody has suggested is aboard. But Deston; they tell me you're Top Dog on this. Is it actually true that the sky's the limit? And that I'm running it without interference?"

"Not even the sky is the limit on this one. No limit. Yes, except in matters of policy, you are the Complete Push."

She glanced at Miss Champion, who said, "If Mr. Deston says so, it is so; he has over-riding authority in this. In two minutes you will be handed an *unlimited* authorization, Doctor Byrd—the first one I ever heard of."

"Oh, wonderful! Thanks a million, both of you! Now if you'll transfer him over here, Miss Cham . . ." Deston's image appeared upon Byrd's screen, ". . . pion— thanks. Mr. Deston, if you'll give Astrogation, here, the coords, we'll . . ." A hand phone rang; she snatched it up. "Byrd . . . Yes, Lew, good news. At last, thank

God, they've found our rhenium and we're jetting. Ac-

and jagged bare-metal-and-rock mountains; and Cecily
Byrd came aboard the exploring vessel.

"I'm very glad to meet you in the flesh, Doctor Byrd,"
Deston said, and as soon as she was out of her space-suit
they shook hands cordially.

"Doctor Livingstone, I presume?" She giggled infec-
tiously. "You'll never know how glad I am to be here."
There was nothing sullen or morose or venomous about
her now; she was eager, friendly, and intense. "And no
formality, Babe. I'm 'Curly' to my friends."

"Okay, Curly—now meet the gang. My wife, Bobby
. . . Herc Jones and his wife, Bun . . . Andy Adams, our
Prime Brain, and his wife, Stella . . . This planet is a
tough baby; a prime stinker."

"So I gathered, and the more you find out about it
the tougher and stinkier it gets. We've fabricated all the
stuff you suggested, for which thanks, by the way, so,
unless there have been new developments in the last
couple of hours, I'll go back and we'll go down. Okay?"

"Okay except for an added feature. Herc and I are
going along as safety factors. We have built-in danger
alarms."

"Oh? Oh, yes, I remember now. Welcome to our city."

Aboard the *Rhene*, Deston said, "But as chief of
the party, Curly, you ought to stay up here, don't you
think?"

"Huh?" The woman's whole body stiffened. "*As* chief

of the party, buster, I'm the best man on it. What would *you* do? Stay home?"

"Okay," and preparations went on.

Extreme precautions were necessary, for this was a fantastic planet indeed. In size it was about the same as Earth, but its surface gravity was almost four times Earth's. Its atmosphere, which was at a pressure of over forty pounds to the square inch, was mostly xenon, with some krypton, argon, and nitrogen, with less than seven percent by volume of oxygen. Its rivers were few and small, as were its lakes. Its three oceans combined would not equal the Atlantic in area, and what was dissolved in those oceans no one knew. The sun Rhenia was a Class B7 horror, so big and so hot that Rhenia Four, although twice as far away from Rhenia as Mars is from Sol, was as hot as Mars is cold. Even at latitude fifty north, where the starships were, and at an altitude of over fifteen thousand feet, at which the floor of the little valley was, the noon temperature in the shade was well over forty degrees Centigrade.

And there was life. Just what kind of life it was, none of the biologists could even guess. They had been arguing ever since arrival, but they hadn't settled a thing. There were things of various shapes and sizes that might or might not be analogous to the grasses, shrubs, and trees of the Tellus-Type planets; but no one could say whether they were vegetable, mineral, or metalo-organic in nature. There were things that ran and leaped and fought; and things that flew and fought—all of which moved with the fantastic speed and violence concomitant with near-four gees—but if they were animals they were entirely unlike any animals ever before seen by man.

No one aboard the *Procyon* had even tried to land, of course. They didn't have the equipment; and besides, it was "Curly" Byrd's oyster and she had repeatedly threatened mayhem upon the person of anyone who tried to open it before she got there.

The personal armor of the landing party—or rather,

happen.

Counting the pilot, five persons composed the party. Director Byrd and Assistant Director Leyton were completely encased. Deston and Jones, however, had left their hands bare, as each was carrying a .475 semi-automatic rifle. Magnums, these, of tremendous slugging power; and all their cartridges—each gunner had three extra fifty-round drums—were loaded with armor-piercers, not soft-nosed stuff. They went down, talking animatedly and peering eagerly, until two silent inner alarms went off at once.

"Hold it!" Jones yelled, and Deston's even louder command was, "High it at max, fly-boy!"

The craft darted upward, but even at full blast she was not fast enough to escape from a horde of flying things that looked something like wildcats' heads mounted on owls' bodies, but vastly larger than either. They attacked viciously; their terrible teeth and even more terrible talons tearing inches-deep gouges into the shuttle's hard, tough armor. As the little vessel shot upward, however, higher and higher into the ever-thinning atmosphere, the things began to drop away—they *did* have to breathe.

Several of them, however, stayed on. They had dug holes clear through the armor; out of which the shuttle's air was whistling. The creatures were breathing ship's air—and liking it!—and were working with ferocious speed and power and with appalling efficiency.

Deston and Jones began shooting as soon as the first two openings were large enough to shoot through, but even those powerful weapons—the hardest-hitting shoulder-guns built—were shockingly ineffective. Both monsters had their heads inside the ship and were coming in fast. The others had dropped away for lack of air.

"Hercules" Jones, big enough and strong enough to handle even a .475 as though it were a .30-30, put fifty hard-nosed bullets against one spot of his monster's head and thus succeeded in battering that head so badly out of shape that the creature died before gaining entrance. Died and hung there, half in and half out.

But Deston, although supremely willing, simply did not have the weight and sheer brute strength to take that brutal magnum's recoil and hold it steady on one point. Thus when his drum was empty the creature was still coming. It was dying, however, almost dead, because of the awful pounding it had taken and because there was almost no air at all left in the shuttle.

Both men were changing drums, but they were a few seconds late. The thing had life enough left so that as it came through the wall and fell to the floor it made one convulsive flop, and in its dying convulsions it sank one set of talons into Cecily Byrd's thigh and the other into the calf of Lewis Leyton's leg. The woman shrieked once and, for the first time in her life, fainted dead away. The man swore sulphurously.

By this time they were almost back to the *Rhene*. The landing craft was taken aboard and a team of surgeons tried for a few minutes to get those incredible talons out of the steel and the flesh; then for a few minutes more they tried to amputate those equally incredible feet. Then they anesthetized both victims and carried the inseparable trio into the machine-shop; where burly mechanics ground the beast's legs in two with high-speed neotride wheels and, using tools designed to handle high-tensile bar stock, curled those ghastly

She straightened up angrily; she was not too sore to fight. "Think again, buster. We're on the job now, not at HQ. It's my job and I'll run it any way I damn well please."

"At HQ or anywhere else, my curly-haired friend, my authority over-rides on matters of policy and this is a matter of policy. You'll take it and you'll like it."

"Over-rides, hell! I'll . . ."

"You'll nothing!" he snapped. "Did you ever get socked on the jaw hard enough to lay you out stiff for fifteen minutes?"

Instead of becoming even more furious at that, she relaxed and grinned up at him. "No, I never did. That would be a brand-new experience."

"Okay. Much more of this sticking out of your beautiful neck and you'll get that brand-new experience. Now let's do some thinking on what to do next. I shot in an order for a special elsie*. . . ."

"Can you . . . those kittyhawks went through superstainless like so much cheese. What plating—neotride?"

"That's right. Here's the funny-picture." He spread a blueprint out on the bed. "I didn't have much of anything to do with it, though; it's mostly Lew's work.

She studied the drawing for a couple of minutes. "That ought to do it; it'd stop a diamond drill cold . . . it'd

*Elsie—L C—Landing Craft. EES.

hold a neotride drill for a while . . . but what *are* those monstrosities, Babe? All that the croakers will give out with is gobbledegook, soothing syrup, and pure pap."

"Nobody knows. All the biologists aboard are going not-so-slowly nuts. They can't do anything from up here."

"All of us. Nice." She bit her lip. "Without rhenium we can't work down there and we have to work down there to get rhenium. Strictly circular progress."

"It isn't that bad, Curly. There are dozens of nice big chunks of the clear quill—thousands of tons of it—right out in the open down there. That's the special elsie's job, to go down and get 'em and bring 'em out here to us. The chief wants a good mess of it rushed in to Galmetia, but there's plenty of it lying around loose to take care of him and build five of your installations besides."

"Wonderful! That makes me feel a lot better, Babe— I'll talk to you now until the croakers throw you out."

to have hundreds of tons of rhenium before they could begin to work.

This little ship was to get it. Her inner layer of armor was four inches thick, forged of the stubbornest super-steel available. The outer layer, electronically fused to the inner, was one full inch of neotride, the synthetic that was the hardest substance known to man—five numbers Rockwell harder than the diamond.

The starship carrying the elsie also brought two formally-typed notices—things almost unknown in a day of subspace communicators and tapes. The one addressed to "Cecily Byrd, Ph.D., Sc.D., F.I.A." (Fellow of the Institute of Automation) read in part: "You are hereby instructed, under penalty of discharge and blacklist, to stay aloft until complete safety of operation has been demonstrated," and the gist of Deston's was: "I cannot give you orders, but if you have half the brain I think you have, you *know* enough to stay aloft until safety of operation has been demonstrated."

Cecily's nostrils flared; then her whole body slumped. "He'd do it, too, the damned old tiger . . . and this is the biggest job I ever dreamed about . . . and I suppose *you'll* go down anyway."

"Uh-uh. He makes sense. Actually, neither of us should take the chance. Anyway, the stuff is right out in the open, where they can sit right down on it and grapple it . . . and besides, my mother told me it isn't sporting to kick a lady in the face when she's down. It isn't done, she said."

"She did? How nice of her! Thanks, Babe, a lot," and she held out her hand.

Thus it was that Assistant Director Leyton and Captain Jones led the down-crew. They both, and two other big, strong men as well, carried .475's; but this time the magnums were not needed. The neotride held up long enough. In spite of everything the rabidly hostile "animals" could do, the elsie grappled five-hundred-ton chunks of the stuff and lugged them up into orbit.

In the meantime the metallurgists, by subjecting the teeth and claws of the dead kittyhawks to intensive study, had solved their biggest basic problem. Or rather, they found out that Nature had solved it for them.

"The composition at maxprop—to get the best mat of longest single crystals, you know—is extremely complex and almost unbelievably critical," Leyton told Deston, happily. "It would have taken us years, and even then we wouldn't have hit it exactly on the nose except by pure luck."

"Well, how do you expect to do in a couple of years what it took Old Mother Nature millions of years? Billions even, maybe."

"It's been done. Anyway, we're 'way ahead of Old Mother in one respect—heat-treating. We've got a growth-cycle already that makes the original look sick."

The new and improved leybyrdite was poured, forged, neotride-ground, and heat-treated. A tailored-to-order mining head was built; and, in spite of the frantic and highly capable opposition of the local life-forms, was driven into the mountainside.

This first unit took a long time, since everyone had to work in armor and anti-grav. After it was in place, however, the job went much faster, as air was run in and the whole installation was gravved down to nine eighty—Earth-normal gravity—and people could work in ordinary working clothes.

Section after section was attached, the whole gigantic

But the director brushed aside the scientists' pleas for elsies in which to study. "I'm sorry, Adams, but first things have got to come first. When we get a full stream of rhenium coming out of that hole in the ground I'll build you anything you want, but until then absolutely *nothing* goes that isn't geared directly to production."

And she herself was everywhere. Dressed in leybyrdite helmet, leather packet, leather breeches, and high-laced boots, she was in the point, in the middle, in the tail, and in all stations, for whatever purpose intended. And, since no two operations are ever alike and this one was like nothing else ever built, she was carrying the full load. But she knew what she was doing, and hers was a mind that did not have to follow any book. She ordered special machinery and equipment so regardlessly of cost that Desmond Phelps almost had heart failure. When she wanted ten extra-special units, each of which would cost over a hundred thousand dollars to build, she ordered them as nonchalantly as though they were that many ballpoint pens; and Maynard okayed her every requisition without asking a single question.

She had her troubles, of course, but only one of them was with her personnel—the revolt of her section heads. Some of them resented the fact that she was a woman; some of them really believed that they knew more about some aspects of the job than she did. She called a meeting and told them viciously to do the job her way and quit dragging their feet—or else. Next day, in four successive minutes, she fired four of them; whereupon the others decided that Byrd was a hard-rock man after all and began to play ball.

She had her troubles, of course—what big job has ever gone strictly according to plan?—but she met them unflinchingly head on and flattened them flat. She knew her stuff and she held her crew and her job right in the palm of her hand. Even Maynard was satisfied; not too many men could have run such a hairy job as smoothly as she was doing it.

The last element was installed. The last tape was checked, rechecked, and double-checked. Maynard, Smith, and Phelps, all in person—a truly unprecedented event, this!—inspected and approved the whole project. Project Rhenia Four, fully automatic, was ready to roll in its vast entirety.

Maynard stared thoughtfully at his project chief. Her helmet was under her left arm. She hadn't seen a hairdresser for five months; her rebellious brick-dust-red curls were jammed into a nylon net. Her jacket, breeches, and boots were scuffed, stained, scarred, and worn. She had lost pounds of weight; faint dark rings encircled both eyes. But those eyes fairly sparkled; her whole mien was one of keen anticipation. Maynard had never seen her in any such mood as this.

"Okay, Byrd; push the button," he said.

"Uh-uh, chief, you push it. It's your honor, really; nobody else in all space would have stood back of me the way you have."

"Thanks. It'd tickle me to; I've never started a big operation yet," and the whole immense project went smoothly to work.

Strained and tense, they watched it for half an hour. Then Maynard shook her hand.

"You *were* worth saving, Byrd. You're an operator; a real performer. I hope you've got over that ungodly insecurity complex of yours. You know what I'm going to do to you if you ever start that hell-raising again?"

She laughed. "You and Babe both seem to have the

less and less tensely and with more and more eating and sleeping, for fifty more hours, during which time a hundred freighters departed with their heavy loads. Then all tension disappeared. Having run this long, it would continue to run; with only normal supervision and maintenance.

"Now for the usual party," Smith said. "Unusual, it should be, since this is a highly unusual installation. How about it, everybody?"

"Let's have a big dance," Barbara suggested. "Dress up and everything."

"Oh, let's!" Cecily almost squealed. She was still in her scuffed leathers, still ready for any emergency. Her hair was still a tightly-packed mop. "We're all rested enough—I just had fourteen hours' sleep and two big steaks. Let's go!"

"We're off, Curly." Bernice took her arm. "We'll help each other get all prettied up. Herc, how about locking the ships together, so we won't get all mussed up in those horrible suits?"

"Can do, pet." Jones gave his wife the smile reserved for her alone; a smile that softened wonderfully his hard, craggy, deeply-tanned face. "For beauty in distress we'd do even more than that."

In about an hour, then, the party began. Bernice and Cecily were standing together when Jones and Leyton came up to them. The red-head was a good inch taller than tall Bernice; she would have stood five feet ten without her four-inch heels. Both gowns were as tight as they could be without showing stress-patterns; both were strapless, backless, and almost frontless; both hemlines bisected kneecaps.

The two men were just about of a size—six feet three, and twenty pounds or so over two hundred. Leyton was handsome; Jones very definitely was not. Leyton was the softer; it was not part of his job to keep himself at the peak of physical fitness. He was, however, by no means soft. Being "softer" than Theodore Jones left a lot of room for a man to be in very good shape indeed, and Lewis Leyton was.

Both men stopped and Jones whistled expressively; a perfectly-executed wolf-whistle. "*This* must be *Miss* Byrd.*" He smiled as he took her hand and bowed over it—and, as a space officer, he really knew how to bow. "Miss Byrd, may I have the honor and the pleasure of the second number, please?"

She dipped a half-curtsy and laughed. "You may indeed, sir," and Leyton swept her away.

Jones danced first with his wife, of course; then led Cecily out onto the floor. For a minute they danced in silence, each conscious of what a superb performer the other was and of how perfectly they matched. She was the first to speak.

"You're looking at my hair. Don't, Herc, please. Nobody in all space can do anything with it, and I didn't have time to let your beauty-shop even try."

"Do you really mean that, Curly, or are you just fishing?"

"Of course I mean it! Look at Bun's hair, or Bobby's, or *anybody's!* They can fix it any way they please and change it any time they please. But *this* stuff?" She shook her intractable mop. "This carroty-pink-sorrel mess of rusty steel-turnings? Nobody can do anything with it whatever. I can't even bleach it or dye it—or even wear a wig. It's bad enough, the color and the way it is now, but

with it anything else, with my turkey egg face. I look

get one tomorrow."

Cecily leaned back—she had been dancing very close —far enough to look into his eyes. "Why, you great big damn liar. . . ."

"Ask her, next time you see her."

"I'll do just that. In the meantime, for the prize-winning big lie of the year, tell me that next to Bun I'm the prettiest girl here; not a hard-boiled hard-rock man in a ball gown."

"I'll tell you something a lot better than that. You've got stuff by the cubic mile that no merely pretty girl ever did have or ever will have."

"Such as?" she scoffed.

"If you really don't know, take a complete inventory of yourself sometime."

"I have, thousands of times."

"Wrong system, then. Change it."

She leaned still farther away from him. "You sound as though you really mean that."

"I do, Scout's Honor. And Bun agrees with me."

"She does? I'll bet she does. You've got a nice line, Herc."

"No line, Curly; believe me."

"It'd be nice if I could . . . but Herc, the chief thinks I have a terrific case of inferiority complex . . . except he called it 'insecurity' . . . and Babe said . . . do you think so?"

"I'm no psych, so I wouldn't know. But why in all

the hells of space should you have?"

She actually missed a step. "Why *should* I have! Just *look* at me! Or can't you imagine what it's like, being the ugliest duckling in the pond all your life?"

"Can't I? You *have* got a complex. Look at *me*, you dumb . . . what do you think *I've* been all my life?"

She stared at him in amazement. "Why, *you're* positively distinguished-looking!"

"Comet-gas! I've always been the homeliest guy around, but I got so I didn't let it throw me."

"Anyway, men don't have to be good-looking."

"Neither do women. Look at history."

"Let's look at Bun instead—one of the most beautiful women who ever lived. You wouldn't have . . ."

"I certainly would have. Beauty helps, of course—and I admit that I like it, that she's a beauty—but over the long route it isn't a drop in the bucket and you know it. She'll still be a charmer at ninety, and so will you. She's prettier than you are, but you've got a lot of stuff she hasn't. What did you think I was talking about, a minute ago?"

"Sex. Anybody can throw that around."

"Not the way you can. But that wasn't it, at all; that's only one phase. It's the total personality that carries the wallop. You've got it. So has Bun. And Bobby. Who else aboard? Nobody."

"I wonder . . ." They danced in silence for a time. "You could be right, I suppose . . . after all, you and Maynard and Babe are certainly three of the smartest men I know."

"You know we're right. So why don't you cut the jaw-flapping and get down to reality?"

"Maybe you *are* right. Thanks, Herc, the thought is one to dwell on. You know what I'm going to do?" She giggled suddenly. "I haven't done it since my Freshman Frolic." She drew herself up very close to him, snuggled her head down onto his shoulder, and closed both eyes.

And thus they finished the dance. He brought her

darling?"

Each woman studied the other. Both were tall and superb of figure. Each projected in quantity—and not only unconsciously—the tremendous basic force that is sex appeal. But there all resemblance ceased. Bernice, as has been said, was one of the most beautiful women of her time. And besides beauty of face and figure, besides strength of physique and of character, she had the poise and confidence of her status and of her sure knowledge of her husband's love. Cecily Byrd, on the other hand, radiated a personality that was uniquely hers and that made itself tellingly felt wherever she was. In addition, she had the driving force, the sheer willpower, and the ruthlessly competent brain of the top-bracket executive she had so fully proved herself to be.

"It'd be fun," the red-head said, thoughtfully. "That would really be a battle."

"As Herc likes to say, you chirped it that time, birdie."

"Ordinarily, that would make it all the more fun, but I'll be working like a dog yet for quite a while—I'll hardly have time enough in bed even to sleep. So let's take a rain-check on it, shall we, my dear?"

"Any time, darling. Any time at all. Whenever you please." Blue eyes stared steadily into eyes of Irish green.

Then Cecily shook her head. "I'm not going to try, Bun. I think too much of both of you . . . and besides,

I might not be able to . . . You know, Bun. . . ." She paused, then went on, slowly, "I never have liked women very much; they're such flabby, gutless things . . . but you're a lot of woman yourself."

"We're a lot alike in some ways, Curly—there *aren't* very many women like you and me and Barbara—for which fact, of course, most men would say 'Thank God!' "

"You're *so* right!"

Not being men, the two almost-antagonists did not shake hands; but at that moment the ice began definitely to melt.

"But listen," Bernice said. "There are hundreds of men around here. Good men and big ones."

Cecily grinned. "But not usually both; and just being big isn't enough to make me come apart at the seams. He has to have a brain, too; and maybe what Herc just called a 'total personality'."

"That *does* narrow the field . . . just about to Lew, I guess . . . but I suppose Executives' Code cuts both ways."

"It's supposed to, probably, but I wouldn't care about that if he weren't such a stuffed shirt . . . but I'm getting an idea. Let's go hunt Babe up." Then, as Bernice looked at her quizzically, "My God, no—who except a half-portion like Bobby would want him? I just want to ask him a question."

They found Deston easily enough. "Babe," Cecily said, "you said there's a lot of tantalum here. As much as on Tantalia Three?"

"More. Thousands of times as much. Why?"

"Then Perce Train ought to come out here and look it over. I'll tell the chief so. Thanks, Babe."

"Perce Train?" Bernice asked, the next time they sat together. "The boy friend?"

"Not yet. We were knifing each other all over the place, back at HQ, but we're both on top now. He'll be good for what ails me. Wait 'till you see *him*, sister —and hang on to your hat."

But there's nothing flagrant about it that I can see, pet," Jones argued one night, just before going to sleep. "What makes you think so except Curly's jaw flapping?"

"I just *know* they are," Bernice said, darkly. "She really meant it, and she's the type to. She ought to be ashamed of herself, but she isn't. Not the least little tiny bit."

"Well, neither of 'em's married, so what's the dif? Even if they are stepping out, which is a moot point, you know."

"Well . . . maybe. One good thing about it, she isn't making any passes at *you*, and she'd better not. I'll scratch both her green eyes out if she tries it, the hussy—so help me!"

"Oh, she was just chomping her choppers, sweetheart. Besides, I'm as prejudiced as I am insulated. I've never seen anyone within seven thousands parsecs of being *you*."

"You're a darling, Herc, and I love you all to pieces." She snuggled up close and closed her eyes; but she did not drop easily, as was her wont, to sleep.

If that red-headed, green-eyed vixen—that sex-flaunting powerhouse—*had* unlimbered her heavy artillery . . . but she hadn't . . . and it was just as well for all concerned, Bernice thought, just before she did go to sleep, that that particular triangular issue had not been joined.

XI

PSIONTISTS

SECRETARY of Labor Deissner was very unhappy. The United Copper Miners, as a union, had been wiped out of existence. Mighty Drivers' all-out effort at New York Spaceport had been smashed with an ease that was, to Deissner's mind, appalling. Worse, it was inexplicable; and, since no one else really knew anything, either, he was being buffeted, pushed, and pulled in a dozen different directions at once.

The Dutchman, however, was nobody's push-over. He merely set his stubborn jaw a little more stubbornly. "I want *facts!*" he bellowed, smashing his open hand down onto the top of his desk. "I've got to have *facts!* Until I get *facts* we can't move—I *won't* move!"

For weeks, then, and months, "Dutch" Deissner studied ultraconfidential reports and interviewed ultra-secret agents—many of whom were so ultra-ultra-secret as to be entirely unknown to any other member of WestHem's government . . . and the more he worked the less secure he felt and the more unhappy he became. He was particularly unhappy when, late one night and very secretly, he conferred with a plenipotentiary from East-Hem.

"The Nameless One is weary of meaningless replies to his questions," the Slav said, bruskly. "I therefore demand with his mouth a plan of action and its date of execution."

"Demand and be damned," Deissner said, flatly. "I will not act until I know what that *verdammte* Maynard has got up his sleeve. Tell Nameless that."

"In that case you will come with me now."

"You talk like a fool. One false move and you and your escort die where you sit. Tell Nameless he does not own me yet and it may very well be he never will

on each side, of course—in South Africa.

"Don't you know, fool," the dictator opened up, "that you will die for this?"

"No. Neither do you. Glance over this list of the real names of some men who have died lately in accidents of various kinds."

If the Slav's iron control was shaken as he read the long list, it was scarcely perceptible. Deissner went on:

"As long as it was to my advantage I let you think that I was just another one of your puppets, but I'm not. If you insist on committing suicide by jumping in the dark, count me out."

"In the dark? My information is that . . ."

"Have you any information as to where those so-huge tanks came from? Where they could possibly have been built?"

"No, but . . ."

"Then whatever information you have is completely useless," the Dutchman drove relentlessly on. "Maynard has been ready. What more is he ready for? That thought made me think. How did he get that way? I investigated. Do you know that computers and automation to the a-mount of hundreds of millions of dollars have been paid for by and delivered to non-existent firms?"

"No, but what . . . ?"

"From that fact I drew the tentative conclusion that MetEnge has industrialized a virgin planet somewhere; one that we know nothing whatever about."

"Ridiculous! MetEnge builds its own automation . . . but to save time they might . . . but such a planet would have to be staffed, and that could not be done tracelessly."

"It was done tracelessly enough so that we did not suspect it. I find that about sixty thousand male graduate engineers and scientists, and about the same number of young and nubile females of the same types, have disappeared from the ninety six planets."

"So?" This information had little visible effect.

"So those disappearances prove beyond any reasonable doubt that my tentative conclusion is a fact. Maynard is not bluffing; he is ready. Now, if MetEnge has worked that long and hard in complete secrecy it should be clear even to you that you and your missiles are precisely as dangerous to them as a one-week-old kitten would be. Before we can act we must find that planet and bomb it out of existence."

"It is impossible to hide so many people, especially young . . ."

"Do you think my agents didn't check? They did, thoroughly, and could find . . ."

"Bah! Your agents are stupid!"

"They were smart enough to put the arm on your men on that list, and if you think Maynard is stupid you had better think again. The worst fact is that twenty eight of my agents have disappeared, too, all of whom had worked up into good jobs with MetEnge and any one of whom could have and would have built a subspace communicator had it been humanly possible. The situation is bad. Very bad. That is why I have not acted. I will not act until I have enough facts to act on."

"*My* agents would have found that planet if it exists. I will send my own men and they will find it if it exists."

"You think you've got a monopoly on brains?" Deissner sneered. "Send your men and be damned. You'll learn. Here are copies of everything I have found out," and he handed The Nameless One a bulging brief-case.

SUBSPACE EXPLORERS

The tremendous new starship, the *Explorer*, built of
leybyrdite and equipped for any foreseeable eventuality,
was ready to fly. The Destons and the Joneses were
holding their last pre-flight conference. No one had
said anything for a couple of minutes; yet no one had
suggested that the meeting was over.

"Well, that covers it . . . I guess. . . ." Deston said,
finally. "Except maybe for one thing that's been niggling
at me . . . but it makes so little sense that I'm afraid to
say it out loud. So if any of you can think of anything
else we might need, no matter how wild it sounds . . .
I'm playing a hunch. Write it down on a slip of paper
and put it face-down on the table . . . here's mine . . .
it'll be three out of four, I think . . . read 'em and weep,
Bun."

Bernice turned the four slips over. "Four out of four.
Perce Train and Cecily Byrd. But what in *hell* do we
want 'em *for?*"

"Search me; just a hunch," Deston said, and:

"Me neither; just intuition." Barbara nodded her head.
"But why didn't we say anything . . . oh, I see. You and
I didn't, Babe, because we thought Bun wouldn't want
her along. Bun didn't because she thought we'd think it
was so she could kick her teeth out. Herc didn't because Bun might think he wanted her along for monkey
business. Right?"

That was right, and Deston called Maynard. "You can
have 'em both and welcome," was the tycoon's surprising

133

reaction to Deston's request. "They're the two hardest cases I ever tried to handle in my life, and I've got troubles enough without combing *them* out of my hair every hour on the hour. They did such good jobs on their projects that they haven't got enough to do. I'd like to fire them both—their assistants are a lot better for their present jobs than they are—but of course I can't. But listen, son. Why lead with your chin? If I can't handle those two damned kittyhawks, how do you expect to?"

"I don't know, chief; I'm just playing a hunch. Thanks a lot, and so-long."

Percival Train and Cecily Byrd boarded the *Explorer* together. "What can you four want of us?" the red-head asked, as soon as the six were seated around a table. "Particularly, what can you *possibly* want of me?"

"We haven't the foggiest idea," was Deston's surprising answer. "But four solid hunches can't be wrong. So suppose you break down and tell us."

"In that case I think I can. That must mean that you and Bobby are a lot more than just a wizard and a witch; and that both Herc and Bun are heavy-duty psionicists, too—I've more than suspected just that of Herc. Right?"

"That's right," Barbara agreed. "So you and Perce both are too." Train's jaw dropped and he looked at Barbara in pop-eyed astonishment. "Which I didn't suspect consciously for a second. How long have you had it, Curly—*known* that you had it, I mean?"

"Just since the dance. You gave me hell, Herc, remember? And before that, the chief and Babe had worked me over, too. . . ."

"I remember." Jones began to grin. "All I'm surprised at . . ."

"Hush, you." Cecily grinned back at him. "I don't get these moments of truth very often, so you just listen. Anyway, after the dance I felt lower than a snake's feet. I didn't feel even like going over to my hand-bag after a cigarette, so I just sat there and looked at it and pretty soon I could see everything perfectly plainly...

...ight. One gone, eleven left.

"Oh?" "Ah!" "So." came three voices at once; and Deston, after counting his cigarettes, said, "Eleven is right. That's a neat trick, Curly—just a minute."

Grasping his case he stared fixedly at it and a Camfield appeared in his mouth, too; but it did not light up. "How do you concentrate the energy without burning the end of your . . ." He broke off as Barbara shot him a thought, then went on, ". . . yeah, that can come later. Go ahead, Perce."

"You four are using *telepathy!*" Train declared.

"Uh-huh. It's easy, we'll show you how it goes. Go ahead."

"There's not much to tell. I've had it all my life, but I've never let on about it until now and I've never used it except on the job; I've been afraid to. I read up on psionics, but it's never been demonstrated scientifically and I didn't want the psychs to start with me. So I kept still. I knew you two were witches, of course—even though that is impossible, too—but I wasn't in your class, so I still kept still. Oh, I could see the stuff plainly enough when I knew exactly where to look, but that was all."

"How do you know that was all? You've been fighting the whole concept, haven't you, the same way I was?"

"Could be, I guess . . . maybe I *have* got something . . . latent, I mean . . . at that."

"I don't suppose we really need to ask you two, then, if you want to come along with us."

"I'll say you don't—and thanks a million for asking us," Cecily breathed; and Train agreed fervently. He went on, "You have room enough, I suppose? And when's your zero?"

"Plenty. Nineteen hours today was announced, but we can hold it up without hurting anything a bit."

"No need to. That gives us over seven hours and we won't need half that. Except for our bags at the hotel all our stuff's in the shed. We'll be seeing you—let's jet, Curly."

Train called an aircab and they were whisked across the city. Nothing was said until they were in the girl's room. He put both arms around her and looked straight into her eyes; his hard but handsome face strangely tender. "This hasn't been enough, Sess. I asked you once before to marry me. . . ."

"I'm glad you brought that up, Perce. I was just going to ask you if you still harbored the idea."

There is no need to go into exactly what happened then. After a time, however, he said, "I knew why you wouldn't, before."

"Of course," she replied, soberly. "We would have been at each other's throats half the time—we would have hurt each other unbearably."

"And this changes things completely," he said, just as soberly. "Exploring the universe with *those* four . . . as well as the unknown universe of psionics. . . ."

"Oh, wonderful!" she breathed. "Just the thought of it—especially that you're so strongly psionic, too—rocks me. It changes my whole world. And besides," her expression changed completely; she gave him a bright, quick grin, "children, especially such super-children as yours and mine, ought to have two parents. Married. To each other. You know?"

"Children!" Train gasped. "Why, I didn't know . . . you didn't tell me you were . . ."

"Of course not, silly. I'm not. I'm talking about the

think they're ordinary babies, too, but Bobby and Bun know very well they aren't. They won't admit it, of course, even to themselves, to say nothing of to each other—Bobby and Bun, I mean, not the kids—so don't *ever* breathe a word of this to *anybody*—besides, they'd snatch you bald-headed if you did. So—*verbum sap.*"

"I *think* you're more than somewhat nuts, presh, but I'll be as verbum sappy as you say. Now, one for the road," which turned out to be several, "and we'll go hunt us up a preacher."

"But we *can't!*" she wailed. "I forgot—just thought of it. Three days—those blood tests and things!"

"That's right . . . but with the physicals we've been taking every ten days—proof enough of perfect health so they'll waive 'em."

"One gets you ten they won't. Did you ever hear of a small-type bureaucrat cutting one inch of his damned red tape?"

"I sure have. All you got to have to push bureacrats around is weight, and we're heavyweights here . . . it'd be quicker, though, to do it the sneaky way—some starship's chaplain."

"Oh, let's!" She squealed like a schoolgirl. "I know you meant 'sneaky' in its engineering sense, but I don't. She has as much cat blood in her as I have. Maybe more."

"She?" Train raised his eyebrows. "Better break that up into smaller pieces, presh. Grind it a little finer."

"Comet-gas! You know who, and why, Bun. If you don't tell her who the chaplain was or what world he was from—registry, you know—she'll *never* find out when we were married."

Train laughed "I see, kitten—but I always did like cats, and I don't leak. Okay, little squirt—let's jet."

Long before nineteen hours, then, the Trains and their belongings arrived at the *Explorer*'s dock. Leaving her husband at the freight hoist, Cecily went up in the passenger elevator and looked Bernice up. "Where's our room, Bun?" she asked, in a perfectly matter-of-fact tone and without turning a hair.

Bernice started to say something; but, as she saw the heavy, plain, yellow-gold band—Cecily had never worn a ring on either hand—she said instead, "Why, I didn't know you were—when did *this* happen?"

"Oh, we've been married quite a while. We didn't want it to get out before, of course, but I thought sure you'd guessed."

"I guessed something, but not that. I'm awfully sorry, Curly, really, but . . ."

"You needn't be, Bun, at all; you had every right to. But I'll tell you one thing right now that I really mean—there'll be no more monkey-business for me. Ever."

"Oh, I'm *so* glad, Curly," and this time the two women did kiss each other. This was the beginning of a friendship that neither had thought would ever be.

At exactly nineteen hours the *Explorer* cut gravs. No one aboard her knew where they were going. Or what they were looking for. Or how long they would be gone.

When Maynard told Deston that he did not have time to cope with two such trouble-makers as Train and Byrd, he was stating the exact truth; for he was busier than ever he had ever been before. It was a foregone conclusion that the opposition, which included the most corrupt and farthest-left government WestHem had ever known, would not and could not accept its two minor

very nature of things, was better than either. And, long
before, Maynard had engineered a deal whereby Stevens Spehn had been put in charge of the combined
"Information Services" of the Galactic Federation—and
it is needless to say what kind of coverage this new
service provided.

Six men now sat at Maynard's conference table. Maynard, as usual, was at its head. Lansing of WarnOil sat
at his left. Spehn sat at his right. Next to Spehn was a
newcomer to the summit table—Vice-President Guerdon
Dann, the Admiral of InStell's far-flung fleet of private-police battleships. In full uniform, he was the typical
officer of space: big, lean, hard, poised, and thoroughly
fit. While older, of course, than a line officer, his stiff,
crew-cut red hair was only lightly sprinkled with gray
and he did not as yet wear lenses. Side by side, below
Lansing, sat two other newcomers, Feodr Ilyowicz and
Li Hing Wong, Russian and Chinese directors on the
Board.

"Yes, it'll be milk," Spehn was saying. "Impossible to
automate, easy to make one hundred percent effective,
and of extremely high emotional value."

"Right," Maynard agreed. "*How* the sobbers will
shriek and scream about our starving helpless babies to
death by the thousands. Any idea yet as to time?"

"Nothing definite, but it'll be fairly soon and the general strike won't be. They're holding that up while they're looking for our base, and nobody is even close yet to suspecting where Base is. Deissner and Nameless are all steamed up about the vanishing boys and girls and automation, but they're looking for them on a new planet out in space somewhere, not on an island on Galmetia. Are the kids still happy in Siberia?"

"Very much so; the bonuses take care of the isolation angle very nicely. They're making a game of being Siberians. They know it won't be too long and they know why we have to be absolutely sure that a lot of stuff stays hush-hush."

"Good. Next, Dutch Deissner is making independent noises and is getting big ideas. Full partnership, no less."

"He'll get himself squashed like a bug."

"Maybe, but so far he's been doing most of the squashing and Mister Big is burning like a torch."

"Umm . . . um . . . mm." Maynard thought for a moment. "So you think EastHem actually will bomb?"

"They're sure to." Spehn glanced across the table at Ilyowicz and Li who both nodded. "Not too long, I think, after the general strike is called—especially when we foul it up. Extra-heavy stuff on all our military installations, and really dirty stuff—one-hundred-percent-lethal nerve gas—on all our biggest cities. Wait a couple of months and take over."

"But retaliation—oh, sure, evacuation of the upper strata, they figure they have too many people, anyway."

"Check. They figure on losing millions of peasants and workers. They plan on getting a lot of people away, but I can't get even an inkling as to where. Do either of you fellows have any ideas on that?"

Li shook his head and Ilyowicz said, "No. I do not believe it can be a developed planet; I do not think that such a project could have been carried out so tracelessly. My thought is that it is a temporary hide-out merely, on some distant virgin planet."

"That makes sense," Spehn said. "How are you making out on the subs and the big jets, Guerd?"

"Satisfactory," the admiral replied. "Everybody with

Li nodded twice. "All really intelligent persons are opposed to government by terrorism. A surprisingly large number of such persons proved to have enough psionic ability so that our so-called mystics could teach them to receive and to transmit thought. Thus we have no cells, no meetings, the absolute minimum of physical contact, and no traceable or detectable communications. Thus, the Nameless One has not now and will not have any suspicion that he and five hundred seventy three of his butchers will die on signal."

The Westerners gasped. East was vastly different from West. "But if you can do that, why . . . ?" Dann began, but shut himself up. That was their job, not his.

"Right." Maynard approved the unspoken thought. "Well, does that cover it?"

"Not quite—one thing bothers me," Spehn said. "The minute we blockade Earth the whole financial system of the galaxy collapses."

"You tell him, Paul," Maynard said. "You're Deston and Deston."

"Covered like a sucker's bet." Lansing laughed and slapped himself zestfully on the leg. "That's the prize joker of the whole buiness. GalBank—the First Galaxian Bank of Newmars—opens for business day after tomorrow. Have you got any idea of what a solid-cash basis even one installation like Project Barbizon is? Or especially Rhenia Four, that's bringing in a net profit of a megabuck an hour? And DesDes owns 'em by the dozen. Hell, we could fight an interstellar war out of petty cash and never miss it from the till. Son, if Dutch and Slobski had any idea of how much hard-cash money we've got it'd scare the bastards right out of their pants."

"I see." Spehn thought for a moment. "I never thought of it before, but the way leybyrdite is taking everything over, no ordinary bank could handle it, at that. And Maynard, I've studied the material you gave us on your board-of-directors government of the Galactic Federation and I'll vote for it. Nothing else has ever worked, so it's time something different was tried."

"It won't be easy, but I'm pretty sure it can be made to work. After all, there have been quite a few self-cleaning boards of directors that have lasted for generations; showing substantial profits, yet adhering rigorously to the Principle of Enlightened Self-Interest. Examples, the largest firms in existence.

"To succeed, our board must both adhere to that Principle and show a profit—the profit in this case being in terms of the welfare of the human race as a whole. Is there anything else to come before this meeting?"

There was nothing else.

"That's it, then. Round it off neatly, Miss Champion—the adjournment and so forth—as usual."

prejudice, inhibition, or bias. He could, and frequently did, toss a laboriously-developed theory or hypothesis of his own down the drain in favor of someone else's—*any*one else's—that gave even slightly better predictions than did his own.

Being what he was, it was inevitable that when the Destons gave Adams his first real insight into telepathy and, through it, into the unimaginably vast and theretofore almost hermetically sealed universe of psionics, he dropped his old researches in favor of the new. He and his wife studied, more and ever more intensively, the possibilities and potentialities of the mind as *the mind*. Scholar-like, however, they needed to analyze and digest all the information available having any bearing upon the subject. Therefore, since there was no esoterica of that type in the *Procyon*'s library, they went back to Earth.

The Adams apartment was a fairly large one; five rooms on the sixteenth floor of Grantland Hall in Ann Arbor, overlooking the somewhat crowded but beautifully landscaped campus of the University of Michigan. Their living room was large—seventeen by twenty five feet—but it was the Adams, not the ordinary, concept of a living room. Almost everything in it was designed for books and tapes; everything in it was designed for study.

First, they went through their own library's stores of philosophy, of metaphysics, of paraphysics, of occultism, of spiritualism, of voodooism, of scores of kinds of cultism and even more kinds of crackpotism, from Forteanism up—or down. They studied thousands of words to glean single phrases of truth. Or, more frequently, bits of something that could be developed into truth or into something having to do with truth. Then they exhausted the resources of the University's immense library; after which they requested twenty two exceedingly rare tomes from the Crerar Library of Chicago. This was unusual, since scholars usually came to the Crerar instead of vice-versa, but Adams was Andrew Adams of the College; one of the very biggest of the Big Brains. Wherefore:

"It can be arranged, Dr. Adams," Crerar's head librarian told him, as one bibliophile to another. "These are replicas, of course—most of the originals are in Rome—and not one of them has been consulted for over five years. I'm glad to have you study these volumes, if for no other reason than to show that they are not really dead wood."

Thus it came finally about that Andrew and Stella Adams sat opposite each other, holding hands tightly across a small table, staring into each other's eyes and thinking at and with each other in terms and symbols many of which cannot be put into words.

"But it *has* to be some development or other of Campbell's Fourth Nume," she insisted. "It simply *can't* be anything else."

"True," he agreed. "However, Campbell had only a glimmering of a few of the—facets? Basics?—of that nume. So let's go over the prime basics again—the take-off points—the spring-boards—to see if possible where our thinking has been at fault."

"Very well. Fourth Nume, the—Level? Region? Realm?—of belief, of meaning, of ability to manipulate and to understand—of understanding of and manipulation of the phenomena of reality existing in the no-space-no-time continuum of . . ."

"Not yet. We may find more. Non-space-non-time manipulation, then, and also n-s-n-t attributes, phenomena, and being. Most important—the *sine qua non*—is the ultimate basic sex. Prerequisite, a duplex pole of power; two very-strongly-linked and very powerful poles, one masculine and one feminine . . ."

"A moment, Stella, I'll have to challenge that nuance of thought. If we are dealing with pure, raw, elemental force—as I think we are—we've been thinking too nicely-nicey on that, especially you. The thought should be, I'm pretty sure, neither masculine and feminine nor manly and womanly but starkly male and just as starkly female."

"You're probably right, Andy . . . you *are* right. So I'll think starkly female; as starkly so as an alley cat in heat. Shall we . . . no, let's finish checking the list."

They finished checking, and neither could perceive any other sources of error in the nuances of their thoughts. They tried it again, and this time it—whatever it was—clicked. Or rather, the result was not a click, but a sonic boom. Both bodies went rigid for seconds; then each drew a tremendously deep breath; as much from relaxation of tension as from realization of accomplishment. Then, poring over a street map of Calcutta, they went mentally to India; to the home of Mahatma Rajaras Molandru, who was one of the greatest sages then alive and who was also a Fellow of the College of Study.

"Is it permitted, Mahatma, that we converse with you and learn?" the fused minds asked.

So calm, so serene was the Great Soul's mind that he neither showed nor felt surprise, even at this almost incredible full meeting of minds. "You are very welcome, friends Andrew and Stella. You have now attained such heights, however, that I have little or nothing to give you and much to receive from you."

While the old Mahatma did get much more than he gave, the Adamses got enough new knowledge from him so that when they left India they no longer needed maps. Their linkage had a sureness and a dirigibility that not even the Destons were to match for many years.

From India they went to China, where they had a long and somewhat profitable interview with Li Hing Wong. Thence to Russia and Feodr Ilyowicz; where results were negligible.

"Andy, I never did like that man," Stella said, when the short and unsatisfactory interview was over. "And on such contact as this I simply can't stand him. Secretive—sly—he wouldn't really open up at all—all take and no give—that is *not* the way a good psiontist should act."

"I noticed that; but the loss is really his. It made it impossible for us to give him anything . . . but that attitude is perhaps natural enough—his whole heritage is one of secretiveness. Where next, my dear?"

They went to Tibet and to the Gobi and to Wales and to Rome and to Central Africa and to Egypt and to various other places where ancient, unpublished lore was to be found. They sifted this lore and screened it; then, after having sent a detector web of thought throughout the space and subspace of half the galaxy, they found and locked minds with Carlyle and Barbara Deston.

"Do not be surprised, youngsters," the Adams duplex began.

"Huh?" Deston yelped. "Clear to hellangone out here? And in subspace besides?"

146

"Distance is no longer important. Neither is the no

doing God-knows-how-many megaparsecs a minute relative to anything? So you've mastered absolute trans-spatial perception?"

"By no means. We have, however, been able to enlarge significantly our hyper-sphere of action. We have learned much."

"That's the understatement of the century. But before you try to teach us any such advanced stuff as that, there's something simple—that is, it *should* be simple— that's been bothering me no end. You got a little time now, Doc?"

"Lots of it, Babe. Go ahead."

"Okay. Well, since I never got beyond calculus, and not very advanced calc at that, I don't know any more about high math than a pig does about Sunday. But you and I both know what we mean by plain, common, ordinary, every-day reality. We know what we mean when we say that matter exists. Check, to here?"

"In the sense in which you are using the terms 'reality' and 'matter', yes."

"Okay. Matter exists in plain, ordinary, three-dimensional space. Matter is composed of atoms. Therefore *atoms* must exist and must have reality in three-dimensional space. So why can't any atomic physicist tri-di a working model of an atom? One that will work? One that human eyes can *watch* work? So that the ordinary human mind can understand how and why it works?"

"That's rank over-simplification, my boy. Why, the

147

very concept of subatomic phenomena and of subspace is so . . ."

"I know it is. That's exactly what I'm bitching about. Basically, nature is simple, and yet you Big Brains can't handle it except by inventing mathematics so horribly complex that it has no relationship at all to reality. You can't understand it yourselves. You don't—at least I'm pretty sure you don't—really understand—like I understand that chair there, I mean—time or subspace or space or anything else that's really fundamental. So do you mind if I stick my amateur neck 'way out and make a rank amateur's guess as to why and why not?"

"I'm listening, Babe, with my mind as well as my ears."

Barbara grinned suddenly. "Out of the mouths of babes —one Babe in this case—*et cetera*," she said.

"Okay, little squirt, that'll be enough out of you. Doc, I think there's one, and probably more than one, fundamental basic principle that nobody knows anything about yet. And that when you find them, and work out their laws, everything will snap into place so that even such a dumbster as I am will be able to see what the real score is. So you think I'm a squirrel food, don't you?"

"By no means. Many have had similar thoughts. . . ."

"I know that, too, but now we jump clear off the far end. Do you read science fiction?"

"Of course."

"You're familiar, then, with the triangle of electromagnetics, electro-gravitics, and magneto-gravitics. That's just a wild stab, of course, but one gets you a hundred that there's something, somewhere, that will tie everything up together—subspace, hunches, telekinetics, witches, and all that stuff."

Adams leaned forward eagerly. "Have you done any work on it?"

"Who, *me*? What with?" Deston laughed, but there was no trace of levity in the sound. "What would I be using for a brain? That's *your* department, Doc."

the laughing-stock of the scientific world—especially since I can't conceive of any possible instrumentation to test it."

"After that, you've *got* to talk. So start."

"The trigger was your flat statement—axiomatic to you—that the atom exists in three dimensions. Since that alleged fact can not be demonstrated, it probably is not true. If it is not true, the reverse—the Occam's-Razor explanation—would almost have to be that space possesses at least four physical dimensions."

"Hell's . . . flaming . . . afterburners . . ." Deston breathed.

"Exactly. The fact that this theory—to my knowledge, at least—has never been propounded seriously does not affect its validity. It explains every phenomena with which I am familiar and conflicts with none."

There was a long silence, which Deston broke. "Except one, maybe. According to that theory, psionic ability would be the ability to perceive and to work in the fourth physical dimension of space. Sometimes in time, too, maybe. But in that case, if anybody's got it why hasn't everybody? Can you explain that?"

"Quite easily. Best, perhaps, by analogy. You'll grant that to primitive man it was axiomatic that the Earth was flat? Two-dimensional?"

"Granted."

"That belief became untenable when it was proved conclusively that it was 'round'. At that point cosmology began. The Geocentric Theory was replaced by the Heliocentric. Then the Galactic. Where are we now? We don't know. Note, however, that with every advance in science the estimated size of the physical universe has increased."

"But what has that got to do with psionics?"

"I'm coming to that. While *intelligence* may not have increased very greatly over the centuries, mental *ability* certainly has. My thought is that the process of evolution has been, more and more frequently, activating certain hitherto-dormant portions of the brain; specifically, those portions responsible for the so-called 'supra-normal' abilities."

"Oh, *brother!* You really went out into the wild blue yonder after that one, professor."

"By no means. It may very well be that not all lines of heredity carry any of the genes necessary to form the required cells, even in the dormant state, and it is certain that there is a wide variation in the number and type of those cells. But have you ever really considered Lee Chaytor? Or George Wesley?"

"Just what everybody knows. They were empiricists —pure experimenters, like the early workers with electricity. They kept on trying until something worked. The theory hasn't all been worked out yet, is all."

" 'Everybody knows' something that, in all probability, simply is not true. I believed it myself until just now; but now I'm almost sure that I know what the truth is. They both were—they must have been—tremendously able psiontists. They did not publish the truth because there was no symbology in which they *could* publish it. There still is no such symbology. They concealed their supra-normal abilities throughout their lives because they did not want to be laughed at—or worse."

Deston thought for a minute. "That's really a bolus . . . what can we—any or all of us—do about it?"

"I'm not sure. Data insufficient—much more work must be done before that question can be answered. As

And next morning after breakfast the four couples sat at a round table, holding hands in a circle.

Very little can be said about what actually went on. It cannot be told in either words or mathematics. There is no symbology except the esoteric jargon of the psiontist—as meaningless to the non-psionic mind as the proverbial "The gostak distims the doshes"—by the use of which such information can be transmitted.

Results, however, were enormous and startling; and it must be said here that not one of the eight had any suspicion then that the Adams fusion had any help in doing what it did. Andrew Adams' mind was admittedly the greatest of its time; combining with its perfect complement would enhance its power; everything that happened was strictly logical and only to be expected.

The physical results of one phase of the investigation, that into teleportation, can be described. Each pair of minds was different, of course. Each had abilities and powers that the others lacked; some of which were fully developable in the others, some only partially, some scarcely at all. Thus, when it came to the upper reaches of the Fourth Nume, even Adams was shocked at the power and scope and control that flared up instantly in the Trains' minds as soon as the doors were opened.

"Ah," Adams said, happily, "That explains why you would not start out without them."

"And *how!*" Deston agreed; and it did.

It is also explained why Cecily had always been, in

Bernice's words, "such a sex-flaunting power-house." It accounted for Train's years of frustration and bafflement. At long, long last, they had found out what they were for.

"You two," Adams said, "have, among other things, a power of teleportation that is almost unbelievable. You could teleport, not merely yourselves, but this entire starship and all its contents, to any destination you please."

"They could, at that," Deston marveled. "Go ahead and do it, so Bobby and I can see how much of the technique we can learn."

"I'm afraid to." Cecily licked her lips. "Suppose we— I, my part of it, I mean—scatter our atoms all over total space?"

"We won't," Train said. Although he had not known it before, he was in fact the stronger of the two. "Give us a target, Babe. We'll hit it to a gnat's eyeball."

"Galmetia. GalMet Tower. Plumb with the flagpole. One thousand point zero feet from the center of the ball to our center of gravity."

"Roger." The Trains stared into each other's eyes and their muscles set momentarily. "Check it for dex and line."

Deston whistled. "One thousand point zero *zero* feet and plumb to a split blonde hair. You win the mink-lined whatsits. Now back?"

"As we were, Sess," Train said, and the starship disappeared from Galmetia's atmosphere, to reappear instantaneously at the exact point it would have occupied in subspace if the trip had not been interrupted.

The meeting went on. There is no need to report any more of its results; in fact, nine tenths of those results could not be reported even if there were room.

An hour or so after the meeting was over, Adams sat at his desk, thinking; staring motionlessly at the sheet of paper upon which he had listed eighteen coincidences. He knew, with all his mathematician's mind, that coincidence had no place in reality; but there they were.

Not merely one or two, but *eighteen* of them . . . which

At this point in his cogitations Barbara knocked on his door and came in, with her mind-blocks full on. He knew what was on her mind; he had perceived it plainly during the wide-open eight-way they had just held. Nevertheless:

"Something is troubling you, my dear?"

"Yes." Barbara nibbled at her lip. ". . . it's just . . . well, are you positively *sure*, Uncle Andy, that the babies are . . . well . . ." She paused, wriggling in embarrassment.

"Normal? Of course I'm sure, child. Positive. I have a file four inches thick to prove it. Have you any grounds at all for suspecting that they may not be?"

"Put that way, no, I haven't. It's just that . . . well, once in a while I get a . . . a *feeling* . . . Indescribable . . ." she paused again.

"It is possible that there is an operator at work," he said, quietly. The girl's eyes widened, but she didn't say anything and he went on, "However, I can find no basis whatever for any assumption concerning such a phenomenon. It is much more logical, therefore, to assume that these new and inexplicable 'feelings' are in fact products of our newly enlarged minds, which we do not as yet fully understand."

"Oh?" she exclaimed. "*You* have them, too? *You've* been working on it? Watching it?"

"I have been and am working on it."

"Oh, wonderful! If there's anything to it, then, you'll get it!" She hugged him vigorously, kissed him on the ear, and ran out of the room.

Adams stared thoughtfully at the closed door. That let Barbara out—or did it? It did not. Nor did it put her in any deeper. The operator, if any, was supernormal; super-psionic. The problem was, by definition, insoluble; one more of the many mysteries of Nature that the mind of man could not yet solve. Therefore he would not waste any more time on it.

He shrugged his shoulders, crumpled the sheet of paper up into a ball, dropped the ball into his wastebasket, and went to work on a problem that he might be able to solve.

century, however, it doubled. In another seventy five or eighty years it doubled again, to four billions. Then, due to limitation of births in most cultures and to famine and pestilence in the few remaining backward ones, the rate of increase began to drop; and early in the twenty second century Earth's population seemed to be approaching seven billions as a limit.

Although cities had increased tremendously in size there was still much farmland, and every acre of it—including the Sahara, irrigated by demineralized and remineralized water from the ocean—was cultivated and fertilized to the maximum possible constant yield. There were also vast hydroponics installations. Complete diet had been synthesized long since; hence Earthly fare for many years had been synthetic for most, vegetarian-and-synthetic for almost all of the upper twenty percent. Cow's milk and real meat were for millionaires only.

The dwindling of Earth's reserves of oil and coal had forced the price of hydrocarbons up to where it became profitable to work oil shale, and it was from the immense deposits of that material that most of Earth's oil was being produced. Very little of this oil, however, was being used as fuel; almost every ton of it was going into the insatiable conversion plants of the plastics and synthetics industries.

Of power, fortunately, there was no lack. It was available everywhere, at relatively low cost and in infinite amount.

Infinite? Well, not quite, perhaps. Inexhaustible, certainly. Also incalculable, since no two mathematicians ever agreed even approximately in estimating the total kinetic energy of the universe. And that super-genius Lee Chaytor, in developing the engine that still bears her name—the engine that taps that inexhaustible source of energy—gave to mankind one of the two greatest gifts it has ever received. The other, of course, was Wesley's Subspace Drive; by virtue of which man peopled the planets of the stars.

However, it was only the bold, the hardy, and the independent, and the discontented who went. Nor was there at first any such thing as Capital: the bankers of Earth were, then as now, highly allergic to risking their money in any venture less certain than a fifty-percent-of-appraised-value first mortgage upon a practically sure thing. Hence everything was on shares.

Elbridge Warner, Barbara Deston's great-great-great-and-so-on grandfather, a multi-millionaire oil man and a rabid anti-union capitalist, was the first big operator to go off-Earth. Following the "hunches" that had made him what he was, he hired a crew of the hardest, toughest, most intransigent men he could find and sniffed out a fantastically oil-rich planet, theretofore unknown to man. He named this planet "Newmars" and claimed it *in toto* as his own personal private property.

Then, having put down a tremendously productive well, he built and populated a balanced-economy colony. He then put down a few more gushers and built an arms plant and a couple of battleships, after which he: 1) Moved everything he owned that was movable from Earth to Newmars, and 2) Fired every union man in his employ. The United Oil Workers struck, of course, whereupon he made or stole—the record is not clear upon this point—some Chaytor superfusers and destroyed every Warner well on Earth. Destroyed them so thoroughly (everyone has seen a tri-di of what a super-

merce and the government of the United States of America forced the United Oil Workers to surrender; whereupon Warner graciously allowed fleets of tankers to haul oil from Newmars to Earth—at shale oil's exact delivered price.

Elbridge never did put down another well on Earth. In fact, as far as is known, he did not even visit Earth throughout the remainder of his hundred years of life. He was not bitter, exactly; he was stubborn, hard-headed, fiercely independent, and contumaceous; and he surrounded himself by preference with people of his own hard kind. Which, with that start and with Warner Oil always dominating the business, is why the oil-men of the planets have never been a gentle breed.

The Asteroid Mining Company followed WarnOil's lead. Iron and nickel, of course, and a few other metals, were available in plenty in Sol's asteroid belt; but a great many other highly important metals, particularly the heavier ones, were not. Wherefore the Asteroid Mining Company changed its name to Galactic Metals, Incorporated, and sent hundreds of prospectors out to explore new solar systems. These men, too—hard-muscled, hard-fighting, hard-playing hard-rock men all—were rugged, rough, and tough.

They found a sun with an asteroid belt so big and so full of chunks of heavy metal that it was all but unapproachable along any radial line anywhere near the plane of the ecliptic. This sun's fourth planet, while it was Tellus-Type as to gravity, temperature, water, air, and so forth, was much richer than Earth in metals heavier than nickel. Whereupon Galactic Metals pre-empted this metalliferous planet, named it "Galmetia", and proceeded to stock it with metalsmen—a breed perhaps one number Brinnell harder even than Elbridge Warner's oilmen.

With colonization an actuality, and productive of profits far beyond anything possible on Earth, a few of the most venturesome capitalists of Earth decided to dip into this flowing fountain for themselves. Lactia Incorporated, the leading-milk-and-meat producer, was the first banker-backed, consumer-oriented firm to take the big plunge. Knowing that it could fly a fifty-thousand-ton tanker from an out-planet to Earth in little more time and at little more expense than was required to ship a five-gallon container from Trempealeau, Wisconsin, to Chicago, Illinois, it found and claimed a Tellus-Type planet whose tremendous expanses of fertile plains and whose equable climate made it ideal for the production of milk and meat. It named its planet Lactia. Then Lactia the firm colonized Lactia the planet with feed-raisers, dairymen, and stockmen, and began to spend money hand over fist.

It required years, of course, to build up the herds, and an immense amount of money, but when many hundreds of millions of cattle lived upon hundreds of millions of fertile acres, the retail price of milk had come down from twenty five dollars a pint to the mythically-old figure of twenty cents per quart. Beef, pork, and mutton were available in every marketplace. Clothing of real wool and of real leather was being sold at prices almost anyone could afford. For, then as now, the businessmen of the planets adhered as closely as they possibly could to the Law of Diminishing Returns.

(With increasing automation, ever-mounting demand, and ever-increasing production as costs were lowered, planetary agriculture eventually, of course, put the synthetic-food industry completely out of business.)

These subsidiary planets, unlike Newmars and Galmetia, were at first dependent upon Earth. However, each one grew in population at an exponential rate. For, despite all the automation that is economically feasible, it takes a lot of men to work even as small a holding as a hundred squares of land. Men need women and women go with their men. Men and women have children —on the planets, as many children as they want. Families need services—all kinds of services—and get them. Factories came into being, and schools—elementary schools, high schools, colleges, and universities. Stores of all kinds, from shoppes to supermarkets. Restaurants and theaters. Cars and trucks. Air-cars. Radio, teevee, and tri-di. Boats and bowling lanes. Golf, even—on the planets there was *room* for golf! And so on. The works.

At first, all this flood of adult population came from Earth; drawn, not by any urge to pioneer, but by that mainspring of free enterprise, profit. Profit either in the form of high wages or of opportunity to enlarge and to advance, each entrepreneur in his own field. And not one in a hundred of those emigrants from Earth, having lived on an outplanet for a year, ever moved back. "Tellus is a nice place to visit, but *live* there? If the Tellurians like that kind of living—if they call it living—they can have it."

But the lessening of Earth's population was of very short duration. Assured of cheap and abundant food, and of more and more good, secure jobs, more and more women had more and more children and cities began to encroach upon what had once been farmland.

One of the most important effects of this migration, although it was scarcely noticed at the time, was the difference between the people of the planets and those of Earth. The planetsmen were, to give a thumbnail description, the venturesome, the independent, the ambitious, the chance-taking. Tellurians were, and became steadily more so, the stodgy, the unimaginative, the security-conscious.

Decade after decade this difference became more and more marked, until finally there developed a definite traffic pattern that operated continuously to intensify it. Young Tellurians of both sexes who did not like regimentation—and urged on by the blandishments of planetary advertising campaigns—left Earth for good. Conversely, a thin stream of colonials who preferred security to competition flowed to Earth. This condition had existed for over two hundred years. (And, by the way, it still exists.)

For competition was and is the way of life on the planets. The labor unions of Earth tried, of course; but the Tellurian brand of unionism never did "take", because of the profoundly basic difference in attitude of the men involved. Some Tellus-Type unions were formed in the early years and a few strikes occurred; only one of which, the last and the most violent and which neither side won, will be mentioned here.

The Stockmen's Strike, on Lactia, was the worst strike in all history. Some three thousand men and over five million head of stock lost their lives; about eight billion dollars of invested capital went down the drain. Neither side would give an inch. Warfare and destruction went on until, driven by the force of public opinion—affected no little by the virtual absence of meat and will f...

work on the problem. They worked for almost a year.

Capital must make enough profit to attract investors, and wants to make as much more than that minimum as it can. Labor must make a living, and wants as much more than the minimum as it can get. Between those two minima lies the line of dispute, which is the locus of all points of reasonable and practicable settlement. Somewhere on that line lies a point, which can be computed from the Law of Diminishing Returns as base, at which Capital's net profit, Labor's net annual income, and the public's benefit, will all three combine to produce the maximum summated good.

Thus was enunciated the Principle of Enlightened Self-Interest. It worked. Wherever and whenever it has been given a chance to work, it has worked ever since.

The planet-wide adoption of this Principle (it never did gain much favor on Earth) ended hourly wages and full annual salaries. Every employee, from top to bottom, received an annual basic salary plus a bonus. This bonus varied with the net profit of the firm and with each employee's actual ability. And the Planetsmen, as the production and service personnel of the planets came to be called, liked it that way. They were independent. They were individualists. Very few of them wanted to be held down in pay or in opportunity to any dead level of mediocrity just to help some stupid jerks of incompetents hang onto their jobs.

The Planetsmen liked automation, and not only because of the perennial shortage of personnel on the out-planets. And, week after week, union organizers from Earth tried fruitlessly to crack the Planetsmen's united front. One such attempt, representative of hundreds on record, is quoted in part as follows:

Organizer: "But listen! You Associated Wavesmen are organized already; organized to the Queen's taste. All you have to do is use your brains and join up with us and it wouldn't take hardly any strike at all to . . ."

Planetsman: "Strike? You crazy in the head? What in hell would we strike for?"

Org: "For more money, of course. You ain't dumb, are you? You could be getting a lot more money than you are now."

Plan: "I could like hell. I'd be getting less, come the end of the quarter."

Org: "Less? How do you figure that?"

Plan: "I don't. I don't have to. We've got expert computermen figuring for us all the time, and they keep Top Brass right on the peak of the curve, too, believe me. You never heard of the Law of Diminishing Returns, I guess."

Org: "I did so; but what has that got to do with . . . ?"

Plan: "Everything. It works like this, see? My basic is six thousand—and say, how much to Tellurian pole-climbers get?"

Org: "Well, of course we would . . ."

Plan: "Not with our help you won't. You'll dig your own spuds, brother. Anyway, say we strike—and that's saying a hell of a lot—ever hear of Lactia? But say we do, and say they raise our basic to—and that's saying a hell of a lot, too, believe me—but say they do, to—hell, to anything you please. Okay. So costs go up, so Top Brass has to raise prices. . . ."

Org: "Uh-uh. Let 'em take it out of their profits."

Plan: "They ain't makin' that much. Anyway, it'd stack up the same, come to the end of the quarter. The point would slide off of the peak and my bonus would get a bad case of the dropsy and I'd wind up the year making

too. It's just that simple. See?"

Org: "I see that it don't make sense. What you don't see is that Capital has been suckering you all along. They've been giving you the business. Feeding you the old boloney and giving you the shaft clear to the hilt and you're dumb enough to take it."

Plan: "Not by seven thousand tanks of juice, chum, and needling won't make us let you lean on us a nickel's worth, either. We get the straight dope and our officers don't dip into the kitty, either, the way yours do. So what you'd better do, meathead, is roll your hoop back to Tellus, where maybe you can make somebody believe part of that crap."

Aboard the *Explorer*, the Adamses and the Destons were discussing the course of civilization. Adams had prepared tables of figures, charts, and graphs. He had determined trends and had extrapolated them into future time. His conclusions were far from cheerful.

"This unstable condition has lasted far longer than was to have been expected two centuries ago," Adams said, definitely. "The only reason why it has lasted so long is because of the stabilizing effect of the planets siphoning off so many of Earth's combative and aggressive people. The situation is now, however, deteriorating; and, considering the ability, the quality, and the state of advancement of the Planetsmen, it will continue to deteriorate at an ever-increasing rate to the point of catastrophe."

"Huh?" Deston asked. "Grind that up a little finer, will you, professor?"

"It's inevitable. The original aim of Communism was to master all Earth. It failed. It also failed to gain any foothold upon any of the outplanets because the basic tenets of Communism are completely unacceptable to the independent and self-reliant peoples of the planets. The fact is, therefore, that Communism is bottled up on something over half of the land surface of one planet, while we 'contemptible capitalist warmongers' are spreading at an exponential rate over a constantly increasing number of planets. The question is, what will this present Nameless One of EastHem—who is none too stable a character—do about this state of affairs?"

Deston whistled, and after a short silence Barbara said, "He will bomb, I suppose you mean."

"Could be, at that," Deston agreed. "Especially since EastHem never will catch up with our production technology. The most important thing, as I see it, is when."

"Within a very few years, I think," Adams said. "By these charts, five years at most, and probably much less than that."

"Nice," Deston said, and thought for moments. "And he won't stick around for the fallout. He and the hard core of the Party will take off for some unknown planet —maybe they've been working on it for years—with the idea of bombing *all* our planets. Is that your idea?"

"That is one of many, but I do not have enough data to give a high probability to any one of them."

"But Uncle Andy," Barbara put in, "Since you never have been anybody's professional crepe-hanger, you've already decided what to do about it. So give."

"I have been able to find only one solution having a probability of success of point nine nine. In psionics, I think, lies the only possible answer. Such masters as Li Hing Wong and the mahatmas can do much, but not psionic development.

"Sounds good to me," Deston approved. "Have you got it going? We'll all get behind it and push."

"How could we have, young man? Even starting in a small way, such a school would require an investment of at least a hundred thousand dollars—which might as well be a million, as far as the Adams resources are concerned."

"A megabuck wouldn't more than start it, the way it ought to be." Deston glanced at Barbara, who nodded. He took a sheet of paper out of a drawer, wrote a couple of lines, and went on, "Doc, for a man with your brains, you've got absolutely the least sense of anybody I know. Any nitwit would know that DesDes would back any such project as that clear up to the hilt. Here, give this to Lansing. It's for twenty five megabucks now, and as much more as you want, whenever you want it."

XIV

THE GENERAL STRIKE

IN their suite, Percival Train put his arm around his wife's supple waist, swung her around, and kissed her lingeringly. "Let's sit down and talk this thing out. We both scanned both kids. We agree that they're both normal—apparently so, anyway—now. So what? Shoot me the load of what's bothering you."

"So a hell of a lot." A cigarette appeared between Cecily's lips, lit itself, and she burned a quarter of it in one long inhalation. "I'll give you both barrels. They *had* mindblocks. Both of them did. Now they either haven't any or are able to hide the fact that they have and I know damn well which one it is. Now. How could a baby who can scarcely walk yet—to say nothing of two of them—have anything to hide or want to? Or be able to if they did? Here's how. They were both conceived in subspace. . . ."

"So what? Don't you think that ever happened before?"

"Not in any ship that ever picked up a zeta charge, it didn't. No woman ever lived through *that* before to become a mother. And both periods of gestation were impossibly long. And all four parents were powerful psiontists; just how powerful you and I don't know and can't guess. And they both, at an age when normal babies are completely dependent, have super-normal intelligence and super-normal powers. . . ."

"Hold it, presh, you're just guessing at that."

"Guessing your left eyeball! Look at what happened! Could any normal man alive, of his own ability, do what we know Upton Maynard did? Or Eldon Smith? Or Guerdon Dann? And look at Steve Spehn. You know as well as I do, Perce, that it's starkly *impossible* to hide an operation as big as that from a spy system as good

166

as FastHem's. And look at me. I never had even a trace

But you got off on the wrong foot and never corrected yourself—so you went clear out to the Pleiades, by way of Canopus, Rigel, and S-Doradus, to hit Venus next door. Didn't you ever hear of Occam's Razor?"

"Why, of course, but . . ."

"Use it, then, and that functional as well as beautiful red-thatched head of yours."

It took her only a couple of seconds. "Why, it's *Barbara!*" she shrieked then. "It's been *Barbara* all the time!"

"Right. So let's examine Barbara. She's been an honest-to-God witch all her life. The greatest and probably the only one-hundred-percenter ever. She's known it and worked at it. That much we know for sure. What else she is we'll never know, but we can do some freehand guessing. She's had her own way all her life. How? Yet it never spoiled her. Why not? Even as a teen-ager, nobody's line ever fooled her. Why not? Above all, why wasn't she ever shot or strangled or blown up with dynamite?"

Cecily nodded her spectacular head. "Competition *must* have tried. That has always been the cut-throatingest of all cut-throat games. And, underneath, she really *is* hard."

"Hard! She's harder than the superneotride hubs of hell itself. Whenever she has wanted anything she has taken it. Including Carlyle Deston. And speaking of Deston, look at what happened to him—and me. He didn't used to have any more psionic ability than I did—not as much. Then, all of a sudden—both of us—*bam-whingo!* And you can't say the kids did that—not to him, anyway. Not only they weren't born yet—you might claim they could work pre-natally—they weren't conceived yet . . . probably, that is . . ."

She laughed. "You can delete the 'probably', Perce. They got married right after their first meetings, you know. Anyway, virgin brides or not, they certainly were not pregnant ones. They both knew the facts of life."

"Okay. She made full-scale, high-powered psionic operators out of Herc and Bun, too; long before the kids were born and probably before they were conceived. So, for my money, it was Bobby who worked all of us over and pulled the strings on the Adamses and on Maynard And Company and did everything else that was done."

"But those babies are *not* normal babies, Perce . . ." She paused, then went on, "But of course . . ." She paused again.

"Of course," he agreed "With cat-tractor-psiontist parents on both sides, how could they be? Especially with said parents working on them—just like we'll be working on ours—from the day they were born? Or maybe even before? I'll buy it that they have a lot more stuff than any normal kids could possibly have; up to and including mind-blocks and even the ability to hide them. When they grow up they'll probably have a lot more stuff than any of us. But now? And *that* kind of stuff? Uh-uh. No sale, presh; wrap it back up and put it back up on the shelf."

"I'll do just that." She drew a deep breath of relief and wriggled herself into closer and fuller contact. "Just the thought of such little monsters as that simply petrified me."

"I know what you mean. You almost gave me gooseflesh there for a minute myself."

"But we can understand Bobby's doing it and play

of the gong. Check, Cecily?"

"*How* I check!" She kissed him fervently. "You were right; I should have talked to you before. I didn't have a leg to stand on."

"*That* allegation I deny." He laughed, put his right hand on her well-exposed left leg, and squeezed. "This, in case nobody ever told you before—I thought I had—is one of the only perfect pair of such ever produced."

She put her hand over his, pressed it even tighter against her leg, and grinned up at him; and for a time action took place of words. Then she pulled her mouth away from his and leaned back far enough to ask, "You don't suppose she's watching us *now*, do you?"

"No. Definitely not. She's no Peeping Thomasina. But even if she were—now that you're you again, my red-headed bundle of joy, we have unfinished business on the agenda. And anyway, you're not exactly a shrinking violet."

"Why, I am too!" She widened her eyes at him in out-raged innocence. "That's a vile and base canard, sir. I'm just as much of a Timid Soul as you are, you Fraidy Freddie, you—why, I'm absodamlutely the shrinkingest little violet you ever laid your cotton-pickin' eyes on!"

"Okay, Little Vi, let's jet." He got up and helped her to her feet; then, arms tightly around each other and savoring each moment, they moved slowly toward a closed door.

The cold-war stalemate that had begun sometime early in the twentieth century had become a way of life. Contrary to the belief of each side over the years, the other had not collapsed. Dictatorship and so-called democracy still coexisted; both were vastly stronger than they had ever been before. Each had enough super-powerful weapons to destroy all life on Earth, but neither wanted a lifeless and barren world; each wanted to rule the Earth as it was. Therefore the Big Bangs had not been launched; each side was doing its subtle best to outwit, to undermine, and/or to overthrow the other.

WestHem was expanding into space; EastHem, as far as WestHem's Intelligence could find out, was waiting, with characteristic Oriental patience, for the capitalistic and imperialistic government of the West to fall apart because of its own innate weaknesses.

This situation existed when the Galactic Federation was formed; specifically to give all the peoples of all the planets a unified, honest, and just government; when Secretary of Labor Deissner, acting through Antonio Grimes, called all the milk-truck drivers of Metropolitan New York out on strike.

At three forty five of the designated morning all the milk-delivery trucks of Depot Eight—taking one station for example; the same thing was happening at all—were in the garage and the heavy steel doors were closed and locked. The gates of the yard were locked and barricaded. The eight-man-deep picket line was composed one-tenth of drivers, nine-tenths of heavily-armed, heavy-muscled hoodlums and plug-uglies. They were ready, they thought, for anything.

At three fifty a fleet of armored half-tracks lumbered up and began to disgorge armored men. Their armor, while somewhat reminiscent of that worn by the chivalry of old, was not at all like it in detail. Built of leybyrdite, it was somewhat lighter, immensely stronger, and very much more efficient. Its wide-angle visors, for instance, were made of bullet-proof, crack-proof, scratch-proof nee glass. Formation was made and from one of the

—it is remarkable how quickly a New York crowd can gather, even at four o'clock in the morning—"keep right on crowding up, as close as you can get. Anybody God damned fool enough to stand gawking in the line of fire of fifty machine guns *ought* to get killed—so just keep on standing there and save some other fool-killer the trouble of sending you to the morgue in baskets. Okay, men, give 'em hell!"

To give credit to the crowd's intelligence, most of it did depart—and at speed—before the shooting began. New Yorkers were used to being chivvied away from scenes of interest; they were *not* used to being invited, in such a loud tone of such savage contempt, to stay and be slaughtered. Of the few who stayed, the still fewer survivors wished fervently, later, that they had taken off as fast as they could run.

Armored men strode forward, swinging alloy-sheathed fists, and men by the dozens went down flat. Then guns went into action and the armored warriors fell down and rolled hap-hazardly on the pavement; for no man, however strong, can stand up against the kinetic energy of a stream of heavy bullets. Except for a few bruises, however, they were not injured. They were not even deafened by the boiler-shop clangor within their horribly resounding shells of metal—highly efficient earplugs had seen to that.

Those steel-jacketed bullets, instead of penetrating that armor, ricocheted off in all directions—and it was only then that the obdurately persistent bystanders—those of them that could, that is—ran away.

The machine-gun phase of the battle didn't last very long, either. In the assault-proof half-tracks expert riflemen peered through telescopic sights and .30-caliber rifles barked viciously. The strikers' guns went silent.

Leybyrdite-shielded mobile torchers clanked forward and the massed pickets fled: no man in his right mind is *ever* going to face willingly the sixty-three-hundred-degree heat of the oxy-acetylene flame. The gates vanished. The barriers disappeared. The locked doors opened. Then, with an armored driver aboard, each delivery truck was loaded as usual and went calmly away along its usual route; while ambulances and meat-wagons brought stretchers and baskets and carried away the wounded and the dead.

Nor were those trucks attacked, or even interfered with. It had been made abundantly clear that it would be the attackers who would suffer.

But what of the source of New York's milk? The spaceport and Way Nineteen? Pickets went there, too, of course; but what they saw there stopped them in their tracks. Just inside the entrance, one on each side of the Way, sat those two tremendous, invulnerable, enigmatic super-tanks. They did not do anything. Nothing at all. They merely sat there; but that was enough. No one there knew what those things could or would do; and no one there wanted to find out. Not, that is, the hard way.

Nor did the Metropolitan Police do anything. There was nothing they could do. This was, most definitely, not their dish. This was war. War between the Galaxians on one side and Labor, backed by WestHem's servile government, on the other. The government's armed forces, however, did not take part in the action. At the first move of the day, Maynard had taken care of that.

"Get the army in on this if you like," he had told Deissner, flatly. "Anything and everything you care to, up to and including the heaviest nuclear devices you have.

We are three long subspace jumps ahead of anything you

and swore. Deissner gritted his teeth in quiet, futile desperation. The Nameless One of EastHem, completely unaccustomed to frustration and highly allergic to it, went almost mad. He now knew that the Galaxians had the most powerful planet in the galaxy and *he could not find it.*

This situation was, of course, much too unstable to endure, and Nameless was the first to crack. He probably went completely mad. At any rate, his first move was to liquidate both Secretary of Labor Deissner and Chief Mediator Wilson. Nor was there anything of finesse about these assassinations. Two multi-ton blockbusters were detonated, one in each of two apartment hotels, and the fact that over three thousand persons died meant nothing to EastHem's tyrant. His second move was to make Antonio Grimes the boss of all WestHem. Whereupon Grimes called a general strike; every union man of the Western Hemisphere walked out; and all hell was out for noon.

The union people, however, were not the only ones who walked out. Executives, supervisors, engineers, and topbracket technicians did too, in droves, and disappeared from Earth; and they did not go empty-handed. For instance, the top technical experts of Communications Incorporated (a wholly-owned subsidiary of InStell) worked for an hour or so apiece in the recesses of their switch-banks and packed big carrying-cases before they left.

Grimes knew and counted upon the fact that West-Hem's economy, half automated though it was, could not function without his union men and women at work. He must also have known the obverse; that it could not function, either, without the brains that had brought automation into being in the first place and that kept it running—the only brains that understood what those piled-up masses of electronic gear were doing. He must also have known that in any fight to the finish Labor would suffer with the rest; hence he did not expect a finish fight. He was superbly confident that Capital, this time as always before, would surrender. He was wrong.

When Grimes found every one of his own communications channels dead, he tried frantically to restore enough service to handle Labor's campaign, but there was nothing he or his union operators could do. (They were still called "operators", although there were no longer any routine manual operations to be performed).

These operators, although highly skilled in the techniques of keeping the millions of calls flowing smoothly through the fantastically complex mazes of their central exchanges, were limited by their own unions' rules to their own extremely narrow field of work. An operator reported trouble, but she must not, under any conditions, try to fix it. Nor could if she tried. No operator knew even the instrumentation necessary to locate any particular failure, to say nothing of being able to interpret the esoteric signals of that instrumentation.

There were independent experts, of course, and Grimes found them and put them to work. These experts, however, could find nothing with which to work. The key codes, the master diagrams, and the all-important frequency manuals had vanished. They could not even find out what, or how much, of sabotage had been done. It would be quicker, they reported, to jury-rig a few channels for Labor's own use. They could do that in a day

missile left the ground, the retaliatory monsters of the West began to climb their ladders.

And in minutes the Nameless One and hundreds of the hard core of the Party died; and thousands of his lesser minions were in vehicles hurtling toward subspacers which had for many months been ready to go and fully programmed for flight.

XV

THE UNIVERSITY OF PSIONICS

EARTH AS SUCH did not have a space navy; there was no danger of attack from space and, as far as Earth was concerned, the outplanets could take care of themselves. Nor did either WestHem or EastHem; with their ICBM's they did not need or want any subspace-going battleships. Nor did any of the planets. Newmars and Galmetia were heavily armed, but their armament was strictly defensive.

Thus InStell had been forced, over the years, to develop a navy of its own, to protect its far-flung network of merchant traffic lines against piracy; which had of course moved into space along with the richly-laden merchantmen. As traffic increased, piracy increased; so protection had to increase, too. Thus, over the years and gradually, there came about a very peculiar situation:

The only real navy in all the reaches of explored space—the only law-enforcement agency of all that space —was a private police force not responsible to any government!

It hunted down and destroyed pirate ships in space. It sought out and destroyed pirate bases. Since no planetary court had jurisdiction, InStell set up a space-court, in which such few marauders as were captured alive were tried, convicted, and sentenced to death. For over a century there had been bitter criticism of these "high-handed tactics," particularly on Earth. However, InStell didn't like it, either—it was expensive. Wherefore, for the same hundred years or so, InStell had been trying to get rid of it; but no planet—particularly Earth—or no Planetary League or whatever—would take it over. Everybody wanted to run it, but nobody would pick up the tab. So InStell kept on being the only Law in space.

every liner, freighter, lorter, and shuttle that could be there was there; MetEnge's every ore-boat, tanker, scout and scow that could possibly be spared; all the Galaxians' every available vessel of every type and kind, from Hatfield's palatial subspace-going private yacht down to Maynard's grandsons' four-boy flitabout. More, every spaceyard of the planets had been combed; every clunker, and every junker not yet cut completely up, was taken over. Drives and controls had been repaired or replaced. Hulls had been made air-tight. Many of these derelicts, however, were in such bad shape that they could not be depended upon to stay air-tight; hence many of those skeleton crews worked, ate, and slept in space-suits complete except for helmets—and with those helmets at belts at the ready.

But each unit of that vast and ridiculously nondescript fleet could carry men, missile-killers, computer-coupled locators, and launchers, and that was all that was necessary. Since there was so much area to cover, it was the number of control stations that was important, not their size or quality. The Galaxians had had to use every craft whose absence from its usual place would not point too directly at Maynard's plan.

The fleet was not evenly distributed, of course. Admiral Dann knew the location of every missile-launching base on Earth, and his coverage varied accordingly. Having made formation, he waited. His flagship covered

EastHem's main base; he personally saw EastHem's first Inter-Continental Ballistic Missile streak upward.

"This is it, boys, go to work," he said quietly into his microphone, and the counter-action began. A computer whirred briefly and a leybyrdite missile-killer erupted from a launcher. Erupted, and flashed away on collision course at an acceleration so appallingly high that it could not be tracked effectively even by the radar of that age.

That acceleration can be stated in Tellurian gravities; but the figure, by itself, would be completely meaningless to the mind. Everyone knows all about one Earthly gravity. Everyone has seen a full-color tri-di of hard-trained men undergoing ten and fifteen gees; has seen what it does to them. But ten thousand gravs? Or a hundred thousand? Or two hundred thousand? Such figures are entirely meaningless.

Consider instead the bullet in the barrel of a magnum rifle at, and immediately after, the instant of ignition of the propellant charge. This concept is much more informative. Starting from rest, in a time of a little over one millisecond and in a distance of less than three feet, that bullet attains a velocity of more than four thousand feet per second. Those missile-killers moved like that, except more so and continuously. They were the highest-acceleration things ever put into production by man.

The first killer struck its target and both killer and target vanished into nothingness; a nothingness so inconceivably hot that the first thing to become visible was a fire-ball some ten miles in diameter. But there was nothing of fission about that frightfulness; GalFed's warheads operated on the utterly incomprehensible heat generated by dead-shorted Chaytor engines during the fractional microsecond each engine lasted before being whiffed into subatomic vapor by the stark ferocity of its own performance.

Missiles by the hundreds were launched; from EastHem, from WestHem, from the poles and from the oceans and from the air; and in their hundreds they were blown

into submolecular and subatomic vapor. Thus it made

of the various oceans. They were hunting, with ultra-sensitive instrumentation, all Earth's missile-carrying submarines. They didn't bother about the missiles launched by the subs—the boys and girls upstairs would take care of them—they were after the pig-boats themselves. Their torpedoes were hunters, too. Once a torpedo's finders locked on, the sub had no chance whatever of escape. There was a world-jarring concussion where each submarine had been, and a huge column of water and vapor drove upward into and through the stratosphere.

This furious first phase of the "police action" lasted—except for the sub-hunt—only minutes. Then every missile-launching site on Earth was blasted out of existence. So also were a few subspacers attempting to leave East-Hem—all Earth had been warned once and had been told that the warning would not be given twice.

Then the immense fleet re-formed, held position, and waited a few hours; after which time Dann ordered all civilian ships to return to their various ports. The navy stayed on in its entirety. It would continue to destroy all ships attempting to leave Earth.

Twelve hours after Earth's last missile had been destroyed, two-hundred-odd persons met in the main lounge of the flagship of the fleet. Maynard, his face haggard and drawn, called the meeting to order. After the preliminaries were over, he said:

"One part of the operation, the prevention of damage

to any important part of Earth, was one hundred percent successful. Second, the replacement of EastHem's dictatorship by a board of directors was also successful—at least, the first objectives were attained. Third, our attempt to replace WestHem's government by a board of directors which, together with that of EastHem, would form a unified and properly-motivated government of all Earth, was a failure. The Westerners did not try to leave Earth, but decided to stay and fight it out. For that reason many key men changed their minds at the last minute and remained loyal to WestHem's government instead of supporting us. Thus, while we succeeded in evacuating most of our personnel, we lost one hundred four very good men.

"The fault, of course, was mine. I erred in several highly important matters. I underestimated the power of nationalism and patriotism; of loyalty to a government even though that government is notoriously inefficient, unjust, and corrupt. I underestimated the depth and strength of the anti-Galaxian prejudice that has been cultivated so assiduously throughout the great majority of Earth's people; I failed to realize how rigidly, in the collective mind of that vast group, Galaxianism is identified with Capitalism. I overestimated the intelligence of that group; its ability to reason from cause to effect and its willingness to act for its own good. I thought that, when the issue was squarely joined, those people would abandon their attitude of 'Let George do it' and take some interest in their own affairs.

"Because of these errors in judgment I hereby tender my resignation, effective as of now, from the position of Chairman of this Board. I turn this meeting over to Vice-Chairman Bryce for the election of my successor."

He left the room; but was recalled in five minutes.

"Mr. Maynard, your tendered resignation has been rejected by an almost unanimous vote," Bryce told him. "It is the concensus that no one else of us all could have

the Galactic Federation concluded its first really important meeting.

Earth's communications systems were restored to normal operating conditions and Maynard, after ample advance notice, spoke to every inhabitant of Earth who cared to listen. He covered the situation as it then was; what had brought it about, and why such drastic action had been necessary. Then he said:

"At present there are ninety five planets in the Galactic Federation. Earth will be admitted to the Federation if and when it adopts a planetary government acceptable to the Federation's Board of Directors. We care nothing about the form of that government; but we insist that its prime concern must be the welfare of the human race as a whole. Earth now has two directors on our board, Li Hing Wong and Feodr Ilyowicz. Earth is entitled to three more directors, to represent the regions now being so erroneously called the Western Hemisphere. They must be chosen by an honest, stable, and responsible authority, not by your present government of corrupt, greedy, and self-serving gangsters and plunderers.

"We will allow enough freighters to land on West-Hem's spaceports to supply WestHem's people with its usual supply of food and of certain other necessities, but that is all. Our milk-truck drivers have been recalled and we will do nothing whatever about the general strike. If you wish to let an organized minority starve you to death, that is your right. You got yourselves into this mess; you can get yourselves out of it or not, as you please.

"We will not broadcast again until three qualified representatives of WestHem have been accepted by us as members of the Board of Directors of the Galactic Federation. Until then, do exactly as you please. That is all."

There is no need to go into what happened then throughout the nations of WestHem; the many nations whose only common denominator had been their opposition to the East. Too much able work has been done, from too many different viewpoints, to make any real summary justifiable. It suffices to say here that the adjustment was not as simple as Maynard's statement indicated that it should be, nor as easy as he really thought it would be. The strife was long, bitter, and violent; and, as will be seen later, certain entirely unexpected events occurred.

In fact, many thousand persons died and the Galaxians themselves had to straighten WestHem out before its three directors were seated on the Board.

There is no agreement as to whether or not the course that was followed was the right course or the best course. Many able scholars hold that the Directorate was just as much of a dictatorship, and just as intolerant of and just as inimical to real liberty and freedom, as was any dictatorship of old.

It is the chronicler's considered opinion, however, that what was done was actually the best thing—for humanity as a whole—that could have been done; considering what the ordinary human being intrinsically is. By "ordinary" is meant, of course, the person to whom the entire field of psionics is a sealed realm; the person in whose tightly closed and rigidly conventional mind no supra-normal phenomenon can possibly occur or exist. And the present state of galactic civilization seems to show that if what was done was not the best that could have been done it was a very close approximation indeed thereto.

was designed from the first to become completely in-dependent of Earth in as short a time as possible. Thus, as well as being longer-established than the other planets, it grew faster in population. Therefore Newmars had a population of about a billion, whereas the next most populous planet, Galmetia, had scarcely half that many people and all the rest of the colonized planets together did not have many more people than did Earth alone.

Geographically, Newmars had somewhat more land than Earth and somewhat less water, but the land masses were arranged in an entirely different pattern. There was one tremendous continent, Warneria; which, roughly rectangular in shape and lying athwart the equator, covered on the average about ninety degrees of latitude and about one hundred fifty of longitude. There were half a dozen other, much smaller continents, and many hundreds of thousands of islands ranging in size from coral atolls up to near-continents as large as Australia.

Most of Newmars' people lived on "The Continent," and some seven millions of them lived in and around the coastal city of Warnton, the planet's only real busi-ness center and the capital city of both the Continent and the whole Warner-owned world.

In establishing the University of Psionics, then, Adams did not have to think twice to decide where to put it. Earth, even though it would furnish most of the students, was out of the question; the U of Psi would have to be in Warnton, Newmars.

Within a day of landing, however, Adams realized that the business of starting such a project as that was not his dish. He simply could not spend important money. He had never bought even an expensive scientific instrument; he had always requisitioned them from some purchasing department or other. He had never in his life written a check for more than a few hundred bucks; he had no knowledge whatever of the use of money as a tool. Wherefore the *Explorer* landed at Warnton Spaceport and Barbara Deston took over. It had been Adams' idea to buy—or preferably to rent—a small apartment house to start with, but Barbara put her foot down hard on that.

She bought outright a brand-new forty-story hotel that covered half of a square block, saying, "We don't want large class-rooms—the smaller the better, since it will be small-group work—so this will suit us well enough until the architects get our real university built. Then we can either sell it or form an operating company and merge it into the hotel chain."

When the project was running smoothly, and after the eight had developed a nucleus of some fifty psiontists, the Destons took the *Explorer* to Earth and the Joneses and the Trains, in two Warner-owned subspacers, started out to cover the other planets, in descending order of population.

The Destons took up residence in their suite in the Hotel Warner and went to work. They scanned colleges and universities, whether or not any such institution of learning had ever shown any interest in psionics. They scanned Institutes of this and that, including several of Psychic Research. They scanned science fiction fan clubs and flying-saucer societies and crackpot groups and cults of all kinds and psychic mediums and fortune-tellers. They attended—unfelt—meetings of the learned societies. They scanned the trades and the professions, from aard-

~~vork keepers and aerialists through electricians and jewel-~~

~~was) learned telepathy in seconds, and, with very few~~
exceptions, all persons with such minds became Galaxians and went to Newmars.

Since the operators knew what to do and exactly
how to do it, the work went fast; and, very shortly after
its beginning, a definite pattern began to form. Every pos-
sessor of a strong latent talent was at or near the top
of his or her heap. If a performer, he or she had top
billing. If a milliner, she got a hundred dollars per copy
for her hats. If a mechanic, he was the best mechanic
in town.

It need scarcely be said that Maynard, Lansing, Dann,
Smith, Phelps, DuPuy, Hatfield, Spehn, Miss Champion,
the seven leaders of the Planetsmen and their assistants
and hundreds of others of the Galaxians were found to
be very strong latents. Or that, even though most of
them were too busy to go to Newmars to study, each
was given everything that he could then take that his
teachers could then give.

On the other hand, not even the Adamses could at
that time get into touch with a non-psionic mind. It was
not that that mind refused contact or blocked the exploring feelers of thought; it was as though there was
nothing there to feel. It was like probing with sentient
fingers throughout the reaches of an unbounded, unde-
fined, completely empty and utterly dark space.

And the conservative ("Hidebound", according to Deston), greedy capitalists of Earth were non-psionic to a man.

The response to this psionic survey was so tremendous that the hotel building, immense as it was, was jammed to overflowing before the first real University building was ready for use.

As Barbara had foreseen, the psionics classes were small, but there were plenty of teachers; people whose former titles ranged from Instructress-In-Kindergarten to Professor Emeritus of Advanced Nucleonics. And these classes were being driven. They wanted to be driven. Each person there had been—more or less unconsciously —unhappy, discontented, frustrated. The few who had known that they had psionic power had been hiding it or disguising it; the others had known, either definitely or vaguely, that they wanted something out of life that they were not getting. Thus, when their minds were opened to the incredible vistas of psionics, they wanted to be driven hard and they drove themselves hard. They graduated fast, and either went right to work or formed advanced-study groups—and in either case they kept on driving hard.

When the *Explorer* emerged near Newmars, Barbara did not wait for the slow maneuvering of landing at the spaceport and then taking the monorail into town, but 'ported herself directly into the main office of the University. Five minutes later she drove a thought to her husband. "Babe, come here, quick! Here's something you're simply got to see!"

He appeared beside her and she went on, "I knew they were working fast, but I certainly didn't expect anything like *that* so soon." Her mind took his up into a small room on the thirtieth floor. "Just *look* at *that!*"

Deston "looked" at the indicated group of four; who, heads almost touching, were seated at a small square table. One was a gangling, coltish, teen-age girl in sweater, slacks, and loafers, with braces on her teeth and her hair in a ponytail. The second was an old friend of Des-

...ter's a big, taut, trim space officer in a uniform sporting...

...doing.

"Uh-uh. I don't want to derail their train of thought."

"You won't. Maybe if you grabbed 'em by the scruff of the neck and the seat of the pants and slammed 'em against the wall a few times you could, but nothing any gentler than that."

"They're *that* solid?" He went in and looked, and his whole body stiffened. He stayed in for five long minutes before he came back to Barbara and whistled through his teeth. "Wow and *wow* and WOW!" he said then. "All of us Big Wheels are going to have to look a little bit out—we're going to have competition. We may have to demonstrate our fitness to lead—if any."

"That's what I mean, and isn't it just *wonderful?* The University doesn't need us any more, so we can start doing whatever it is that we're going to do right now instead of waiting so long, like we thought we'd have to."

"They've done a grand job, that's sure. Let's do some long-distance checking—see how Spehn and Dann are making out."

They were making out all right. Since both were now psiontists, Intelligence and Navy were barreling right along. Graduates from the University of Psionics had been pouring into both services for weeks. Both services were expanding rapidly, in both numbers and quality; and, since the opposition was practically non-psionic, the Galaxians' advantage (Spehn and Dann agreed) was increasing all the time. Also, the opposition was not really united and could never be united except superficially because its factions were, by their very natures, immiscible. How effective *could* such opposition be?

Unfortunately, Spehn and Dann were wrong; and so were the Destons. It is a sad but true fact that a college graduate at graduation knows more than he ever did before or ever will again; and so it was with these young new psiontists. They thought they knew it all, but they didn't. They had a long way to go.

tance here.) What had been the Interstellar Patrol was now the Grand Fleet of the Galactic Federation.

Fleet Admiral Guerdon Dann, being a psiontist, could understand and could work in subspace. Therefore he could perceive subspace-going vessels before they emerged into normal space, a feat no non-psionic observer could perform. Thus he perceived a very large number of vessels so maneuvering in subspace as to emerge in a roughly globular formation well outside his own globe of warships. He perceived that they were warcraft and really big stuff—super-dreadnoughts very much like his own—and that there were four or five hundred of them. That wasn't good; but, since their purpose was pellucidly clear, he'd have to do something. What could he do? His mind raced.

He wasn't a war admiral—pirates didn't fight in fleets. He didn't know any more about fleet action in space than a pig did about Sunday. There'd never been any. Missile-killers were new and had extreme range, and no repulsor except a planet-based super-giant could stop one after fifteen seconds of flight at 175,000 gravities. However, they carried no screen, so they'd be duck soup for beams, especially lasers—if they could spot them soon enough, and he'd have to assume that they could.

Torps had plenty of screen, but they were slow; hence they were duck soup for repulsors. What he *ought* to have, dammit, was something with the legs of a killer and the screens of a torp, and there was nothing like that even on the drawing boards. Before leybyrdite nothing like that had been possible.

Beams, then? Uh—*uh!* They'd englobe shipwise, four or five to one. His ships could then immerge—if they were fast enough—or get whiffed out.

He got into telepathic touch with his officers. "I don't know whether we can do anything to those boys or not. Probably not. We certainly can't if we let them get close to us—they'll englobe us four or five to one if we make like heroes, so we won't. Be ready to immerge when I give the word. Try killers at fifteen seconds range as they emerge and send out some torps on general principles, but that's all. We're going to execute a strategic withdrawal—in other words, run like hell."

Computers computed briefly; impressed data upon mechanical brains. Missile-killers and torpedoes hurtled away. The first strange warship emerged and the first missile-killer flashed into a raging, space-wracking fireball miles short of objective.

"I was afraid of that," Dann thought on, quietly. "I don't think they'll follow us—I think I know what they're after—so we'll run. Numbers one to fifty, to Galmetia; fifty one to one hundred, to Newmars; and everybody, get under an umbrella, just in case they do follow us."

En route to Galmetia—the flagship *Terra* was of course Number One—Dann had a long telepathic conversation with Maynard, and on landing he went straight to GalMet's main office. Maynard was waiting for him, with a staff of some fifty people. Maynard said:

"You all know that the purpose of the enemy fleet was not specifically to attack our fleet or our planets, but to break our blockade of Earth. They broke it, and announced that any planet refusing to resume full trade with Earth would be bombed. So," he shrugged his shoulders and grimaced wryly, "we give in and it is now business as usual. We have of course taken the obvious steps; we are beefing

The meeting went on for four hours; but beyond the obvious fact that there was a planet—and not a Johnny-Come-Lately planet, either, but one long-enough established to have plenty of people, plenty of industry, and plenty of money or its equivalent—the meeting got nowhere. At adjournment time Maynard flashed Deston a thought to stay behind, and after the others had gone he said:

"You told me you didn't know anything. I didn't ask you then and I'm not asking you now what you're figuring on doing about it. But you're going to do something. Correct?"

"Correct. I don't know what anybody *can* do, but we're going to work on it. They have leybyrdite; but they almost certainly did not develop it themselves."

"Cancel the 'almost'. We've never limited its sale—we can't. Anyone could have bought any amount of it. Dummy concerns—untraceable—is my guess on that. We know that a lot of Tellurian capital has always operated on the old grab-everything-in-sight principle, and everyone knows what Communism does. Either of them could and would run a planet as that one has obviously been run for many years—in a way that would make the robber barons of old sick at the stomach. But since it doesn't make sense that Labor has been doing it . . . it almost has to be either Capital or Communism."

"It looks that way." Deston frowned in thought. "But I don't know any sure-fire way of finding out which, if either . . . so I'd better go get hold of some people to help me think. 'Bye."

Deston did not walk out of the room, but 'ported himself to Barbara's side in the University office. "Hi, pet," he said, kissing her lightly. "I got troubles. How about busting in on that squirrelsome foursome that Horse French is in? I want to cry in their beer."

"Uh-uh, let's not bust in; they'll have to come up for air pretty soon. Let's wait 'til they do, then 'port up there with some lemon sour and Gulka fizz and cherry sloosh and stuff for a break."

The foursome did and the Destons did and Deston said:

"Well, well, Frenchy old horse, fancy meeting *you* here!" and four strong hands gripped and shook hard. This was the Communications Officer to whom Deston had reported the survival of the liner *Procyon* so long before. "Nobody ever even suspected you of having a brain in your head. All beef—nothing but muscle to keep your ears apart, I always thought."

"Hi, Runt! You? Think? What with? But I'll tell you how it was. So many captains got married that they couldn't find room for enough desks for 'em all to sit at, so they loaned me to this here Adams project—on pay, too. Nice of 'em, what?—but you've never met my wife. Paula, this renegade fugitive from InStell is Babe Deston—the unabashed hero of subspace, you know."

"I know." The slender, graceful, black-haired, black-eyed girl with the almost theatrical make-up, who had been watching and listening to this underplayed meeting as intently as Barbara had, gave him a firm, warm handshake and turned to Barbara. "And you're Bobby, of course. These men of ours. . . ." She raised one carefully-sculptured eyebrow, "but *we* don't have to insult each other to prove that we're . . ."

"Hey!" Deston broke in then. He had been studying the way Paula walked—he'd never seen anybody except Barhara move with such perfect automatic unconscious

rest of us a chance." The coltish but attractive teenager, having gulped the last syrupy bits of a full half-liter of cherry sloosh, came in. "I'm May Eberly. I can't tell you two wonderful people how glad I am that you started this and let me in—I never *dreamed*—well, anyway, it's *exactly* what I was born for. The others, too. You know what they call us? The Effeff—the Funny Four, no less—but I don't care. I *love* it! And this," she waved a hand at the oldster, "is Titus Fleming. He's got pots of money, so we call him 'Tite', but of course he isn't, just the opposite, in fact he spoils us all rotten, and . . ."

"Hush, child," Fleming said, with an affectionate smile. Then, to Deston, "May has an extraordinarily brilliant and agile mind, but she is inclined to natter too much."

"Well, why not?" the youngster demanded, engagingly. "When we're en rapport I don't talk at all, so I have to make up for it sometime, don't I? And Mr. Deston —no, I think I'll call you 'Babe', too. Okay?"

"Sure. Why not?"

"Horse, there—I never heard him called that before, but I like it—says if everybody's forbearing enough to let me keep on living long enough to grow up, which will surprise him a megabuck's worth, I'll be a gorgeous hunk of woman some day." She executed a rather awkward pirouette. "I can't do this anywhere near like Paula does yet, but I'm going to sometime, just see if I don't."

"I'd hate to bet one buck against Horse's megabuck that you won't." Deston agreed. The girl was certainly under fourteen, but the promise was there. Unmistakably there. "Or that you won't live to break a hundred, either."

"Oh, thanks, Babe. Oh, I just *can't wait!* I'm going to be a *femme fatale,* you know—all slinky and everything—but you prob'ly didn't come all the way out here just to chatter—I think Tite's word 'natter' is cute, don't you?—so maybe before Horse bats my ears down again I'd better keep still awhile. S'pose?"

"Could be—we're in a jam," Deston said, and told them what the jam was. "So you see, to get anywhere at all, we've got to do some really intensive spying, and the only way to do that is to learn how to read non-psionic minds, and the poop is that if anybody in total space can deliver the goods on that order, you four are most apt to be the ones."

"Oh?" May exclaimed. "That's a really funny one, Babe—we must *really* be psychic. . . ." She broke off with a giggle as the others began to laugh. "No, I mean really—much more so even than we thought—because that's *exactly* what we've just been working on—not to be just snoopy stinkers, either—or stinky snoopers?—but just to find out why nobody could ever do it before—we aren't very good at it yet, but it goes like this—no, let's all link up and we'll show you. Oh, this is going to *really* be fun!"

The four linked up and went to work, and the Destons tuned themselves in; very slowly at first; more as observers than as active participants in the investigation. The subject this time was a middle-echelon executive, the traffic manager of one division of far-flung Warner Oil. He was a keen-looking young man, sharp-featured, with a very good head for figures. His king-size desk was littered with schedules, rate-books, and revision sheets. From time to time his fingertips flicked rapidly by touch over the keys of a desk-type computer.

The four were getting a flash of coherent thought once

"You weren't ready, so Doc wouldn't have tried to give it to you, so who did?"

"Mr. and Mrs. Throckmorton."

"They would," Barbara said then. "Fortunately, they've learned better now."

"But *you* two can give it to us."

"We could make a stab at it, but we'd rather not. We need more practice. We'll call Adams and Stella and watch."

The Adamses came in, and wrought; and this time, since the pupils were ready, the lesson "took."

"*Now* we'll git 'im!" May exclaimed. "Come on, what's holding us up?"

"I am," Deston said. "Don't go off half-cocked; we've got a lot to do yet. Before anyone can do a job he has to know exactly what the job is and exactly how to do it, and we don't know either one. So let's examine your four-ply entity—the tools you're using. There's no three-dimensional analogy, but we can call Horace and Paula an engine, with two vital parts missing—the spark-plug and the flywheel. . . ."

"But I want to learn that fourth-nume stuff *now!*" May declared. She was, as usual, 'way out ahead. "I don't *want* to wait until I'm old and decrepit and . . ."

"Tut-tut, youngsters." Fleming reached out and put his hand lightly over the girl's mouth. "That attitude is precisely what makes you the spark-plug; but if you and I had the abilities we lack instead of the ones we have, neither of us would be in this particular engine at all."

"That's right," Deston said. "Now as to what this engine does. Postulating a two-dimensional creature, you could pile a million of him up and still have no thickness at all. Similarly, no three-dimensional material body can be compressed to zero thickness. The analogy holds in three and four dimensions. However, there are discontinuities, incompatibilities, and sheer logical impossibilities. Hence, ordinarily, a four-dimensional mind, which all psionic minds are, cannot engage any three-dimensional, non-psionic mind at all. All possible points of contact are of zero dimensions. . . ."

"But wait up, Babe," French broke in. "We can see three dimensional objects, so why can't we . . ."

"We can't really see 'em," Deston said, flatly. "We can see what and where they are, but they're absolutely immaterial to us. So forces, already immaterial, become imperceptible. Clear?"

"As mud," French said, dubiously. "There's a . . ."

Paula broke in. "I see! The Fourth—they just showed us—remember? Manipulate—immaterial . . . non-space-non-time?"

"Oh, sure." French's face cleared. "What we were doing, Babe, was blundering around in the Fourth, making a contact once in a blue moon by luck?"

"That's about it. Now, another analogy. Consider transformation of coordinates—polar into Cartesian, three-dimensional into two-dimensional, and so on. What a competent operator in the Fourth actually does is manipulate non-space-non-time attributes in such a way as to construct a matrix that is both three- and four-dimensional. Analogous to light—particle and/or wave. You follow?"

"Perfectly," the Frenches said in unison. "Four on our side, three on the non-psi's side, with perfect coupling."

snowflake or one instantaneous pattern in a kaleidoscope. What two telepaths do is *not* tune one mind to the other. Instead, each one of a very large number of filaments of thought—all under control, remember—touches its opposite number, thus setting up a pattern that has never existed before and will never exist again. . . ."

"I get it!" French exclaimed. "Reading a non-psi's mind will be a strictly one-way street. We'll have to go *through* the matrix—which doesn't exist in telepathy —and match whatever pattern we find on the other side —which won't change."

"That's right—we hope! Now you can go."

They went; and this time the traffic-manager's mind was wider open to inspection than any book could possibly be. To be comparable, every page of such a book would have to be placed in perfect position to read— and all at once!

Paula stood it for something over one second, then broke the linkage with what was almost a scream. "Stop it!"

She drew a deep breath and went on, more quietly, "I'm glad it's you who will have to do that, Babe, not I. That was a worse thing than anything a Peeping Tom could ever do. It's shameful—monstrous—it's positively obscene to do a thing like that to anyone, for any reason."

"Why, Paula, that was *fun!*" May exclaimed.

"But Babe," Paula said, "that was *nothing* like telepathy . . . but of course if wouldn't be."

"Of course. In telepathy the exchange of information is voluntary and selective. This way, the poor devil doesn't stand a chance. He doesn't even know it's happening."

Paula frowned. " 'Poor devil' is the exactly correct choice of words. Are you going to have to use us like that on the other poor devils you are going to . . . I can't think of a word bad enough."

"No. I just tried it. I can do it alone now, perfectly. But that's the way it is; opening new cells and learning new techniques. I had the latent capabilities. You others did, too."

"I *can,* but if you think I ever *will* you're completely out of your mind," Barbara declared, and Paula agreed vigorously.

"But I want to and I *can't!*" May wailed. "Why oh why can't I grow up *faster!*"

"We don't want you to grow up at all, sweetie," French said. "We don't want to lose our spark-plug. Ever think of that angle?"

"Babe, will I *really* have to leave this Funny Four then?"

"You'll not only have to, you'll want to," Deston replied, soberly. "That is one of the immutable facts of life."

"Okay, this is lots more fun than being old would be, anyway. What'll we try next, Paula?"

"I'd like to go back up into the Fourth Nume and really explore it—turn it inside out—that is, if there's nothing more important at the moment?" Paula quirked an eyebrow at Deston.

There was not. Goodbyes were said, and promises were made to meet soon and often, and the Destons 'ported themselves away.

Maynard called a special meeting of the Board to

order and said, "Since you all know what the Tellurian

rapidly accelerating downward spiral. A bad recession, or even a severe panic, would follow. Any such result *could* be avoided, of course, if WestHem's government would cut taxes in the full amount of defense spending; but has any one of you an imagination sufficiently elastic to encompass the idea of that government giving up half its income and firing *that* many hundreds of thousands of political hangers-on?"

There was a burst of scornful laughter.

"Mine isn't, either. As you know, defense stocks are already plummeting. They are dropping the limit every day. Due to public panic, they will continue to drop to a point below—in some cases to a point much below—the actual value of the properties. I propose that we start buying before that point is reached. Not enough to support the market, of course; just enough to control it at whatever rate of decline the specialists will compute as being certain to result in our gaining control.

"Having gained control of the largest—excuse me, I'm getting ahead of myself. I assure you that this program is financially feasible. I am authorized to say that in addition to GalBank, whose statements you all get, Deston and Deston, Warner Oil, InterStellar, and Galactic Metals will all put their treasuries behind this project."

There was a burst of applause.

"Since we are very large holders of these stocks already, there is no doubt that we can obtain control. We will then re-hire all the personnel who have been laid off and convert to the production of luxury goods, preferably of the more expensive and less durable types. We will finance the purchase of these goods ourselves . . ."

This time, they clapped and whistled and stamped their feet.

". . . and put on a massive advertising campaign for such basic spending as modernization, new housing, and so on. All of this, however, will be secondary to our main purpose. None of you have realized as yet that this is the first chance we have ever had of forming a political party and actually *electing* a government of WestHem that will govern it. . . ."

There was a storm of applause that lasted for five minutes. Then Maynard went on:

"The Board seems to be in favor of such action. Mr. Stevens Spehn, who has done a great deal of work on the political aspects of this idea, will now take the floor."

Company on Compday, January First in the Year One; and this day—also a Compday, of course—was the two hundred twenty sixth anniversary of that date: Jan. 1, 226. There was no celebration or ceremony—in fact, there were no words in the language to express any such concept—but, since it was Compday, all Operators worked only half a shift.

In the Beginning the Company had decreed that there were to be three hundred eighty four days (plus an extra Compday, to be announced by the Highest Agent, once every few years) in each year. Each year had twelve months; each month four weeks; each week eight days—Compday, Sonday, Monday, Tonday, Wonday, Thurday, Furday, and Surday. All Operators were to work exactly half of each of those days except Compday, upon which they were to work only a quarter; the other quarter was to be devoted to being happy and to thinking pleasant thoughts of the Company, of its goodness in furnishing them all with happiness and with life and its comforts.

No other World had ever been created or ever would be, nor any other People. The Company and The World comprised the Cosmic All.

The World had not changed and it never would change; The Company had so decreed. Not to the People directly, of course; the Company was an immaterial, omniscient, omnipotent entity that, except in the matter of punishment, dealt with People only through Company

Agents. These Agents were not People, but were super-men and superwomen far above People; so far above People that the lowest-caste Company Agents had qual-ities that not even the highest-caste People could under-stand.

Upon very rare occasions the Company, whose symbol was A A A A A A A, appeared in a form of flesh to the Highest Agent, the Comptroller General of The World, whose symbol was A A A A A A B; and, emitting the pure mercury-vapor Light of the Company and in the sight and the hearing of the highest-caste Company Agents, uttered sacred Company Orders.

Company Agents of various high castes transmitted these Orders to the Managers, who told the Assistant Man-agers, who told the Chiefs, who told the Assistant Chiefs, who told the Heads, who told the Assistant Heads, who told the Foremen, who told the Shift Bosses, who told the lower-caste People who were the Operators what to do and saw to it that they did it.

At the time of the World's creation The Company had issued a three-fold Prime Directive; which was immutable and eternal: ALL PEOPLE MUST: 1) Be happy. 2) Produce more and more People. 3) Produce more and more Goods.

If a Person obeyed these three injunctions all his life, his immaterial Aura—the thing that made him alive, not dead, and that made him different from all other Persons—when he became dead was absorbed into the Company and he would be happy forever.

On the other hand, there were a few who did not follow the Prime Directive literally and exactly. These were the mals—the malcontents, the maladjusts, the malefactors—the thinkers, the questioners, the unbelievers —the unhappy for any cause. They were blasted out of existence by the Company itself and that was the end of them, auras and all.

And that was fair enough. Every Person was born into a caste. He grew up in that caste. He was trained to do what his ancestors had done and what his descend

oo it was, is, and ever shall be. Selah. It is written.

Following the Prime Directive was easy enough; for most people, in fact, easier than not following it.

Since happiness was simply the state of not being unhappy, and there was nothing in the normal life to be unhappy about, happiness was the norm.

Producing People, too, was a normal part of life. Furthermore, since the Company punished pre-family sexual experience with Company wrath just a few volts short of death, the family state brought a new and different kind of happiness. Every female Person's job assignment was to produce, between the ages of eighteen and thirty, ten children, and then to keep on running her family unless and until she was transferred to some other job. Since every nubile girl wanted a man of her own, and since children were a source of happiness on their own account, not one woman in a thousand had to be brainwashed at all to really like the job of running a family.

And as for producing Goods—why not? That was what People were created for, and that was all that men were good for—except, of course, for fathering children. Also, there was much happiness to be had in keeping a machine right at the peak of performance, turning out, every shift, an over-quota of passes and an under-permittance of rejects—zero rejects being always the target.

No Person in his right mind ever even thought of wondering what the Goods he produced were for, or what became of them. That was Company business and thus incomprehensible by definition.

On this Compday forenoon, then, in a vast machine-shop in City One of the World, a young man was hard at work—sitting at ease in a form-fitting chair facing an instrument-board having a hundred-odd dials, meters, gauges, lights, bells, whistles, buzzers, and what-have-you.

Occasionally a green light would begin to shade toward amber and a buzzer would begin to talk to him in Morse code; whereupon he would get up, walk around back of the board to his machine, and make almost imperceptible manual adjustments until the complaining monolog stopped. If, instead of stopping, the signal had turned into a Klaxon blare, he would have been manu-facturing rejects, but he was far too good a machiner to make any such error as that. He hadn't turned out a single reject in eighteen straight shifts. He knew everything there was to be known about his machine—and the fact that he knew practically nothing whatever else had never bothered him a bit. Why should it have? That was precisely the way it should be in this, the perfect World: that was precisely what the all-powerful Com-pany had decreed.

He was of medium height and medium build; trimly, smoothly muscular; with large, strong, and exquisitely sensitive hands. He had a shock of rather unkempt brown hair, clear gray eyes, and a lightly-tanned, unblemished skin. He wore the green-and-white-striped coveralls of his caste—Machiner Second—and around his neck, on a hard-alloy chain, there hung a large and fairly thick locket. This locket, which had been put on him one minute after he was born and which his body would wear into the crematorium, and which—he firmly be-lieved—could not be opened or removed without causing his death, had seven letters of the English alphabet cut deeply into its face. This group of letters—V T J E S O Q —was his symbol. As far as he knew, the only purpose of the locket was to make him permanently and un-

Her short-bobbed hair was deep russet brown in color. Low on her forehead blazed the green jewel of her rank. This jewel, which resembled more than anything else a flaring green spotlight about the size of a half-dollar piece and not much thicker, was mounted in platinum on the platinum drop-piece of a plain platinum headband. Under her sweater she, too, wore a locket; upon which was engraved the symbol A C B A A B A.

"Be happy, Veety!" the Agent snapped.

"Be happy, Agent." The machiner raised his arms and put both hands flat on the top of his head.

"At ease, Veety! Follow me!"

Whirling on the ball of her left foot, she led the way down a narrow corridor; sharp right into a wider one; sharp left into the main hall and straight into the crowd of operators going off shift. She did not even slow down —the crowd dissolved away from her like magic. They fell all over themselves to get out of her way; for to touch a Company Agent, however accidentally or however lightly, was to receive a blast of Company wrath that, while not permanently harmful, was as intolerable as it was inexplicable.

Through the huge archway, along a wide walkway she led him, to the second archway on the right. She stopped and whistled sharply through her teeth. The exiting operators stopped in their tracks, put hands on heads, and stood motionless.

"V T J R S Y X—forward!" she snapped, and a green-and-white-coveralled, well-built girl—People had to be good physical specimens or they did not live to grow up—came up to within a few feet of the Agent and stopped. She was neither apprehensive nor pleased; merely acquiescent.

"Be happy, Veety!"

"Be happy, Agent."

"Job transfer. Come with me and this other veety to that aircar over there."

The Agent slipped lithely into the single front seat of the vehicle, at the controls; the two Machiners Second got into the back seat. The aircar bulleted upward, screamed across City One to Suburb Ten, and dropped vertically downward to a high-G landing on the beauti-fully-kept grounds of a small plastic house.

"Out," the Agent said, and led the couple into a large, comfortably-furnished living room. "Stand there . . . hold hands . . . V T J R S Y X—job transfer. You're eighteen today, so you stop machinering and start running a family. Permanent assignment. The Company knows that you two know each other and like each other. That liking will now become love. The Company knows all."

"The Company knows all," the two intoned in unison, solemnly.

"Press your right thumbs here . . . you are mated for life. This house is yours—permanently. Four rooms and bath to start. It's expandable; one additional room per child. Here are your family coupon books; throw your single-person ones into the disposer. This special mating coupon gives you free time from now until hour seven-teen, when you go to the band concert at Shell Nineteen. Amuse yourselves, you two." The Agent smiled suddenly, a smile that made her hard young face human and beau-tiful. "Have fun—in the bedroom, perhaps? Be happy, both of you." The Company Agent executed a merry

round out a thing after bed-hour last night that *everybody* has got to know. . . ."

"Shut up!" the young man barked. "We don't want to know one single damn thing that we don't know already."

"But listen!" the stranger whispered, intensely. "This is *important!* The most important thing that ever happened in the World! There's a meeting tonight—I'll pick you up—but I tell you this right now. There ain't any such thing as the Company. It's just those damn snotty Agents and they're just as human as we are; they've been suckering us all our lives. If we had the gadgetry they've got we could knock them all off and take . . ."

"*Shut up!*" the girl screamed, and sprang away from him in horror. "You're a mal—you're unhappy—that means *death!*"

"Death, hell!" came the whispered snarl. "I got the straight dope—the real poop—last night and I'm still alive, ain't I? We're going to get some special insulation tonight and I'm going to grab one of those high-nosed bitches of Agents and choke her plumb to death after I . . ."

The man stopped whispering and screamed in utterly unbearable agony. His every muscle writhed and twisted, convulsively and impossibly. After a few seconds his body slumped bonelessly to the pavement; limp, motionless, dead.

"How terrible," the girl remarked, in a perfectly matter-of-fact tone of voice. Then, with arms again around each other and as blissful as before, the two lovers stepped over the body and went on their interrupted way. Mals had no right whatever to live. Therefore the All-Wise, All-Powerful Company had put that mal to death. Everything was perfect, in this their perfect World.

And in one minute flat a ground-car, a light-truck type, came up beside the corpse and stopped. Two husky men, wearing the dark-gray-on-light-gray of Sanitationers Fourth, got out of it, picked the body up, and tossed it nonchalantly into the back of their truck.

Perce and Cecily Train 'ported the *Explorer* to a point in space well outside Pluto's orbit; well out of detector range of any of the strange warships englobing Earth. Aboardship this time, in addition to the regular complement of spacemen and psiontists, were a couple of dozen graduates of the University, who were making the trip for advanced study.

"If any of us'd thought of it and if we'd stayed and if we'd had the techniques we've got now, we could've 'ported bombs aboard those jaspers and blown 'em clear out of the ether," Train said, while they were getting ready to go to work.

"One if's enough, why use three?" Deston countered. "But I got a lot better idea than that one, especially since Bobby is just slightly allergic to killing people in job lots. We'll find out where they come from, 'port each one of 'em back to his own house, tuck him gently into his own bed and present all those nice subspacers to Fleet Admiral Guerdon Dann, with the compliments of the University of Psionics—for a small consideration, of course."

"*Now* you're chirping, birdie!" Barbara exclaimed. "You *do* get an idea once in a while, don't you? That one is really a dilly. Ready, everybody? Let's go."

They went . . . and they studied . . . and the more they studied the more baffled they became. The captains of the ships were to a man from Tellus. They were

That, or anything else pertaining to logistics or supply, was none of their business.

The Vice-Admirals and Admirals had wondered; but, since they had not been told, none of them had ever asked. Asking impertinent questions was a thing that simply was not done.

The Fleet Admiral did not know; neither did the Base Commander on Teneriffe. They got their orders via non-directional subspace radio from the Company of the World—"World," of course, meaning Earth. It wasn't only a company, really, it was a new government, still very QT and TS, that was going to take over Tellus and all the planets, they both supposed. They had the power to do it, so why not? To any hard-nosed man of war might is right, and if they wanted to play it cosy and call themselves The Company of the World that was all right, too.

And as for the lower echelons . . .

"My . . . God. . . ." Cecily said slowly, aloud, into the dense silence that had lasted through a long fifteen minutes of stupefied investigation. "The Eternal, Omniscient, Omnipotent, Omnipresent Company created the World and the People on Compday—Company Day, that is—January First of the Year One. No other World nor any other People—capitalized, please note, even in thought—ever were created or ever will be. Will some or one of you nice people please tell me what in all the infinite reaches of all the incandescent and viridescent hells of all total space we have got ourselves into now?"

"I'll never know, Curly." Deston, who had been holding his breath for a good two minutes, let it all out at once. "And the poor dumb meatheads *believe* that comet-gas with every cell of their minds . . . and take everything that's going on right in stride—it's all Company business and as such is naturally incomprehensible to the mind of man . . . 'My God!' is correct, Curly. Check."

"But look! Look in here!" Barbara put in, excitedly. "Not the caste system—above it—Company Agents! Angels, suppose? Or something? None here with the Fleet; all back on the World. Those spotlight-jewels— *gorgeous!* I'd love to wear one of those myself. Power-packs, do you think?"

"Maybe," Jones said. "That's certainly something we'll have to look into. But what do we do now, Babe?"

"I know what *I'm* going to do—report to the boss in person—you people stay right here 'til I get back." Deston disappeared.

Maynard was alone, so Deston 'ported himself unceremoniously into the private office. "I don't want even Doris in on this until you let her in," he explained, then reported everything.

As he listened, Maynard's face turned gray.

"So you see, chief," Deston concluded, "it's an unholy mess. What was it you said? A planet . . . 'run for years in a way that would make the robber barons of old sick at the stomach.' You said it. You *certainly* said it. Have you got any idea as to who could be monster enough to pull a stunt like that?"

"More than an idea, son. This explains a lot of things I've wondered about, but I couldn't let my mind run wild enough. Two of 'em are why Plastics, one of the biggest of the big, never played ball, and how they got that way. It's Plastics, and Lord Byron Punsunby is head man."

"That makes sense, so I'll do a flit. . . ."

"Not yet ... that's such a staggering thing ... what

... A perfect self set-up.

"Check. And one of their castes is of top-notch engineers who don't know anything else and put everything they've got into it. And castes of scientists and so on."

"That's right. As a 'troncist I'm here to testify that that locket is one beautiful job of work. Transmits everything except what the guy ate for breakfast, and maybe even that."

"To Central Intelligence ... each checked as frequently as desired ... or even recorded ... God, what a system!" Maynard shook his head. "And those Company Agents. Special castes, too. Charged, of course. Insulated boots. Magic no end. They could even *live* in a charged environment."

"Could be. I told you, it's a mell of a hess."

"One more thing. You've never thought of the real problem here, apparently. How can we—how can *anybody*—rehabilitate any race that has been driven that far off course?"

Deston's jaw dropped. "Huh? Wow! It's a little soon, though, isn't it, to have to think about that?"

"I'll have to think about it, I'm afraid, whether I want to or not ... but that's more in my department than yours, I suppose ... well, I'll let you go now. Thanks for reporting. Good luck."

"Luck, chief. 'Bye," and Deston 'ported himself back into the main lounge of the *Explorer*.

Since the Plastics Building was one of the largest office buildings on Earth, it was very easy to find; and it was even easier to find the blatantly magnificent private office of "Lord" Byron Punsunby, the president of Plastics Incorporated. Deston got into his mind and put it through the wringer. Punsunby knew a great deal that was new. He knew all about the business end—by what devious routes the goods were smuggled into the markets of Earth, how and through what underground channels they were sold, how incredibly vast the hidden holdings of Plastics were, and how all this skullduggery had been performed—but even he did not know the general direction from Sol of Plastics' ultra-secret planet, The World, which had never been given a name.

It was and had always been Company policy that no Tellurian should know The World's coordinates. Only two living men were to know them; the Comptroller General of the World, who came to Earth to report to Punsunby after the close of business of each of The World's calendar quarters; and the captain—who was also the only navigating officer—of the one ship that ever made the direct run from The World to Earth and back. There were only two records of those figures in existence; one in each of the personal safe-deposit boxes of those two men.

Deston kept on reading. Yes, there were a few unscheduled vists; more than he liked of late . . . he didn't like to use subspace radio, it *could* be tapped . . . changing conditions . . . trouble . . .

Ah! That was what Deston wanted. There hadn't been enough generations yet to wipe out all the genes of throwbacks to the independent, intractable type. Conditioning might not hold; it was possible that some of them were even smart enough to pose as tractable, although the electronicists swore that their instruments were far too sensitive and comprehensive for that. Whatever the cause, in any case of real trouble checking the lockets even once every day wasn't enough. Occasionally Pun-

Sure.

"Herc?"

"Okay by me."

"That's three. Talk to some of the graduates, will you, Perce, so we won't have to make the shifts too long? I'll take the first shift, starting now."

XVIII

HUNCHERS

COMPANY AGENT A C B A A B A was a busy girl. She mated a dozen more couples that afternoon, then shot her aircar out to Suburb Fourteen, which was under construction. It was a beautiful layout, the girl thought, as she brought her car to a halt and looked the suburb over from a height of ten thousand feet. Rolling, heavily-wooded hills, a nice lake sparkling in the sunshine, and two winding streams. Lovely landscaping and curving, contoured drives. Over sixteen hundred of its two thousand homes should be done now—but were they? There wasn't a single house on Thirtieth Drive yet!

Frowning, she took a map of the suburb out of a compartment and scanned it. Then she compared it carefully with the terrain below. There was no one at work there this afternoon, of course, but she knew the call-code of the foreman of the project, so she punched it forthwith.

Her screen brightened, showing the head and shoulders of a man, who put both hands flat on his head and said, "Be happy, Agent."

"Be happy, Kubey! You're 'way, *way* behind sked on Sub Fourteen. How come?"

"I know, Agent, but there wasn't a thing I could do about it. Five of my best people went mal on me last week and the replacements they sent me were absolute gristleheads. All five of 'em fouled up their machines so bad I had to get a whole crew of . . ."

"That's enough. Be happy, Kubey!"

"Be happy, Agent."

She snapped the set off and gnawed at her lower lip. An Agent didn't yap at damn stupid dumb jerks of People—it wouldn't do any good to, anyway, they didn't know anything. A B F A D A A was the last who'd

rolling on and I'm going to have to start installing on it before it's finished!"

"So what? There'll be all the finished houses you'll need, long before you'll need 'em, so . . ."

" 'So what?' " she almost screamed. "Because it never happened before with anybody else and because it's absolutely contra-Regs, *that's* what! And you know it as well as I do! It's your business to keep ahead of me, and by . . ."

"Shut up!" The man's grin had disappeared; his face was stern and cold. "I know my business as well as you know yours, Acey."

"Well, then, why . . . Oh! But Abie, if you're having as much mal trouble as *that*, why didn't you tell me?"

"You just said why not. It's Abie business, not Acey, so just keep your tights on. And keep all this under your headband if you don't want to get bopped bow-legged." He cut com; and after a moment of lip-biting indecision, she did the same.

Then, shrugging her shapely shoulders, she set course for Suburb One and the immense apartment house in which she and eight-hundred-odd other AC's lived. She landed on the roof, parked her little speedster in its stall, and walked a hundred yards or so to a canopied, but unguarded hole with a stainless-steel pipe emerging from it. She slid unconcernedly down the slide-pole's three-hundred-foot length to the thirty fourth floor, where the general offices were. She walked seventy yards along a main corridor, turned left into a narrower one, went fifty yards along that, and turned left again into a large room half full of desks. Some twenty girls, of about her own age and size—and with pretty much her own spectacular shape—and as many young men, were already there. Some were at desks, working; some were at scanners, studying; some were sitting or standing by couples or in groups, talking or playing games; some singles were reading. All wore the headlight-like green jewels. The girls all wore the same uniform she did; the men all wore yellow whipcord battle-jackets, black whipcord breeches, and high-laced red-leather boots.

"Hi, Bee-ay!" one of the men called. (Since everyone in the house was an Acey, other letters of each symbol were used intra-house). "You jump a mean knight; come on over and play me some chess."

"Not enough time on the chron, Apey, I've got to red-tape it for a good hour yet," and she strode purposefully to her desk.

She had hardly seated herself, however, when a big, good-looking, fair-haired young fellow came over and perched hip-wise on the corner of her desk.

"Hi, beautiful," he said, swinging one big boot in a small arc. "What do you know for real sure that's new?"

"Hi, Crip—mental, that is—nothing at all. Should I?"

"Nope. Everything is perfect in this our perfect World." He squared his shoulders as though he had made a momentous decision and glanced quickly around. No one was within earshot; no one was paying any attention to their customary *tête-à-tête*.

Reaching into his pocket, he took out two soft, almost transparent pouches. He bent over, pulled his locket out from under his jacket, said, "Well, beautiful, I'll see you after," slipped one of the pouches over his locket, tightened its drawstring, and put the now insulated locket back where it had been. Then, handing her the other pouch, he indicated silently that she was to do the same.

The girl's eyes widened and her face went suddenly

you've been flirting with the flamers and if you go there's nothing left for me. That's the way you look at it, too, isn't it?"

"Of course, darling. I wouldn't live an hour, after. You came out because you noticed I was going off the beam?"

"How could I help but notice? But I wonder—is your hunch the same as mine? Something so wild—so utterly utter—that there are no words for it? That goes, some way or other, clear up to the Company itself?"

"That sounds like the same pattern, so I guess it's the same hunch. Something *way* out; beyond all understanding, sense or reason. I can't get even a clue to it. But these . . . ?" She indicated the lockets. "Coms? Up to the Three-A's, maybe? And you blocked 'em? I'd never have thought of anything like that—but of course girl Sciencers First don't really. . . ."

"I don't *know* that they're coms; I was afraid to do any testing. But I knew something was riding you and I had to do something. But all I blocked was audio—if anybody is on us they're getting everything else and the well-known fact that we're in love will account for tension and so on—I think. I suppose you've heard the gossip that twelve Aceys from this house went absento —probably mal and probably flamed?"

"I've heard—and with that and this horrible hunch I've been jittering like a witch. It got so bad that I yapped at a Blue this afternoon—Old Baldy A B F A D A A himself."

"Almighty Company fend you!" he gasped. "You *are* asking for a flame!"

"Not in that, Beedy. No fear of *him* howling. He *can't* howl. He's so far minus sked on Sub Fourteen that I'm going to have to go contra-Regs. . . ." She explained the housing situation, ". . . so I could kick him right in the face and he couldn't even kick me back because I'm strictly on sked. He *said* he'd bop me bow-legged if I leaked about it, but that was all."

The man whistled softly through his teeth. "*That* much mal trouble?" He thought for a moment, then threw off his dark mood. "Retrieve the insulator and slip it to me when I get back."

He moved quietly away, then came back with appropriate noise. He resumed his former position, put both pouches into his pocket, and said, "I just had a cogent and gravid idea, my proud and haughty beauty. How about us taking five and going down stairs and tilting us a couple of flagons?"

"I'd love to, my courteous and sprightly knave, but I've simply *got* to get this red tape out first. An hour, say?"

"An hour's a date, you beautiful thing, you." He took his leg off the desk and straightened up. "I've got some red-taping of my own to do. So, as Old Baldy would say, keep your . . ."

"*Beedy!* Is *that* nice?" She laughed up at him; two deep dimples appeared. "Besides, as you very well know, I *always* do!"

In an hour the paper-work was done. (While People all got half a shift off on Compday, Company Agents got theirs on any day other than Compday). Bee-ay and Beedy tilted their flagons, ate supper together, and went to their rooms. Not only to separate rooms, but to separate wings of the immense building.

She, however, did not sleep at all well; and when she

her out of the driver's seat and into the back, where he let her struggle; holding her only tightly enough to prevent her escape. In the meantime a smaller man, also dressed in a full-coverage suit that looked like asbestos but wasn't, cut three wires of the aircar's power supply and got into the front seat. The car shot straight up out of sight of the ground, darted northward, and came to ground on the flat top of a high, bare-rock mesa.

"Are you going to behave yourself?" the big man asked.

She nodded behind the glove and he released her completely.

"What the hell goes on?" she demanded, sitting up properly and putting her hair to rights with her fingers. "You'll get the flame for this."

"I think not," he said, quietly. "You're not frightened, I'm very glad to see."

"*Frightened? Me?* Of any person or People ever born? High Company beyond!"

"Good girl. We've made a few poor picks, but you and your friend A C B D will make out."

"Beedy? You've got him, too? Where are you taking us, if I may ask?" The last phrase was pure sneer.

"You may not ask," was the calm reply.

Then the big man, working deftly despite his heavy gloves, lifted the girl's locket and cut its chain with a heavy angle-nose cutter. He then twitched the band from her head, tied the locket to the band with the chain, and threw the bundle, in a high arc, out and away. When it came down there was a flare of greenish brilliance brighter than the sun, the white glare of a small pool of incandescent lava, and after a few seconds, the odor of volatilized rock.

"So?" the girl asked, quietly. "So there goes a bit of Company power. But you . . . Oh!" She broke off sharply as she saw the smaller man touching the aircar here and there with the looped end of a heavy wire held in one gloved hand. "Oh? High resistance? How high?"

"One point two five megohms," the big man said. "We have no intention whatever of doing you any harm whatever."

"You know, some way or other, I've rather gathered that?" and she extended a beautifully-shaped bare arm for the wire's touch. A minute later, while both men were shedding their insulation, she spoke again. "You're going to give me some explanation of all this, I suppose?"

"We are indeed, Miss Acey Bee-ay, as soon as we get to where we're going and your friend joins us. It's altogether too long and too deep and too involved to go into twice for the two of you. We'll take off now."

The aircar went straight up to twelve thousand feet, then hurtled north northeast at its top speed. It held course and speed for over three hours. It crossed mountain ranges, lakes, forests, and rivers. Finally, however, it slanted sharply downward, slowed, stopped, and descended vertically into a canyon—a crevasse, rather—but little wider than the car was long and half a mile deep.

It landed near a man wearing a greenish-gray uniform, who had a sidearm in a holster at his hip. This guard saluted crisply and put his hand against a slight projection of the rock, whereupon a section of the canyon's wall swung inward, revealing a long, straight, brightly-lighted tunnel. The three got out of the car and the guard stepped aside, drawing his weapon as he did so.

"As usual," the big man told the guard. "It's harmless.

and its transmitters have been cut. You won't need the

after dismissing his smaller companion, ushered the girl into a small, plainly-furnished office.

"They aren't here yet, I see. Take a chair, please." He sat down behind the desk. "We'll wait here; it won't be very long."

Nor was it. In about fifteen minutes the door opened and three gray-uniformed men, one of them pushing a wheeled chair, entered the office. Beedy, without headband or locket, was chained to the chair. His uniform was torn off, both eyes would soon be black-and-blue "shiners," and his flesh was puffy and bruised, but he was still full of fight. When he saw the girl, however, he stopped struggling instantly and stopped her with a word as she leaped to her feet, screamed, and ran toward him.

"If you'd used your brain, meathead," he said, glaring between swollen lids at the man behind the desk, "and told your gorillas to tell me you had *her* here, it would've saved all five of us some lumps."

"Well, I can't think of everything," the big man admitted. "I did tell her we had you, come to think of it, which perhaps accounts for her cooperation." He studied his three men. The smallest one of them was of B D's size, but each of the three bore more marks of battle than did the captive. "I was not informed that you are such an expert at unarmed combat. Free him, you, and get out. With the chair."

"*Free* him?" one of the captors protested. "Why, he'll . . ." and one of the others broke in:

"But he damn near *killed* Big Pietr, boss—they're taking him up to sick-bay now, and . . ."

"You heard me," the boss said, without raising his voice a fraction of a decibel, and the three obeyed.

As the door closed, the two went into each other's arms, the girl moaning over her lover's wounds.

"It's all right, now that I know *you* aren't hurt. You aren't, are you?"

"No, not the least bit, in any way," she assured him. "But they hurt *you*, and if you think . . ."

"Hush, sweetheart, listen. I got more of them than they did of me, so, with you here safe, if they won't carry a grudge I won't." He cocked a blood-clotted eyebrow—with a slight wince—at the man behind the desk. "No grudge, I take it?"

"Splendid! No grudge at all."

B D turned to B A. "Wasn't this in your hunch?" he asked.

"Your getting all beat up certainly wasn't, but the rest of it . . . well, I guess it could fit the pattern . . . but don't try to tell me it was that clear in yours, either!"

"I won't; but it does fit the pattern."

"You two are far and away the best we've found yet," the man at the desk said then. "Since I'm going to be your instructor, you may as well start calling me 'Basil'."

"Bay-sill? That doesn't make sense," the girl said.

"It's my name. We don't use symbols—I'll go into that later. You are beginning to realize that your knowledge and experience have left you almost entirely ignorant of man, of nature, and of the cosmos. Exposure to that knowledge will be such a shock to your minds that you will feel much better together than apart. To that end, would you like to be married—'mate,' is your word for it—immediately?"

"But we can't," the girl said. "Not for half a year yet."

"Sure we can, and we will," B D said. "My hunch is

any response and he went on. "If so, I hope to persuade you to help us look for others like you. Now, before I take you upstairs to the sick-bay and thence to your suite, where you will find clothing and so on, I am going to give you some of the basic elements of the truth. I shall give them to you brutally straight. You will be shocked as you have never believed it possible to be shocked. You will not be able to understand any part of it at first, but you must not ask me any questions until tomorrow morning, when I will begin instructing you in detail. By that time you will have given the matter sufficient thought so that you will be able to ask intelligent questions. You wish to marry each other, you said?"

"We certainly do!"

"Splendid! You can make decisions, as well as think. I have very high hopes indeed of you two. After the short visits I mentioned I will arrange for your wedding. Then, if you wish, you may dine and retire to your suite until eight hours tomorrow.

"Now for your first introduction to the truth. This world is not the only world in existence and you people —you upper echelons are just as much people as those you call People—are not the only people. There are thousands of millions of other worlds, more or less like this one, throughout an immensity of space so vast as to be beyond imagining. There are thousands of millions of human beings—members of the human race, to which both you and we belong—inhabiting many of those

223

worlds. One such world, my native planet Earth, has a population of almost seven thousand million people.

"Your concept of the Company is completely false. There are hundreds of thousands of companies, each a self-perpetuating group of men. Not supermen in any sense, but ordinary men like me. Your company was and is only one of the multitude of companies of Earth. It was founded by and is still operated by a group of greedy, utterly callous capitalists—money men—of Earth. It was founded and is being operated specifically as a world of slave labor. Every person born on this world is a slave; a slave without freedom, liberty, or personal rights of any kind.

"We, on the other hand, represent a society of worlds of freedom-loving people. We have come here to liberate all the inhabitants of this world from slavery; to enable you to take your rightful place—and that place *is* yours by right—in the fellowship of all the civilized worlds. Our creed, the creed of all free peoples everywhere, is this:

"We hold these truths to be self-evident, that all men are created equal, that they are endowed by their Creator with certain inalienable Rights, that among these are Life, Liberty, and the Pursuit of Happiness.

"These things I have told you, young friends, are fundamental. They are basic. They are absolutely necessary prerequisites for any learning of the truth; so think them over very carefully until tomorrow morning.

"When your instruction is complete, I am sure that you will be glad to work side by side with us to unite your world with our society—The Union of Soviet Socialist Republics."

Also, he could handle those Tellurian affairs much better if he were there in person—especially if he could drop GalMet entirely for a while—and why not? Young Smith had plenty of jets . . . wherefore he called Smith and Miss Champion into his inner office.

"Miss Champion, take notes, please. Mr. Eldon Jay Smith I believe, the Executive Vice-President of Galactic Metals, Incorporated?"

"That is precisely what I have the honor and privilege of being, sir." Smith put his right hand over his heart and bowed. "As of the present moment, sir; that is, sir, I mean, sir."

"You'll start executing as of the present moment, sir," and Maynard told him what he had in mind, concluding, "So sit on the throne, bub, 'til I get back—and don't let the block line drop down through the bottom of the chart."

"Drop? You kidding? Now we can get something done —it'll zoom right up through the top. How about it, Dorry?" He winked at Miss Champion, who, always the perfect First Secretary—always, that is, in Maynard's presence—did not wink back. She merely smiled.

"But suppose I take her along?"

"Go ahead. Do that. Wreck the outfit. I've been wanting to quit and go fishing, anyway."

"Yeah. I know. I know just what I'd be wrecking— anyway, I'd bet on the fish. 'Bye, Don; 'bye, Doris," and Maynard strode blithely out.

The girl gave Smith a long, level look. "You're the only human being alive with the sublime nerve to give *him* the needle that way. Just suppose he climbs your frame for it some day?"

"He set the pace, didn't he? Anyway, I'd get along."

"Pfooie! Nobody could blast you out of here with an atomic bomb and everybody knows it. You really know him don't you? I've always thought I was the only one who did."

"I know he's the universe's best—and that these damned yesmen and toadies around here make him just as sicka da bel' as they do me—and that's a great God's plenty."

"That's what I meant, Don . . . and you're not *too* bad a stinker yourself, in some ways." For weeks, ever since they had become psionic, a current of something—like electricity plus—had been flowing between these two, and it was getting stronger all the time.

"Thanks for them kind words, Dorry. You're slipping. First thing you know you'll . . ."

"I'm not slipping and whatever it was you were going to say, I won't. No telepathy, no rapport. I've been a career business woman ever since I was fifteen—a good one—and I'm going to keep on being just that."

He smiled; more a grin than a smile. "That's the way to talk, Dorry. Strictly business. If there's any one thing in this wide fat world I really love, it's business."

"Let's get at it, then." Miss Champion, now all briskly efficient FirSec, picked up her book. "I'll remind you, Mister Smith, that you are wasting time that is costing the company a dollar a minute. In exactly four and one half minutes you have an appointment with Felton of Barbizon about enlarging the operation there; at nine plus forty five with Quisenberry of Belmark, ditto; at ten plus ten with Andersen of Pharmics. . . ."

Maynard landed on Earth at Chicago Spaceport. He took a copter to the big old building on Michigan Avenue that was GalFed's headquarters. Stevens Spehn's office was on the twenty sixth floor, in front, affording a

with a little stretching, reach anything on its plate-glass top. He was leaning 'way back in his swivel chair, with both feet perched up on the corner of his desk. When Maynard came in Spehn pointed his cigarette at a huge overstuffed chair near the desk, but facing the huge front window. Maynard sat down, lighted a long, thin cigar, crossed his legs, and spoke aloud. "So you're rolling, Steve. So you like your PsiCor, eh?"

"Oh, brother!" Spehn got up, walked around to the older man, shook him solemnly by the hand, and resumed seat and pose. Then: "Oh . . . broth . . . *therr!* One hundred percent convictions so far and not a possible miss in sight. Psionic Intelligence agents are things that . . . well, maybe some cloak-and-dagger men have dreamed about such things, but we've *got* 'em. Over ten thousand already and more coming and they're all batting a thousand. Boss, the Big Brains claim that while ethics is related to psionics, ethics is not and cannot be made an absolute. Do you buy that?"

"In the abstract, as a generalization, yes. In practice, and in the specific case of our own culture as it now is, perhaps not. I might almost say probably not."

"Very, very cautious about going out on a limb, aren't you? So bite yourself off a piece of this and chew on it and give your taste-buds a treat. The opposition hasn't got any psiontists worth a tinker's toot and never will have any."

Maynard did not question this statement. All experience had shown that any psychics of much ability, immediately upon perceiving the vastnesses of psionics, went to Newmars and the University of Psionics as a matter of course. Spehn went on:

"It's a truly wonderful thing to *know*, for certain damn sure, everything that goes on. So we're steam-rolling 'em to the queen's own taste. This next election will be honest; the kind of election the Founding Fathers had in mind. GalFed should be in the saddle shortly after that. Of course there'll be some fuss, but Guerd should be ready by then. You're sticking around?"

Maynard nodded. "Longer than that, Stev. Until GalFed is, both in name and in fact, THE GALACTIC FEDERATION; until Tellus—a united Tellus—is both in name and in fact the capital of all civilization."

Spehn thought for a moment. "That's a big order, boss, but I wouldn't wonder if we might be able to deliver the goods."

After half an hour more of discussion, Maynard went up one floor and had a long discussion with Fleet Admiral Guerdon Dann.

He then tuned his mind to that of Li Hing Wong, who brought Feodr Ilyowicz in for a three-way. Things were going as well as was to be expected. The Iron Curtain and the Bamboo Curtain, which had faced outward, had been replaced by Psionic Curtains facing inward. Since the fleet englobing Earth, whatever it really was, did not seem to care what happened to either Russia or China, there had not been very much effective opposition. People were dying, but that couldn't be helped. The only way progress could be made was by killing off the commissars and the warlords and all such corruptionists; and, since corruption had been the way of life for centuries, reclamation would necessarily be a slow process.

As each district was reclaimed and put under a psionic Peace-lord its people were given as much self-government as they could handle—which wasn't very much. They would have to grow up to self government

ting in the stock market.

The Plastics Building, in Chicago, Illinois, WestHem, Tellus, occupied the entire eight hundred block west; bounded by Halsted and Peoria Streets on the east and west, and by Washington and Randolph Boulevards on the south and north. Its main bulk, built of steel-reenforced synthetics of various kinds, was eighty five stories high, and a comparatively slender tower reached up fifteen stories higher still. This tower housed the private offices of the Biggest of the Big of Plastics, Incorporated; and its entire top floor, the one hundredth of the building, was devoted to the series of exceedingly private offices, in ascending order of privacy from the private elevator, of the least accessible man on Earth—President Byron Punsunby himself.

To say that these offices were sumptuous is to make the understatement of the year, but that is all that will be said. At three o'clock one Wednesday afternoon, while President Punsunby was sitting at his most sumptuous desk, alone in his most sumptuous, most private office, clear across the tower from the elevator, a call came in on a communicator that was his alone, in a mish-mash of noise and herringbone that he alone could unscramble. He stared at it angrily for a few seconds; his big, fat body tensing, his big, fat face stiffening, and his small blue eyes growing even harder than their hard wont.

He'd been getting altogether too damned many calls on that com of late and he hadn't liked any one of them. And this was the worst. It wasn't subspace, or even long distance; it was *local*—and this was one purely sweet-scented *hell* of a time for him to have to leave Earth . . . why couldn't the ape handle a few things himself?

He unscrambled the mish-mash; Erskine Cantwell, the Comptroller General of The World, appeared.

"Where are you?" Punsunby snapped. "Spaceport?"

"Yes. Just landing."

"Come in. I'll be alone."

Cantwell did not enter the Plastics Building by any of the usual routes. He approached it via subway, opened an almost invisible door into the second subbasement, walked along a deserted hall, opened a completely invisible door by speaking a series of six coined words, and took the ultra-secret elevator straight up into Punsunby's ultra-private office.

"Well?" Punsunby demanded, savagely. "I told you to take whatever steps might prove necessary. Why the hell didn't you do it, instead of coming here again?"

"What do *you* think?" Cantwell sneered. "That I'm here for the fun of it? I'm only the Highest Agent, remember? Six A's and a B, with only a violet headlight. It takes the one and only discarnate God Himself—the one and only holder of seven straight A's—the All-Powerful and Eternal—the one and only being able to pour the pure mercury-vapor light of God onto his poor dumb creatures—*you*, you fat-head, are the only living human being who can modify Article Ninety of your precious Second Directive, and by all the devils in hell you . . ."

"Christ almighty!" Punsunby broke in. He had been turning not-so-slowly purple as he listened to this *lese-majeste*, but at the words "Second Directive" his face began to pale. "But that's the basis of the whole caste system—it's *never* been modified. Things *can't* be that

230

bad. Ersk—there *must* be some other way of handling

"You're so right. That's the trouble with any rigid system," Cantwell said, much more calmly. "When it starts to crack it's apt to shatter. But that's the way you Tops have always wanted it, so you're stuck with it. So let's get at it."

"All right. I'll have to make a couple of calls."

There was no more talk of business until they were in SUITE ONE of the subspacer. Then Punsunby said, "Go ahead, Ersk. What do you think it is?"

"I know what it is, now. Sabotage. Expert, organized, directed, and highly efficient sabotage. Worthy of the Commies at their very best."

"The Commies? But I . . ."

"I didn't say it was and I don't think it is. I don't see how it could be. I can see only one possibility. I never have believed in mindreading; but what else can it be?"

"The Galaxians." Punsunby thought for minutes. "Mental stuff—that's why you want our mentalists to work openly with operators without losing caste. But no person has ever—knowingly, that is—has ever even seen a three-A, Ersk. It'd scare 'em to death."

"It'll have to be worse than that. They'll have to shed their pretty colored spotlights, put on lockets, and *become* operators. How the hell else can we find out what is going on? All we're doing now is knocking hell out of production by killing thousands of dumb bastards who don't know whether Christ was crucified or shot in a crap game."

"Well, how about hiring some of their psychics away from 'em? Price would be no object."

"We can't. They're *ethical*. And if WestHem ever finds out what we're doing they'll stop the Earth in its tracks and throw us the hell off bodily. Don't kid yourself about this, Lord Byron, or you'll wind up square behind the eight-ball."

Punsunby wriggled and squirmed all the way to The World; but his every idea was crushed by Cantwell's relentless logic. Therefore, as soon as the starship landed, the two Supreme Beings of The World went directly to the immense building housing Information Central and donned the gorgeously-colored, heavily-jeweled regalia of their respective positions. Punsunby sat on the splendidly ornate Throne of The Company; Cantwell on a much smaller and somewhat plainer throne at his master's feet.

Punsunby put on a wisely beneficent smile, Cantwell pressed a hidden switch, and each of the thousands of Agents in Information Central's vast building was bathed both in the pure mercury-vapor Light of the Company and in the warmth and abundance of the Company's good will. Each put hands on head; each was suffused with happiness at this all-too-rare personal contact with The Company Itself.

"Children of the Company—*my* children—be happy," Punsunby told the raptly-listening thousands. "In view of the unprecedented difficulties which the World is now experiencing, The Company decrees that Article Ninety of its Second Directive is amended by the addition to it of Section Fifty Six, as follows: 'All members of all Mentalist castes in category A A A are permitted and directed to work, with no effect upon caste, at whatever undertakings and in whatever fashions Highest Agent A A A A A A B shall set up and direct.' Be happy children."

232

The Company lights all went out, the golden thrones

Thus, even before Cantwell's subspace drive, they learned everything that Cantwell himself had ever known about The World and had put the *Explorer* into orbit around The World's sun. And thus, long before the disguised psychologists of The World had made any significant progress in their investigations, the Galaxians were ready to go to work.

"Shall we take a quick peek at Information Central?" Deston asked, "To see which of those colored-head-lamped buzzards are doing what to whom?"

"We shall *not!*" Barbara declared. "If I *never* know exactly which button a murderer pushes to kill a perfectly innocent person it will be three days too soon. We can cripple all the instrumentation of that whole Information Central without . . ." She paused and frowned.

"Exactly," Jones said. "That *would* tear it."

"Well, maybe," Barbara conceded. "So we'll hunt up whoever's causing it and put *them* out of business, and *then* stop it. We know it isn't the Galaxians, so it must be the Communists."

"If we couldn't find the place, how could they?" Deston asked. His thoughts took a new turn then, and as he thought his mind-blocks began unconsciously to go up. "Okay, we'll hunt 'em up. We know how they work. They won't be close in—too easy to spot. They'll be 'way out somewhere, and quite possibly underground. It will be a job, fine-toothing that much territory, but there's a lot of us. We'll divide it up . . . like this. . . ."

It was super-sensitive Bernice who finally found the Russians' carefully-concealed, deeply-buried headquarters.

"Good going, Bun!" Deston applauded. Then, after a quick probe, he went on. "*New* Russia! That's really one for the book. First thing, let's get those Company Agents up here—those two there, I think, are going to be the answer to Maynard's prayer. Their language has been sort of—censored?—let's see how they take to telepathy."

A C B A and A C B D, being very strong latents and well on the way to making psiontists of themselves without even knowing that such a science as psionics existed, learned telepathy in seconds. More, they went into a hammer-and-tongs mind-to-mind session with the Funny Four even while the six leaders were arguing with the other ex-Agents. All these were latents, however; hence, after the University of Psionics had been explained to them, they were more or less eager to go. They knew less of reality than even the little that the two "hunchers" knew; but, like latents everywhere, they did want to learn.

Wherefore, after Barbara had had a flashing exchange of thought with Stella Adams, the new recruits were delivered to her in her office in the University. Beedy was still bruised and battered, but no one—except his new wife, of course—paid any more attention to that than he did himself. Everyone knew all about what had happened, and they all approved of him and he knew it.

"Babe!" Barbara burst out then. "What's on your mind? You've been blocking solid—give!"

"I didn't mean to, actually, but I wouldn't wonder. I don't like the only possible answer a bit, and you won't either. We never even *heard* of that planet New Russia. And how did they find this world? I've been racking my brains and the only possible answer I can come up with is that Feodr Ilyowicz has always been a double agent —suckering us but good, all along."

"Oh, no!" came a storm of protest, and Jones added,

234

sia! Bernice broke in.

"He has to, or he wouldn't last an hour," Jones said, grimly. "All that means is that, compared to a planet and years of time, EastHem's expendable—for as many years as is necessary. So I'll buy it after all. What do we do next? Scout New Russia?"

"I don't think so, we need dope first, and, as I started to say, we can find out. Flit us to one of Jupiters's moons, you Trains, and we'll put . . ."

"High it, fly-boy, and find the beam!" Jones snapped. "We can't 'port those jaspers down there back to New Russia and we can't leave 'em here and we can't very well kill 'em in cold blood."

"Okay, Control Six, I'll try it again," Deston agreed. "Um . . . um . . . mm. How about putting 'em—being sure we get 'em all, of course—into an empty hold here in the *Explorer?* Keep 'em in durance vile for the duration? Intern 'em?"

"That's a cogent thought, friend," Barbara said, and the others agreed. "I wish we could do a lot worse to 'em than that."

It was done.

"Can I land now, Control Six?" Deston asked, plaintively, and the others laughed.

"Okay, fly-boy, you're on the beam now."

"Thank you, Control Six. As I was saying when I was so rudely interrupted, let's flit to somewhere near Tellus and put the snatch on Ilyowicz and see if our guesses are any good. No, better let me do the grabbing alone—if he has any warning whatever we'll never get him, and if I'm wrong about him I'll apologize abjectly."

The Russian had no warning whatever. Before he could begin to thing about setting up the psionic barrier through which no psionic force could act, he was in the *Explorer*. Nor did Deston have occasion to apologize. It became evident instantly that Ilyowicz would fight to the death, and in another instant six of the most powerful minds known to man were tearing at his mental shields.

He held those shields with everything he had, but he did not have enough. No human mind could have had enough. His shields failed; and, a moment after their failure, such was the irresistible flood of mental energy driving inward, Feodr Ilyowicz died. In that moment before death, however, the six learned much.

He had always been a double agent. He had always lived for Russia, he was dying for Russia. Not the Russia of Earth—that was expendable—no one cared what happened there for a few years or a few decades—but the great New Russia that already possessed one whole planet, was taking possession of another at this moment, and would very soon possess all the populated planets of civilization. Everything he had learned he had passed on to New Russia. It had a University of Psionics that would soon surpass that of Newmars. He had traced Punsunby to The World long ago, and had advised the Premier himself as to what should be done about it. If it had not been for that stupid oaf Ovlovetski he would have gone to The World himself and made such arrangements as to . . .

That was all. Feodor Ilyowicz was dead.

Thoughts flew for minutes; then Deston said, "There may not have to be any scandal. I'll yank his first assistant—his nephew, Stepan Ilyowicz, you know—and we'll see what *he's* like."

The nephew was deeply shocked at what had happened, but he opened his mind fully and completely.

While his uncle had always been a solitary, secretive

It was agreed that Maynard would have to know the whole truth, and would have to decide what to do with it.

Maynard was shocked, too; and for minutes deeply thoughtful. "Well," he said, finally, "that teaches us something. There'll be no more gentlemanliness or courtesy on the Board with respect to mental privacy. Never again. No, we can't have a scandal at this point; it would be disastrous. I'll take care of it. Thanks, all of you—both for this and for the fine job you've done on the whole project."

And Maynard did take care of it. It was announced with due pomp that Feodr Ilyowicz, the beloved, revered, and highly honored Second Tellurian Member of the Directorate of the Galactic Federation, had died almost instantly in his sleep of a massive cerebral hemorrhage.

XX

THE ELECTION

"Oh, Babe, look!" Barbara laughed delightedly and hugged Deston's arm against her side. "And she's four months pregnant, too."

Deston "looked." Cecily Train was romping like a schoolgirl with Teddy and Babbsy. She was on her hands and knees on the rug in the main lounge, shaking her head and growling deep in her throat; the kids, with all four hands buried in her thick red mop of curls, were tugging at it and shrieking with glee.

"Uh-huh; nice," Deston agreed. "And you aren't quite as sylph-like yourself as you were a while back." He glanced down at a slight bulge.

"Uh-huh. Bun, too. It's catching, I guess. There's some kind of a germ around, must be. S'pose we'd better fumigate the ship or something?" Her voice was solemn, but her eyes danced. "But that wasn't what I meant, that she might hurt herself—I'm *so* happy for her. Who'd ever have thought that such an out-and-out stinker as she used to be would turn out to be such a wonderful person? Why, even Bun loves her now."

"Something made her change her ways, that's for sure. Love? Psionics? It's a shame to break that joyous rough-house up, but we've got a lot of . . ."

"We don't have to yet, my sweet and impetuous. It can wait a few minutes. I'm going to join that rough-house myself—the kids *need* exercise, you big dope."

Wherefore it was fifteen minutes later that the Big Six went to work. The fleet englobing Earth was the first thing on the agenda, and disposing of the multitude of People aboard those hundreds of huge starships was a problem. So Deston shot a thought across space and —much to his surprise—Bee-ay and Beedy materialized beside him in the *Explorer*.

course; but we *could* be. On most things we're getting to be pretty good—the Fourth Nume, even. We can't do long-distance 'porting yet, except on ourselves, but Stella says we'll be ready for anything in a couple of weeks. Then Mr. Maynard says we can go back to The World. He said, 'See if you can work out a program of rehabilitation that will begin to show results in the generation now being born.' He's wonderful, isn't he?"

"He's wonderful at putting people to work, that's for sure. But what we wanted to know is, how can we put all those people back on your world without lousing everything up over there?"

"Oh, easy—that'll be perfect! It won't bother them a bit—'Acts of the Company,' you know. There'll be enough of them, maybe . . ." the fusion scanned the fleet, ". . . almost enough, anyway, to put everything back to normal. The Three-A's will instruct and take care of caste, and the Aceys will give them all job transfers, housing coupon books, and so on. Everything will be perfect. And that was a good idea, putting a psionic shield around The World, in case the Russians—but wouldn't it be a good idea to release it long enough to blow up their headquarters?"

"It would indeed. . . ." Deston began.

"But no atomics!" Barbara said, sharply.

"Maybe not, at that. Half a dozen two-thousand-pound charges of cyclodetonite will do the trick, with no more jar than a very small earthquake, and I know where they keep the demolition stuff. . . ."

They placed the bombs; then watched a small mountain on The World erupt and then subside. They could find no trace of what had once been there.

"That's it," Deston said then. "Now if you two will show us exactly where to put each one of—but listen! There are *thousands* of 'em—your Aceys will be running themselves ragged—and those three-A's will smell—hell, *everybody* will smell a rat—they can't help but smell such a rough job as that."

"Oh, no," the two assured him, but they did grin at each other. "The Ways of The Company are just as inscrutable to them as to everyone else. And after such a mal—such a disaster—it would be perfectly natural, wouldn't it, for The Company to do whatever is necessary to get its World right back into full production?"

"My . . . God . . ." Cecily breathed. "But that does make a weird kind of sense, at that."

"Another thing," the Aceys went on. "It'd take simply forever to 'port them one at a time to the homes they used to have, even if they still have 'em. There's a great big recreation park back of our house—I'll show you where—so you can 'port 'em there in what you call job lots. That would be even more impressive and Company-like, don't you think?"

"I'll tell that whole cockeyed world it would," Deston agreed, and that was how the job was done.

After it was done Train, who had been looking around on his own, laughed, suddenly. "Somebody did smell your rat, Babe. Cantwell. He called Punsunby and they're both having litters of kittens all over the place."

They all looked, and Jones and Deston laughed, too; but the girls didn't think it was funny to see even two such men as those suffer so much.

"Well, whatever they decide to do, it'll keep 'em out of mischief for a while," Deston said, "so let's clean it up. Thanks a lot, you two," and the Ayamenyi girl

...

can about New Russia without touching off any psycnic
alarms—I doubt very much if they've got anybody in
your class for delicacy of touch. The rest of us will go
along, to cover you if we have to, but you'll do all the
feeling around. Okay?"

"I'll give it the good old college try, Babe," silver-
haired Bernice said, and Operation New Russia was begun.

While all these things were going on, and for some
time before, the political campaign throughout all West-
Hem had been waxing warmer and warmer. It was now
in full, hot swing. With full prosperity restored—and
everyone who could either see or hear knew how that
had come about and who had brought it about—the Galaxians were really making hay.

They had made so much hay that the Sociocrats and
the Consercans, the two major parties before this unprecedented break-up, had merged as the only way of
beating the snowballing Galaxians; and the Communists
and the Liberals had joined them after being promised a
place at the trough. This fusion party, the Party of Freedom and Liberty, was called the "FreeLibs."

"That old cliche about 'strange bedfellows' was never
truer," Spehn said to Maynard one day. "I never thought
I'd live long enough to see renegade capital, labor, Commies, gangsters, radicals, and facists all eating out of

241

the same dish. How long can such an alliance as that last, even if they beat us this time?"

"It's up to us to see to it that they don't beat us even this time," Maynard replied, comfortably, and lit another cigar.

Time went on; the campaign grew hotter and hotter, and at the calculated time the Galaxians filed criminal charges against almost a hundred Big Names of the opposition.

The "Ins" screamed and howled, of course. They'd been framed. They'd been jobbed. Swivel-tongued demagogues ranted and raved about freedom and liberty and patriotism and motherhood; about tyranny and oppression and muzzling and dictatorship and fascism and slavery and corruption and soullessness and greed. They accused the "upstairs" of everything they themselves had been doing and were still doing.

The Galaxian psiontists, however, had the facts. Events, names, dates, places, and amounts. They knew exactly what had been done, who had done it, and for how much, and they could prove their every allegation.

Truth and honesty and facts are much easier to present and to prove than are lies. Wherefore the Galaxians, in addition to publicizing their facts in newspapers, magazines, tapes, brochures, pamphlets, and flyers, also took a lot of time on the communications networks of vast InStell. According to law, InStell had to allot as much time to the FreeLibs as to the Galaxians—but it was probably neither accidental nor coincidental that little or no "network" trouble ever developed on Galaxian time.

Psiontist-lawyers took solid facts to court and inserted them solidly into jurors' heads. Corruptionists, extortioners, boodlers, political and legal, and big-shot racketeers —lords of vice and crime—began to go one by one behind bars.

And the vast, lethargic, unorganized public began to stir . . . began finally to move. . . .

As Election Day drew near, the "fuss" predicted by

echelons, the boys and girls who got out the vote, had
not been touched.

It was a thoroughly dirty campaign; nor were the
Galaxians exactly lily-white. While most of the mud they
threw was true—even though some of it could not be
proved except by psionic evidence, which of course was
not admissible in court—they did at times do quite a
little extrapolating: but not when they could get caught
at it very easily.

The Galaxians had another great advantage in that
every important political meeting was attended by at
least one high-powered psiontist; and at these rallies,
Galaxian or FreeLib, those experts inserted the truth
into minds theretofore closed to reason. These minds
thought, of course, that they had perceived the truth for
themselves.

Registration soared to an all-time high of ninety eight
point nine percent of all eligible voters.

Maynard knew that the Galaxians would lose every
stronghold of organized Labor and every district controlled by ward heelers. He knew that they would win
in all suburbs and "out in the sticks." It was in the middle
regions that the issue would be decided, and he knew
exactly where those regions were. He also knew that,
in spite of all the illegal work the Galaxians had done
in those regions, they would lose a lot of them. The decision would be close: altogether too close.

On the morning of Election Day, then, especially in those doubtful regions, tension hit its peak. Voting was far from clean, on both sides, but in that skullduggery the Galaxians again had two great advantages. First, their ringers and repeaters had been set up so far in advance and so carefully as to avoid suspicion. Second, they had the psiontists. Not one in every precinct, of course, but one could 'port to any polling-place in less than one second of time.

And whenever a mind-reader stared into an imposter's eyes and told him who he really was, where he really lived, when and where and who had paid him how much, and dared him to sign that false name, the imposter ran: but fast.

Even so, it was very close. It see-sawed back and forth all night. Maynard and his staff were worn and drawn when, at ten o'clock next morning, it became mathematically certain that the Galaxians had lost the presidency and had not won control of either the Senate or the House.

"I can't say that I'm not disappointed," Maynard said then, "but—considering the lethargy of John and Mary Public, that we are a completely new party, and what the FreeLibs promised everybody—we did very well. We elected such a strong minority that the opposition will have to maintain a solid front, which will be very hard for them to do. If we keep on working, and we will, we should be able to win next time."

known to us, has made an intensive psionic study of New Russia. Her report is already on tape; but, since you are all psiontists, I have asked her to give you, mind to mind, everything she found out, so that you will be able to perceive and to feel the many sidebands, connotations, and implications that can not possibly be put into words. Mrs. Jones, will you take the floor, please?"

Bernice took Maynard's place in the speaker's box and an almost absolute silence fell; a silence that, even at the speed of thought, lasted almost half an hour. When she sat down, all two-hundred-odd members of the Board breathed gustily and stared at each other with emotions and expressions that simply cannot be described. Maynard resumed his place at the speaker's stand and spoke into the microphone:

"You see that Communism has not changed one iota in over two hundred years. It is a rule based solely upon violence and fear. It is a rule of terror, of spies, of informers, of secret police of the lowest, most brutal type —police who use by choice the most callous, the most hideous techniques of all the older regimes of the iron heel; those of the GESTAPO and the OGPU and the SLRESK and the KARSH. There are no civil liberties, no rights of any kind except those based upon the power to kill. There have been, there are now, and there will continue to be assassinations and purges; slaughter at the whim of one power-mad man or of a group of such men.

"It is my considered opinion that Communism should have been wiped out before atomic energy was developed. It has never been willing to cooperate with any decent civilization. It was forced into a kind of coexistence by the certain knowledge that if it did not at least pretend to accept coexistence it itself would be destroyed in the world-wide holocaust that would inevitably follow any attempt at conquest by armed force. Its basic drive, its prime tenet, however, has not changed. Not in any particular. Its insane lust for dominance will never be satisfied until all civilization lies prostrate under its spike-studded clubs. Before colonization, it devoted its every effort, fair and foul, to the mastery of the entire Earth; since the first planet was colonized its innate compulsion was, now is, and will continue to be the complete mastery of civilization everywhere; whereever in total space our civilization may go.

"It is my carefully-considered personal opinion that this cancer in the body politic, if it is not extirpated now, will soon become inoperable. At the time when we acquired the fleet that had been englobing Earth, the Communists had built on their hidden planet a war-fleet almost as large as our own. They were and still are building more superdreadnoughts. They intended to attack us as soon as their superiority was sufficient to warrant an all-out bid for supremacy. It was only the acquirement of that fleet that gave us overwhelming superiority as of now. How long will our superiority last? They are building much faster than we can without converting to a war footing. Shall we do that, and try to perpetuate the cold war? An attempt that will certainly fail sooner or later? The only question, as I see it, is: Do we want war now, while by luck we have the means to win; or later, when we very probably will not have?

"I use the words 'very probably will not' advisedly; with reference to our ultra-high-acceleration screened battle torpedoes, against which we ourselves have no defense except a planet-based repulsor. It is practically

246

certain that the Russians do not have them in production

munitions plants, and entire areas that are probably munitions plants, that are hidden under psionic shields.
The meaning of that is clear.

"I now ask the supremely vital question: Ladies and
gentlemen of the Board— Shall we fight now or not?"

There was some discussion, but not very much. Every
person in the hall knew the whole story with psionic
certainty, and the spirit of Patrick Henry still lived. The
vote was unanimous for immediate war.

The Galaxians' Grand Fleet, six hundred thirty five
superdreadnoughts strong, was in subspace on its way
to New Russia. Fleet Admiral Dann, in his flagship *Terra*,
felt happy, proud, and confident. Since bombs could not
be teleported though competent psionic screening and
the Communists had plenty of competent psiontists, the
battle would have to be fought along conventional lines.
However, that was all right. He now had overwhelming
superiority. He also had the TIMPS; which, he was sure,
would win the battle. The worst that could happen was
that he couldn't get them all. A lot of them would get
away by immerging . . . unless that thing Deston and
Adams were working on would . . . maybe . . .

That was the only thing about this whole operation
he didn't like. He called Adams, aboard the *Explorer;*
which subspace-going laboratory, while traveling in the
same direction as the fleet and at the same velocity,
was in no sense any part of it.

"Doc," Dann thought at him, "I'm going to try again. I know there are only fourteen of you aboard this time, but God damn it, there's only one Andrew Adams. You're the most important man alive, and nobody in his right mind would call the Big Six expendable, either. The rest of us are—that's our business—but if *you* get killed there'll be hell to pay and no pitch hot. I'd probably have to take cyanide or face a firing squad. So won't you please, *please* go back home and stay there?"

"We will not," Adams replied. "Your solicitude for us does not impress me, and that for yourself is absurd—it is on record that we are working independently of your fleet and against your wishes. We are conducting a scientific investigation, which may or may not result in the destruction of one or more Communist warships. It may or may not result in the loss of one or all of our lives, although we believe that we have a rather high probability of safety. In any case, the data we obtain will be preserved, which is all that is important. Whatever else happens is immaterial—the results of this investigation, young man, are necessary to science," and Adams cut the telepathic line.

Dann sat back appalled. He had heard of selfless devotion to a cause, but this . . . and not only himself, but also his wife and the other twelve top psiontists of all known space . . .

But Admiral Dann had very little time to ponder abstractions. Grand Fleet emerged. Not in tight formation, of course—really fine control was to come later—but most of the subspacers came out within a few thousand miles of where they had intended to. And every Galaxian ship, as it emerged, hurled death and destruction. The TIMPS were launched first, of course; they were the Sunday punch. Thousands of killers erupted, too, and hundreds of ordinary torps. They were not expected to do much damage—and they didn't—but they would fill the ether full of fireworks and they might keep the Communist needlemen busy enough with their lasers so that some of them might get through. At least

heads exploding as thick as sparks from a forging ram, and eight of the Communist ships of war were volatilized at that first blast.

But fifteen seconds at battle tension is a long time; plenty of time for a smart commander—especially one who has been warned that the enemy may have a weapon against which he has no defense—to push his IMMERGE button and flit for the protection of an umbrella. Therefore, five seconds after the first Commie ship had been blown to atoms—twenty seconds after the battle's beginning and long before Grand Fleet could begin englobing tactics against individual Communist ships—the Battle of New Russia was over. Not one Communist warship remained in space.

There was some defensive action, of course. The Commies had launched a lot of long-range stuff, too, but it was all ordinary stuff; stuff that could be handled. Defensive and repulsor screens flared white and beamers and lasermen were very busy men indeed for a few minutes, but not one Galaxian vessel was very badly damaged or had to immerge.

Admiral Dann had followed the last few Commies into subspace with his sense of perception, but they had simply disappeared—with no sign of damage or of violence. Okay: if they re-emerged to continue the battle that would be all right; if they never re-emerged that would be still better. Wherefore, after ordering full detection alert, both up and down, he relaxed—still

strapped down at his con-board—and waited to hear
from Maynard.

It is exceedingly difficult, as all psiontists know, to
work the Fourth Nume of Total Reality. What, then, of
the Fifth? It had been known, theoretically, for many
years, as the realm of two abysmally fundamental and
irreconcilably opposed aspects of that Reality.

First, there was DISCONTINUITY. This was the
aspect of complete unpredictability. The infinity-to-
the-infinitieth power of all possible and impossible events
could and would happen; simultaneously, in regular or
in irregular sequence, or at complete random, or in all
of these ways at once; completely without justification,
reason, or cause.

Second, there was something that was called, for lack
of a better term, CREATIVITY. This was the hyper-
volume locus of the basic male principle, although sex
as such was only an infinitesimal part of it. It was the
aspect or phase—Quality? Ability? Primal Urge? Power? Force?—backing and binding all being and all doing.
It was the—the Will? The Drive? The Compulsion?—
to be, to do, to develop, to grow—TO CREATE. It was
the enormous "natural tendency" toward the continuing
existence of a universe of order and of law. Call it what
you please, it is that without which—or without the application of which: language is *so* helpless in psionics!
—this our universe could not have come into being and
would not even momentarily endure.

Carlyle Deston, the only human being of his time to
work the Fifth, reached it the hard way. He had a hunch,
but he could neither show it nor explain it to his fellows.
They got behind him a few times and pushed, but nothing happened. He, however, did not forget it. It kept
on niggling at him, and he kept on nibbling at it, until
the two Aceys graduated. They had something he
needed and lacked; a subconscious—and therefore in-
eradicable by experience, education, or knowledge—

learned. However, he knew what he knew: wherefore a crew of the finest technicians of Galmetia, working under his minute supervision, built a machine.

It was like no other machine ever built by man. Everything, apparently, was input. It could take half the power of the gigantic leybyrdite-built generators of the gigantic leybyrdite-built *Explorer*, but there was no visible or perceptible output of any kind. There were no controls; no buttons or meters or dials or gauges. All the immense power of that machine would be controlled purely by thought. If that machine performed at all, it would perform at the immeasurable speed of thought.

His hunch was that the thing would work. Since he could work the Fifth Nume alone (no woman can even perceive that Nume) as well as he and Barbara together could work the Fourth, he was practically certain that it would work. Certain enough to let the others who had insisted on coming along, even Barbara, do so: but no one else. And most certainly not the kids. Something might happen.

Shortly after Dann's last protest to Adams, the psiontists aboard the *Explorer* gathered in the control room, around Deston's enigmatic "Z-gun."

"But what *could* happen, Babe?" Bernice asked, nervously.

"Don't worry, Bun. What is going to happen, as nearly as I can express it, is that I'm going to transform the coordinates of those ships from the continuous phase to the discontinuous phase of Reality; using just enough energy to control the balance."

"You are not answering her question," Adams said. "There is an indeterminate and at present indeterminable probability that any disturbance of equilibrium will initiate an irreversibly accelerating transformation of the entire cosmos, so that . . ."

"Wow!" Cecily exclaimed. "It's bad enough, thinking of destroying one whole planet, but the whole *cosmos!*"

"Compared to the discontinuous imbalances always there?" Deston protested. "Have a heart, Doc! And you two gals, listen—what Doc calls a probability isn't even an actual possibility—it's out beyond nine sigmas—exactly as possible as that an automatic screw machine running six-thirty-two hex nuts would accidentally turn out a cash-register full of money. If it wasn't safe do you think I'd have Bobby here? Hell, I wouldn't be here myself!"

"Young man, your reasoning is deplorable," Adams said. "Your data is entirely insufficient for the computation of sigma in this case. Furthermore, the term 'probability,' in its meaningful sense, is defined by . . ."

"Meaningful sense and all, we'll drop all that stuff right now," Barbara said, unusually sharply for her. "Besides, it's about time to, isn't it?"

It was, and Deston stretched out on a davenport and closed his eyes. When the first Communist warship appeared in subspace he stiffened suddenly and it vanished. As more and more warships immerged and were caught in whatever it was that Deston and his Z-gun were doing, nothing seemed to be happening in the *Explorer* at all. The machine never had done anything, apparently, and Deston's body was stiffly rigid all the time.

Adams, leaving Stella behind, bored into that psionic murk with every iota of his psionic might. He perceived much—no two of those disappearances occurred in exactly the same way—and he would remember every detail of everything he perceived.

When the ghastly performance was over Deston got

full of canaries. "Fabulous! Utterly priceless!" he enthused, to anyone who cared to listen. "Thus is probably
the greatest break-through of all time! The data we
have obtained here will undoubtedly be the basis for a
completely new system of science!"

Just before the adjournment of the board meeting following the fall of New Russia, Maynard said:

"Since science has not yet devised a recorder of
thought, I will sum up briefly, for the minutes, the
sense of this meeting.

"The political situation on Earth, while better than it
was, is still bad. We have discussed strategy and have
formulated plans by virtue of which we expect to win
the next election.

"Plastics' serf world presents many problems, but
they appear to be more a matter of time than of intrinsic
impossibility. The psionists of that world are working
out a program of rehabilitation that promises excellent
results.

"The ordinary citizens of New Russia will not present
any problems. The non-psionic commissars and hard-
core Party members will not be allowed to present any
problems. The New Russian psionists do, however, present a very serious problem; one that has taken up practically all of the time of this meeting.

"Psionics is necessarily ethical, but ethics is not at present an absolute. Thus most of the New Russian psiontists, steeped from infancy in Communist doctrine and never exposed to any except Communist thought, are as thoroughly convinced that Communism is right as we are that it is wrong. This difference of opinion in these cases, while total at present, is probably not irreconcilable. It is believed that when these uninformed persons have studied all aspects of the truth they will of their own accord come around to our way of thinking.

"There are some well-informed Communists psiontists, however, who believe so thoroughly that Communism is right that they would rather become martyrs to its cause than renounce it. Feodr Ilyowicz, a man of wide learning, knowledge, and experience, was one. What can be done about such men as he was?

"Are we right? We do not know. We cannot know.

"All we can do—what we must do—is what eighty percent or more of this Board believes to be right.

"Our prime tenet, the solid bed-rock foundation upon which the Galactic Federation is being built, defines 'right' as that which, in the opinion of at least four fifths of the membership of its Board of Directors, is for the best good of humanity as a whole.

"It is a fact that about seventy percent of all known human population is non-Communist. This Board is in virtually unanimous agreement that about ninety six percent of all people now under Communist rule as we know it would be vastly better off under Galaxianism; would live much fuller, freer, and better lives than under Communism. Thus, we believe that Galaxianism is for the best good of about ninety eight and eight tenths percent of all humanity known to us.

"More than the required four fifths of us have agreed upon three points. First: each such psiontist as Feodr Ilyowicz was will be watched. Second: no general ruling will be made, but each such case will be decided upon its own merits. Third, the penalty of death will not be imposed.